The Meet Cute

The Meet Cute

Isobel Mahon

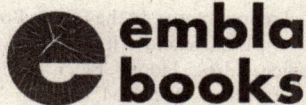

embla
books

First published in the UK in 2025 by

embla books

An imprint of Bonnier Books UK
5th Floor, HYLO, 105 Bunhill Row,
London, EC1Y 8LZ

A CIP catalogue record for this book is available from the British Library.

ISBN: 9781471418976

Also available as an ebook and an audiobook

1

Typeset by IDSUK (Data Connection) Ltd
Printed and bound in Great Britain by Clays Ltd, Elcograf S.p.A.

MIX
Paper | Supporting
responsible forestry
FSC® C018072

The authorised representative in the EEA is Bonnier Books
UK (Ireland) Limited.
Registered office address: Floor 3, Block 3, Miesian Plaza,
Dublin 2, D02 Y754, Ireland
compliance@bonnierbooks.ie
www.bonnierbooks.co.uk

This book is dedicated to:
Daisaku Ikeda (1928–2024)

Chapter 1

The row of faces stared at her blankly.

'Six grand to film your armpit?' said Bryony, her frizzy blonde hair framed by a halo of flashing lights from a tired-looking Christmas tree which was starting to make Cassie feel slightly ill. The restaurant was full of groups, mostly consisting of women shrieking with laughter, apparently having the time of their lives. Cassie was meeting her old school crowd from Rockwood Manor – or 'the girls', as they still referred to themselves – for their Christmas meet-up, which in recent years always seemed to be relegated to the post-Christmas lull.

'You make it sound insane, but it's a deodorant commercial. I've officially one of the most famous armpits in the UK – and Ireland, of course,' Cassie announced, expecting at least some hilarity. Silence. Jeez, tough crowd.

'And did you have to be a member of . . . whatever it is . . . Actors' Equity for that?' Norah's tone was incredulous.

'Well, technically, yes.'

'Not all of her, just her armpit.' Celine chortled, always the comedienne. Cassie could feel her heart beginning to sink into the new green suede Doc Martens boots she'd treated herself to out of a chunk of the six grand.

1

'I mean, any one of us could've done that. It's not really acting, is it?' said Norah.

Cassie knew in her heart the truth of the old adage 'When you're explaining, you're losing,' nonetheless she could hear her tone becoming more insistent.

'It's not just the armpit thing, obviously. It's the girl-power spirit that we're creating in the ad. It's subtle, but that's what creates the magic.'

There was a pause.

'Magic?' they chorused.

'I mean, they were such an amazing group of women on the ad, really vibrant and empowered. It was so inspiring, being with them for the two days – and we've actually stayed in touch. We've a WhatsApp group called "Stay cool".'

'Two days, six grand? Girls, we're in the wrong business,' said Celine.

'Well, of course, it's not that simple, you have to hit your mark for the camera and things like that.'

'What's that?' said Bryony.

'Well, it's basically an X on the floor.'

There was no point in trying to explain that you were one piece in a multimillion-pound jigsaw and whatever you did, big or small, you had to get it right.

'Yeah, that's what I've always thought. Anyone could do it,' observed Norah in exactly the same authoritative tone that had earned her the level of Higher Executive in the civil service. She was also the mother of twin boys who were simultaneously cutting their back teeth and therefore had precious little time for nonsense of any sort.

Oh God, please, somebody change the subject, thought Cassie.

'Well,' said Louise kindly, her soft face dimpling, 'at least you got paid, that's the main thing, isn't it?'

'It sure is,' agreed Cassie gratefully.

'I still think it's a racket, not to mention a closed shop,' persisted Norah, which was probably why she was about to be promoted to Higher Executive, Higher Scale and soon thereafter, no doubt, Assistant Principal Officer.

Louise raised her glass. 'Welcome home, Cassie, and happy belated thirty-seventh birthday, sorry we missed it.'

There was a chorus of cheers.

'Thirty-seven already? My birthday's not till July. I thought I was the oldest,' said Bryony.

Silence.

'I was thirty-six last month,' volunteered Celine.

'I'm not till next September,' said Norah. 'Cassie, how come you were always one of the oldest in the class?'

'Oh, I don't know, I think my mother forgot to send me.'

They all tittered politely. Mercifully, Norah continued her conversation with Bryony, who was way ahead in the baby stakes, with a ten- and a six-year-old, and had become quite an authority for the others.

'It's almost fizzy, isn't it . . .?'

Cassie was catching snatches of the conversation, which was taking on a surreal quality.

'The teething nappies. Yellowy . . . like—'

'Ochre, that's the colour!' chimed in Celine who was apparently in the process of renovating an old bungalow.

'That's the exact shade we've chosen for the statement wall of the back sitting room, it's so cosy.'

Cassie held out her glass gratefully as Louise gestured towards her with the half-empty Prosecco bottle. 'Are you not having any?'

Louise shook her head and made a coy face.

'Oh my God, congratulations!' Cassie mouthed. 'How long?'

'Twelve weeks,' said Louise with pantomime secrecy, to which Cassie obligingly responded by miming zipping her mouth.

'Oh, it's OK, they all know,' said Louise, which caused Cassie's heart to sink just a little. She was officially the only childless member of the group and for a moment felt painfully conspicuous, even though everybody's attention had moved on to the gripping topic of children's eating (fussy, for the most part) and sleeping – patchy to non-existent, apart from Celine's nine-month-old who seemed to have the sleeping powers of a tiny Rip Van Winkle. She desperately wanted to add something to the conversation like, 'I thought I was pregnant once but it turned out to be a false alarm,' but recognised in time this was no place for it.

Among the white noise of chatter, she wondered how her old friend group could have changed so much and yet so little. She'd always felt like the odd one out, working to fit in when to everyone else it all seemed so effortless.

In Sixth Year, Norah had been the head girl; Bryony, with her unruly blonde hair and devil-may-care attitude, had been the popular one. Celine, with her dry wit, had been the class joker and Louise had always been the nice one who never spoke ill of anyone. Sometimes that had irritated the feistier members of the gang but now, as a grown-up who'd spent a long time out in the world, Cassie could well recognise the value of simple kindness.

She was always labelled as the arty one, which felt like being told she was the one with the particularly bad case of impetigo. If she'd gone to an artier school, like the comprehensive where nobody had hair their own colour beyond the age of twelve, she might have blended in and been totally unremarkable, but Mam and Da wouldn't hear of any of that namby-pamby, off-the-wall nonsense and had marched her down in her navy uniform to a decent, traditional all-girls school.

'Declan's a design engineer so he combines technical ability and creative thinking. I mean, that's the future right there, isn't it?' announced Norah, who never missed a chance to remind everyone she had won the jackpot in life. 'He's a problem-solver, it just flows out of him: he's adapted the baby sling so he can carry both Karl and Louis at the same time.'

She was commanding the full attention of the group, not to mention the couple at the next table, who discreetly swivelled in their direction so as not to miss any decent tips.

'Anyhow, he's fixed it so that instead of them being either front or back, they're attached on either side of him so he can cook and hoover at the same time. They love it.'

The girls murmured their appreciation but as Cassie's gaze inadvertently slid to the couple at the next table, she could see they too were struggling to envisage this contraption.

'He's actually going to patent the idea. Just wait, it's the engineers will save us all.'

Crikey, Cassie thought, it sounded like a sort of Wild West-style holster where you could whip one of the twins out and point them at someone in an emergency. This was a totally un-maternal thought to have about a friend's babies, but she just didn't get the hype. They secretly knew it and she knew they knew it.

'And you'll be next.' Celine nudged Louise conspiratorially. 'One of our meet-ups soon is going to be a baby shower, waay-haay, I can't wait.'

Cassie beamed and cheers-ed along with everyone else but she felt a stab in the gut, not that anyone else noticed. It hadn't even occurred to any of her friends to ask her if she had any plans in that direction. Not that she wanted them to . . . exactly. Just then, Celine, whose tolerance for booze seemed to have plummeted in the years since the Leaving Cert holiday in Corfu, slurred slightly in her direction.

'What about you, Cass? You going to make a solo run while there's still time?'

'Or . . . wait a minute, have you been hiding somebody back in London?' said Norah.

'Well, if I have, I can't find him.'

There was an uneasy laugh.

'Not since I finished with Gav, that is.'

There was a general murmur of sympathy.

'How long ago was that?' asked Bryony.

'Three months, give or take – but sod it, it's still Christmas, let's just be silly,' said Cassie brightly, eager to break the tension.

They all laughed, and she'd just refilled her glass and was settling in to have a giggle with the girls when babe-a-licious Bryony – as she used to be referred to by the boys at school – glanced at her phone and squawked.

'Oh, my holy jeez, it's half ten! My life is going to be hell if I'm not asleep by eleven.' To Cassie's dismay, the others immediately agreed and started waving and calling for the bill.

'Pete's outside, he says he'll give everyone a lift, since we're all on a loop. Oh, wait, there's only four seats.'

Bryony looked guiltily at Cassie, who was actually feeling a rush of relief.

'Don't even think about it, I can get the Luas back to Mam's.'

'Are you sure? You're so good,' said Louise.

Everyone hugged her under the canopy outside the door of Casey's Irish Cuisine (reimagined) and said it'd been 'such a blast', before piling into Pete's silver Lexus which pulled out into the dazzling lights of the rain-soaked traffic.

Cassie mooched back down the road, the thick bushes alongside the path shielding her from the worst of the rain. Thankfully, a tram was on its way as she arrived on the platform. Diving into the sparsely populated carriage, she huddled into a window seat. There were about six stops to go, so she allowed her gaze to soften and follow the movement of raindrops trailing down the window as

7

they crossed the M50 bridge, over the big roundabout and down towards the busier stations, heading in the direction of town. She hadn't ever expected to be single and back in Dublin at her age. It wasn't that she'd planned to marry Gavin, exactly, it wasn't like that. She just thought they'd keep going as they were. Why wouldn't they? A life where she was a jobbing actress, temping between gigs, and Gav came home between tours. Until one day, he didn't. Thirty-seven last Sunday but she didn't feel it, whatever this was supposed to feel like. She let her mind drift back over the evening and how her friends had regarded her septum piercing with scepticism.

'Oh yes, my niece got that done to annoy her mother but she takes it out for school,' Norah had commented. They'd also expressed surprise at her boots, which wouldn't have elicited a second glance in cosmopolitan Camden. The girls had serious jobs: Celine was a solicitor, Louise was a speech and language therapist, Bryony ran her own lucrative little business from home importing baby and early-years equipment, and Norah was surreptitiously working towards taking over the country in the near future. When they'd asked about her job, she'd fudged, describing herself as 'temping in offices, admin sort of thing'. She didn't add that her colleagues consisted of a mixture of directionless youths and non-specific freelancers like herself, who recognised each other: actors, writers, dreamers. Miscellaneous, marginalised individuals whose lives were characterised by 'staying available', which was code for avoiding any sort of commitment that could compromise their 'dreams' or 'the big break', no matter how vanishingly unlikely that outcome might have become.

Oh hell, this was her stop. She leaped up and managed to squeeze out just before the doors slammed. Out into the early January night, with the tired Christmas lights sagging in the windows of apartment blocks. A whole chessboard of different lives stacked one on top of the other and each a little world onto itself. In London, everyone was from somewhere else, and once you'd arrived, you were as much part of it as anyone else. Here in Dublin there were private lives, family ties, with roots that ran deep into the earth. Although she'd been born here and grown up here, in that moment Cassie felt like a stranger.

Chapter 2

Cassie noticed a warm light coming from the sitting room as she closed the front door behind her. Mam didn't have much time for keeping up with the polished wooden-floor idea. Fads came and went, and you could be sure that one of these days the wall-to-wall carpet and fluffy rugs style would be making a comeback. Especially with the price of heating, as she was wont to declare on occasion.

'Let's see how long your minimalist fad lasts! The whole bloody house open from foundation to rafters, and the wind free to whistle from one end to the other, like your auntie Patricia's house. Let's just see. And I'll be sitting here, cosy, with my pouffe and my nicely lined curtains, thank you very much.'

Cassie froze in indecision. One part of her wanted to creep upstairs to the peace of the childhood bedroom she'd moved back into since her homecoming a week before Christmas. The other yearned to trudge through the door and slump down onto the big cushiony sofa that threatened to swallow anyone smaller than Giant Haystacks.

'Is that you, Cassie?' Mam called. Without waiting for a reply, she went on, 'Well, did you have a nice time?'

For Mam, time had stood still – Cassie's unmarried, childless state probably contributed to that. She pushed

10

open the door to the glow of the figurine table lamps and gas flame set into the wall, Mam's one concession to modernity.

'The kettle's boiled, would you ever refill the pot there, love? I've just been watching the most boring film God ever made. I dozed off a bit in the middle, but I don't think I missed anything. *Room* . . . You know the one. Where they end up in the shed?'

'God, Mam, that's a very harrowing film, did it not upset you?'

Mam pondered for a moment. 'Do you know what struck me about it? Just how much you can make out of a small space with a bit of ingenuity.'

'Seriously?'

Cassie could feel her irritation levels beginning to rise; undeterred, Mam ploughed on.

'But d'you see what I'm saying? This isn't a big room by any standards, at least not in comparison to your auntie Patricia's, don't get me started . . . but people always comment when they come in here how big it looks.'

Everything that occurred in Mam's world was ultimately a reflection of her.

'So, did you think it was good?'

'Ah, well . . . sure, they all got out in the end, didn't they?'

Cassie was about to declare that she really didn't think that was the point of the film, when she felt her shoulders sag.

'Grand, give me the teapot.'

Out in the kitchen, she rummaged through the pine cabinets.

'Would you like a piece of Christmas cake, Mam?'

'Ah no, it'll only keep me awake.'

What was this powerful mixture of frustration and comfort that filled her as she surveyed the kitchen, with its flowery mugs and fake marble counter. The whole space seemed to exert a gravitational pull on her, back to the warm, familiar world from which she couldn't wait to escape all those years ago.

'So, they all have babies, have they?' Mam asked as Cassie walked through with the tea.

'All except Louise but she's pregnant after a load of IVF.'

'God love them, that's very expensive, but, sure, isn't he a barrister?'

'Still, it's hard on Louise.'

Mam made a sympathetic face.

'And what did they say to you? Are they all delighted now that you're back home from London?'

'Honestly, Mam, time moves on, they're all very tied up in their own lives.'

'I suppose they are. They've moved on, I suppose.' Mam stopped herself but the thought reverberated around the room. *And you haven't.*

Cassie sipped her tea and scanned the gallery of photos that crowded the walls and mantelpiece. Graduation photos, communion photos, her sister Maxine's wedding photo from 2003 – she'd worn a dress of ivory sateen with huge ruffled skirt and leg-of-mutton sleeves.

Mam hadn't held back with her comments after a few gin and tonics: 'For the love of God, did she have to go down the aisle dressed in a cinema curtain?' Ownie, her chap, looked surprisingly normal. How is it that men always ended up looking way less weird in retrospect? As chief bridesmaid, Cassie was right there next to Maxine, decked out in a mauve Grecian-style affair and beaming.

Of course, that was a long time ago.

'You were such a lovely little thing.' Mam was gazing wistfully at the photo of her daughter in a Kermit-green dress with a Celtic design on it, her hair styled with sausage curls and holding an Irish dancing medal.

Cassie felt a pang in her chest. *I was seven. God, in my mother's eyes I peaked at seven.* A part of her wanted to shout, *Mam, I'm so sorry for being a disappointment, I'll make it up to you, I promise,* but then the other side hollered back, *I don't owe you anything, my life is my own.* Or is it ever? Do we really owe it to our parents to make them happy, make them proud? As Da had said to her in the hospice on one of his last good days, 'You couldn't make some people happy if you tried.'

Though he didn't specify who.

* * *

She closed the bedroom door behind her before switching on the light to reveal a candyfloss-pink time capsule: the room she'd left at eighteen-and-a-half and only ever returned to for a week here and there during summers and at Christmas. There really hadn't been any point in updating it; anything she needed came home in her suit-case. She settled on the bed, propped pillows up against the headboard, wrapped a fleecy rug around herself and gazed around at the photos of the old gang, from their Leaving Cert holiday in Corfu. All real, printed photos from 1999, a time when everything had felt more solid, before the virtual world took over.

There was one of Bryony in her low-rise denim shorts, with Celine in her stripy mini, clowning on the edge of a pier; one of Norah holding a guidebook and pointing at something cultural in the blinding white sun that made everything feel like a dream, while the other girls made faces and Louise waved at the camera. It was a perfect moment, she mused, and we had no idea.

Her old certificate from Mountway drama school was framed on the wall. She thought of her teenage self walking up the steps of the impressive, modern build-ing in Peckham, thinking, *Crikey, this is bigger than I expected*, and feeling her already anxious heart take off as though someone had jammed their foot on the accel-erator of a go-kart.

She closed her eyes and drifted back to that day, in the waiting room, dressed in her black leggings and tunic top that she'd chosen to look like a young actress ready for rehearsal. That couldn't be wrong, could it? But perched on her plastic chair – sweaty hands clutching her three speeches on paper that was about to come apart at the creases – that wasn't how she felt at all. Beside her had been a stunningly pretty girl, wearing loose dunga-rees over a perfect top which Cassie would never have even thought of wearing, let alone been able to find in Dublin. Oh God, being prepared didn't come close to being up to the mark, you had to be fabulous. The other guy and girl waiting nervously looked admittedly a bit cooler than herself, but at least they weren't light years ahead. From inside the holy-of-holies somebody could be overheard engaging in a very loud and exuberant audition, culminating in a resonant thump which suggested they'd just leaped off a high piece of furniture, to the evident joy of the adjudicators, who clapped and laughed uproariously. The atmosphere in the waiting room chilled palpably. From somewhere she found the presence of mind to breathe 'into the diaphragm'. To her relief, the very pretty girl could hardly be heard at all, while the next girl gave an intense, tearful performance which sounded unnervingly good. By the time the thin guy with bleached blond hair went in ahead of her, from somewhere she'd remembered the last thing her drama teacher had told her: 'Just get out of your own way. Keep it simple.' Which turned out to be the best advice she'd got from anyone ever, about anything.

'What have you got for us today?' said a man with flowing grey hair and half-moon glasses, who looked like he wouldn't have been out of place conducting an orchestra.

Cassie found she was able to do her best, plus add a bit of magic that she'd spun from who knew where. To her delight she was met with a round of applause at the end. The grey-haired man muttered, 'Well, that was a pleasant surprise.'

She'd sailed back down the steps of the modern building like a different person. No longer feeling like an
impostor. She'd a right to be there. Her black outfit was
fine, her Irish accent was fine, her speeches were fine –
she'd been herself and it was fine.

Three weeks later the letter had landed on the mat.
She'd been so terrified, she'd forced Mam to open it while
she'd hidden in the cupboard under the stairs with her
fingers in her ears, singing tunelessly until she'd heard
Mam's voice shriek from the kitchen, 'You got it, Cassie,
they've accepted you!'

The family had gone out for a Chinese meal to celebrate, and Da had raised a glass of Merlot in jubilation and
declared for the whole place to hear, 'I always knew it, we
have a star in the family.' The whole restaurant had clapped.

'Do you want a hot-water bottle?' Mam hollered from
the bottom of the stairs, startling Cassie out of her reverie.

'No, I'm fine, thanks, Mam.'

'Are you sure now? You've an outside wall there.'

Cassie decided to ignore this last comment and let her
mind drift back to her first day at Mountway. She'd run
straight into the peroxide blond guy and tearful girl who'd
been sitting beside her at the audition. They'd all screamed
and hugged as though they were long-lost friends.

'I looked at you and I thought, she looks like a professional,' confided the guy, Pal. Paldon's family, it turned
out, were originally from Tibet, though he was a London
boy, through and through.

Cassie gasped in disbelief at the irony. 'I thought you
sounded bloody brilliant; I was terrified,' she admitted

to Josie, who'd become a firm and loyal friend from that moment onwards. That had been the beginning of four happy years of excitement, sometimes terror, but more than anything the sense of being truly, truly alive.

She'd found an agent – or rather, Bea Benowitz had found her at the graduation show. Bea ran a small agency in an upstairs office on the Holloway Road, but actually that suited Cassie just fine. She preferred a smaller, more homely agency that felt approachable, rather than somewhere very big and high-powered where you were terrified of the receptionist. Bea had been wearing the same Revlon lipstick for thirty-five years and smoked a million cigarettes a day, but Cassie loved her. Whenever she felt low, particularly waking up on a Monday morning, she was reassured by the sound of Bea's raspy voice down the phone, assuring her that it was 'All down to timing, darling. Don't worry, we'll get you something nice.' It gave her a sense of security in a world where it was all too easy to feel like you were in freefall. Bea had been as overjoyed as herself when she'd been cast in the panto the following Christmas. She was 'on her way', as Bea put it, though she didn't specify where to. And that's when she'd met Gavin. That was when her future began.

* * *

'So, it's definitely over, then? I thought you two were engaged,' said Mam sadly as they set the table for Sunday lunch.

'I never said that.'

'Well, somebody did. And you were together for a long time . . .'

'But we split up in October. Not exactly my choice.'

'Oh, I'm sorry to hear that,' said Eric kindly. Eric was Mam's new friend.

Mam busied herself shifting dishes around to make room for the carrots and Brussels sprouts, deliberately avoiding eye contact. It was not unknown for her to blur the boundaries between wishful thinking and fact, especially where her younger daughter was concerned.

'I was telling Eric he was some sort of photographer for a while, wasn't he?'

'Food.' Cassie sighed. 'He was a food photographer for a year, until he got fed up and went back to being a tour manager.'

'Just food photography, is that a thing?'

'Of course, how d'you think they do ads and posters and things?'

Mam was obviously bringing this up to raise the tone of the conversation for Eric's benefit. He was dressed in the sort of outfit that actors used to wear to read bed-time stories on the BBC – flannel shirt with a cravat tucked in – and was very polite, expressing surprise and admiration as each new dish arrived on the table. Mam was clearly delighted. 'Friend' was obviously code for 'boyfriend'.

'Of course, food photography is essentially the direct descendant of the still-life painting,' he said. 'We've always been fascinated by food in all its forms. It's a very deep instinct.'

'That's very insightful, Eric,' said Mam proudly.

Cassie couldn't have imagined Mam telling Da he was very insightful, or he'd just have guffawed and done his best *Carry On* impersonation, cracking himself up in the process. Eric was clearly bringing out another side of Mam. It was funny to think old people could change like that. Cassie had always feared she'd be heartbroken to see a new man in Mam's life, even though he'd been sensitive enough to choose the seat opposite her and leave Da's big carver at the head of the table empty. In truth there was nothing the least bit objectionable about Eric; it was just that in her absence he seemed to have become part of the family. She'd come home to a world where everybody seemed to know the new rules except her.

'So, when're you planning to head back?' he asked affably. Suddenly, she felt herself the focus of attention again.

'I'm not sure.'

'An open return, that must have cost you,' observed Mam.

'I don't have any particular job coming up right now, so I have some flexibility,' she replied airily. Which obviously meant 'out of work'.

'So, what were you doing up to the time you came back?' enquired Eric, not unkindly.

'You were on the BBC!' Mam broke in.

'I was in an episode of *Casualty* as a patient. Basically, it works that the more seriously ill you are, the bigger the part. I had an unexplained rash – apparently, the script-writers had been planning to make it meningitis but then they decided the character was just allergic to the mould in her council flat. So, that meant I was relegated to the "C" story.'

Eric nodded.

'But you did have screen time with that lovely doctor with the white hair that's been in it since the 1980s . . .'

'No, he hasn't, Mam—'

'And you were doing some theatre in education work too, weren't you, love?'

'Sort of . . . I worked at the Tomb Raider Live experience, which was quite fun.'

'And the big sciencey one.' Mam seemed to be trying to promote her as the next Carol Vorderman.

'I was actually subbing for a friend of mine at Slime Planet.'

'But it's fantastic, isn't it, helping to make science an exciting, relatable subject for children. Don't run yourself down.'

This was all for Eric's benefit. He nodded sagely. Cassie winced as her memory catapulted her back to the shock of cold green slime cascading down on her head and 500 kids chorusing 'Slime! Slime! Slime!' like the mob at the Colosseum.

'It's all a business in the end, isn't it?' said Eric evenly.

Cassie could've hugged him.

* * *

Josie looked a bit different on Zoom. Everybody did – you were flat, after all. A two-dimensional image, like you were an astronaut phoning Earth from outer space. It felt a bit like that too.

'If you change your mind and feel like coming back, you can always crash with me and Pal for a few weeks. I really miss you and I know Pal does too. By the way, a friend of mine is just opening a café in Islington – street food and eclectic interior kind of thing, and I'm sure I could get you a job.'

'Don't tempt me, Jos. I can't explain it, I just feel like I can't go back.'

'I understand, if that's how you feel, sweetie.'

'Ever since Bea passed . . . and Gavin buggered off. It's like London changed for me. It feels like the end of an era. I miss you and Pal terribly, but I can't keep floating along day-to-day with no proper plan. I have to try and build something solid before it's too late and people start feeling sorry for me and referring to me as "you used to be . . ."'

Josie looked hard at her.

'You know, in my family we say every crisis is an opportunity. The universe never closes one door, but it opens another.'

'I know, Josie, but I just feel like I'm stuck in the hallway and I haven't the energy to keep trying all the feckin' doors one after another. I feel like all that time I was buzzing along and holding on to my dreams, real life was happening somewhere else, and I've just woken up. Sorry for being a moany Mona. I'd better go.'

'Wait!'

There was something in her tone that jolted Cassie to attention.

'Just before you go, I've been meaning to tell you but . . . Look, I've a bit of news.'

'Ooooh, I'm intrigued.'

There was a pause that felt anything but empty.

'I'm pregnant.'

Time stopped. Dead.

'Shit, Jesus, what? How? When? I mean, that's fabulous.'

Nothing, nothing on earth had prepared her for this.

She registered that Josie was blinking a lot. She could also see in the thumbnail screen that her own face had collapsed and she was looking unnervingly like the Churchill dog. She pulled herself together instantly.

'That's . . . That's incredible! Oh my God, Jos, I didn't even know you guys were trying.'

'We weren't, that's the thing. It just happened.'

Fate had taken a hand, or rather it had taken Josie's hand and presented her with this most wonderful of gifts. Not Cassie. Not her with Gav in all the years they'd been together. Why was she so floored? Surely, she could've realised it was always a possibility.

'Oh my God, I'm so excited for you. I couldn't be more excited.' She was aware of the concern on Josie's face.

'I'm sorry, I was going to save it for a better time.'

Normally, they could be savagely, delightfully honest with each other but this was too big, too unknown, too painful for honesty.

'What? There isn't a better time. This is the better time. It's amazing. That's what it is.'

'Thanks, Cass, you're being great about it. I was . . . Never mind. I'd better go now. We're going down to the Duck for Sunday lunch. It'll be mashed potato and flat water for me. Pal's so excited, he's planning to go for the full-on all-you-can-eat buffet to celebrate. With beer. I'm not sure I can watch him.'

Despite her wish to be sensitive, Josie's joy and excitement bubbled through and for a split second Cassie hated her. Then she laughed.

'That is so adorable.'

Josie was one year younger than her. Was that what had made all the difference?

'Bye, darling, you take care of yourself.'

She could hear Josie speaking but the words weren't going in. 'No, you take care, sweetie, thrilled for you.'

She clicked 'End Meeting for All' and burst into tears.

* * *

'Dog walking?'

After the shock of the phone call with Josie, Cassie had had a good bawl and a shower, and was now standing dressed in a tracksuit, holding a mug of not-particularly-warm coffee from Mam's 2002 coffee maker.

'Now, hear me out.' Mam was on a mission. 'It's a gap in the market. That's the number-one principle of any successful business. See a need, fill a need.'

'Right now, I need to be left alone. Does that count?'

'No. Listen to me: Maura's had her hip done so she's out of action and your auntie Patricia's had her bunions done so she's going to be on that scooter thing for weeks. They can't all keep relying on neighbours and, God help us, friends. And between ourselves, neither of them's short of a few bob.'

Cassie opened her mouth to protest then closed it again. It wasn't actually the worst idea in the world. She wasn't really qualified to do anything apart from act, or maybe teach – she'd made her peace with that. But dogs needed to be walked, and she had two legs so that was a start.

'You'll need a catchy name. Some sort of a play on words. Now, let's think . . . Waggy Walks isn't bad.' Mam began a list of excruciating alliterations: 'Waggy Wanders—'

'That makes them sound lost.'

'Pooch Parade.'

'Too . . . up itself.'

After twenty-seven versions, they finally settled on the first one. Mam scanned her phone.

'There's a Waggy Walks in Melbourne and one in Solihull, but that's grand – it's nowhere near here. Look, I'm not saying you have to do it forever. It'll just be a nice thing to do until you decide what to do with the rest of your life.'

'Exactly. What *I* decide to do, Mam.' Cassie knew she was being childish and ungracious, but she just couldn't hold it in.

'Now, you're going to want a nice colour scheme for your branding, something that'll appeal to your clientele.'

'You mean *your* clientele.'

Mam gave a martyred sigh.

'I could be out enjoying myself and instead I'm here on a wet Sunday, helping you to get a business off the ground and the least I could hope for is the remotest bit of gratitude.'

'Sorry, Mam.'

'That's all right. We'll start afresh.'

In fairness to Mam, she mocked up a template which Cassie had to admit looked passably professional.

'That's nice, Mam, thanks.'

'Right. Time to get started.'

Chapter 3

Tuesday dawned with a sky the colour of porridge. In a way it was a relief. If you were going to feel crap, you might as well do it on a crap day. No point in wasting a blazing blue sky and dazzling New Year sun on a big grump.

'You'll have to put up with a blow-by-blow account of her renovations – nobody gets away without that, God forbid,' warned Mam.

Cassie didn't care.

After a breakfast of a boiled egg and half a slice of toast in an attempt to be good, even though that probably meant she'd be starving by eleven, she packed up her leads, dog treats and roll of poo bags – the tools of her new trade – and set off towards her first job. Today was the first day of her life without illusions, she told herself. She remembered what Josie had said earlier: 'Whatever it is, just do it. Let go of your expectations. Expectations are disappointments waiting to happen.'

Which was a quote Josie had stuck to her fridge.

Stop expecting life to deliver exactly what you want, and just get on with it. She was decked out in her warmest of clothes against the frosty January weather: polo neck, Aran sweater, long puffa coat, sturdy boots and a woolly hat – it all added a good three sizes to her figure and none of it in the right places. Oh well, bugger-all difference it was going to make at the dog park, she thought gloomily as she stomped up the hill towards Patricia's. The front door had a touchpad that apparently recognised her fingerprints.

'For feck's sake,' she'd overheard Mam mutter, 'if you're too fancy for a keyhole, what's next?'

She pressed the doorbell and waited for Augusta, Patricia's cleaning lady. She was led into what looked like an unprepossessing hallway, but when you went through a nearby door, it opened out into what looked like a full-on tropical glasshouse straight out of the Botanic Gardens, but was in fact the kitchen.

'Cassie, love, is that you?'

A hand waved from behind a wingback armchair. 'Come round here and let me have a look at you. All muffled up like a Christmas turkey, aren't you great? Well, I couldn't be happier to see you. The boys and girls haven't had a proper walk for a week. And tell me, how is poor Iris? I think of her down there on her own sometimes. Tell me, is she doing all right in that little house? Sad, really . . . Gosh, dropping in there is a walk down memory lane.'

Mam obviously hadn't said a word about Eric, and it wasn't her place to blab about her mother's love life, but in a flash, she could see exactly why Mam had it in for Auntie Patricia and her condescending attitude. You had to admit, though, her house did look like something straight out of *Grand Designs*.

Without warning, she roared over her shoulder, 'Augusta, let them in.'

A moment later a cacophony of frantic barking ensued as a pack of white fleecy bullets tore into the kitchen and began doing laps of the kitchen island, skidding around the corners.

'Oh . . . I thought there were only one or two.'

'No, we're six little rascals, aren't we? But we're going to be very good for our auntie Cassie, aren't we? Because she's new at this and mightn't be very used to it.'

Finally, after an exhausting ten minutes, between herself and Augusta they managed to wrangle the spring-loaded Bichons onto leads. All the while, Patricia regaled her with the names and personalities of each one: 'This one is Snow, short for Snowdrop – don't be fooled by her, she's very entitled.'

'Little feckers,' muttered Augusta at the back of the armchair.

By the time she'd steered them down the hill and across the road towards the park, Cassie was already overheating. Surely it couldn't be the perimenopause yet. The sun had come out and the morning had grown unexpectedly warm. Far too warm for her outfit. She desperately needed to snatch the bobble hat off her head, not to mention scratch her nose, but with three dogs in each hand, all trying to go in opposite directions, she felt like something out of *Ben-Hur*.

She lifted the latch on the inner gate, only to notice at that moment that there were about five large energetic Labrador types joyfully lolloping around as their owners watched listlessly. The Bichons were beside themselves with excitement and, taking pity on the little things, she reached down and unclipped the leads, causing them to shoot off in all directions, diving and rolling. Soon they were soaking brown blobs, almost indistinguishable from the sticky, thawing mud. This was Pandora's box in action: how the hell was she going to get them back? Apart from that, the big bouncy Labradors seemed totally oblivious to their size and were joyfully launching themselves on the tiny bodies. She noticed to her further horror a frisky black Labrador attempting an intimate act with one of her charges.

'Oh God, no, please, help, they'll be killed.'

If there was one thing Cassie hadn't banked on, it was the possibility that things could go horribly wrong with her aunt's babies. She felt panic rising in her chest.

'Napoleon!' projected a booming woman's voice. 'Desist at once. You're embarrassing me and, what's more, you're embarrassing yourself!'

Cassie opened her mouth to intervene when, from nowhere, a massive dark shape filled her field of vision. She felt an almighty thump in her solar plexus, which knocked the wind clean out of her. Next thing, she was lying flat as a plank, staring up at the wintery sky. Scraggy blades of grass framed her face as everything felt very peaceful. A deliciously cool feeling was spreading along the back of her head and neck, and she'd the distinct feeling of water trickling into one of her ears.

'Woman down!' bellowed the hearty voice as Cassie realised her hat had flown off and she was lying on her back, partially sunk in mud. A group of ladies and a tall figure in a balaclava were staring down at her.

'Thor, bad boy!' admonished the tall figure to a crestfallen Great Dane who, Cassie now registered, was wearing a Superman outfit complete with little cape. The figure, evidently male, held out his hand to her.

'I'm really sorry. Thor's not vicious, he's just super excited to see a new person.'

Cassie registered that she was staring into blue-grey eyes with surprisingly long eyelashes.

'Wait,' projected the hearty lady. 'Step back, sir.' As she said that, she kneeled down in the mud and produced a safety pin from the pocket of her waxed coat.

'Don't move a muscle, dear. I'm a trained army nurse.' She proceeded to jab the pin into Cassie's hands and lower legs, causing her to yowl with pain. 'There's no obvious spinal damage anyhow,' she pronounced rather terrifyingly.

'Thank you all, thank you so much,' said Cassie, attempting to scramble to her feet. Unfortunately, she found that the suction power of mud combined with the bulk of her outfit left her struggling like an upturned beetle.

'Never mind,' declared the hearty lady, whose name turned out to be Phyllis. 'We've all taken a tumble at some time or another. Rite of passage around here.'

Out of the corner of her eye, Cassie could see the figures of a man and a dog slipping through the gate. On a positive note, word appeared to have spread among the Bichons that there was a human face at ground level, and she felt her face plastered with tiny licks.

'Grab them, please,' she wailed, and between the assembled crowd, they gathered up the tiny brown blobs and clipped them back on their leads. Finally, she managed to roll over and scramble to a standing position. Mam had suggested that she bring cards and hand them out, but with a layer of mud drying on her back like an off-duty hippo, it just didn't seem like the moment to mention Waggy Walks or her supposed professional status. Timing was everything. She resigned herself to thanking the ladies and squelched off with what was left of her dignity.

Limping back up the hill, she registered the tall bal-aclava-clad figure loping off in the opposite direction with the chastened shape of Thor. A surge of fury ran through her. There was no way he was getting off scot-free like that. No way. 'Excuse me,' she heard herself bellow across the grass. 'Excuse me!!!'

That tall figure looked around in confusion, then spotted her and waved slightly. Idiot, he didn't seem to have a clue how serious this was.

'I just think,' she roared as she approached him, 'that you should have a lot more control of your dog. He's enormous and very dangerous.'

It seemed to be taking a moment for the penny to drop, though it was hard to know for sure under his balaclava.

'Yeah, sorry, he gets excited.'

It was a pleasant voice, which wasn't making it easy to stay cross with him, but she wasn't giving up that easily. 'Yes, well. I could have been badly injured and I think we all need to be more responsible. That's all.'

It sounded a bit self-righteous, but she was totally in the right, she reminded herself.

'OK, sure. You're right.' He nodded and looked decidedly contrite. 'I'll remember that for next time.'

He trudged off up the hill, leaving her feeling annoyingly guilty.

'OK, well . . . Bye, then,' she called after him, for no good reason.

At that moment she caught sight of her shadow and realised with a shock that she looked like a hot-water tank in boots. Yes, well. She wasn't trying to impress anybody. At least she'd made her point with Mr Balaclava.

The stares at her dishevelled appearance didn't bother her at all. Today had gone about as badly as it possibly could have and yet she'd survived.

Back at her auntie's house, Cassie registered the horror on Augusta's face when she and the dogs appeared at the door.

'It's all right, nobody's hurt.'

She soon realised that Augusta wouldn't have given a shite if the whole lot of them had sunk in quicksand.

Cassie was led into a delightful wet room lined with sand-coloured Italian tiles; the sort of bathroom Mam could only dream of. This, she was informed, was the dogs' bathroom. The next half hour was spent showering the dogs, which resulted in her getting fairly soaked herself. Still, as the room was warm and steamy, it proved a dizzying if not totally unpleasant experience.

'Heaven help you,' said Patricia, seated in her beautifully appointed conservatory, when she handed Cassie a fifty-euro note. The six little bodies were now snow-white once again and curled up in their beds, fast asleep like little angels.

'You've obviously done a great job with them.' Patricia was dressed in cashmere leisure trousers and a voluminous cashmere sweater which engulfed her like an exquisite beige hug. She appeared to have absolutely no idea of the chaos going on in the outside world.

'I'll see you back here tomorrow,' she purred.

Cassie inhaled with the intention of explaining that another day might actually be more than her nerves could stand, when something stopped her. She'd no other source of income. Life had to be lived, after all.

'Sure, thanks, I'll see you then.' She beamed at Patricia before heading as fast as she could towards the statement front door.

* * *

'Holy God, what happened? Were you dog walking or mud wrestling?'

'Don't ask.'

'What did that old wagon have you doing? Was it desperate?'

'No, actually, it was great,' she heard herself reply.

The image of the mysterious Mr Balaclava flashed in front of her eyes, much to her annoyance because, frankly, he'd no right to be there.

Now she was home, with the prospect of her own hot shower and a mug of coffee, the day felt more like a little adventure.

That evening she offered to make dinner for Mam and Eric. Chicken curry and rice. She found it a strange experience to see the two sixty-somethings settled on the plush sofa side-by-side with a gin and tonic, talking through the *Irish Times* crossword together.

They'd clearly established themselves as a steady couple somewhere in the months since she'd been home on a flying visit during the summer. Whenever over the years Mam had asked her why she could only stay a few days, she'd always replied, 'I'm so busy. I'll stay longer at Christmas.'

But then Christmases had come and gone, and it was always the same story. What had she been so busy doing? Waiting tables. Waiting to hear if she got the part. Waiting for Gav to come home from tour. A lady in waiting. And in the meantime, she'd had a static view of home preserved in her mind. Funny, wasn't it? Like in dreams, where you remember places as they were in the past, preserved forever. She knew Da was gone but in her mind the picture had remained exactly the same, just without him. It was only now, watching the two of them together, that it struck her that Eric wasn't the visitor. She was.

* * *

The following Friday she was heading back into the dog park, as had become her routine. By then the weather was milder, so she'd shed her heavier layers and was now dressed in a pale-pink fleece and jeans, and feeling a bit less like a hot-water tank than on her very first visit. To her relief the place was almost deserted, although she had to admit that she felt just the smallest pang of disappointment not to see Napoleon and Phyllis, as well as a certain tall someone and his dog – but she rapidly quashed that feeling. An uneventful half hour followed, watching dirty snowballs delightedly chasing each other round the field as she lounged on the bench, scrolling on her phone, watching influencers suggest outfits she couldn't have afforded if she'd sold an organ. Finally, she began to scrabble around, trying to gather her charges up to leave, when she noticed the tall figure approaching in the distance. He was accompanied by his equally tall dog, who this time was kitted out in tartan. Involuntarily, she felt a lurch in her heart and a flash of heat whoosh up her face.

'Stoppit,' she warned herself severely. 'None of that shite now, just cop yourself on.' She deliberately busied herself with clipping on leads, her face studiously turned away from the gate, all the time furious with her heart for insisting on beating like a marching samba band.

'Glad to see you're showing them who's boss this time,' came a voice from behind her. Feck off, she thought. Who actually needed smart-arse comments on a miserable Friday in January, when it was his actual freaking pony-sized dog who'd caused all the trouble in the first place.

'Excuse me?' she replied, feigning confusion, though there wasn't anybody else he could possibly have addressed.

'I hardly recognised you without the mud,' he said with a boyish laugh. Which made it even harder to feel indignant.

'I hardly recognised you without the balaclava,' she retorted, then kicked herself for the lame comeback. She had to admit he was good-looking, with wavy reddish-brown hair and blue-grey eyes that changed colour depending on the light and drew you in – if you were of a mind to be drawn in, which, of course, she wasn't. Why were men given false-looking eyelashes like that when they patently didn't need them? A clear misallocation of resources in the grand scheme of things.

'Well, I'm fine after being knocked flat by your dog, thanks for asking. Except that it took a week to get the mud out of my hair.' What was she telling him that for? She kicked herself. This guy was a stranger, for God's sake.

He exhaled a little laugh. 'Yeah, look, I'm really sorry. I felt bad afterwards, so did Thor, but he just doesn't know his own strength.'

'Yes, well. No harm done. Just a bit of mud, even if I did look a total sight.' As she said that, she noticed she reached to just the height of his ear . . .

'I've played Gaelic football for years. I can tell you, a bit of muck doesn't faze me.'

'Really? I played hockey but I was very bad. I'm more of a swingball girl myself.' What sort of weirdness was she spouting?

'Not so much into contact sport, then?' He seemed to be focusing mainly on his mucky Timberland boots. He's shy, she realised.

'No, I've always been afraid I'll get hurt.'

'That's part of the fun, isn't it?'

'Spoken like a real man.' She was trying hard to keep her mouth straight and not to smile at him, which was proving increasingly difficult.

He took a deep breath, as though about to hurl himself into empty space. 'Would you . . . fancy a coffee?'

'But you just got here, what about Thor's exercise? Maybe somebody else will turn up that he can flatten?'

The Great Dane looked mournfully at her. Perhaps he was missing his superhero costume. Balaclava man shrugged.

'We can come back.'

This was new, this was good, this was somebody actually changing their plans to accommodate her.

'Well, this sure is thirsty work,' she quipped in a Wild West accent. Jesus, just be freaking normal, or is that too much to ask? She kicked herself. 'What I mean is . . . Yes, thanks, I'd love a coffee.'

Ten minutes later they were settled at a little round table in the courtyard of the café, as Cassie tried to ignore the glares from other customers. The place was allegedly dog-friendly but in moderation, for God's sake. Thankfully, the six little Bichons had exhausted themselves and were quite happy to flop in a twitching, snoring heap. Thor, on the other hand, proved to be an extremely neurotic dog with a bad case of separation anxiety and refused to be comforted until his dad returned with a skinny latte – extra hot – and coconut milk cappuccino.

He put down the takeaway cups and a plate with two slices of cake – one carrot, her favourite, and one lemon. Presenting not-previously-agreed-to cake demonstrated a certain confidence, she decided. Balaclava man then reached out his hand for a handshake, which struck her as quaint and sweet.

'I'm Finnian, but people call me Finn. It's after some saint, though that's not really me.'

'You're not saintly, then? Glad to hear it.' She smiled. Cheeky cow, be cool, she scolded herself . . .

'I'm Cassie, short for Cassandra. I'd love to say it was because they were really into Greek mythology or something, but I think it was just that my mum was watching *Only Fools and Horses* while she was pregnant.'

Finn smiled. She knew in that moment that secretly she'd only ever be able to think of him as Mr Balaclava, dog-father and man of mystery. He pulled off his heavy gloves and she found her gaze swivelling like a lighthouse beam to his left hand. Bare. *You are so shallow and pathetic*, she scolded herself. You are meeting this person for a random experience and without expectations, with an open mind, simply as another human being. But on the other hand, no rings – this was great. She took a sip of the hot foamy drink and, sighed. The sun had come out and, despite it being midwinter, there was a glow of heat. Some consolation at least for living in one of the few countries on Earth which could actually do with a bit of global warming.

'So, do you come here often?' she said, ironically, of course. They both laughed.

'Far too often.'

'How come I've never seen you before, then?'

As Josie would say, if she could've turned round fast enough, she'd have kicked her own arse for being too forward. Did he raise an eyebrow? Too subtle to tell.

'I work shifts, so poor old Thor here gets a pretty chaotic walking routine.'

'I'm hardly one to point fingers at chaotic dog walking.'

'I didn't like to bring it up but with the six dogs you just reminded me of a really old movie set in Antarctica. It was these scientists with a team of sled dogs—'

'*Eight Below*, you saw it? Nobody else I know has seen it. I watched it with my dad one Christmas, both of us were crying, even though my dad tried to pretend he had an allergy. Especially when the dogs—'

'Were left behind to cross Antarctica alone in the storm of the century.' His eyes glittered with intensity.

'But the scientists flew back in to save them, no matter the danger,' she finished.

'Leave no one behind.'

'That's right.'

Oh my God, Finn had got it. He'd had the same reaction as herself and Da, maybe even at the very same moment. For a while they looked at each other, and then she laughed.

'That was our all-time favourite. I just didn't think I'd find myself accidentally re-enacting it in my mid-thirties . . . Does thirty-seven still count as mid-thirties?' *Damn, did I actually say that out loud?*

'Really?' He gazed at her with his head on one side, as though he were trying to choose between two televisions

39

in a shop. 'I'd have given you thirty-one . . . thirty-two max.'

'Thank you. That's what my agent always says – or said, before she passed.' She was taken aback by the catch in her voice. Why was this happening? Finn tactfully took a sip of coffee.

'Sounds like you miss her.'

Nobody else had mentioned this and she felt a glow of gratitude.

'You know what, it sounds so stupid. Like when a pet dies and people don't get it. She was kind of like a second mother to me. Just a chain-smoking one on the other end of the phone.'

'It's not always the obvious people, is it? I think love turns up in random spots and they're not always where you expect.'

'I remember phoning in on the Monday morning as usual and getting Sunita, her assistant, which was weird. And she just blurted out that she'd found a message on the phone from her son to say that Bea had died that night. Of nothing. She just died. And then it hit me that this twenty-something kid was standing in that cramped little office by herself with this terrible news and I just said, "Hang on, I'll be there in an hour." And I remember the two of us looking at Bea's desk with the lighter in the little penholder and her favourite mug that she'd never use again, and the ashtray with the last stub of a cigarette with the lipstick mark, and all the hopeful headshots on the big noticeboard behind her chair. And it felt like the end of an era . . .'

40

It was only then she felt a tear rolling down her cheek and swiped it away quickly.

'So, I suppose that's why I'm back here. Well, that and . . . something else.'

Finn wordlessly passed her a handful of paper napkins. She blew her nose.

'I'm sorry, that was . . . a lot, I don't know where it came from. Who was it said that life is just a list of things you've lost? But that's ridiculous. Most people don't think that.'

'You'd be surprised.'

'How did we get from old movies to death?' She snorted a laugh which turned out to be snottier than expected. She blew her nose again but somehow didn't feel as embarrassed as she might have with someone else. He picked up a fork and began on the lemon cake. She found herself smiling.

'How did you know that carrot cake is my favourite?'

He shrugged. 'Hunch.'

Her coffee was getting a little cold in the January air.

'I don't know a thing about you, sorry – all I've done is blather on about myself. What do you work at?'

'Tech – I'm an electrical engineer.'

That was good, and simple, and something about the way he said it didn't invite much investigation. He had a bare ring finger and a steady job. Jeez, Mam would be on the blower to Auntie Patricia before the day was over. She'd better keep her trap shut. It turned out he lived in one of the apartments not far away. Nice apartments. She liked the thought of him living in one of those upmarket places. She liked to think of him happy. Just then one of the Bichons stirred, causing a chain reaction among the other five. They'd timed out.

'Like kids.' Finn exhaled and she was so distracted by untangling the leads that she didn't think about that until afterwards.

'Can I see you again?'

She could feel his shyness, which made the invitation more affecting. 'I'd really like that,' she said and couldn't help her smile.

'Have you got an Insta handle?'

This was just a little looser than she'd hoped, but yes, she did. And for a tech kind of guy that was probably absolutely normal.

'I'll DM you.'

'And I'll reply,' she quipped in a voice that was more carefree than she felt. 'Ciao, and thanks for the coffee.'

'Thank you,' he said with a wave, before heading off with the anxious Thor.

Chapter 4

'What are you talking about? You did nothing wrong,' Zoom Josie reassured her.

'You don't think saying "I'd really like that" was too pushy?'

'Oh, for Pete's sake, imagine if you hadn't. You know all those ninety-nine-year-olds who are interviewed about what they regret most in life. Do they ever regret telling someone they liked them? Never. Not one, it just doesn't happen.'

'Thanks, Jos, that really helps.'

'Hang on, I just need to get another Actimel. God, it's the only thing that helps with the acidity.'

Josie hurried away, leaving an empty chair, and while she waited, Cassie looked down at her phone to see a message notification. Oh crap. Bottoms. Knickers. Just then Josie reappeared.

'God, I wouldn't be caught dead drinking these normally, but now I literally panic if I start to run out. I had Pal cycle down to the all-night shop at 3 a.m. on Saturday night.'

'Don't move, Jos, I've just got a message from Finn99 this very second. What's "99"? The date, the ice cream?' Cassie knew she was just trying to mask her nerves.

'Shut up, just open it.'

Cassie pressed and read: 'Can I cook you dinner to make up for Thor? He says he's sorry and wants you to come. One request: no Bichons.'

'He's talking through his dog, that's a good sign. Very,' said Josie between gulps. There was something about her pregnancy that made consuming anything take on an astonishing urgency.

'What'll I say?'

'Don't overthink it. What do you want to say?'

'Well, yes, obviously. Here goes . . . "Tell Thor thank you and I'd love to come. OK, no Bichons." Send. Do you think it's too soon for dinner?'

'Oh, for fuck's sake.'

They both cheered delightedly and high-fived each other across the miles.

'That was a perfect reply, just perfect,' said Josie. 'You were totally in sync.'

'That was kind of what I was going for,' said Cassie, thrilled for once that she hadn't screwed up.

* * *

They'd agreed to meet at seven o'clock at his apartment. But so many decisions: wine – red or white? Red could make her teeth go purple but white was too girly and might trigger her occasional allergy and bring on a sneezing attack. Red, then. Trousers or skirt? Jeans, keep it casual. But what about the top? Too skimpy would give the wrong impression. Plus, he might have the place at guy temperature, not girl temperature, and she'd be freezing. What was the right impression for dinner with a man she knew almost nothing about . . . Hiking jumper? Too hefty. Sparkly top? A month too late. Cream boat-necked top tucked into jeans and cute earrings? About right, just don't slosh any of the red wine on it.

Mam had been riveted by the prospect of Cassie going on a date.

'Don't attempt to go out that door without showing me exactly what you're wearing,' she'd warned happily. 'I can leave the alarm off for you in case you're late back, and sure even if you're not back, January is the lowest month for burglaries. I saw that on *Garda Patrol* one time. Apparently, the criminals are all at home watching Netflix, same as the rest of us, God love them.'

Eric was coming over that evening and Cassie had the distinct impression Mam was trying to get rid of her but just didn't want to say so. As she was heading for the door, Mam stopped her.

'Is that all you're wearing? Is it not a bit plain?'

'I just wanted to keep things low-key.'

'You can be low-key when you're dead.'

She couldn't help noticing that Mam had changed into good jeans and a gorgeous floaty blouse over what looked very similar to the kind of simple top she herself was wearing. She had to admit that her mother looked decidedly more glamorous than she did. It was certainly a long way from the cosy fleeces she'd worn when Da was alive. Still, fair play to her. Cassie smiled to herself.

* * *

Finn opened the door wearing dark jeans and some sort of dark-green shirt that, she couldn't help noticing, had two buttons open. She could smell his aftershave, which was . . . musky and something else she couldn't quite identify, and he had a slight stubble which made her wonder what running her lips across that roughness might feel like . . .

'Hey, come on in.'

The place behind him looked, well, kind of neutral. She noticed two bedrooms and apparently no flatmates, thank God. For a moment she felt overcome with shyness. After a week of secretly fantasising about Mr Balaclava, despite admonishment from her sensible self, here she was, stepping straight into his life. Into his apartment. He appeared a little bit flustered and stuck for words too. Thankfully, she remembered Da's old saying: 'When in doubt, just be nice. Ye can't go wrong.' Bless him. She smiled. Finn looked relieved and smiled too. They both stood like lemons, smiling at each other for a moment.

'Wine? I've white in the fridge.'

'Lovely, thanks.'

Feck the occasional allergy, she decided.

He vanished into the little open-plan kitchen behind the breakfast bar, with its pale marble countertop and dark wood, as she settled onto the green sofa and looked around. There wasn't much to give away any clues about him as a person; in fact, if she were being honest, it all looked a bit bare. Was that a good thing? The place had that sweetish apartment smell that wasn't of a person, more a situation. There was a big TV with a PS5 and an enormous dog bed by the gas fire, which was hissing away. Thor, true to his attachment issues, was staying close to his dad, especially with a stranger in the house. She'd noticed a set of golf clubs in the hallway, when he'd taken her coat as soon as she arrived.

'I like your place.'

'Thanks. It's OK.'

There was something mournful about his tone. She was almost going to ask if he owned it, but something stopped her; it seemed highly unlikely. He handed her the chilled glass of wine and she took a larger gulp than she'd intended, due to nerves, which emboldened her.

'Since I came back from London, I've been staying with Mam. Just for now.'

She felt a flush of embarrassment hearing the words out loud but, as Josie had pointed out, there was absolutely no point in pretending to be anything you weren't. Spit it out and see how he takes it. Finn nodded gravely and shrugged. He seemed unbothered. Despite that, there was something intangible that felt . . . off. Like he was watching an inner movie at the same time as sitting in the room. And she didn't know how to fix it, even though it felt like something that should be fixed. Why would you invite somebody for dinner and then be only half-there?

'Finn?'

'Sorry, I'm tired. I was on call last night, in case the system went down. Which it did.'

Oh dear.

'You're a gamer?' she said, indicating the PlayStation.

He looked confused for a moment then lit up.

'Yeah, overgrown kid here. I've a pile of games in the cupboard.'

'Me too, I still keep all my old stuffed toys. You can hardly get into my bedroom.' This was better, more like their coffee date.

'Do you eat chicken? I forgot to ask: are you vegan or—?'

'Because I'm some weird-ass actor?'

'Something like that.'

Mercifully, they both burst out laughing.

'I eat fucking everything. I have no morals.' The heaviness in the room wafted upwards like the scented sheet in a fabric conditioner ad, as he gestured towards the table with a smile.

'Madam, your seat.'

'Why, thank you.'

He vanished for a moment then reappeared with plates of aromatic Thai red curry served with wild rice and raita on the side. She realised that after all the getting-ready stress, she was actually starving.

'I hope it's OK,' he said. 'New recipe.'

She tentatively tried a forkful of food, which caused her to involuntarily close her eyes in bliss. 'Oh my God, Finn, this is heavenly! Where did you learn to cook like this?'

'Ah, I've always been interested in food, just a hobby,' he said diffidently, though she could tell he was pleased.

'You know, my dad was an amazing chef and he did most of the cooking. It was one of the biggest things I missed when I left for London. Whenever I taste really good cooking, it just feels like home.'

After a beat he nodded. 'That's lovely.'

'So, what made you ask me out, then?' she asked, aware she was fishing for a compliment.

He laughed awkwardly. 'You're very direct.'

'Sorry.'

'No, I like it. You just struck me as different. I mean . . . you're not like most of the people I meet – in a good way.'

'I'm quirky, is that what you mean?'

He hesitated, and she recognised he wasn't that suggestible.

'That makes you sound odd. No, more like unique.'

'People say that. I always suspected being unique was a bad thing.'

'Most people are, well . . .'

'Trying not to stand out, whereas I can just land flat on my back in the mud and haul myself out without embarrassment? Yeah, that does come from being an actor. Day one, you learn to stop being afraid of making a fool of yourself.'

He suddenly looked serious and she recognised the intensity in his eyes under the easy-going facade.

'I like that you're real, you're not afraid. Too many people are afraid of being themselves.' She wondered who he was referring to.

'Gavin, my ex, used to say that I was like one of those wobbly toys with the round bottom that you could bat in any direction.'

'The ones that keep bobbing back up?'

She'd meant it to be funny, but as soon as the words were out in the room, Cassie felt exposed.

'He meant it in a nice way. A slaggy way. Although now I'm saying it out loud, it doesn't sound that funny.'

'Sorry, I didn't mean—'

'Oh no, I'm sorry! I realise I've just stumbled into ex territory on a first date.'

He'd started to gather up their plates, so he busied himself momentarily behind the kitchen counter, then clicked on his sound system. The sound of Green Day's 'Boulevard of Broken Dreams' filled the room. Love his choice of music, she thought, but was there an underlying message in the lonesome lyrics?

'So, Cassie, what about your ex? Were you married?'

'To Gav? No.'

He refilled their glasses and sat back down. She could feel the intense focus of his attention, which had the effect of making her listen clearly to herself, perhaps for the first time.

'He wasn't . . . We just weren't that type of couple, you know? When he arrived anywhere, there would always be a big kerfuffle. He was that sort of character who turned up the volume in a crowd: "Waay-haay, Gav's arrived," you know? Looking back, I can see he was at his best in a crowd. When he was alone with me, I always had this niggling feeling that I wasn't quite enough for him. I should've realised that was on him, not me, but you live and learn. He ended up working with bands as a tour manager. Actually, he toured with some pretty big names. In fairness, he was really good at the job. He is one of those people great at everything they do . . .' She found herself petering out.

'So you felt you weren't enough for him? But you're gorgeous, surely you must realise that. I mean, you could have anybody.'

He reached out a hand and felt a tendril of her honey-blonde hair.

She studied his face, searching for any signs of insincerity, but there were none.

'Really?'

'How can you not know? Did nobody tell you?'

She shrugged. 'I have a weird nose.'

He took her chin between his fingers and angled her face sideways. 'What's wrong with it? It's beautiful.'

'It's a button. I look like a guinea pig.'

He burst out laughing. 'Guinea pigs are adorable. I used to have one as a pet. But seriously, no you don't.'

For a breathless moment she waited for him to kiss her, but he drew back.

'It's perfect, suits your face.'

She resisted the urge to reach out and run her finger along the arc of his well-shaped mouth.

The sound of 'Mr. Brightside' by The Killers came over the speakers. Was he hacking into her old Spotify account?

She realised he was smiling at her.

'About Gav, you were saying . . .'

'So, we originally met on my first real acting job, which was *The Three Little Pigs* panto in East Grinstead. I was the little pig who lived in the house of straw, so that meant I was mostly finished by the end of act one, and that's how I was able to flirt with Gavin backstage.'

'Hang on a minute, I thought in the story of the three little pigs, they all bunked in together as the wicked wolf blew each house down. How did you get out so early?'

'The director was a socialist, he was intending the whole panto as a metaphor for housing standards. Thank God nobody noticed.'

'Sounds like you brought the house down. Sorry.'

Cassie laughed and rolled her eyes. 'First dad joke of the night.'

The sound of 'Shut up and Dance' by Walk the Moon filled the air. Finn turned up the volume.

'Oh my God, I love this,' she shouted over the noise.

Without warning, Finn grabbed her hand. 'Come on, do you dance?'

'Do I hell?' She laughed, allowing herself to be pulled to her feet. That was sudden. Balaclava man as a dancer, no way had she seen this coming.

'I used to dance all the time, but I haven't for ages.' It was true, it was a long time since she'd felt like dancing. Too long.

There was something about watching someone dance that told you more about them than words ever could. They rocked around the room, ignoring a series of thumps on the ceiling from the neighbours upstairs. Feck them, it wasn't even ten. It was funny, they'd never met at a school disco when they were sixteen, never swigged vodka in a field or snogged behind the school hall, but it didn't matter – those kids were still inside them, just waiting for a chance to burst out with the joy of feeling totally, ridiculously alive. They went through his playlist – a few oldies: 'Since U Been Gone' by Kelly Clarkson, 'Lost Weekend' by Lloyd Cole and the Commotions – until they finally heard the soulful strains of Adele. Wordlessly, they moved together, and she felt his heart pounding as he pulled her against his taut body and slid his hands down her back.

'This is what I've wanted to do from the first time I saw you,' he whispered.

It seemed unlikely to Cassie, given their first meeting, but who cared? She caught a faint musky smell rising off his body and the prickle of his stubble against her skin. She felt his mouth on hers, his tongue forcing her lips apart as she closed her eyes.

A moment later she held up her hand. 'Hold on, don't move for a moment. I need the loo.'

At some point, without Cassie noticing, they'd started a second bottle of wine and she was feeling more than a little floaty. Outside in the hallway, dizzy from desire, she found herself facing a row of identical doors. She could hear Finn's voice shouting something vague and indistinct above the music, which she blithely ignored in her current state, and grabbed the nearest doorknob and twisted. Next thing she knew, a whack of something hard walloped against her forehead and sent her staggering backwards against the wall. As her shock abated, she realised it was a child's scooter, which was followed by an avalanche of toys: coloured things, squeaky things, bouncy things, hard things . . . She screamed and slapped her hand to her forehead to find a definite bump coming up.

'Finn!'

'Shit, shit, I tried to tell you. I was going to.'

Far from being the strong, silent type, all of a sudden it seemed Finn couldn't talk fast enough.

'What the . . . fuck? Why didn't you tell me?'

She picked up a plastic unicorn and hurled it at him, followed by the controller of a remote-control car.

'Jesus, how many kids have you?' she yelled.

'Three. I have three,' he gabbled, trying to shield his head after the first projectile made contact.

'And I've just been clobbered by a Barbie . . . fuck-ing . . . scooter,' she wailed. 'Why would you do that? Hide it all? Why wouldn't you just tell me?'

'I didn't want to ruin things. I really like you and I was afraid you'd have this reaction.'

'Well, I wouldn't have if you'd just told me the truth.'

'I wasn't trying to deceive you. I swear. Wait here,' he said and disappeared into the kitchen, returning with two pots of frozen yoghurt, one of which he was holding to the bruise on his own head, the other he handed to her.

'What are you giving me that for? Is that dessert?'

'It'll stop the swelling.'

She took the frozen tub and held it to the bump.

'I can't believe this is happening, I feel like such an idiot. I can't believe after everything that happened with Gav, I've walked into it all over again.'

'Cassie, please . . . it's not like that.'

'I mean, do I actually have a sign on my forehead saying *big eejit*? Do I? Because if I do, tell me! Please. You'd be doing me a favour!'

'Stop, stop, listen to me, will you? I'm an idiot.'

'You said it. Well, don't worry, because that makes two of us,' she retorted.

There was another thump from upstairs.

'Aw fuck off,' she roared.

'Please, just calm down, we don't want the Gardaí called. Let me explain.'

Cassie stood, panting, all shouted-out and, to her dismay, she felt her chin start to wobble uncontrollably. 'How old are they?'

'Samantha is fourteen, Conor is eleven and Cici is five, nearly six.'

She picked up a doll and ran her hand over its long auburn hair. 'I used to have a doll a bit like this.'

It felt strange to be looking at the children's toys when they weren't around. As though she were getting a glimpse into something she shouldn't be a part of. 'I'm sorry, this is too much. I'm out of here.'

'No, no, wait. Please, come back in and we can talk about it.'

'Talk about what? You made a fool of me. Thank you for the evening, though, I was actually having a lovely time up until now.'

She grabbed her coat.

'Let me give you a lift home at least. I don't want to see you walking in the dark.'

'Finn, you can't drive, you're drunk.' She sniffled.

A part of her was screaming, *Just calm down, give him a chance to explain*. But it was too late, she was already on her way out the door, and a minute later she found herself clattering down the stairs, stifling tears.

Chapter 5

Mam was on her way to bed when Cassie stumbled in the door, trying to look more sober than she felt.

'Three children?' Her face was a picture. She hurriedly deleted a text on her phone. 'Well, I'm glad you told me or I could've walked right into it with Patricia. I was just about to text her to tell her you'd met someone . . . But you like him?'

'Well, I did.'

Cassie whipped off her hat and clumsily explained the bruise and what had happened. She took out her phone and gazed ruefully at the cracked screen. 'I think a scooter fell on it.'

'Love, I always say a broken phone is just God's way of telling you to go and visit someone. Look, he should've been honest with you. He did the wrong thing but probably for the right reason, nobody's perfect, and sure, even at least you hadn't slept with him on the first date . . . although maybe it doesn't matter so much at your age.'

Which was a bit rich, given that she was heading for the stairs with two mugs of tea.

'Mam, I don't believe you just said that.'

She felt the urge to hug her mother but instead they ended up doing a little mime around the two brimming mugs (why did Mam always overfill mugs?). That would have to suffice.

'Love you,' she called as the back of her mam's dressing gown disappeared round the turn of the staircase.

She sent a panicked text to Josie, even though she knew she'd be asleep:

> *Total fucking full-on catastrophe. Nightmare. HELP!*

She immediately felt guilty for burdening her poor pregnant friend. None of it was making sense and she was feeling pretty drunk so there was nothing for it but turn out the light and sink into oblivion.

* * *

Grey light was leaking in around the curtains when Cassie's phone buzzed. It was Finn. Oh crap. Her heart lurched. Was she awake enough for this?

> *Need to talk. U there?*

Was she? Or was she going to hold out and play unavailable? No, that would be totally stupid shite. If she'd learned anything from letting countless things slide with Gav, it was to face things head-on, no matter what.

> *Yes.*

Let him do the talking, if she could manage to keep her trap shut. Her jaunty ringtone chimed (changing that bloody thing was next on the list).

'Hey.' His voice had a deep resonance, but the tone was soft. Cassie felt her heart flip. Stay strong, she ordered herself.

'Hey, you.' Her voice sounded warmer than she'd intended. She could hear his breath.

'Sooooo-o, you got home.'

'I'm alive, if hungover.'

'Look, Cassie, I'm really sorry. I should've been upfront with you about having kids, I was a total dick.'

Don't back down, be honest, she told herself.

'You said it. Look, maybe underneath you actually wanted to keep part of your life private.'

She knew she was being provocative. Let's see how he handled it.

He sighed.

'I don't know what I was thinking. I just haven't done this in a long time. Very long.'

Could she believe him? Every fibre of her wanted to, but her head had to stay in control. Cassie knew only too well that once her heart got in the driving seat, they were all liable to go over a cliff.

'I don't know what to think, Finn. What would have happened if I hadn't opened that door? When were you going to tell me? I mean, how long have you been separated?'

She heard him inhale after a long pause. 'No, that's a fair question. Three weeks.'

'Three weeks? Is that all?'

On the other hand, her head chimed in crisply, think of him like the January sales. You have to get in on day one or all the good stuff's gone . . .

'OK . . . let me just explain: I've been separated from my ex-wife but living under the same roof for five years. From my children, I will never be separated.'

OK, that wasn't so bad.

'And so that's why you stayed in the family home?'

'For one last Christmas, yeah.'

In spite of all the stern warnings, her heart was already melting into a puddle on the floor. Stoppit now, she warned herself.

'OK. I'm sorry I went off the deep end and chucked those toys at you, I'm not normally that deranged.'

'Me neither. I don't know what I was thinking, I had my head up my arse. I suppose I was afraid if you knew, you wouldn't want anything to do with me.'

'Why would you think that?'

'Because . . . you're so independent and bohemian.'

'Really?'

Was that how she came across? Frankly, that was exactly what she was trying not to do.

'I think you just sound like you're trying to be a good dad.'

She could hear the relief as he exhaled.

'That's right. So, do you think we could . . . maybe try again sometime?'

Cassie was trying furiously not to let the smile show in her voice. Cop on, she scolded herself. There were red flags here and they weren't the sign of a carnival.

'I don't know, let me think about it . . .'

Just then she could hear a whistle and a booming announcement in the background.

'Oh, I'm sorry, Cici's just finishing her swimming lesson so I've got to go. I'll text you later.'

Cassie clicked off the phone, climbed back under the duvet and hugged Bonnie, her old stuffed rabbit. Maybe, just maybe, things were looking up. Even if something told her it might not be quite the fairy tale she was hoping for.

She'd hung around until nearly twelve before Zooming Josie, who was looking less than radiant.

'God, you're so lucky it's even on the cards. I can't bonk at the moment. All that jolting makes me want to puke.'

Cassie felt a rush of relief to see her friend's face and tried to explain the whole roller-coaster of events. Josie, bless her, was reassuring.

'OK, first of all you did nothing wrong, apart from hurling the controller at his head, which wasn't great, but understandable. Of course, he should've let you know his situation so you could make up your mind what you wanted to do.'

'Exactly, and before I drank most of a bottle of white wine. And, oh, Josie, we were having so much fun and he's so gorgeous and I haven't felt like that, honestly . . . ever. Then I find out he has three kids and he's a really committed, hands-on dad. I know I said it's all fine and dandy, and one part of me really believes that but another part wonders if there's even room for me? I'll be in fecking no man's land, and that's what I'm afraid of. I feel shit, I've a banging hangover coming on and I don't know what to do. What should I do, Josie? Should I get out of it? But I'm not even totally sure I'm in it.'

Josie had been listening patiently to this rant.

'What would you have done if you'd known the situation in advance? Would you have agreed to go out with him?'

That was a no-brainer.

'Are you kidding me, one hundred per cent yes. But I'd have been more cautious . . . I wouldn't have dived in like that.'

'Who knows, maybe it was for the best.'

'When I first met him, his dog was wearing a Superman costume and it never even occurred to me that could mean he had kids. I didn't want to believe it was anything but him being a fun guy.'

'Cass, it's not necessarily a bad thing . . . it's just . . . different to what you thought.'

'But Jos, he's a grown-up, with an ex-wife and three kids.'

'Don't be so horrified, Cassie. We're the weirdo Peter Pans living in a world where time doesn't exist. Except, take one step outside it and you'll find that it bloody well does.'

'But Jos, at least your baby will be a mini you . . . and Pal. And it'll love you. It won't be able to help itself.'

'I know, terrifying thought, isn't it?'

'But Finn already has a family, so how can there ever be enough love left for me? I'll always be the also-ran.'

'Babe, things don't work like that. Love isn't like a pie with only so many slices.'

'I know, you're right,' said Cassie, though inside she didn't feel nearly as sure.

* * *

Cassie spent an hour and a half at a local gym where you could pay per session, in an attempt to clear her head and sweat off the small bucket of white wine she'd drunk the night before and hopefully regain some equilibrium. The place looked full of people – mostly singles like herself, she observed – sweating away, trying to get control of their lives, or was that just her? She returned home to find Eric sitting alone at the table, playing solo Scrabble. She liked Eric, even if he did seem at this stage to be a fixture. He had a flowery mug of tea and a leftover mince pie, and seemed to embody the sort of inner peace and stability that felt a million miles away to her. He looked up and smiled.

'Your mum's at her book club, though why they meet at five on a Sunday evening, I don't know.'

Cassie wasn't entirely sure what opinion to have about his presence, so she did what her mental health app always suggested and checked in with her gut. It turned out her gut had no strong feelings either way so, relieved of the need to feel indignant, she sat down beside him. He paused and looked at her closely.

'Nice time last night?'

'Eric, I need your help.'

'Your mum told me a bit. No details, mind.'

'You're a man. I mean . . . What's Finn thinking?'

Eric picked up three more tiles. '"Extrapolate". Oh good, an X and a double word score.'

How could anyone that laid-back relate to her turmoil? He contemplated the letter holder.

'I imagine he's feeling a number of things.'

'I mean, would you see a load of warning signs around him? Should I run?' she asked.

Eric smiled. 'Warning signs for whom?'

Ouch, he had a point.

'You mentioned that you were with a chap in London before you came back, and he had no children. How did that go?'

'Well, that's the thing, Gav should've had plenty of time but he always seemed to have something better to do than prioritise us or plan for the future – with me, anyway.'

He shrugged. 'So, really it's down to the person, not just the circumstances, isn't it?'

He picked up the pencil he was using to record his scores and drew a sketch of a little boat surrounded by waves.

'See, if the boat is empty, you would think it'd be safer, wouldn't you? It's not carrying any weight, after all. But paradoxically . . .' (that was such an Eric word, thirteen letters including an X and a Y) 'it's the opposite. If you put some weight in it, it'll sit lower and steadier in the waves. Responsibility, or baggage, whatever you want to call it, is like that – it makes a person's life more stable, not less.'

This made a great deal of sense but suddenly Cassie felt judged. She had carefully avoided responsibility up to now, after all. And how had that gone?

'I'm not running away from responsibility if that's what you mean . . . I'm facing up to things. That's why I'm back here in Ireland.'

Eric nodded but that moment her phone rang and she looked down to see the name Finn flashing on the screen. 'I'd better go.' She smiled ruefully but he waved good-naturedly as she rushed out of the room. She ran upstairs, shut the door behind her and threw herself on the bed.

'Hey, how did your day go?' he said.

She could hear the warmth in his voice.

'Middling, mostly spent working through my hangover.'

'Lucky you, I didn't get a minute, Con had his MMA, but Cici actually managed a few strokes without holding onto her float.'

'Aw, good for her.'

'Yeah, she was ridiculously excited. We had to drop into McDonald's on the way home to get a McFlurry.'

'That's sweet,' she said, and a part of her meant it, truly; she was genuinely delighted that he was sharing with her the details of what was most important in his life. But the mean little voice inside her broke in: what about me? God, what am I like, her better self retorted. I am not allowing

65

myself to get into competition with a five-year-old. Now was the moment to behave better than she felt.

'I'm impressed, especially since you took a bit of a hammering last night.'

She heard him chuckle. There was a brief pause. 'So, will I see you again?' His voice was soft and persuasive.

She hesitated. Go on, say it, she urged herself, don't chicken out. 'Finn, there's something I need to ask you. I didn't like to bring it up last night but . . . three weeks is an incredibly short time. What am I supposed to think? This could be just a glitch for you. Like an experiment in living outside the family. It's not like that for me. I'm on my own. If you decide to bugger off home—'

'Cassie, stop. I've been on my own for a long time. I know it hasn't looked like that but, believe me, it's felt like it.'

She reminded herself of her New Year's resolutions:

1. *No attached men (Finn?)*
2. *No rebounders (Finn?)*
3. *No unstable narcissists (Gav)*

It was a risk. She took a deep breath.

'Are you still there?' he said.

'So, about this meet-up, when were you thinking?'

She heard him smile. 'Next Friday?'

'OK, sounds good, but let me see, I'll have to confirm with you on Thursday,' she replied, feeling just a little bit in control. She could get used to this.

Chapter 6

'Are you mad?'

Mam's face was incredulous.

Cassie had just arrived home from her dog walking on Tuesday and was peeling off her layers and looking forward to a nice mug of fresh coffee and a ham salad sandwich. The last thing she needed was one of Mam's dire life-warnings.

'You're making him wait until *Thursday*? I only hope you're not a sorry girl. Remember that song by The Weather Girls?'

'No.'

'Ah, you do, "It's raining men, halleluiah, it's raining men . . ."'

'Oh, that one . . .'

'Well, it isn't. That's nonsense, and if he's as dishy as you say, he won't be on the shelf for long. He's in a difficult situation with all those kids, for the love of God don't make it any harder for him.'

Trust Mam to take the man's side every time.

'Stop it, will you, you're scaring me.'

'I'm only saying it for your own good. If this chap has a flaw, it's being too committed. Men like that don't grow on trees, and if you do see him again, try and glam up a bit. As your father always used to say, you don't go fishing without bait.'

'Mam!'

'What? It's supposed to be a date, not a trip to Aldi. Now, do you want mustard on the ham?'

By Wednesday, Cassie was in a state; the conversation with Mam had rattled her more than she'd realised. Josie looked pale and drawn on the screen but was the only person Cassie really trusted for reassurance.

'She's your mum, Cass, you know what she's like.'

'Yeah, but she has a point. What was I thinking, playing it cool? I've been freaking out about it ever since. What if he's changed his mind?'

Josie smiled tiredly. 'He won't have. Anyhow, if he did back off that easily, you'd be dodging a bullet.'

She felt a surge of gratitude towards her old friend.

'Thanks, Josie, I don't know what I'd do without you. I'll make it up to you someday soon, I swear.'

'Just be happy that tomorrow's Thursday. Text him early, for God's sake. And then let me know.'

The following morning, perched on the edge of the bed, Cassie managed to hold out until 9.15 a.m.

Hi, things have worked out. You still on for tomorrow?

She was wondering about adding some funny, sexy quips or winky emojis but there was no point in putting her foot in it – better to check the mood first, before making an eejit of herself.

There followed the most stressful three hours she could remember. Finally, at 12.48 p.m. the phone buzzed.

Crazy day at work. Been thinking of you. Mine 7 p.m.?

OK, pretty literal, no banter, but it was all she needed. She read it over three times, told herself to calm the fuck down and then hugged the phone as she rocked out around the room to 'Happy' by Pharrell Williams.

The following evening, she paced around, hurling outfit after outfit on the bed. By six thirty she'd decided to ditch the jeans. Ten minutes later, she was starting to panic.

'Wear a nice dress, why don't you? You'll be dead long enough,' hollered Mam from the foot of the stairs.

Suddenly, the planets aligned and she remembered the cute black mini she'd worn with ankle boots to a concert last year. It showed off her legs but was floaty enough not to make her feel like a pack of sausages. Perfect. She whacked on eyeliner and mascara and enough makeup to look her best without being fully Insta-ready, which could be off-putting to guys. A few spritzes of Miss Dior and she was off.

Standing outside his door, clutching a bottle of wine, her hands felt sweaty and her heart wouldn't slow down. How come she'd been so calm earlier? Before she could finish her deep-breathing exercises, Finn swung open the door, so her heart palpitations would just have to bloody well look after themselves.

She noticed he was wearing a dark denim shirt and his hair looked barely dry. This time, instead of the slight awkwardness, he kissed her lightly on the lips and led her towards the kitchen and past the cupboard of doom, which was firmly closed. Thor clipped across the wooden floor like a sorrowful pony and nuzzled into her hand.

'Oh, look, he knows me.'

'He's an introvert, he doesn't take to many people so when he does, they can't leave or he pines.'

Not for the first time Cassie wondered where Thor's thoughts ended and Finn's began. By this stage he'd hoisted a steaming roasting dish of duck breasts onto the hob and was spooning what smelled like a heavenly orange glaze over them before slipping them back in the oven with a practised hand.

'Fifteen minutes,' he announced.

'Plonk?' said Cassie, dumping the bottle on the counter, although it was actually a good Chablis and well above her doggie-walking budget. Without comment, Finn pulled a complicated-looking corkscrew out of a drawer and passed it to her. Oh hell, she'd seen those on telly but was likely to make a complete horse's arse of doing it herself. He looked at her expression and laughed.

'Give it here.'

He picked up the bottle and, without looking, extracted the cork seemingly in a single movement and poured them both a glass of cold crisp wine.

'Cheers.'

For the first time she could feel his glance appraising her body.

'I like your . . . dress,' he pronounced slowly. 'It's sexy. You should wear them more often.'

Cassie felt a surge of heat run through her, even though it was exactly the effect she'd been hoping for. She took a large gulp of wine to settle herself – so much for subtle tasting.

'I just wanted to make it up to you after last week,' he murmured, apparently examining his shoes. *He's as nervous as I am*, she realised.

'No, I'm sorry, I overreacted. I shouldn't have—'

'Hurled those things at my head?'

'You were pretty gentlemanly about it.'

'I thought about your reaction and I realised you were right. I was trying to hide a part of myself. I was being an arsehole.'

She laughed in surprise; somehow, she hadn't expected cool, detached Finn to come out with naughty words. *He finds it hard to be himself*, she thought. Not that hard, clearly, for in the next moment, he took a step towards her and took the glass from her hand, pushing her against the kitchen counter. His lips were on hers and he pulled her in closer still, so she could feel his hardness pressing into her belly. He bit her lip gently, teasingly, as his hand slid under the flimsy material, caressing her thigh.

Oh. My. God. *This is all going waaay too fast*, said a voice in her head, although the other voices didn't seem to give a hoot.

'Finn?'

'Mmm?'

'I'm starving.'

'So am I.'

'But—'

'Ssssh . . .'

She felt his tongue caressing hers.

The food could wait.

Chapter 7

At 8.45 the following morning, she found herself sitting on the side of Finn's bed sipping a coffee and wearing one of his shirts, which was blue and made of the sort of high-quality cotton that crackled slightly.

It was turning out that far from being a day of leisure, Saturday was wall-to-wall action for Finn's kids. Samantha had hip-hop in town at ten, Conor had football at eleven and Cici had choir at two.

'So, children don't have the weekend off anymore? I don't remember having all those activities as a kid. The most exciting thing I remember was watching *Swap Shop* or *Live and Kicking* with a bowl of Frosties on a Saturday morning, then the afternoon being endless. Are kids never bored anymore?'

She watched the definition of his muscles under the pale, faintly freckled skin as he moved around the room without a trace of vanity or self-consciousness. He had a lean, toned physique that he seemed to take for granted as he chose his clothes for the day: Calvin Klein jeans and a dark-green hoodie. It didn't seem fair, she thought, a guy could have twenty kids and it would never change his body. She took a sip from her cup and reflected on how intimate they had been last night and yet how strangely separate he felt this morning.

He sat down beside her on the bed, gripping his mug of coffee with both hands. She touched his hair, which was slightly standing on end. He was even better-looking up close in the daylight, she decided. He nodded and for a moment she had him back.

'We didn't have a damn thing to do, did we? And as for sports clubs, are you kidding, you had your bike . . .'

'And your skates and your skipping rope. I don't even remember what we did. Playtime was sort of endless, but it was great.'

'It's so different now. And no, kids never do seem to get bored, or exhausted.' He leaned in and kissed her.

'You've got to go,' she reminded him. 'Hip-hop at ten.'

At least that gave her some vestige of control in a situation where she was having the uneasy feeling of being in the way.

'I know, sorry,' he said.

She grabbed her clothes and made for the bathroom. Gazing at herself in the mirror, she let her shoulders droop. Who the hell was she? A questionable woman. She'd just slept with a man who, while definitely not exactly belonging to someone else, didn't appear to be entirely free either, and who could only keep a thin slice of himself for her. He was supposed to be separated, but she could feel the pull of those other lives around him. On a happier note, she looked astonishingly well, probably the combination of hormones and excitement. They should bottle that and sell it. Every woman's peak moment.

He was fastening on a high-tech-looking watch when she walked back into the bedroom.

'Come here,' he said. 'I'm going to miss you.'

She could feel his voice resonating through her body.

'I'd love to stay, you know that. I'll call you later, OK?'

But already, she could feel he was in parent mode. That wasn't a bad thing, she reminded herself. It showed character. It just trumped everything else.

He offered her a lift but, sure, couldn't she cut through the apartments and across the park on foot. She flipped up the collar of her long wool coat around her face and waved sanguinely as he drove past in the black Ford Ranger with the rack of halogen lamps on the roof for his on-site work. God, even his car was sexy. He indicated briefly at the corner then disappeared out onto the road, leaving her feeling . . . bereft. That was absolutely ridiculous, she scolded herself, because what was he but an adult being a good dad? And here she was, like a sulky twenty-something, expecting him to lounge around in bed, have lazy sex and then trail out for some brunch around 2 p.m. Instead, he was on a timer. She'd timed out in his schedule and he'd moved on.

Chapter 8

As usual the girls' meet-up managed to be just off-season, and consequently their Valentine's night out was on 7th February, when you could get a table at a restaurant without having the food hurled at you by stressed-out staff. The restaurant was discreetly festooned with red swags of netting and garlands of hearts. Slightly off-season they might be, but the girls had taken the opportunity to dress up for their night off from mama duties. They were eagerly sharing their plans for the following week, starting with Celine, whose baby had flipped from his enviable sleep cycle and was now waking on the dot of 4.40 every morning. Cassie found herself fixated on the top she was wearing, with the complicated system of straps, until it dawned on her that Celine appeared to have her head through the wrong hole.

'I said to Robbie, I don't care where we go, all I want is for the floor to stop spinning,' she proclaimed.

Norah, in a black dress which she referred to as her camouflage, was her usual practical self. 'Nothing fancy, I said to Declan. It's a taxi, the two-course special and a ride when we get home. He's grand with that. Once he knows what to expect.'

Cassie marvelled at Norah's candour, but it just showed, relationships were all about finding the right person. Bryony, of course, was wearing a gorgeous crossover pink dress and shared that they were going on a three-night break in Paris while the children would be looked after by her parents.

'Freedom. It's all ahead of you, girls.' She smiled magnanimously.

'And only about a thousand broken nights' sleep in between,' lamented Celine.

Louise shared that she and Mike were going out but that she'd be on the no-secco.

'What about you, Cass, got a hot date?' boomed Bryony, not known for her discretion.

'Actually, I've met someone.'

Bryony actually gasped.

'Where?'

She shared the story to hoots of laughter and realised the girls were genuinely delighted for her. This was genuine, bona fide New News.

'It's like a romcom.' Louise clapped her hands.

'Come on, come on, girl, show us a photo,' said Norah

She and Celine zoomed in on the photo on Cassie's phone, which they were examining in forensic detail.

'He's got very long eyelashes,' observed Bryony.

'You do know there's some poor woman going round with bald eyes to compensate for that?' said Celine, just before a distracted expression crossed her face. She reached down her cleavage and rummaged around, before pulling out a large rubbery spider.

'Oh, that's where it went,' she muttered and shoved it in her handbag without missing a beat.

'So, what's he like?' said Norah.

'He's lovely. He's fun and he's a great dancer.'

'Dancer? God, girls, do you remember that?' said Norah with a detectable edge to her voice.

'Oh, look, here he is on Facebook,' announced Bryony. They went very quiet as she and Celine scrolled through a few photos.

'Are those his kids?'

'Er, yes, he's separated.' Josie had advised her to come straight out with it.

'Right.'

After a few seconds of growing discomfort, where Cassie was picking up distinctly judgy vibes, she decided to get all the details out in one go.

'OK, to be honest he didn't actually tell me about his ex or the kids until . . . actually the middle of our first date,' she confessed.

'God, that is scurrilous!' burst out Norah. 'I'd hate to be still out there in that shark pool – sorry, but I don't know how you face it.'

'Now, now, less of the smug married, Nor,' broke in Bryony. 'Anyway, we shouldn't discount the power of the earth-shattering bonk.'

That shut her up.

'Oh, for God's sake, girls,' said Louise. 'These things happen all the time. It's hardly surprising that a man in his forties has children. I mean, if he hadn't, you might be wondering.'

Norah looked a bit more tight-lipped and started searching on her phone.

'I think Declan might know him if he works in engineering,' she said. Cassie squirmed; the last thing she wanted was her new relationship stuck under the microscope of public scrutiny but, as Mam had opined, 'Sure, what can you do in a place this size? In a week they'll be on to someone else.'

God, in London nobody would've thought twice about it, let alone actually known him. There was only one effective strategy in a situation like this: distract, deflect . . .

She turned to Louise and beamed. 'So, how far on are you now?'

Louise lit up. 'Nearly sixteen weeks. My morning sickness is about three per cent better. I finally managed to eat toast and a banana this morning.'

Bingo. Within seconds the girls were competing with morning-sickness stories and vying with each other for their most outrageous cravings.

'For the first sixteen weeks with Sam all I could eat was tinned lentil soup,' said Celine. 'Robbie had to escape to the spare room, the farts were so bad.'

Everyone roared laughing.

'I was in hospital with hyperemesis gravidarum,' announced Norah. 'Same as Kate Middleton. I lost two stone.'

As nobody seemed to have anything to top that, the conversation began to drift back to Cassie.

'And have you met the kids yet?' Bryony enquired. 'Could be tricky.'

'Oh, for God's sake, she's only just met him – of course she hasn't met the kids,' said Louise.

'Right,' persisted Bryony. 'And the youngest is how old?'

'Almost six.'

Cassie was conscious that this was uncomfortably close to one of Bryony's children, as she passed Cassie's phone back with a wry expression on her face.

'Brave girl.' Said in a way which portended trouble ahead that Cassie hadn't even dreamed of.

They made their way outside into the bitter early February night. As usual, the reliable Pete was waiting in the Lexus with the engine purring as the girls piled into the back.

'Need a lift, Cass? Luckily, I'm on the dry,' said Louise.

Cassie gratefully settled into the passenger seat of the Dacia Duster and relaxed for the first time that evening.

'Don't mind them. People can be a bit weird if someone breaks out of the ordinary. What matters is that you're happy. Truth be told, we're all a teeny bit envious.'

Cassie looked at her in disbelief.

'What could you possibly have to feel envious about? You've all got your lives totally sorted. I'm the odd one out.'

'I don't think anybody's got it all sorted.'

There was something about the way Louise spoke that felt more loaded than a general remark.

'Is everything OK?' she asked.

There was a pause.

'I feel so guilty saying this because I'm so lucky. Everyone keeps reminding me how lucky I am and how delighted they are for me. But I don't know if I can trust Mike anymore. I haven't said that to anybody else. They all seem to have a version of how my life is going and I can't bear to wreck their illusions.'

'Sorry, Louise, I'd no idea . . .'

'I mean, don't mind me, I'm probably imagining that he's out chatting up girls.'

'In my experience, you're probably not. Look, I know I'm not one to set myself up as a shining example of anything, but feeling like you have to squash your life into a particular shape to match other people's version of things doesn't work. It'll always break out in the end.'

'Everyone in my family is so happy for me. Especially my mum, it's her first grandchild and they've waited so long. But I didn't even see Mike before I left this evening. He sent me a text to say: *b late from work. C you later*. When the girls are all sharing stories, all I can do is smile and hope they don't see through me.'

'You and me both. OK, well, let's make a pact. No hiding. I'm here for you,' said Cassie.

'So, what about you? I know the girls were all laughing but it's not exactly simple, is it?'

'I'm off the map,' Cassie confessed. 'I don't know the rules of going out with a parent. I mean, what's reasonable to expect? How d'you find the balance between being a clueless, demanding diva and a complete doormat with no needs of their own?'

They were stopped at the lights of a busy junction, so Louise had time to look at Cassie for a moment, her face tinted slightly green in the orange streetlights.

'I suppose all you can go with is what feels OK. One step at a time.'

That all sounded really sensible. Except that not all steps were equal, Cassie mused – it all depended where they were taking you.

Chapter 9

'Sorry . . . what?'

'We're getting married.'

It was a blustery Saturday morning and Cassie had come home from her dog-walking duties with her cheeks ruddy and her hair standing on end to find Mam and Eric sitting together on the sofa with coffee and Danish pastries laid out on the coffee table. That was remarkable enough, added to which she noticed Mam had put heated rollers in her hair that morning and was clearly wearing makeup, which was a sure indication of an upcoming photo opportunity.

Cassie realised she really shouldn't have been that shocked by the revelation; also, both Mam and Eric couldn't have been sweeter or more considerate in their tone.

'When?'

'Well, we thought early July.' Mam gazed up at Eric. 'And we'd like you to be one of our bridesmaids, with your sister Maxine, of course.'

Oh sweet, suffering Jesus, that was a whole other level of dreadful.

'Wow, I am absolutely thrilled and . . . kind of surprised? If I'm being honest.'

Fucking stunned was what she meant.

Mam slipped her hand into Eric's and began, as though speaking to a small child, 'Eric and I met at a time in our lives when we'd both lost somebody very dear to us. And we'd like to spend the rest of the time left to us together. And we're so happy to share it with you first of all.'

She'd never looked happier, Cassie thought, even with Da. She was conscious that this was Mam's big moment and kept smiling, but underneath she felt . . . what? A twinge of jealousy that her mother had managed to win the lasting devotion of not one, but two fine men. A flash of indignation on Da's behalf – I mean, for the love of God, he was only dead less than three years. On top of that was a wave of guilt for feeling like this. It made no sense; she had grown deeply fond of Eric and you could've seen from the International Space Station that they were perfect for each other, so what was her problem? Change. *I hate change.* Just don't cry and ruin everything, she warned herself severely.

'And we can go wedding-dress shopping together. We didn't get to do that the first time round.' Mam beamed. 'We can link up with Maxine online from Toronto so she can give her opinion.'

Cassie's smile froze. Oh crap.

Eric was very wisely saying nothing, but he leaned in, waving his iPad. 'Little photo to mark the occasion?'

Predictably, she looked like a startled ostrich, while Mam and Eric looked like the golden-years couple from a multivitamin ad.

Half an hour later Cassie was rinsing the cups in the kitchen when Mam slipped in beside her with an air of anticipation about her.

'Thank you for taking it all so well, love. I understand it might have been a shock for you.'

'It's OK, Mam, I'm really happy for you both.'

Cassie smiled bravely as Mam went on, 'I know things have been a little distant between you and Maxie over the years and I hope this is the perfect time to put all the silliness behind you. Life's too short for that sort of nonsense.'

Cassie was just about to protest that it wasn't that simple, when Mam raised her hand.

'There's just one other thing and there's no point in putting it off. I hope you understand, because I know it'll work out for the best in the long run . . .'

That sounded ominous.

'So, I'm sure you'll understand that when Eric moves in, we'll be wanting the house to ourselves.'

'Of course, that goes without saying,' said Cassie out loud with a smile.

Inside her, her ten-year-old self was wailing, *I'm being evicted from my own home.*

The next moment her sensible side kicked in: face it, we're all adults, even though blood, in this case, didn't seem to be thicker than water.

'You don't want to be stuck here with us oldies, you want to be up and out, getting on with your own life. Trust me, you'll thank me in the end.'

Cassie had an image of herself like some perky prairie dog popping out of a burrow.

'Oh sure, I'll start checking out Daft. I'm sure there'll be loads of properties on that.'

She knew she was being passive–aggressive but there did feel a distinct difference between moving out and being turfed out on your arse.

* * *

'A bridesmaid with Maxine? How do you feel about that?' Josie's face was full of concern.

'Freaked, obviously. She still thinks I'm a waste of space. I'm thrilled for Mam, sort of. Eric is a dote, but how am I supposed to find somewhere to live in this jungle of a housing crisis? You don't know how bad it is here. I know it's not easy in London, but trust me, there's no comparison.'

'Something will come up, it always does.'

'In the absence of my own confidence, I'll have to borrow yours. What am I going to do, Jos? Mam's already started down the road of Bridezilla, I'm going to co-bridesmaid with the sister I've barely spoken to apart from *Happy Christmas* texts for years, and I've barely heard from Finn since our last date.'

'Nothing since?'

'OK, once this week he texted: *Missing you, place feels v quiet*. It was just the facts but that's to be expected, he's an engineer. Oh, and then I got a: *Hope u slept well, had dream about you.*'

'Stop, stop, whoa, what sort of dream?'

'How do I know? He's a tidy texter, not a big, long psycho texter . . . And when I asked, he did text back: *Tell u at the w/e.* And that's the last I heard. In fairness, maybe that's why I'm being such a miserable bitch about Mam.'

'Hold that thought, I need the loo. Every time I take a sip of water, I have to go.'

Just then Cassie's phone beeped.

'Jos, wait, it's him: *Are you around this evening?* Am I?'

'I don't know, all I can think about is my bladder. Wait there.'

Exactly two minutes later Josie reappeared, looking infinitely more relaxed.

'OK, now I can think. At such short notice? You most certainly are not. That is sounding way too casual for my liking.'

'Come on, Jos, it's only late lunchtime.'

'Cas, I am thinking of your own good. If you make it too easy for him now, you'll ruin everything.'

'It's a bit late for that, don't you think?'

'Nonsense, it's never a minute too late to place value on yourself.'

'How am I supposed to do that?'

'Cass, if you weren't *afraid* of him not coming back, what would you do?'

'This is your *The Rules* book, Jos. When did you turn into Marjorie Proops?'

Josie was looking at her steadily with her 'you know I'm right' expression. 'I bet your mum didn't sleep with Eric on the first date.'

'Nooo, please don't give me that image. He was probably dressed in a smoking jacket and cravat like Sergei the meercat anyway.'

Josie burst out laughing.

'Don't laugh, this is serious. If I don't see him tonight, then next weekend he'll have his kids and that'll be two whole weeks, and he'll just forget about me. Plus, he's probably on Tinder and has hundreds of other options anyway.'

Cassie could hear the plaintive tone in her voice and it wasn't a pretty sound.

'Only hundreds? I'd say thousands, possibly millions.'

'It's not funny, Jos.'

'Whatever scares the hell out of you, lean into it.'

Which was possibly the worst advice ever given to anybody, but in her current state of uncertainty at least it was something to hang on to.

'Nobody says you can't have a smoochy phone call. That'll make him want you more, not less.'

'I don't know,' Cassie said. 'This feels all wrong.'

'It feels unfamiliar. That doesn't mean it's wrong. Do you want to slide into the "friends with benefits" zone, or do you want something more?'

'Something more.'

'Sorry, I don't think I heard that?'

'Something more,' Cassie muttered like a child who's been persuaded that they really don't want that second ice cream.

'I've got to go, Cass, my boobs are killing me. I need to stick two packs of frozen peas in my bra. Let me know how it goes.'

And she was gone.

Cassie was left to debate her two options alone. She could text back:

> *So sorry, can't ☹. Unfortunately made other plans*

That would be the wise and dignified thing to do, even if it did make her sound like a miserable bitch. Alternatively, she could reply:

> *Sure, when and where?*

This would be the pushover thing to do . . . or . . . could there be another option? Something that would steer the line between a booty call and the friend zone. OK, the last date had got a little – fine, a lot – out of hand and the no-nonsense side of her recognised that she needed to row back. She flinched at the endless excuses she'd made to herself about Gavin.

No. Just no. This was a new start. She would not do the same old thing and expect a new outcome. Not anymore. So she texted:

> *Oh dear, wasn't sure we were still on so made alternate plans. P.S. what was the dream about?*

She waited. The phone pinged.

Need to tell you in person.

Her heart lurched.

Phone me at six?

The reply arrived quickly:

☺

As five o'clock passed, she found herself showering and putting a mask in her hair, because she needed to anyway. She then changed into her favourite loose jeans that hung on her slim frame and paired them with a blue-grey cashmere V-neck sweater that just happened to look and feel effortlessly wonderful. The secret weapon in any girl's wardrobe.

This is so sad, she chided herself, you're dressing for a date when you've just told him you're unavailable. Well, if you're not sure what you want, she reminded herself, just look at what you find yourself doing. Just then her phone rang.

'Is that the dream-interpretation agency?'

She sighed. 'Wrong number.'

She heard him chuckle.

'Look, I'm really sorry, I should've contacted you way earlier. To be honest, it's been such a crazy week, it went clean out of my mind,' he said.

Be sweet but unavailable, she reminded herself.

'What a shame, but never mind – next time,' she purred. That was good, leave the way open for him to make it up to you.

'Like I said, it's a long time since I've done this. I'm out of practice.'

'Oh, I don't know . . .' she murmured coquettishly. 'You seem to be doing OK.'

He gave a short laugh. At least it didn't sound like he was spending every spare waking moment scrolling on Tinder.

'So, what was the dream?'

She heard him inhale. 'Nothing much. I just dreamed you were there with me in the apartment, except that it was on wheels, and we were driving somewhere and when I woke up, well . . . you weren't there.'

There was a pause. OK, that was pretty straightforward. Freud would've been out of business if the world was full of Finns; on the other hand, it was lovely – how often did you get a role in someone else's dream?

'And I realised I missed you.'

Oh, bugger the pretence.

'I missed you too.'

OK, Josie would be proud of her. She'd made him a little sorry for screwing up the date but not sorry enough to be discouraged. For the first time in her life Cassie began to feel a little empowered in the dating game.

'Where are you now?' she couldn't stop herself asking.

'Across the road from your house, in the car.'

This was either very stalkerish or very endearing. She chose to go with the latter. For God's sake what was she thinking? He'd shown remorse about being late, he'd dreamed about her, dammit, he'd even driven to her door. There was self-respect and then there was being a total eejit.

'Just say, if your alternate plans didn't start until later, would you have time to come for a drink?'

She contemplated that. For about one millisecond.

'Yes. It'd have to be a bit quick, though.' No point in sabotaging all the good work now.

'I get it.'

She could hear the smile in his voice and was trying to purse her lips to stop herself from beaming.

'OK, just give me a minute,' she said airily.

Don't fall over yourself now, she thought, adding a touch of blusher to her perfectly made-up face and finishing with a spritz of perfume. She briefly caught sight of herself in the mirror: a woman with honey-blonde hair in a long brown coat, collar turned up against the cold. She could turn heads. Mam met her at the door.

'God, love, there's some weirdo loitering in a car across the road. He's been there for ages. Do you think I should call the Gardaí?'

'It's all right, Mam, he's for me.'

* * *

'I don't know, I thought our last date went pretty well.'

Cassie could see Finn's raised eyebrow; his face was illuminated by the streetlights as he spoke. They had parked above the city and were gazing out across the bay. Cassie gave him a playful tap.

'So did I, but think about it, you have a complicated life at the moment and I do not.'

He smiled pointedly at her. 'Apart from me?'

Interesting . . . That implied he saw himself in her life.

'Apart from you. We've been so intimate and yet . . . God, I'm embarrassed to hear myself saying this, but I feel like I know very little about you.'

'Funny, that's exactly what my ex used to say.'

'So, she thought you were unreadable as well.' She smiled. 'And were you?'

He gave a rueful laugh. 'Maybe. Seems like it.' His shoulders slumped a little. He's really not used to this, she thought.

'So, what happened?'

'No blame,' he began, which was a good sign. 'Nobody else involved or anything like that.'

'You just . . . fell out of love?'

He gave a snort of laughter.

'Is that funny?'

'No, it's just I have asked myself that too: were we ever "in love" at all?'

'Don't make it sound like a disease.'

He seemed to be struggling to find the words and it struck Cassie that perhaps this was the first time he'd talked about it.

'Maybe we were, for the first summer we were together. She'd just finished teacher training, I was work-ing in my first graduate job, making decent money, and for those few months it seemed as though everything came together. It was like someone had turned down the force of gravity. OK, you have permission to laugh.'

'No, that's lovely. I've never heard it described quite like that before, but it sounds special. I mean, if that's not being in love . . .'

'Thank you, for some reason that makes me feel better. Like I didn't just make it all up.'

There was a sadness in his voice. 'It was that stage in our lives where you have all the independence and none of the responsibility.'

Cassie thought back over her long freelance career.

'That can wear pretty thin after a while. Trust me.'

Finn made that sound where people exhale through their nose and finish with a harrumph to express a feeling of regret. There's no word for that, Cassie thought. And there should be. People do it all the time.

'I wonder how many couples run for years on the memory of a feeling.'

'Lots, probably. They live on the feeling they got on their first date. Forever trying to recreate it. Though not my parents, now I think of it. They always seemed to laugh so much. Da would grab Mam and they'd jive around the kitchen whenever Abba or the Bee Gees came on the radio, and then she'd pretend to do the dance of the seven veils with a couple of tea towels. What were your parents like?'

'Not like yours, by the sound of it. They were very separate.' He seemed to be searching for the right words. 'They were always very busy. It was all a bit chaotic, now I think of it.'

Instinct told Cassie to leave it, he'd tell her in his own good time.

'My ex-wife is very organised.'

'Good for her.'

'Looking back, I think that's what we ran on. A sixteen-year marriage and three kids based on one summer of love and a whole lot of lists.'

'You stuck with it, though. Maybe there was more to it. It's my theory that we don't always know why we do something. Sometimes we start things for one reason and end up doing them for another.'

'I changed.'

'Was that a bad thing?'

'I turned into an adult. I got stuck there. I sort of didn't recognise myself anymore.'

'Well, good for you. Sorry, I only mean that about the adult bit. That's something I'm still working on.'

'Why d'you think I'm here?' He leaned in, took her face between his hands and kissed her. She felt her insides melt. He reached down with the other hand, fumbling with the lever, when suddenly the seat shot back, sending them both into fits of giggles.

'Wow, smooth move . . .'

'Come here . . .' He pulled her astride him, allowing her to lean her head against his forehead as his hands explored the soft skin under her top, and she teased her mouth against the rough stubble of his upper lip. 'Well, if you wanted to feel not like an adult, snogging in the car with a woman who still lives with her mammy is a good place to start.'

'I love talking to you, Cassie Kearney, I love being with you. I knew that from the minute I saw you.'

'What? Lying flat in the mud, totally winded by your dog, who by the way has serious attachment issues – you thought: that is the woman for me?'

'That, and the fact you were gorgeous.'

'With my grilled-tomato face and mud-caked hair?'

'It was the natural look, I'll admit.'

'At least I don't have too much to live up to. I'm hardly likely to destroy your illusions.'

He touched his lips against her hair.

'That's what I like. Don't change, OK?' He sounded serious.

'I'm not sure I can. But I might have to try. I'm not looking to wreck the moment or anything, it's just that I've spent way too long letting my heart rule my head. I'm really still trying to sort myself out. And you were hoping for something simple.'

He looked at her intently. 'Why did you come home from London, when you had a whole life there? And a career in acting?'

'Of sorts.'

'Have you given that up?' His tone felt curious but totally without judgement.

'When I went as a teenager, I had such confidence. I felt like I could do anything. Sounds cocky, but it's what you need. And then I came home one summer to visit and . . . something unfortunate happened. It was my fault. And it kind of . . . triggered some crisis, some self-doubt – I haven't really analysed it, though I probably should – but looking back, after that, everything began to unravel. And the phone stopped ringing. I still feel guilty for Bea, she'd such belief in me.'

Finn watched her, waiting for her to continue. But she didn't. The heart had gone out of her.

'Finn, I'm sorry, I think I need to go home now.'

'For your prior engagement?'

She pulled up a smile. 'Yeah. Right.'

After they parked in front of the house, Cassie reached out in the dark and clutched his hand.

'Thank you for asking me about all that,' she said.

'No. Thank you. I don't talk enough about that sort of stuff.'

She could feel his struggle.

'I kind of guessed.'

They sat for a moment in a silence that felt like stroking a soft-haired cat.

'Admit it, this was a pretty classy date.'

She laughed. 'A tepid glass of Pinot Grigio out of a paper cup for me and a Heiney zero from Spar for you, drunk by the light of the dashboard.'

'Anywhere is fun with you, Cass.'

She allowed that to sink in.

'OK, next time let's take it up a notch – you better take me to the movies. You pick the film.' There was something so uncomplicated and sweet about the movies. Like they were rolling back time to the place where life was still innocent.

He leaned forward and kissed her. She could feel the stubble as his tongue probed her mouth, eliciting an involuntary gasp. It was time to go.

'Night,' she whispered and scrambled out of the car.

Chapter 10

The following morning Cassie lay in bed, gazing at the pink-hued light that filled the room, and thought back over the night before. How long was it since she'd been on a date? Twenty years? Almost. She let her mind wander back to Finn's long, pale hands and the slightly uncertain air he had at times, which somehow made her feel calmer. Never in their time together did she remember Gav looking unsure. She thought about Finn's ex never feeling she knew him. In spite of his laconic manner, Cassie didn't feel he was hiding from her. To whatever extent he knew himself, he was letting her see. And that was a lovely thought. Unfortunately, it didn't last long. Oh God, I'm being kicked out, she panicked.

Finn has a lovely apartment, was her next thought. Oh no, don't you dare, broke in her sensible self. You can sleep in the garage; you can sleep in the garden shed or in the car before it comes to that. Mam's brisk, matter-of-fact request that she find herself somewhere to live had been shocking – not only from a logistical point of view, which was bad enough, but more, it seemed to hint that this was her mother's house, not hers. Cassie didn't know if she was quite ready for that. Even at thirty-seven,

98

she was still her mother's child. It felt like she'd been orphaned. Ridiculous, but true.

Enough wallowing, proclaimed her no-nonsense self, let's get this show started.

'Alexa!' Soon the sound of an M People club classic filled the room. She jumped out of bed, swiped open the curtains and joined in karaoke-style at the top of her voice while rocking around the room in her pyjamas: 'Moving on up, moving on out, nothing can stop me . . .'

Right, let's plug into the world and see what's out there for me. She showered and pulled on her new leggings, platform Uggs and a cornflower-blue hoodie over a white T-shirt. Dressing for spring, dressing for the future. 'Moving on up, moving on out,' she rocked out the door and went downstairs to make coffee.

'Oh, pet, you look lovely, like a Wedgwood plate.'

'Thanks.' She eyed the stewed-looking pot of coffee doubtfully. 'Sorry, Mam, but if I'm looking for a flat, I'm going to need a serious, proper cup of coffee – no offence.'

She fished out the stove-top coffee pot she'd brought home from London and made herself a huge cup of piping-hot Italian coffee with foaming hot milk. Mam looked sheepish.

'Look, love, I was only giving you a heads-up for the long run. I wasn't expecting you to move out right away.'

'It's fine, honestly, I think you've done me a favour. I need to stand on my own two feet. You're right not to make things too comfortable for me.'

Armed with her power-latte, she sat down at the laptop and began a search of property letting sites. She had two options: try to find someone with a spare room and looking for a flatmate or rent an apartment herself and look for a second person – at least that way she'd have a bit more control. Good plan, she reasoned. However, by midday it had become abundantly clear that her ideas were wildly naive and totally out of touch with reality. She found herself scrolling past one depressing dive after another, or else ads charging exorbitant rent for anything she could inhabit with a modicum of self-respect. Once, she grew highly excited at the sight of a gorgeous double bedroom with a view through enchanting dormer windows, at an affordable price, only to realise it was in Belgium.

'There's always something,' chirped Mam, sticking her head in the door. 'You just have to look hard enough.'

This was absolute twaddle, seeing as the last time Mam had been flat-hunting was in 1974 with a copy of the *Evening Herald* stuck in her handbag, the ads circled in biro.

She thought of the girls, with their husbands and their houses, and how once you had established a home of your own, the alternative scenarios simply melted away. They'd be appalled or simply couldn't imagine anymore what it'd be like to join the crowds of people desperately phoning or standing queueing for somewhere to rent. Plus, she didn't even have a steady job at the moment. No, no, no, this was not a good road to wander down. She thought fondly of the cosy little flat she'd left behind in Archway with Gavin. Their freewheeling life together. Or rather, his freewheeling life and her keeping the home.

Nope, that ship had sailed, that sort of thinking led only to pain. She'd given London her youth and what was she left with? A lot of memories, a few regrets and a narrow window to make up for lost time.

There was something inherently lonely in feeling like you were between homes, even if you hadn't left yet. She longed to reach out to a friend. Not Josie, who was out at the Victoria and Albert with Pal, working through their bucket list of couples' activities to do before the baby arrived. But who? She ran through the possible reactions of her gang: Bryony and Celine would enjoy the disaster stories, but did she really want to be the butt of the jokes? Norah, for all her brusqueness, might actually take a more practical view and see it as a failure of government policy rather than Cassie's fault for finding herself in such a vulnerable position. Still, she'd be bound to judge. No, there was only one person she felt safe enough to open up to. She looked at her watch: twelve thirty. God, let's hope it isn't a bad time. She ran down her list of contacts and pressed call.

'Hi, Louise.'

'Cassie, hey. It's great to hear from you.'

There was no mistaking the enthusiasm in Louise's voice.

'I hope it's not a bad time. I'm phoning for . . . nothing, honestly, just for a chat.'

'Love it,' broke in Louise. 'A phone call about nothing, they're the best type. How are you?' Despite her plan to be upbeat, in the face of Louise's unexpected warmth she found herself telling the truth.

'Ish, how about you?'

'Ish back at you.'

There was something in Louise's tone that alerted her.

'Hey, are you OK?'

There was a hesitation from the other end of the phone.

'Mike went out to play golf yesterday.'

Cassie remembered the wide smile and confident air of the handsome Mike.

'OK, that's his thing, isn't it?'

'Except that he went out at noon yesterday and didn't come home until after one in the morning, and now he's still in bed snoring and I want to wake him to ask him where the hell he was. And if you find yourself needing to do that, well . . . So, when I saw your name coming up on the phone, honestly, I couldn't have been happier.'

'I was afraid you'd be tied up, everyone's so manically busy these days.'

'Feck 'em, I'm not.'

As briefly as possible, she explained to Louise the drama about Mam's wedding plans and how she was essentially being booted out of the love-nest.

'Oh, that's disturbing. I don't care what age you are . . .' After thinking for a moment, Louise went on, 'You'll want to kill me for this but it's probably for the best in the long run. You need your own place, girl. It could be fun.'

'That's what I've been trying to tell myself but it's so minging out there.' Despite her best efforts, she heard her voice crack. 'I'm sorry, Louise, I actually phoned you for a laugh. I didn't mean to be such a big baby.'

'I get it. Believe me. Everyone keeps telling me how fantastic my life is, except the one person I really need to hear it from.'

And there it was. The world wasn't necessarily crammed full of dewy-eyed ecstatically happy people.

'You're a lovely person and you deserve nothing but the best.'

'You know what,' said Louise, 'I think I might actually be able to help.'

'You're kidding? I've been flicking through the rooms to rent. One advertised a "charming room with mezzanine". Seriously, when I looked closely, it was just a big shelf nailed to the wall with a ladder up to it. If you turned over in bed you could plummet to your death, and any nookie could cause a full-on earthquake,' lamented Cassie. 'I was just getting over that when the next one said, "bed for rent". You don't even get the room and when I phoned, they explained it's a timeshare on the bed!'

Louise burst out laughing. 'Fancy living, or what? You could invite the girls round to dinner . . . Can you imagine Norah's face. She'd have to bring her Dettol spray and latex gloves.'

They both rocked with laughter.

'And Celine would be posting it on Instagram for likes, and I'd be made a total show of and have to go round with a bag over my head,' said Cassie.

'Wait, don't panic yet! My sister has a friend who's looking for a flatmate . . . again . . .'

Excitement prevented her from registering how Louise's voice petered out.

'Are you serious? Please don't get my hopes up, not after the morning I've had.'

'Do you mind . . . very loud people?'

'Loud? At this stage I'd share with a howler monkey if I could afford it.'

'In that case you'll be fine. Ramona's fun. In fact, she pretty much defines the term.'

Chapter 11

The speed with which everything fell into place made Cassie's head spin. On Sunday they had the 'I have a friend . . .' conversation and by Monday evening she was driving in Louise's car towards Ramona's apartment in posh Dublin 4. They made their way through the glass doors and across the marble floor of the entrance, past the floor-to-ceiling windows and the enormous artwork in the foyer, and took the burnished lift up to the fourth floor.

'Why are we here, Louise? There isn't a hope in holy hell I'll be able to afford this. What's she like? What do you know about her? I mean, how come this amazing apartment is available instantly?'

'Ramona is a little . . . different,' explained Louise carefully.

'That's OK, so am I.'

There was something about Louise's demeanour that made her panic slightly. Too late for that. Here they were at 16D, Ramona's door. As they knocked and waited, Cassie could feel the tingle of excitement at the prospect of living in such a ritzy location, light years away from the depressing properties she'd been viewing online. Perhaps it would all work out, perhaps fortune favoured the bold and all of her risky decisions would be proved right. Just then the door swung open.

'Well, hey, babies!!'

Standing in front of them was a six-foot-two woman, at the very least, in her gold platform sandals and spandex shorts, not to mention a white skintight crop top. On a bitter March evening. Cassie immediately felt like a contestant from the *Housewife of the Year* competition circa 1972, dressed in her cosy jacket and sensible boots.

'Well, look at you, aren't you just the cutest thing?' boomed Ramona with a put-on country-and-western crackle in her voice, though underneath her accent was genuinely American. 'Come on in.'

Pivoting on her high heels, she paraded her toned and barely covered bum into the adjoining room, projecting over her shoulder as she vanished, 'D'you girls drink gin?'

Cassie looked open-mouthed at Louise. She'd never seen such beautiful makeup in real life, only on *Drag Race*. It was only when Louise clocked her expression and whispered, 'Ramona is . . . just Ramona,' that she managed to recover herself.

'Well, don't huddle in the hall like a little herd of sheep!' They shuffled after her into what was presumably supposed to be the sitting room but, to all appearances, looked like a club of some sort – or to be more precise, a lap dancing club. The curtains were closed, giving the space a gloomy feel. One wall was painted black, one purple and the other consisted of strips of smoked mirror from floor to ceiling. The only furniture apart from an L-shaped black leather sofa and a massive TV was a chrome pole fixed between floor and ceiling, and a phone on a tripod. Striking it might be, cosy it definitely was not.

'Wow, fabulous,' breathed Cassie.

'Sorry, sweeties, I was rehearsing for my act. Come on, I'll show you the rest of the place. Lulie, did you get a little chunky since I saw you last?'

'I'm pregnant.'

'Thank God, I thought you'd been hitting the pizza.' She gave Louise a playful slap on the bottom.

Louise looked a little taken aback so Cassie gave her a reassuring smile. Without further consultation, Ramona pushed one of the mirror panels, which slowly opened to reveal a well-lit drinks bar, including, apparently, a fridge from which she served Beefeater Blood Orange gin and tonics.

'Hey, preggers, you're off the booze I suppose?'

'Er yes, thanks, just a few ice cubes for me. I can't even look at a tonic. I can barely even say the word without getting a wave of—'

'How does the human race ever reproduce, when pregnancy is just so *boring*?'

Cassie's jaw practically hit the floor. This was, without exception, the most insensitive, rude, boorish woman she had ever met. But at the same time, she reflected, there was something hilariously anarchic about the whole situation that made her feel a laugh bubbling up inside her.

Ramona towered over her five-foot-five frame as she handed her the eye-wateringly strong gin and tonic.

'Haven't I seen you before somewhere?'

Cassie knew better than to coyly reply, 'Yes, on *Casualty*.' This only gave the other person a chance to reply, 'No, not that, I never watch it.' So she said nothing and let Ramona work it out.

'I know what it was! You were all in your bra and panties, that's why I didn't recognise you!' she hollered.

Cassie practically felt herself blasted against the wall with the impact.

'You were one of those chicks waving their oxters around – that deodorant. *I knew it.*'

She seemed to take an almost childlike delight in recognising her.

'I didn't recognise you with your clothes on.' She burst into raucous laughter and then, without warning, made straight for the door.

'Come on, let me show you your room.'

There seemed to be an understanding that Cassie had magically passed some invisible test and was now as good as moved in. She snuck a glance back at Louise, who gave a helpless shrug as they trooped down the hallway to a kitchen of cream cabinets with black marble surfaces and a breathtaking view over the city. It was obvious from the show-house feel that the occupant had probably never cooked a meal there. The apartment was fitted out to an impressively high standard, about which Ramona seemed utterly nonchalant. 'Fridge,' she droned, flicking open the massive American-style appliance that seemed to contain not much more than a large bottle of vodka, a family-sized carton of orange juice and a wedge of cheese. Not much of a domestic goddess, but no surprises there.

'Myyy roooom,' she drawled as they passed a dark space. 'Your roooom.' She flung open a room and switched on the light to indicate a double en-suite room with built-in wardrobe, whose open doors seemed to suggest someone had left in a hurry.

Seated at the glass table in the kitchen, a few moments later, Cassie reminded herself to take some ownership of this situation and not be railroaded by Ramona's powerful presence.

'OK, first of all, your place is amazing – and what an incredible location, oh my God, but—'

'Yada, yada, I know what you're going to ask. How much is the rent? Well, how much'a you got?'

'Well, I've a dog-walking business, part-time, and some savings but I am planning to get a more serious job.' She put a little laugh in her voice to try and minimise the tension, but it still sounded lame.

Glancing around the apartment, she felt the strength drain out of her. This was a fantasy. What was she thinking? She'd need more than a serious job to pay for this lot. She'd need a sugar daddy. Ramona produced a vape from a tiny jewelled handbag and took a pull.

'I own the place so . . . whatever.'

That nonchalance again. It struck Cassie that Ramona must either have one hell of an income or come from a background where money wasn't an issue. A fizz of excitement started in her tummy – this might actually, unbelievably, be possible after all.

'Five hundred?' Ramona threw out airily, as though she were starting an auction at Sotheby's.

'A week?'

Ramona looked at her and snorted with laughter. 'Jeez. I'm not that much of a witch. A month, obvs!'

What?? Five hundred a month was nothing. She could easily afford that. Cassie found herself involuntarily leaping up from her chair and hugging Ramona.

'Oh my God, yes. Yes, thank you. That'd be . . . amazing.'

'So, we've a deal. First of every month, and don't bring anyone back unless I've vetted them first.' Another throaty laugh.

'Deal.'

'I'll be away until the weekend, so make yourself at home. I don't actually cook but someone told me there's pots somewhere – oh, and help yourself to the OJ and vodka . . . See you then.'

Cassie looked at Louise and only then did it dawn on them both that Ramona was on her way out. This was a girl who clearly didn't sit around watching life happen second-hand.

Five minutes later they were walking down the path towards the car park. Cassie was feeling buffeted by conflicting feelings.

'I never dreamed I could get something like that, Louise. I can't thank you enough for introducing me.'

'Well, one thing I can promise you is that you won't be bored.'

'I've just realised I never asked her anything about herself. I didn't feel like I could, what does she do? She only looks about thirty, if that, how does she own that place? I mean . . . what is she?'

'I don't know, exactly. My sister Trish is in events management and knows her as a burlesque dancer. Apparently, she's pretty celebrated in those circles. But she's some sort of TikTok influencer as well.'

'None of that sounds like it'd buy you a sniff of that apartment. As my ma would say, maybe she comes from a long line of bling-bling.'

'Maybe she does. I wouldn't be surprised. Don't super-rich people kind of feel like they can make their own rules?'

'I wouldn't know,' said Cassie.

'Neither would I.'

They both laughed, a companionable, relieved laugh. Six-foot-two in her platform sandals and hot pants or not, Ramona had taken her in. At least she was back on track towards her own independence, whatever that might look like.

* * *

Finn had his arm around her as she leaned against his shoulder, both of them munching their way through a big box of popcorn as they watched the movie in the small, intimate cinema. As the titles began to roll, everyone else got up with a flap of their seat and shuffled out from between their rows while they sat on, watching the credits. The closing music drifted, haunting and meditative, through the empty cinema, as the endless list of names scrolled by.

'I adored it,' she said. 'There's something about music in movies. I once heard it described as creating a back door to the emotions. Good choice.'

He smiled and kissed the top of her head as they meandered out of the cinema and down the hill towards the warm yellow light spilling through the windows of the thatched pub.

'I like the way you put words on things that I feel, but I've never named,' remarked Finn, apparently addressing a stop sign. She understood his awkwardness and tightened her arm around his.

After she found them a comfortable seat at a table in a corner, Finn returned with a pint of Heineken for himself and a glass of Sauvignon Blanc for her.

'I love the way you can order for me without asking, and it's always the right thing.'

He gave her a sideways glance, but she could tell he was pleased.

'You're welcome. So, tell me all about this new flatmate.' He settled back comfortably.

But before she could reply, she registered a look of consternation on Finn's face. Oh God, what now? He hastily put down his drink and said, 'Let's get out of here.'

'What? We've just sat down, Finn. What's going on?'

She snuck a glance in the direction of his gaze, only to lock eyes with one of the most hostile stares she'd ever encountered.

'Come on—'

'No! Wait, I've just got my drink and I'm not leaving. Tell me who that woman is.'

'It's Janine, my ex-wife's sister.'

'And does she not know you're separated?'

'Oh, she does, yeah.'

'Well, then, feck her.'

'You don't get it. She's a weapon.'

'What the hell? You owe her nothing and neither do I.'

'Oh, God, she's coming over. Christ.'

The burly middle-aged woman was barging towards them through the tables, drawing alarmed glances from the other patrons. With her elbows raised and her chin jutting, she looked extremely intimidating. But if life as a performer had taught Cassie anything, it was not to be afraid of a scene. Embarrassment was no threat to her, no siree. Janine had picked the wrong girl for that. Oh yes. Maybe Cassie was secretly missing performing or maybe meeting the fearless Ramona had given her extra confidence, but if this bitch wanted a ding-dong, then a ding-dong she would get. Audience or no audience.

'So, Finn, you're out and about already?'

The decibel level of her voice was designed to brow-beat and humiliate.

'Hello, Janine,' said Finn through gritted teeth.

Janine swivelled her attention round to Cassie like a rocket launcher taking aim.

'And who is this lady? I don't believe I've had the pleasure?'

What a wagon. At least Cassie had had the foresight to whip her drink off the table on the off-chance Janine might try to tip it over her. No point in wasting good wine. She was no psychologist, but she could certainly spot a chick with a ton of inner rage who was only too delighted to find an excuse to take it out on someone in the name of loyalty or whatever.

'Cassie.' She smiled pleasantly. 'My name is Cassie.'

'Well, "Cassie", are you aware that this man is married to my sister?'

The rest of the bar was getting way more action than they'd bargained for on a lacklustre Thursday evening and were lapping it up. This was a tricky situation, Cassie recognised – the moment she reacted, Janine would have her hooked. The old quote about mud wrestling with a pig sprang to mind. Something about . . . 'You'll both end up dirty and the pig will only enjoy it.' Apart from that, this was Finn's battle, and anything she did could only make things worse.

'That's enough, Janine, we all know the situation. Marisha and I are living separately. This is none of your business.'

Which was a perfectly fine and accurate reply. Unfortunately, Janine appeared to be one of those people for whom facts were irrelevant or, worse, all part of a conspiracy. She was also hell-bent on involving the entire pub in the drama. Cassie sensed that the only way to play this was to be composed, slightly surprised and utterly unapologetic, thereby making her opponent look unhinged.

'And I wonder if my sister or her *three little children* were here now what they'd make of it.'

'Marisha is well aware of the situation and, anyhow, we're not in the way of bringing our children into pubs at night.'

'Is that so? Well, maybe then we should phone her!' announced Janine, triumphantly whipping out her phone. Mercifully, help came from an unexpected source in the form of a group of men who had become quite invested in the dispute.

'Ah, shut oop, ye ole slag.'

'Yeah, the fella's separated. That's what he's after sayin'. Fair an' square. Leave them alone.'

'She's only raging 'cause your other one is way better lookin',' a third chortled.

This caused a degree of hilarity at the table but wasn't doing anything to improve Janine's temper.

'Let it go, Janine,' muttered Finn. She hesitated for a moment but had the sense to read the room. She lowered her voice. 'Just you wait, Finn, just you see how much access you get to those kids after this.'

At that, she swept out of the pub. Cassie felt shaken and Finn looked positively grey.

'Don't you mind her, son,' said one of the men kindly. 'She's only an old wagon. I know the type.'

'What a 'mare,' observed another. 'Reminds me of my ex. See that?' he said, jabbing his finger at his balding head while looking in Cassie's direction. 'She done that to me.'

The problem was that Janine did potentially have some power. Mean, vindictive power maybe, but power nonetheless. They sat in silence, flinching at the surreptitious glances and mutterings around them.

'God, I'm sorry, maybe we should've left . . .'

'Babe, you were absolutely right. I've nothing to be ashamed of. Maybe it wasn't the wisest thing to come here in the first place, but if not now . . . when?'

Babe. It was a long time since she'd been called that. It felt lovely.

'I thought you stayed calm and handled it brilliantly.'

'Yeah?'

She squeezed his hand. 'Yeah. You couldn't have dealt with it better.'

She knew that if they'd been in private, he'd have kissed her.

'Thanks, but there's no point pretending. She could make life hell for me.'

'Your child custody hasn't been made official yet?'

He shook his head.

'Right now, it's all based around goodwill, which works fine . . . until it doesn't. And the last thing I need is that one sticking her oar in. The only good thing is that Marisha doesn't particularly like her. And Marisha's job is high pressure, so breaks from the kids actually suit her. She always seems in pretty good form when I collect them.'

This provoked an unease in Cassie. She loved the feeling of being trusted with painful family stuff but, on the other hand, there was something unnerving about the familiarity with which he still spoke about his ex-wife. The rest of the pub appeared to have lost interest in their drama and gone back to their own conversations. None-theless, it was a relief to see the tables clearing and the crowd thinning out. The men who'd come to their rescue stood up to go, and one of them leaned over to speak to Finn.

'This'll pass,' he said and patted his shoulder. 'Don't let the haters call the shots.'

It was a kindly remark and it seemed as though Finn welcomed it, especially as the other man exuded an air of quiet authority. Finn nodded and Cassie noticed that he was looking down busily at his phone, holding back tears.

'Let's go,' she said, reaching for her coat.

They stood outside together in the cold night, in the same spot they'd been only a couple of hours earlier, but Cassie could feel a shift in the air. The season was changing.

Chapter 12

Mam couldn't stop talking about the new apartment.

'And tell me, is there a kitchen island?'

'Yes.'

'Five hundred a month, that sounds like an awful lot.'

'It isn't.'

'Well, I can come with you on Saturday to help you carry some stuff. You don't want to be up and down in the lift like a yo-yo.'

Cassie sighed. That much she could concede to. Mam was also bursting with curiosity about Ramona, not to mention feeling more than a little guilty about the speed of her daughter's exit.

'I'll make you a batch of scones to get you started. I'm sure your flatmate would like that.' The thought of Ramona in her gold hot pants bothering about scones felt so incongruous that she inadvertently scoffed.

'Oh, all right, then, I won't. But, believe me, there's very few people in my experience that don't appreciate a good scone.'

It turned out she was right.

* * *

Saturday at 11 a.m. on the dot she and Mam, both laden down with cardboard boxes, knocked on the door marked 16D. From inside they could hear the beat of loud, pounding music, which stopped dead. A moment later the door was flung open by Ramona, her bleached hair tied up in a brightly coloured headband; she was dressed in red leggings, the chunkiest pair of runners Cassie had ever seen, which added another couple of inches to her height, and a T-shirt that said: 'Attitude Matters'.

'Come in, babies,' she hollered. 'I was just hoovering.'

Which seemed unlikely, as the hoover wasn't even plugged in. This time the curtains in the living room were thrown open to create a somewhat more lively feel, but the shiny pole was still the focus of the room. A pile of richly coloured ostrich-feather fans was strewn across the sofa.

Mam clapped her hands like a child at Christmas.

Cassie's heart sank. Mam had a way of becoming obsessed by people she saw as exciting, a remnant perhaps of her own uneventful life. There was more than a little Shirley Valentine in her. Cassie's fear was that, having asked her to clear out of the family home, Mam would now try to follow her.

'Attitude matters, it certainly does! A girl after my own heart,' she cried. 'Oh my God, look at the pole – go on, show us how you do the dancing.'

There was no need to ask twice; Ramona hit the sound system and as the strains of Ariana Grande filled the room, she handed her phone to Cassie and explained, 'For my Insta feed, just press play and keep it centred, OK?'

She grabbed the pole high up, flipped her body upside down, did the splits and rotated slowly, lowering herself to the ground. Cassie had seen things like that on film, but up close it was even more obvious just how much strength and control were required.

Mam was enchanted, clapping like a small child at a circus show, which in fairness, it pretty much was.

'Isn't that fabulous! See, now, *that's* performance. *That's* entertainment.'

Cassie was stung by the implied unfavourable comparison, and for one awful moment was terrified that Mam would clamour to have a go herself, but fortunately just then she remembered the scones and produced them triumphantly, like a magician pulling a rabbit out of her tote bag. Ramona accepted the box like a winning cheque from the Lotto. In absolute fairness to Mam's tact, she declined a coffee, with the excuse that she'd arranged to meet Eric in Roly's Bistro round the corner for brunch – where they served the most scrumptious omelettes, she explained – and she'd hate to spoil her appetite, but another time would be absolutely gorgeous. As Mam made her exit, waving and blowing kisses, Ramona watched her go. 'You're so lucky, your mother is amazing . . . I mean, there she is heading off to meet her little man to have their little omelettes, it's so cute.'

Which was all true. It was just . . . Sometimes it was easier for other people to see that than it was for her.

And she'd no doubt that Mam probably felt the same way about her.

* * *

Later that evening, Cassie unpacked her clothes and hung them up in the cavernous wardrobes. She placed Ronron, her balding stuffed rabbit, on the bed, plugged in her lava lamp and arranged her budget toiletries in the chi-chi en suite. She gazed doubtfully at the incongruity between the high-end setting and her humble possessions. Just then, there was a loud knock, causing Cassie to jump.

'Hey, hon . . . can I come in?'

Cassie pulled open the door and Ramona, now dressed in a gold dress with a skater skirt and red platform shoes, paraded in and plonked herself on the bed.

'Oh, hi, I was just putting my things out.'

An unreadable expression crossed Ramona's face as she looked around, taking in every detail almost hungrily.

'My Lord . . . this room really transforms with every new person who lives here.'

OK, so had the place been host to a succession of occupants?

'I'm going out clubbing later,' she announced, which explained the even more arresting outfit than usual, as well as her makeup, which was as good as what last season's *Drag Show* winner wore. *Is there anything this girl can't do?* Cassie thought.

'Let's open a bottle of wine and order a little Chinese to celebrate your first night – how about that?'

It was exactly what Cassie felt like doing. She had to admit there was always a bleakness about the first night in a new apartment, and she'd had more than a few of those over the years.

Cassie seated herself on a Perspex chair at the glass table in the kitchen, as Ramona presented her with a large, very chilled glass of Sauvignon Blanc. In fairness, she couldn't have been kinder or more welcoming; none-theless, Cassie was a little anxious: she'd taken a wild leap into the unknown and was now looking around to see where she'd landed.

'Come on, let's take a shot for Insta.'

Ramona leaned in and snapped the two of them, cheers-ing the lens. She studied the photo, switched on the beauty filter and smoothed out any imperfections in the faces, highlighting cheekbones and shading hollows so they both looked dewy-faced and glowing and all of about twenty-three.

Pre-show drinks with my new BFF/flatmate.

She added the caption and hit send without a moment's dithering. This was a professional. Wow, thought Cassie, 'BFF' on the first day. That was either very flattering or slightly off. She decided to go with flattering. It was clear Ramona's world was composed of one part reality and a whole lot of spin, but what the hell, it was fun. You could get way too much reality.

It felt exciting to be part of an aspirational world that other people could flick through and envy. Just then she remembered Da's old advice that he'd dole out if she was nervous when heading out to a party as a teenager: 'Just be yourself, love,' he'd say. 'Then ye can't go wrong.'

Those simple words had always felt solid and reassuring, but up here in this polished world, watching the uber-glamorous Ramona flicking through her Instagram with fifty-five thousand followers, it struck her that just being the bog-standard version of yourself mightn't cut it after all.

Ramona was commenting as she scrolled. 'People will recognise you, you'll see. Your face – well, your armpit – is everywhere. I have to keep my sponsors happy. They love to know what I'm doing, where I'm going, what I'm wearing.'

Cassie nodded. She thought back over her own life. Who was following her right now? Josie was probably sitting at home watching Netflix, as the faithful Pal brought her cream cheese on water biscuits with cucumber – her latest obsession. The girls were probably busy baby-wrangling or else had managed to get their kids settled and were flopping onto the sofa and gratefully pouring themselves a drink. Finn would have Cici, Conor and Samantha with him, the mythical three children who had a place in her imagination as they occupied his pale apartment. She glanced down at WhatsApp, only to realise that over the past frantic half hour with Ramona she'd missed a message from him.

> *Kids going to family party tomorrow (surprise!)*
> *u free to drop over 1 p.m.?*

Her face lit up.

> *Surprise!! ☺ Think I might just manage that!*

She looked up and caught Ramona staring at her.

'Just my chap,' she explained. 'At least, he is sort of my chap but we're only new, so still feeling our way. No expectations, if you know what I mean. I actually didn't expect him to be free this weekend.'

A shadow of unease crossed Cassie's mind, but it didn't have time to settle.

'Got a photo?' Ramona beckoned insistently towards her phone. Cassie laughed, enjoying her no-holds-barred familiarity.

'Handsome,' she pronounced, 'in an IRL sort of way. Wholesome.'

She was looking at him with curiosity, like he was a rare animal that had been captured in the wild.

'Nice sweater. Very . . . normal. But then, so are you.'

That could've been insulting said in a different tone, but in this case, it sounded almost wistful.

'Ramona, I have to ask you . . . I'm really curious. Your style . . . aesthetic?'

Ramona eyeballed her. 'What am I, you mean?'

'Well, I wasn't going to put it quite like that, but . . . how would you label yourself?'

'Honey, I try not to label myself at all. But if you were to force me . . . I would say I'm a bio queen. Preferred pronoun she, with a capital S.'

'So . . . you're a woman, but in drag. Sometimes. Gotcha.'

'Good for you. Not everyone does. See, the drag queens have been celebrating what it is to be a woman, in a radical version, for years. Now some of us feel it's time to reclaim that for ourselves. Not *from* them, you understand, they're welcome to it, but for us as well, the cis women.'

'OK . . .'

'Take the female icons of the past, chicks like Elizabeth I, Marie Antoinette in her wigs, they weren't just biological women – their femininity was political.'

It struck Cassie that the example of Marie Antoinette was a bit doubtful but she thought better than to say so.

'See, every time you step out of the house dressed like this, it's innately political.'

'Er, OK . . .'

'It's two fingers to the patriarchy and two fingers to gender norms.'

'OK, but you're a woman . . . dressed as a woman.'

'Honey, how many women do you see dressed like me?'

Cassie looked down at her own comfy sweatpants and hoodie. She was a woman, and one with a decent figure, to be fair, but she really wasn't celebrating it. She made a mental note to make a bit more of an effort in future. Ramona had a point. One really shouldn't take one's sex for granted. It was kind of lazy, when you came to think of it.

'I'm really curious, what was your family like? I mean, what sort of woman was your mum?'

Ramona's reaction was barely a flicker, but Cassie was aware of her energy closing down.

'Sorry, I really didn't mean to pry. Just tell me to mind my own business.'

'No, it's OK, dear old Mom.' There was a note of bitterness in her voice. 'I didn't know her very well. She had her issues. She was an addict, among other things. I was mostly brought up by my grandmother . . .' Her voice petered out.

'I suppose it's hard to be brought up by someone of a different generation, even if they're a good person.'

Cassie was conscious of trying to rescue the situation.

'She got stuck with me, poor woman. She's filthy rich, by the way. I got a shit ton of money when I turned twenty-one, hence this place, so at least I owe her that.'

There was something about Ramona's brittle tone that didn't make Cassie feel like she could probe any further.

'Well, I just want you to know I'm incredibly grateful for you renting to me at mates' rates. I really don't take it for granted.'

This seemed to jolt Ramona out of her slump. She perked up.

'Cassie, what're you like? You're such a goddamned chatterbox, look at the time. I have to get my ass out the door, this night won't start on its own. Don't wait up.'

With that, she drained her glass, grabbed her orange faux-fur jacket and disappeared out the door. Cassie waited until she heard it close with a bang then finally released a long breath. Phew.

She lay in her new bed that night and looked around. Hers was the smaller bedroom, nonetheless there was a floor-to-ceiling window to her right covered by expensive-looking curtains. The polished floor was made of real wood, not laminate, and the wardrobe fittings closed with a discreet clunk. Everything had the air of a life where you bought exactly what you wanted, not just what you could afford.

Chapter 13

Finn helped himself to a warm, flaky croissant and a mug of fresh coffee as they sat bundled up together on the sofa, wrapped in a fleecy rug against the bleak greyness, as the rain pounded against the window and the gas fire flickered.

'I'm so sorry this happened. Why would Marisha take the kids away for the weekend without warning?'

Finn shrugged gloomily. 'It's all based on goodwill, just like I said.'

'Finn, if my being in your life is going to ruin things, maybe we shouldn't—'

'Is that what you want?'

She detected a note of uncertainty in his voice.

'No, it's . . .' She was on the verge of blurting out *the last thing I want*, but realised that was going to sound needy. 'It really isn't.'

'Me neither, but I wouldn't want you to feel stuck with somebody who's pinned down by sandbags.'

Cassie laughed incredulously. 'Not the word I'd have used. All I see is someone who's trying hard to be a good dad.'

He smiled. 'I'm trying to keep everyone happy.'

Cassie found herself on the verge of replying, 'Well, don't worry about me,' but switched tack just in time.

'So, what makes you happy, hmm?'

She was fishing for compliments and she knew it, but what the hell.

'Being here with you. Not having to watch myself all the time.'

'Why would you have to do that?'

'Have you ever had the feeling that you're a nuisance, just by being, just by breathing?'

'Is that how you used to feel? Sounds horrible. So, what happened?'

'We'd been skirting around each other for months, we both knew it was over, there wasn't any option.'

'So, she got the house and the kids, and you got the dog. Tough negotiator.'

He gave a rueful laugh. 'Wouldn't you be happier finding yourself some rich guy who could whisk you off to Paris to stay in a five-star hotel, sip vintage champagne in the piano bar, have a fabulous dinner served by ten waiters . . .'

'I'd probably spend the whole time desperately trying not to flip a snail down my cleavage. Still, it is a bit of a notch up from a sad movie and popcorn, followed by a big fight in the local pub with Maleficent, saved only by the Three Amigos at the next table.'

'Seriously, I was panicking. I was nearly going to make a run for the door,' Finn confessed.

'She'd only have chased you down and decked you with her knock-off Michael Kors handbag.'

By this stage they were both wiping tears of laughter from their eyes, more from relief than anything else.

Sometimes it was the worst experiences that made the best glue, Cassie thought.

* * *

That afternoon, after it had stopped raining, they took Thor for a walk to the mucky dog park. The sun hung low over the north-facing slope fringed by tangled bushes and bare branches. The whole place would only really dry out when the season turned to spring and the sun arched higher in the sky.

The first person they walked into was the intrepid Phyllis, in her quilted jacket and bobble hat. 'Poly,' she hollered. 'Poly, come and see who's here.' As though her pooch was going to stick out his paw and start a conversation.

It struck Cassie that in the absence of a husband, Napoleon had slotted into the role, which was quite sweet if a bit scary. She gave Cassie a sidelong glance.

'Sooo, I'm going to stick my neck out here and ask if you two are an item now?'

Of course, she realised with a shock: he must've been here previously with Thor and his kids, and more than likely his ex. The doggie community know him as a family man and here she was, an interloper.

Just then Thor bounded off and was busy love-bombing some other unlucky person at the other end of the field. Finn raced after him just in time to prevent a lawsuit. Phyllis stepped closer to her. 'I've known Finn and his wife for years, coming here,' she confided. 'This

mightn't be my place to say but I think this is the best
thing for him.'

'Thank you. I really appreciate—'

'Just don't be surprised if not everyone feels the same
way. Be careful. She's very well-known.'

Cassie was bursting to ask her what she meant, when
she saw Finn and a chastened Thor trotting back in
their direction. Phyllis's face betrayed nothing of their
exchange, but Cassie couldn't help thinking: what had
she blundered into?

* * *

That evening she returned to her apartment and called
out to see if anyone was home but was met only with her
voice echoing back from the hard surfaces – funny, she'd
never noticed that before. For a moment her heart sank
at the bleakness of the unfamiliar surroundings. She
didn't go near the cavernous sitting room but wandered
into the kitchen and searched through the contents of
the big fridge. At least she'd done a grocery shop, so the
shelves looked slightly less bachelorette than previously.
She assembled the ingredients for a cheese-and-tomato
omelette and started to cook. She also made herself a
large, comforting mug of tea, and carried everything
into her room, where she waited for Josie to answer the
Zoom call. She was bursting to hear her friend's take on
all that had happened.

'Where are you?' Josie looked confused at the bare
walls.

Cassie tried to explain briefly about the apartment, Ramona and her pole dancing, not to mention the dates with Finn. She expected Josie to be rocking with hilarity and disbelief at the news but found her friend oddly low-key.

'What's wrong?'

She noticed Josie's chin wobbling. Cassie kicked herself for her insensitivity.

'I'm sorry, I'm so full of my own shit. Please, talk to me, what's going on?'

'You're moving away. You're turning into somebody else and so am I.'

It was as though somebody had pulled up a roller blind and suddenly Cassie had a clear view of what was happening in her friend's life.

'But I thought you were so happy, I thought everything was perfect for you and Pal. Whenever anybody asks me about my friends, I use you as a shining example of how to get your life right.'

'But that's total crap. All I am is a woman who's having a last gasp at pregnancy and yes, I am happy, but I'm also terrified it's going to destroy whatever career I've built, and I'll never be able to get it back. I'll be nothing. I'll vanish. I'll just be one of those invisible women.'

'That's ridiculous. You could never be that.'

'And you think I'm the person who always has the answers, and I'm not and I don't.'

Josie had made the decision to move into arts administration about five years into her acting career. Now the manager of a small theatre in North London, she'd always claimed it was the best decision she'd ever made.

'But Jos, you'll just go on maternity leave and then come back, what's wrong with that?'

'That's not how things work, you know that. Once you're out of sight, somebody younger and hipper moves in and there's no space to go back to. I've already had to accept disappointment once before, when I left acting, and that was OK, I made my peace with that, but I don't think I can face it again.'

She pulled a tissue from her sleeve and cried noisily. Cassie was at a loss.

'And now I hear you've found this swanky apartment with an exciting cool person and a new boyfriend. Friendships don't survive long distance. I'll just become an old friend, someone who's not important anymore. Who you have to feel guilty about not keeping in touch with.'

Cassie couldn't believe her ears, but Josie had always been there for her with unrelenting good sense, so she was one hundred per cent entitled to a meltdown. Hormonally driven or not.

'What a load of utter crap!'

'It's not!'

'It is. You're just blurting out all your worst, most hideous fears, and as your best mate, I'm the perfect person to do it with.'

'But it's all true,' she wailed.

'I'll tell you what's true. You are building a person. And the reason you don't feel like yourself anymore is because you're not yourself. You're two people.'

Josie sniffed and nodded mutely.

Cassie ploughed on. 'But that's going to change. And change and change again. And I'll be the one afraid of being left out because you'll have all your chummy-mummies and I'll just be your barren mate. But I'll still be here.'

She felt herself growing teary. Josie had dried her eyes, but this caused her to dissolve into sobs again.

'I could never forget about you,' Cassie said decidedly.

'Me neither, so are we good?'

Cassie gave a snort-laugh and nodded.

'So now, tell me about this guy with the fifty kids and the psycho ex. He sounds perfect for you.'

They both burst out laughing.

'You know what I think?' Josie went on. 'I think, screw him. I'm sure he's nice but right now what you need is a job.'

'That's just because right now you're obsessed with jobs.'

'You know you've been here before, Cassie, making a guy the centre of your life instead of yourself.'

An image of Gav flashed into her mind, causing her stomach to lurch. She winced at the thought of how she'd compromised her life to be with him for fifteen years. How had she let it go on for so long? Perhaps she didn't know how to live life without him? Or maybe she thought he was as good as she could do? She believed other people's estimation of him rather than trusting her own experience, until finally she was left high and dry. All of those reasons, probably, and now here she was again, trying to carve out a little bit of another man's life. Josie was right, she needed a job.

'I'll phone a career consultant tomorrow, I promise.'

'And I'm not leaving our Zooms more than a week again. I can't trust you not to go off the rails.'

Cassie spluttered her tea, laughing at the irony.

'Bloody cheek.'

* * *

Wandering back towards the open-plan kitchen, her heart leaped at the sight of a dark shape hunched at the table. It took a few seconds to register Ramona sitting on a chair, gripping her knees. She was dressed in a stained T-shirt and towelling robe. Her gelled white-blonde hair was plastered flat and only the streaked remnants of her makeup from the night before were still visible. She looked virtually unrecognisable. It just showed perhaps Ramona's fabulous public face didn't tell the whole story.

Chapter 14

Nursing a get-your-life-back-on-track latte from her favourite oversized mug that read: *IF YOU CAN DREAM IT, YOU CAN DO IT*, as Walt Disney said, Cassie was setting to the task of starting her career again from scratch, when she noticed a message from Mam on her phone.

> *Hope all's well, and not having too much fun without me* ☺.

Bet she means it, Cassie thought. A part of her mum would love to be out clubbing with Ramona. She hit the call button and waited.

'Hello, Iris's phone, how can I help?'

Wow, they really were a couple if they were answering each other's phones. After an initial flash of irritation, she noticed there was something about Eric's voice that caused her shoulders to drop with relief. Perhaps he was exactly the person she needed to speak to right now.

'Hi Eric, I don't even know where to start . . .' She poured out how overwhelmed she was feeling at the prospect of searching for a job, while trying not to sound like a needy child. 'And the thing is, Eric, apart from acting, there really isn't anything I'm qualified to do. I could kick myself for leaving myself in this situation.'

There was a pause at the end of the phone, which she had learned to interpret not as awkwardness but simply as Eric giving her his full attention.

'You know, I think I know someone who just might be able to help you. He's an old friend of mine, but don't worry, he's not nearly as old as me. But he's a fabulous guy, I'll give you his number.'

Cassie felt a glow of gratitude for his kindly manner that made everything feel manageable. Buoyed up by Eric's optimism, she set to phoning the contact he'd given her, a Philip Ackerman, career consultant at the company Work-Shi. Now surely everything would fall into place.

'Mr Ackerman is in a meeting. If you have an enquiry, I suggest you put it in writing with your curriculum vitae and he may get back to you.'

Cassie ended the call, feeling crushed – this chilly response from his PA was not what she'd expected, but what was she thinking? It was only realistic to have to write in and take your turn. She composed an email and hit send; Philip Ackerman suddenly felt a lot more important and less accessible than she'd been led to believe. Everything was harder in the doing than the thinking, whatever Walt Disney said.

Just then her phone buzzed.

'Cassandra, is it? Phil Ackerman. Always a pleasure to hear from someone who knows my old friend Eric.

If you're free this afternoon after four, pop into the office and we can have a chat, you have the address.'

He sounded small and plump and twinkly – and . . . Phil, well, she could relate to someone called Phil.

* * *

Cassie jumped in the shower and as she stood under the jet of water, she let her mind wander. Did she secretly want to return to acting? It wasn't that she didn't want to, it was more that the stress of the auditioning process had played havoc with her state of mind over the years. I do love it, she mused, but I just want some stability in my life. The image of Ramona sitting hunched in the kitchen the night before haunted her for some reason. Perhaps every high had to be paid for by a low, and right now she had to get off the seesaw.

From her wardrobe she chose a pair of Calvin Klein jeans, a pale blue shirt and a light navy blazer. In fact, it was her costume from an ad she'd done the previous year as 'working mum, mid-thirties'. She'd bought the clothes for a knock-down price at the end of the production. At last, she was getting into costume for her own life.

* * *

At the office of Work-Shi, Cassie found herself face to face with possibly the friendliest person she had ever met. Phil Ackerman, to her surprise, turned out to be not at all like his voice had led her to believe. He was tall and bookish-looking, and undeniably handsome in a priestly sort of way. He must have been in his early fifties, but he looked good for it, and had round glasses and a manner that made her feel instantly at ease, as though she'd done him the greatest possible honour by taking the trouble of coming in for a chat that was entirely for her own benefit.

He led her into his office, which had a panoramic view of the entire quays. Cassie tried to summarise in five minutes the many tentacles of her career, her recent return home and hopes of a new start.

'By the way, I saw your ad.' He smiled in a way that wasn't in the least bit creepy, then straightened his face and continued, 'I read your CV and it's a little, shall we say, unconventional but that's not a bad thing, not a bad thing at all.'

Bless him, thought Cassie, I've just found a career consultant who'd be played by Tom Hanks in the movie of my life.

'Now, in terms of the "big five" . . .' Here he raised a large, well-manicured hand in illustration. 'Starting with *openness to experience*, I'm thinking of Slime Planet, so that would need to be around . . . ninety-eight per cent.'

'More that I was desperate for a job,' she said ruefully.

Phil waved this aside and went on. '*Conscientiousness*, we'll give it fifty-five per cent . . . *extroversion*, say sixty per cent. Sometimes I find actors like to appear more extroverted than they are inside. *Neuroticism*, well, now, that I wouldn't know – you'd have to tell me that yourself.'

'Well, I am a bit neurotic, but I can bounce back.'

'And finally, *agreeability*. Well, that's a no-brainer, if you're a friend of Eric's. I'll give you a ninety-five per cent on that.'

This struck Cassie as a slightly unsystematic way of doing a personality test, based almost entirely on guesswork and goodwill, but was she complaining? Not on your life.

'Now, I'm going to start with the bog obvious, if you'll forgive the expression. Have you thought of children's entertainer, clowning, that sort of thing?'

Cassie didn't even have time to reply before he raised his hand in an almost biblical gesture. 'No need to utter a word, your face says it all.'

'Sorry, I . . .' To her mortification, Cassie realised she was going to cry.

'There, there,' Phil soothed as he dug a tissue out from somewhere.

'I'm so sorry,' she wailed. 'I'd no idea that was such a big deal for me.'

'That's all right, sometimes these things come at us from heaven knows where. Happens all the time.'

Cassie was sure it didn't, but was grateful to him for saying it anyway. She struggled to compose herself but the last thing she wanted was to look unprofessional, or worse, unstable.

'In my experience,' he said, 'we should all cry a bit more. The world would be a much better place. Now, I'm going to say something very obvious, but what about working in a school? Do you speak fluent Irish?'

She weighed it up for a moment then shook her head.

'Pity. I've a well-paid job here in an Irish-speaking school if you could, but moving on . . .'

Damn, she thought, so much for teenage bullshit opinions about Irish being boring when you were trying to start a new career in your thirties.

'Oh, we might have something,' he exclaimed. 'It's a school, part-time.'

Cassie nodded enthusiastically; after all, she'd a score of ninety-five per cent agreeableness to live up to.

'It's a primary school, and it's not a widely known fact, but you don't need to be qualified to be a substitute teacher. Once you get in the door, you never know, you might get to enjoy it.'

'Brilliant, Phil. Please put me forward for it.'

'And . . . away it goes,' he said with the air of a children's magician.

She felt like hugging him.

Cassie skipped back along the quays, feeling a surge of enthusiasm she hadn't felt for a long time.

She couldn't wait to share the news with Finn.

* * *

'Teaching? Are you sure that's really you?'

Her heart sank like an undercooked sponge cake.

'Well, it hasn't been, up to now, but the idea of teaching actually appeals to me.'

He shrugged. 'Then go ahead.'

'Well, thanks.' She paused. 'I was just hoping for a bit more encouragement.'

'Sorry, I'm not sure what else you want me to say.'

'Well done, that's great, good for you . . . Any of those to show you're happy for me.'

He put his arm around her and kissed her cheek.

'All I want is what's best for you.'

Which did strike her as a notch down from out-and-out enthusiasm.

They started hiking up the narrow, heather-lined path up the Little Sugar Loaf mountain. It was Finn's week on late shift, so they had time for a walk but also, she suspected, to avoid running into anyone who might recognise him, although she pushed away the thought. She gave him a sidelong glance but his face gave little away.

'Phil said they'd be in touch within a week. Isn't that good? I mean, at least it's promising.'

'Working in a school? That's kind of ironic.'

'Is it? How?'

He buried his hands in his pockets and squared his shoulders in a way that made him seem defensive.

'My ex is a teacher.'

'Well . . . OK, but plenty of people are teachers. I haven't stood inside a school since my Leaving Cert. I don't know how I'll be able to handle being on the staff. I still feel like a teenager.'

She became aware of Finn's distance. 'Look, I realise this must feel like déjà vu for you, with your ex. But for me it just feels like something solid and grown-up at last.'

Finn gave a rueful laugh.

'Tell me about it.'

'I'm not going to change – I'm still me – but I have to live, dammit, and I can't do that on what I earn walking those little feckers every day, cute as they are.' A light breeze carried with it the feeling of spring.

'Race you to the top.' She took off up the hill, her legs carrying her effortlessly forward. Well, at least walking the pups had left her fitter, if not richer. She could hear Finn gaining on her and accelerated until she gasped to a halt.

'It's not fair, you have longer legs.'

He caught up with her and grabbed her around the waist, pulling her to him and kissing her. In that moment the gorse-covered landscape, the bright blue arch of sky, the breeze that ruffled their hair – everything vanished and all she could feel was his arms holding her, his mouth gently searching for hers, her body moulding into his. Even then, there was still something unreadable about Finn. Perhaps it was only in those moments of silent intimacy that she could come closest to glimpsing the person he truly was.

They strolled to the summit and gazed out to sea.

'D'you think in time we could be just a normal couple that people don't look at as questionable? I know we're not technically doing anything wrong but it's all about perception. You know what people are like.'

Finn thought for a moment.

'I think some people will never change their perception.'

'In that case, feck them.'

'And some people will just take time to adjust.'

'Fair enough . . . And then there's my family and friends, who'll have no agenda at all. So, which side would your parents be on?'

Finn shrugged.

'That bad?'

'My family don't really like change. Unless it's their own decision.'

A bulbous grey cloud was nudging towards them, casting a shadow on the landscape below.

'From where I'm sitting, change keeps happening, whether you like it or not.'

Suddenly, she'd a flashback of the text Gav had sent her that morning in London. She'd just finished cleaning the house, ready for him to come home from tour. The flat felt fresh and scrubbed, and she'd bought a new string of fairy lights and tacked them round the big mirror to make the place look fun and welcoming. She was happy.

Then a ping from her phone. The memory of it as vivid as a red beach-ball on blazing white sand.

> *Crashing with a mate for now. B in touch to explain.*

And that was all. The text had been so innocuous on the surface, so indirect, it'd taken her a few minutes for the implication to sink in. He wasn't coming back. She'd been dumped.

'Cassie?'

There was something comforting about the view of the sea and the fields stretched out in front of them, largely unchanged for a hundred years at least.

'We used to come up here when we were kids, myself and Maxine, with our dad. I used to love looking down and allowing myself to feel dizzy, and just hang on to the rocks to feel safe. I still do.'

She felt the rough granite under her hands as they sat side-by-side on a massive boulder. He leaned into his backpack, took out a bar of chocolate and broke it in half.

'There's no such thing as a view without chocolate.'

'I bet you're a lovely dad.'

He gave a wry smile. 'I'm not sure everyone would agree.'

'Finn, do you think your kids would like me?'

She knew she was fishing, but the little girl in her wanted reassurance.

'Of course, they would. Who wouldn't love you?'

Well, maybe kids who wouldn't see her as just Cassie. She felt a sudden desire to be part of his world, to be accepted in it, but she heard Josie's insistent voice in her head. Don't fall over yourself to be accepted. You're worth more than that.

Josie, her rock, who was now rushing to join the world of parents, where Cassie could be a tourist at best, an intruder at worst, but never a native.

'It's time for me to head off.' Finn sighed.

'Already?'

'I'll make it up to you, I promise. Come over Thursday after six, I'll cook dinner.'

That felt better.

'Done.' She smiled.

* * *

Back at her car, the sun had gone in and she felt the harsh March wind whipping her cheeks. There was something about separating from Finn and seeing him switch off as soon as they kissed goodbye that left her with a pang of loneliness. She just needed to grow up, she mused, while negotiating the traffic along the N11; she needed to allow him his space without feeling abandoned. Despite that, she found herself veering off at the next set of lights and heading up towards Mam's. She didn't have the energy to be cool and self-reliant; she felt like sitting beside a fire in the familiar surroundings and letting the hectic world go by for a little while.

'A school?' enthused Mam. 'Now, that'd be lovely. I always said you'd make a super little teacher. But of course, you had to go off and do the risky thing.'

Mam rolled her eyes towards the ceiling and made them do a little shimmy of exasperation. Cassie picked up a slice of lemon drizzle cake and sank her teeth into its spongy comfort.

'Still,' she went on, 'I'm delighted you met that nice fellow, Phil. Terribly sad.'

She allowed the dramatic pause to hang between them.

'What's sad?'

Mam inhaled. 'Well, all right. He married quite late. But men often do. Anyhow, it was all working out brilliantly.

She was a district nurse and apparently everyone loved her and was very happy for them. They had a house in a lovely spot in Crossmolina, Co. Mayo, and the next thing, wasn't she expecting? And it's twins.'

This was clearly one of Mam's stories where everything was going enviably well for people, heralding the fact that it was all about to go to shite.

'Now, she was a few months off her due date and they had the whole house set up for the twins, and of course there was great excitement. But then . . . didn't she go into labour, just one night, no reason in the wide world – they couldn't believe what was happening. So, what could they do but pile into the car and start heading for Castlebar Hospital. But of course, it's a very long drive and the roads are very bad. She's in the back, in agony, and poor Phil is nearly beside himself. Should he stop and see to her, or should he just keep going, poor fellow, what could he do?'

'God, Mam, that's ghastly.'

'They got to the hospital, but didn't it turn out to be placenta previa. They did everything but, in the end, all three of them passed away.'

The thought of something this awful happening to lovely, kind, positive Phil was heartbreaking. He'd reached out to her as a friend, even though she'd only met him once.

Mam continued, 'So, in the end he sold up the lovely house and moved back to Dublin, and what could he do but try to pick up his life as best he could. And that's the story. Some people make the choice to bounce back, some can't.'

What had hers been? If she were honest, it had been to run away. Just then her phone pinged. She rummaged round in the tote bag with the princess cats on it.

'Oh my God, it's Phil. That's serendipity.'

Cassie read aloud: '*Please present at Oakdale national school, eleven a.m. on Thursday morning.* Shit. That's only two days away.'

'They're desperate, that's what it is. Sure, the dogs in the street know that the poor teachers are priced out of the housing market. Anyway, that's great.'

Cassie felt a combination of excitement and panic.

'How do you prepare for a temporary teacher post? Do you think I need to look up some extra online training?'

'Not a bit of it. Look, you can knit, crochet, sing, play guitar, use glue and scissors—'

'Mam, I think that's more the pupils than the teachers.'

As usual, Mam was wildly, unrealistically optimistic. But maybe that was for the best. She needed a cheerleader, not a heckler. She'd borrow Mam's confidence to get started, and after that, life could take care of itself.

'So, what're you going to wear for your interview?'

'Same as for Phil's, I was thinking.'

'Oh God, no. Not jeans. Not to an interview. That'd suggest you were unreliable.'

'But lots of teachers wear jeans.'

'Look, when you're made permanent, you can wear an Elvis costume to work if you want, but in the meantime look respectable. I'm telling you, head teachers can be sticklers, that's why they're in the job. So, trust me, go for plain boring black trousers.'

'Do you really think so?'

'Err on the side of caution.'

What would the world be like if humanity had always erred on the side of caution? We'd never have migrated out of Africa, never have set sail towards a distant horizon. Still, she did need a new pair of black trousers.

Chapter 15

She'd decided on a smart pair of ankle grazer trousers, which she'd teamed with a navy blazer. It was the costume she'd worn on a bank commercial a few years ago. God, she should've watched more educational TED Talks, she should've boned up further on the latest educational theory and formed opinions of her own. Oh well, too late now.

She knocked at the glass window of a little beige office where a tired-looking lady in a baggy pink cardigan was staring at a desktop screen. The woman's gaze suggested she'd had it up to the back teeth with hassle and just wanted a quiet life, which Cassie found rather reassuring. Perhaps someone too high-powered was the last thing they wanted. The woman glanced around wearily.

'Hello?'

'I'm Cassandra Kearney, I've an appointment to see the principal.'

The secretary's pale blue eyes focused on someone behind her. She heard the sound of air being inhaled through nostrils and swung round to find herself excessively close to a balding middle-aged man with heavy eyebrows and deep stress lines on his forehead.

'Roger Newcombe, please come in.'

The tall, bespectacled figure held out his hand formally towards her, which was a little awkward given their proximity, then indicated an adjoining door. He led the way into an office about the size of a department-store changing room, where the air felt thick with chalk dust and years of responsibility. He squeezed in behind a desk, which had the effect of either keeping her out or barricading him in. There was a little sign saying: 'Roger Newcombe, Principal' on the desk, as though he needed reminding himself of his position. He leaned back in his chair and paused.

'This is a fine school you have here, Rrr— Mr Newcombe.'

'Well, we try. It's all about budgets, of course, making them stretch . . . I don't know what they think I am.'

The last bit felt almost as though he'd forgotten she was in the room. His no-nonsense square glasses gave the impression that whatever he gazed upon would be viewed in an entirely serious light. He was wearing a green check shirt and knitted tie that some fashion-forward art students might have worn ironically, though probably without the egg stain; however, this clearly wasn't the case with Roger Newcombe. Clothes were purely functional and, all in all, Roger Newcombe was one of the most thoroughly responsible people she'd ever met, although he was probably no more than five years older than herself.

'Perhaps you could tell me about your teaching experience?'

What was he playing at? He had her CV in front of him, which gave zero evidence of anything of the sort. Oh hell, just wing it, she thought.

'None . . . precisely, but I have worked extensively in musical theatre and in an educational setting as a . . . facilitator.'

She was chancing her arm and they both knew it.

'Ah yes, Slime Planet, I noticed. Not a name I see on every résumé. I brought my son there once, as a matter of fact. I remember we quite enjoyed it.'

That was an unexpected moment of self-revelation.

'Although, as far as I remember, any "facilitators" we saw there seemed to end up as part of the experiments, rather than conducting them.'

Damn. He had her there.

'I simply did what the job required,' she replied, trying not to sound desperate.

He contemplated her through the thick lenses and then seemed to cheer up.

'Well, let's hope that even on its worst day, nothing like that should happen to you here. I'll be honest, we are chronically short of a substitute teacher so could you start at eight thirty on Monday morning? And if you wouldn't mind not parking in the space where Mr Daly, the groundsman, parks the electric buggy? I'm sure you saw the charging point.'

'Of course, thank you. I won't let you down.'

She sat waiting for his response, but he seemed to have already moved on, almost having forgotten she was still in the room. She sat awkwardly for a moment.

'So, shall I . . .?'

He looked up as though surprised she was still there.

'Yes, yes, that's fine. See you on Monday.'

She couldn't quite shake the feeling that this man was treating her like a six-year-old. Still, a job was a job, even if her status was one step below the golf buggy.

* * *

By half past twelve she was pushing open the door to the apartment, while awkwardly balancing a celebratory piping-hot latte and pastrami roll along with her shoulder bag. She was met by the pounding beat of Lady Gaga's 'Paparazzi' coming from the doorway. Edging into the hall, she peeped into the sitting room to find Ramona rotating upside down on the pole, gripping it between astonishingly high platform shoes and dressed in a barely there leotard. Cassie gaped as she spun downwards, supporting her entire weight using only her stomach muscles, then performed aerial splits and lowered her legs slowly down to the ground. Cassie spontaneously burst into applause, narrowly escaping scalding herself with the small tidal wave of coffee. Ramona looked up in surprise and smiled.

'Oh my God, that was incredible. I mean, where did you learn to do those acrobatics? You're a total gymnast, even apart from the dance routine.'

She expected Ramona to light up in response to her enthusiasm and was just a little disappointed at the low-key reaction.

'Yeah, I grew up doing gymnastics back home. I used to compete a lot as a kid.'

'Your family must have been so proud of you . . . you're sensational.'

Ramona shrugged. 'They weren't really around much, and my grandma used to just put me in a cab. I mean, it worked fine. Until it didn't.'

'So, you'd nobody to cheer you on?'

'Like those dance moms who live entirely through their little sprogs? No, I didn't have one of those.'

There was a wistfulness in her tone. It struck Cassie that Ramona mightn't have minded being fussed over. What she'd got was travelling alone in a taxi.

'Hey, fancy half a pastrami roll? Finn's cooking for me tonight so I'm saving myself.' She did a little hula dance with the roll.

'You're on, I'm freaking starving.'

The pair of them trooped into the kitchen, where Ramona shoved a pod into the coffee maker and whipped two plates out of the cupboard, all in what seemed like a single movement. She was phenomenally well co-ordinated, that was for sure.

'So where do you perform?'

'I'm with an agency, we get hired for big events like corporate conferences. Which is just code for being perved at, but hey, all part of the job.'

Cassie laughed.

Just then Ramona noticed her outfit. 'Girl, you're looking like you've been put through a refit. Who are you now, corporate Barbie?'

Cassie chuckled. 'Thanks for noticing, it's teacher Barbie, actually.'

She explained the whole saga of the interview and it actually felt such a relief to unload her feelings over strong coffee, scrumptious sandwich and Ramona's bullshit-free gaze.

'Sounds wholesome, I like it. Don't think I could do it but, you know, part of me envies you.' Again, Cassie detected the loneliness in Ramona's tone.

'Really? If I could do what you do, I'd swap.'

'You wouldn't, trust me. Once you get used to doing anything, it's a job. You must know that from acting.'

Cassie nodded. It was true. This was an incredibly hard way to make money, however enviable and magical it might require your body to become.

'So, you're seeing your beau this evening for a special date. What're you going to wear?'

'Jeans and a black top?'

'*Stop!*' Ramona raised her palm. 'Don't offend my ears. Girlfriend, this is a *Thursday* night and therefore *pre-weekend*, and therefore you have to look bewitching with your killer figure in your most alluring outfit. You have got to stun him.'

Cassie let her mind wander over her sensible, well-washed underwear, her cosy jumpers, graphic tees and stripy tops. None of it seemed quite up to the job of stunning anyone. Ramona could see her hesitation.

'Don't panic. We can salvage this. Trust me.'

Cassie had the feeling she was being sucked into Ramona's world, which was going to leave her own humdrum version of life face down in the dust.

'Girlfriend, we are going to turn you into a *goddess*, you are going to go out of here this evening *on another level*. He will not recognise you.'

Cassie could hear alarm bells at the idea of being unrecognisable; on the other hand, Ramona's confidence was infectious. Seriously, what could go wrong?

Under her flatmate's surveillance, Cassie went through her drawers and pulled out a tangle of lacy underwear. They settled on a silver-and-aqua set from Victoria's Secret which she'd fallen in love with the previous year in a moment of excitement after hearing she'd been booked for the deodorant job. The labels were still on, so she'd never worn the items, which said something about how much time she'd spent with Gav in the last few months.

'These are passable,' announced Ramona, now leafing through her wardrobe. She fished out a red satin mini slip dress with diamanté straps which was perfect for either a heaving nightclub or a country with a climate considerably warmer than this one.

'Perfect, now what about shoes?'

Cassie was dragged into Ramona's room and saw it in its totality for the first time. It looked more like the wardrobe department for Cirque du Soleil than the average person's bedroom. Angel wings, silver boots, wigs, an ominous-looking Crocodile Dundee whip – not to mention a five-foot-high Perspex champagne glass which was currently full of richly coloured feather boas and ostrich fans.

'Ramona, is that for . . .?'

'My burlesque act. Only damn problem is travelling with it. Try hauling that lot through airport security. I'm going to have to find someone to make one for me in the States.'

In a bowl on the dressing table were a number of objects she didn't recognise.

'Sorry for being nosy, but what are those C-shaped things? Are they hair accessories?'

Ramona looked at her in astonishment and then burst out laughing.

'No, sweetie, the other end – they just keep everything in place during my act.'

'Right, gotcha.'

Cassie felt a bit silly – what else were these, after all, but Ramona's normal work clothes.

'Now, these'll be fun.'

She pulled a couple of pairs of sky-high platform ankle boots off a rack and headed back to Cassie's room. As it happened, they were about the right size. Cassie slipped into the red netting, six-inch heels and laced them up. They felt surprisingly stable when she tried to walk in them.

'Course, they are, they're dance shoes. I mean, you're going to look a klutz if you go over on your ankle in the middle of your act. OK, now, I'm going to do your makeup. Do you trust me?'

What the hell, it was a drizzly grey Irish day.

'Just make me sparkle.'

Ramona applied a smooth layer of light-reflecting foundation, followed by skilfully swept eyeliner. By the end of thirty minutes of elaborate brushstrokes, blending and shading, Ramona swung the chair around for Cassie to catch sight of herself in the professional makeup mirror.

'Is that me?'

The exotic, stunning creature staring back at her was unrecognisable from the neat, modest little temporary teacher she'd been costumed for that morning. She was back in another costume.

'It's fabulous. If you ever want to give up performing, you can just become a makeup artist,' said Cassie.

Ramona looked genuinely proud of herself.

'He's going to go crazy when he sees you, chick, just you wait.'

Chapter 16

'Thank God, you're here.'

Finn's face looked almost straight into her own, such was the number of extra inches the boots had given her, but he barely seemed to register that. He looked crazy, all right, but definitely not in the way she'd hoped. Cassie smiled encouragingly, attempting to break through his agitation, but he vanished into the bedroom, leaving her holding the bottle of wine she'd had no difficulty keeping chilled in the raw evening.

'What's wrong?'

'Everything's gone to shit is what's wrong.'

It dawned on her that whatever drama she was costumed for bore no relation to the drama that was engulfing Finn at this moment. She followed him into the bedroom, where he was pulling on extra layers of T-shirts under a fleece and lacing up sturdy boots.

'Finn, please tell me what is going on.'

He flopped on the bed, picked up his phone and looked at it distractedly. She'd never seen him like this.

'Marisha's mother has been taken ill and she's gone down to Limerick. And at the same time the person who was on call at work has gone sick, and I've been called in as replacement until eleven.'

Cassie was starting to feel less like Catherine Zeta-Jones in *Chicago* and more like Krusty the Clown, which just went to show it was all about being the right person in the right place at the right time.

'But if it's not your day to see them and she's just springing it on you . . .?'

Even as she spoke, she knew it was a mistake. His look was utterly dismissive.

'That's not how it works. I'm their dad. Anyway, she has all the power right now. If she wanted to cut back my access to the kids, she could do it, like that.' He snapped his fingers.

'But don't married people have equal rights to their children?'

He looked up at her with a hollow expression.

'In theory, but things are never that simple, she could turn them against me.'

'I'm sorry, that was clueless of me, I understand.'

Oh boy. She placed the rapidly warming bottle of Sauvignon on the bedside locker and sat down beside him.

'OK, let's take a breath and break this down. Marisha's in an emergency so, of course, you want to help. You certainly don't want to give any ammunition to that weapon of a sister from the pub.'

Finn seemed to have gone into a panic state, which didn't allow for problem-solving.

'Anything but that.'

'OK, you have to turn in for work. You can stay here until . . . when?'

'They're due here at six thirty . . . I'll have to leave ten minutes later.'

'OK, so why can't I be called in as an emergency babysitter? No need to say who I am or how you know me. I can stay with the kids, and then you'll be home and everyone will be safe.'

'I can't ask you to do that.'

'For heaven's sake, I suggested it. I love kids, it'll be fine.'

She wasn't nearly as confident as she sounded but, come on, they weren't babies, how hard could it be?

'Would you really do that for me, for us? It's only the two little ones, and maybe Samantha. She's supposed to have a sleepover with a friend, but the last I heard they'd had a row – don't ask me, this happens all the time . . . but don't be surprised if she turns up at the last minute, that's Sam.'

Oh hell. A fourteen-year-old could be a great deal harder to convince than a six-year-old. What, oh what, had possessed her to allow Ramona to dress her up as a stripper for a weekday night at home? Still, nothing for it but to plough ahead.

'So, I go and make myself scarce, sit in the car for half an hour then come back just before quarter to seven, when you introduce me to Cici and Conn as "the babysitter".'

'I hate to think of you sitting in the car, it's just—'

'So it doesn't look like a set-up, I get it.'

Finn smiled. 'They know how to get themselves ready for bed. Cici needs a story, but apart from that, you don't have to worry.'

'Not a problem.'

Finn was beginning to come down from his panic by this stage. He looked at her closely. 'Do you think you could just rub off a bit of that red . . . stuff. You know, babysitters are usually . . .' Realisation dawned on his face. 'Oh God, I'm really sorry. It looks great, it really does, it's just—'

'Oh God, this is so embarrassing. To be honest, Ramona did me up. It was all her idea – I was planning to come in jeans and a jumper. I mean, I don't normally veer towards the Vegas showgirl style of makeup. Look, it was supposed to be a fun surprise for our date, OK? Rubbish timing, I'm afraid.'

She was starting to feel like a lilo that'd been punctured and was gradually losing its bounce. On the other hand, here was an opportunity to be supportive in her new relationship because, after all, everyone knew that messy break-ups were a nightmare, and rather than being marginalised she could help out and perhaps even get to know the kids in an informal way. Not her choice, exactly, but that was life – you just had to be ready to bat whatever ball came at you.

* * *

Cassie spent nearly forty minutes lurking in a darkening car park outside the local Tesco with a stewed cup of coffee and soggy egg-mayonnaise sandwich, regretting that she'd saved herself earlier. When she finally pulled into a space in front of Finn's apartment block and switched off the engine, she realised her hands felt sweaty and were shaking slightly against the steering wheel. She had a flash of panic. What if the kids kicked up and wouldn't settle? Was this actually immoral, and would Marisha be within her rights to phone the Gardaí about her children being minded by a stranger without her permission? She batted the thoughts away. It was too late for any of that. All she could do was show up, be nice and go ahead with the plan.

* * *

'This is Cici and she has to be in bed by eight.'

'Eight thirty.' Cici's hazel eyes were round like a marmalade kitten's. Her voice was insistent and Cassie could see exactly how, under other circumstances, she could be highly persuasive.

'Eight,' said Finn firmly, clearly not in the mood for being cajoled. 'And this is Con, his bedtime is quarter to nine because it's Thursday.'

Con was clearly going to grow up to have the same build as his dad; he stayed motionless, his eyes fixed on the PlayStation controller in his hand. 'We don't normally see you on Thursdays anymore, Daddy,' he replied in a flat voice.

Finn flashed her a glance. 'Con likes things to stay the same, but I've explained to him it's an emergency and Cassie is going to look after you tonight.'

Con looked up at her. *I totally get this child*, flashed through her mind.

'You know, I don't like change much either. I prefer it when things stay the same too.' She smiled at him.

'If it's an emergency, then does that make you a super-hero?'

'Interesting question, Con. What do you think?'

'I think you're not as big as you look, you're just wearing tall boots.'

Which was a more astute observation than perhaps he realised.

Cici looked up at her in wonderment.

'Can I try them on, Daddy, can I? Then you can take a photo and show Samantha I'm as grown up as her.'

She exchanged a glance with Finn, That'd be another story for her mother, but what the hell.

'Course you can, pet, if Cassie doesn't mind.'

Tied into the sparkly red boots with the steeple-high heels, Cici held on to the wall with one splayed hand and carefully began a sort of spacewalk up the hall.

'Look at me, Daddy. These are like stilts,' she shrieked in excitement. 'I'm bigger than Con.'

'You look like a Transformer,' said Con.

'I do not. You look like a shithead.'

'Cici, that's enough.'

Cassie practically exploded with laughter. For the first time she was getting to observe Finn in his dad role. It felt almost voyeuristic. Cici had wobbled up to her and now the height difference was at least six inches fewer than it had been. The child reached out a chubby index finger. 'I like your red sparkly eyes, can I touch them?'

Cassie obligingly leaned forward.

'Eeew, it's crusty.' Cici gave a shiver.

'I know, it'll probably be stuck on for days.'

Cici contemplated this idea and giggled. 'That'll be funny.'

'You know what, yes it will,' Cassie agreed warmly.

'I'd better be off.' Finn pulled on his jacket. 'The kids know everything, they can explain it all to you.'

Just then his phone buzzed, he read the message slowly and rolled his eyes.

'What?' she mouthed.

'Kids, go and put your things in the sitting room.'

He turned the phone round to show her.

> *Sorry DD, actually busy, I have a life.*

'That's it? What's DD, darling daddy?'

'If only. Nope, it's her new "joke" name for me, *Deadbeat Dad*.'

'Oh babe, I'm sorry, that's rotten.'

His phone beeped again.

> *Pawning them off on babysitter. Nice one dd ☹. btw Con sent pic of babysitter shoes. Classy. she a hooker?*

Cassie gawked in disbelief, instinctively moving to put her arms around him, but he stepped back and put out his hand.

'Oh, sorry, sorry. I forgot.'

'Yeah, just . . . I can't.'

'Sure, of course.' Adult-up, she reminded herself, it's a game, we can sort it out later. 'Bye kids, be good for Cassie,' he called. 'I'll be home later . . . Oh, and eat whatever she cooks for you.' Then he was gone and she was left reeling from some of the most hostile texts she'd ever seen. Let it go for now, she told herself.

In fairness, rustling up a meal for two children should be nothing. Any of the girls would've probably been able to whip it up blindfolded while tied to a chair, but for her this was totally out of her comfort zone. What would Jamie Oliver do? He'd airily juggle the most wholesome ingredients in a pan while humming . . . pom, pompity, pom. Oh, good Lord.

'Let's look in the kitchen, kids,' she announced in her most CBeebies presenter's voice. 'Yaaay!' Cici played along delightfully while Con gripped his remote controller like a talisman.

'Let's see what's in the fridge . . .'

What met her was . . . nothing. Just eggs, and in a manky drawer a gnarly onion and wrinkled tomato. And sriracha sauce. Jamie Oliver would be weeping. *I'll fucking kill him*, she thought momentarily, *leaving me to manage all of this*. Then she nudged herself – what about that ad where the dad whips up an omelette? It could work.

'So, kids, how about my super-special spicy omelette surprise?'

'Yaaay!' cheered Cici, almost toppling off the boots in the process. 'What's an *omplet*?' This child was adorable, Cassie realised, but also a totally unreliable source of information.

'Con has to have all his food so none of the things touch,' she explained gravely. 'The peas can't touch the mash and the chicken can't touch the nip.'

Turnip, Cassie deduced. Crikey, that was pretty specific. Where on earth was she going to find a meal like that at this hour? She recognised she'd about five minutes before their hunger would time out. She waved her phone. 'Let's order something!!'

'Yaaay,' cheered Cici.

'Like what?' said Con, flatly.

Oh God, good question. Think. Fast. 'Chips! With . . . a sausage. And a side order of peas.' She was trying to make it sound like they'd won the Lotto. In fairness, she'd done a lot of improvisation.

'Yaaay.'

'We're not allowed takeaways. Mum says trans fats cause lifelong damage to our arteries.'

'*Yes*. Your mother is right. If you had them a lot. But . . . tonight is an *emergency*, so . . .'

'Yaay.'

CiCi should be hired out to shows up and down the country as an audience plant. Con studied the skirting board and began to recite, 'In case of an emergency, remain calm and inform the relevant authorities. In case of fire do not open a window . . .'

He was beginning to hyperventilate. Oh God, she could feel her temperature soaring despite the skimpy outfit. Top priority was to manage his anxiety before it spiralled out of control. Act confident.

'Excellent advice, Con. Thank you for that. Glad to say it's not a fire, but we can remain calm and phone the relevant authorities.'

He blinked at her in silence for a good thirty seconds with a glance eerily reminiscent of Finn's.

She brandished her phone. 'And in this case, the authorities are Just Eat.'

There was a long pause.

'I like chips,' he pronounced, with great effort.

'We all do. Let's call in the order.'

* * *

Twenty minutes later they were unpacking the little parcels out of the carrier bag which had been delivered to the door, and both children seemed to be happy with the contents. Maybe Marisha, with her sky-high standards, had done her a favour. These kids seemed a hell of a lot easier to impress than most. They laid out two plates and counted out the food meticulously: ten chips for Cici, fifteen for Conor, a jumbo sausage each and a spoon of peas, placed in a spot of the recipient's choosing.

After dinner Conor seemed to be magnetically pulled towards one end of the sofa, with Thor at his feet. 'He always sits in that seat. It regulates him,' Cici explained earnestly before she vanished out the door and could be heard rummaging in the cupboard of doom. Conor was engrossed in loading up a computer game when Cici clumped back into the room, holding the familiar long-haired doll who was now wearing a white pillowcase safety-pinned under her chin.

'This is St Teresa of Ávila,' Cici intoned with such solemnity that Cassie practically burst out laughing but stopped herself just in time.

'Really? How did she get her name?'

'Because she is so good and when I'm not here, she minds my daddy.'

'Well, that's beautiful, Cici, does your daddy know?'

She shook her head.

'The magic doesn't work unless it's a secret.'

The trust in the little girl's face caused a lump in Cassie's throat. Cici took the doll back and kissed her head. 'It's her bedtime. She has to go before me because she's younger.'

Cassie followed her into the second bedroom, which had bunk beds and a single bed – bit of a squash, she observed. Cici tucked the doll into the corner of the lower bunk.

'Con sleeps in the top one and Samantha sleeps over there, but she says she hates sharing with us. She says we're farty, but I'm not,' she confided indignantly.

God, having to share with two younger siblings couldn't be the most ideal situation for a teenager – no wonder she was trying to dodge whenever she could.

'Would you like me to read you a story?'

'I'm nearly six, I can read myself,' said Cici, pulling out a battered copy of *Rhinos Don't Eat Pancakes*, which she proceeded to read through without actually looking at the pages. Clearly, she knew it off by heart, which struck Cassie as a very comforting idea right before sleep. She remembered having books like that, endlessly re-read and stuffed under the pillow until the pages began to fall out.

'Now you have to put it on the locker, so it's right on the corner and looks like a sandwich,' Cici explained. Cassie had to adjust the angle of her moon-shaped night light before she crept out of the softly lit room, leaving the door slightly ajar. It felt both novel and strangely familiar. Being a kid hadn't changed that much over the decades. I could've done this, she thought. She could've coped with a child, even though during all the years with Gav it'd seemed like such an impossibly big leap and one which they'd agreed wouldn't 'suit their lifestyles'. That was bullshit. She'd actually have managed fine. The thought jabbed her in the heart so savagely that she quickly squashed it down.

Con was wedged into the corner of the sofa, with his feet resting against Thor who, despite the gruesome events on the screen, had settled into a soporific trance and was snoring gently. She plonked down beside him.

'So, what's the plot?'

She hoped she wasn't going to be that infuriating adult buzzing in the kid's ear but thankfully he didn't seem to see it that way.

'It's this town that's overrun with zombies because of a radioactive experiment that went wrong,' he explained.

'We're the survivors and we have to fight our way into the reactor to shut it down.'

As you would, she thought. She watched for a few minutes as he explained the properties of his various weapons.

'Con, watch it!' Cassie slapped her hand over her mouth as a swarm of jerky black figures filled the screen and his thumbs jabbed frantically at the controls.

'I'm trying . . . Fuck,' he roared as a pixellated red splosh filled the screen. 'I died.'

'There were too many. What could you do?'

Sometimes life was just like that. No matter how hard you tried, it all became too much.

'Are you allowed to play this at home?'

He shook his head.

'You won't tell my mum, right? I'm only allowed to play *The Sims* and *Minecraft*, but they're lame.'

'Don't worry. Your dad's house, your dad's rules. So, what do we do now?'

'I could re-spawn and try again.'

She looked at her watch and thought, what the hell, it was a Thursday night. She picked up the second controller.

'You game?' He looked at her with curiosity for the first time.

'A bit. I used to play with someone . . .' She and Gav had played *Final Fantasy* on his nights at home from tour; it was how he unwound and her way of reconnecting with him.

'I've never played this one but I'm sure I can pick it up.'

Just then his pocket began to buzz.

'Hi Mum, Dad's not here, he's in work. The babysitter's here.'

Although they were at opposite ends of the sofa, Cassie could hear the outraged voice piercing through the peaceful atmosphere of murder and mayhem. She watched tension return to Con's face as he handed her the phone with a shrug.

'Sorry . . . who are you?' came down the phone at her. This was not fair. She wasn't prepared for this shite.

'My name is Cassandra and I was called in to babysit for a few hours.'

'Where did he get you?'

Oh my God, the sheer rudeness and aggression took her aback. What was it that felt so familiar? That woman in the pub who'd no compunction about making a scene in front of the entire place. Her first impulse was to tell this bitch to fuck off. She was here out of her own good nature to dig Finn out of a hole and see that these children were safe and cared for and, inexperienced as she might be, she was doing a perfectly good job.

When she didn't respond immediately, the voice became even more insistent. 'Are you government-registered? Are you Garda-vetted? Where can I find your full name?'

Oh, come on, she felt about one more aggressive question away from hanging up, phoning Finn and telling him she never wanted to see him again. She replied in the tone she'd used for Viola in *Twelfth Night* two years ago in pub theatre.

'I was contacted at very short notice by Mr Reynolds who, it seems, was called into work in an emergency.'

'Very well, I am going to level with you. My older daughter has forwarded me a photo which I have examined, and I need to ask you a question. Are you an escort? Not that I am in any way prejudiced against your profession, but I would like to know.'

Oh Lord, she could murder Ramona for landing her in this.

'I can assure you I am not. It's simply a costume . . . I am a performer. It was all very last minute.'

Her story was about as watertight as a colander. There was an intake of breath and Marisha's tone softened slightly.

'I see. Well, in that case it's not your fault.'

That was something, at least. Obviously, Mrs Boiled Spuds was the type to attack first and ask questions later.

'For future reference, I like to be kept in the loop where my own young children are concerned and, as it happens, their father is not picking up his phone.'

Thankfully, Con had had enough sense to pause the murderous sound effects while his mother was listening. Cassie realised he was frozen to the spot and breathing shallowly as he took in every word. So much for doing all the right things, if your kid was afraid to breathe when you were around. Still, she'd the sense to keep her trap shut – this woman was threatening and could be trouble.

'By the way, how old are you? You certainly don't sound like a teenager.'

She hadn't thought this through properly at all. If this woman had a mind to, she could level any accusation against her.

'I am a responsible adult, and I can assure you that I am simply waiting for the children's father to come home so I can leave.' A knot of anxiety gripped her stomach. The conversation could have gone two ways, but thankfully Momzilla recognised that berating the person in charge of her children mightn't be the wisest plan.

'Well, thanks for stepping into the need for care, however inappropriate. My issue is clearly with their father, not with you. Hand me back to my son, please.'

Cassie overheard some instructions about breathing exercises and how many times to switch the bathroom light on and off, then the phone went dead.

'D'you think I'm in trouble?' he asked in a subdued voice.

'No, I am, if anyone.'

'Is Daddy? Sometimes she gets very cross with him.'

'There's just been a little mix-up around your dad's work, that's all.'

Poor kid, no wonder he liked to have some control over his vegetables, not to mention killing zombies in his spare time.

'OK, five more minutes, then bed.'

Just then her phone buzzed. She slipped out into the hallway.

'Finn? You have no idea what—'

'I have, believe me, I've been getting texts. And from Sam too, who's really going for the *pawning them off with a babysitter* line, I'm sorry. I'll make it up to you, I promise.'

'That's twice. Look, I get it, she was within her rights to be annoyed. She was pretty tough about it, but why didn't you just level with her?'

There was a pause she recognised – it felt exactly like his son's.

'It's really not that simple.'

'You're scared of her. Don't worry, I get it.'

It was true, Cassie realised, she still had the knot in her stomach, even though she'd handled herself in the moment.

'I recognise that as a modus operandi: scare the wits out of someone then be sweet to them afterwards so they're grateful and compliant.'

'Look, I've got to go, we're finishing up here. I'll be back within an hour, max.'

'Fine.'

She looked back towards the sitting-room door from which a small crack of light was falling on the ground like a folded fan. Poor kid was in there, straining his ears, trying to make sense of it all.

* * *

His bedtime routine seemed to last forever, with an elaborate ritual for brushing his teeth – one hundred strokes – then tapping the basin with his toothbrush fifty times, then counting each of the bathroom tiles as he touched them.

'Ninety-two. That's a nice even number.'

Cassie nodded, surprised by her own patience.

At the bedroom door, he baulked. From inside, Cici's steady breathing was audible.

'Cassie, I can't go in unless you check.'

'Under the . . .?'

He nodded. She crept in and looked under the bed; there was nothing but a stray shoe. She raised her thumb, and he made a dash for the ladder, clambered up and burrowed under the duvet.

'Cassie,' he hissed, 'will you be hanging out with us again?'

'I don't know, why?'

'So, we'll have time to play *Nuclear Zombie* again?'

'Would you like that?'

'Yeah. We could change the setting up to normal difficulty because I could definitely do that. And then we could turn off auto-lock for enemies.'

'Sounds like a great idea, Con, but I'm not sure exactly when I'll be back.' No point in lying to the poor kid. 'I would like to, though. Maybe ask your dad?'

'My dad is always busy working or . . . just busy.'

That was interesting.

'We'll see, night night.'

Here she was, like every adult that had ever palmed off a child with some empty platitude. Con struggled to relate to people and he'd chosen to trust her. She knew how fragile trust could be.

She crept back into the sitting room to find, to her horror, Thor contentedly chewing on the strap of Ramona's shoe – thankfully, he was only getting started. She wrestled it from him then curled up on the sofa, trying to breathe. Nothing felt more attractive at that moment than a cold glass of white wine, but she was driving so that was out of the question, dammit.

Shortly afterwards, she heard the key and Finn put his head around the door. He was noticeably more relaxed than earlier.

'Hey, how did you get on?'

'With your younger kids, adorable, they're little darlings. With the call from your ex-wife, let's say I'm still getting over it.'

'Look, this was crazy and I'm so sorry, and I can't thank you enough. I can't imagine what I'd have done without you.'

He watched in amusement as she buckled on the shoes.

'Even if I did come dressed as a stripper.'

He broke into a soft laugh. 'That is actually some outfit.'

'Thanks. It didn't get quite the outing I'd expected.'

'Or that it deserved. I mean it, I'm taking you for dinner one Saturday. Do you think Ramona would lend you it again?' He pulled her towards him. 'It's all over for tonight, we can relax.'

In spite of herself, Cassie felt her body respond to his hand sliding round her waist.

'I can't, not now. I'm the babysitter.'

'They can't hear.'

'But I can. It'd feel inappropriate.'

There was something about Finn that didn't quite seem to register the fuzzy things.

'Daddy, can I have a glass of water?' The piping little voice of Cici, who had just entered the room, caused her heart to plunge. Oh help, had she not had enough frights for one night?

'Of course, lovie, the babysitter's going now because Daddy's home. I'll bring it in to you.'

They telegraphed to each other as Cassie pulled on her coat. That was what adults did above kids' heads, wasn't it, but by the look on Cici's little face, most kids seemed well able to crack the code.

Chapter 17

In the background of Josie's sitting room, Cassie could see a pale-yellow chest of drawers sitting on a sheet of newspaper.

'We found it in the market last Saturday for a tenner. Pal is repainting it for the baby's room. We're really trying to upcycle and be as sustainable as possible.'

Oh, to have a life where your main focus was on restoring light furniture and reading baby-development books. Cassie felt mean-spirited but, well, what was the point in pretending?

'It's beautiful. But what do you think about the situation? And please don't tell me I shouldn't have offered to dig him out of a hole.'

'Hello . . . I was going to say that you did great, I'm really proud of you. That was a potential disaster and you turned it into a fun experience for those poor kids.'

Cassie felt her chin wobble.

'What's wrong?'

'I enjoyed it. Oh Jos, it was fine. It was lovely. I suppose I've instinctively avoided children . . .'

'Well, we know that's connected to what happened with Maxine.'

Cassie couldn't face going there.

'I didn't realise I've been so afraid of looking after kids alone, but I did fine. You should've seen me.'

'I don't doubt it. I believe in you. Always did.'

'Thanks.'

Despite Josie's bright smile, there was a brittleness in her manner. Nobody else would have noticed but Cassie saw her fidgeting.

'Jos, I know you, what's going on?'

Josie hesitated and looked away. 'There's something I have to let you know.'

Oh shit, she felt a warning note sound in her chest.

'Pal and I discussed it and—'

'Oh, come on, just tell me.'

'We got an invitation. To a wedding.'

'Whose?'

'Gavin's.'

In her heart, the tide went out, like right before a tsunami, when the world sucks in a massive breath before all hell is let loose.

'You're joking. You're fucking joking. He only ended it six months ago. If that's what you'd even call it.'

'I know, I know, we were as shocked as you, believe me.'

'Who is she? Oh my God, Josie, he must have known her already.'

'Stop, wait, don't panic. I think it's a whirlwind thing, I don't think he was cheating.'

The next question loomed over her like a thunder cloud.

'Do we know her?'

'Are you sure you want to know?'

'*Just fucking tell me.*' She really hadn't meant to shout. 'Sorry, sorry, Jos.'

'It's Kirsty, the stage manager.'

'The one who's about twenty-four? Fucking hell.'

'I think she's twenty-six. It wasn't going on while you were together, we're pretty sure of that. It was just one of those things.'

Everything felt very far away. In the silence, she could hear the faintest ringing in her ears.

'Cass, Cass, are you OK?'

She could hear Josie's voice but it just didn't feel that important.

'It's OK. People move on, Jos. What can you do? I can't control it.'

'Cass, you sound weirdly calm. It's OK not to be. I mean, who would be? I wouldn't. Fuck no, I'd be screaming.'

'If I get angry and hysterical then he wins.'

'It doesn't work like that. Stop being so freaking calm, please, you're scaring me. Oh God, I wish I was there to give you a hug.'

'It's OK. I'm a grown-up.' But inside she felt like one of those cartoon scientific experiments where the nutty professor adds one more chemical to the test tube and the whole thing explodes, foaming over the top like a big gloopy volcano that takes over everything.

'Josie, I've got to go. I don't feel that well. I'll chat to you later.'

Without waiting for a reply, she hit 'End Meeting', grabbed a pillow and howled.

* * *

At ten to eight on Monday morning, she pulled into a parking space, of which there seemed to be plenty, and hoped there wouldn't be someone cursing her behind her back. She reminded herself to breathe mindfully and control catastrophic thinking. Roger Newcombe met her just inside the front door. He was wearing an almost identical jacket to the one he wore for her interview, except in a browner hue. She'd been bracing herself for his previous dismissive tone but instead relief flooded his face.

'Thank heavens you're here. Three staff have phoned in so far, two with the vomiting bug, the other with a herniated disc, and my vice principal is still out. Can you stand in with Fourth Class?'

'Absolutely.'

First rule of improvisation: say yes to everything and take it from there. Despite the shock of Josie's news, she'd spent Sunday evening combing the internet for teaching tips so at least she'd made a list of what to ask, which was just as well, as she could feel her mind moving into overwhelm.

'Could you please let me know which subject matter I'm to teach them? Also, who is the main teacher?'

He looked at her strangely. 'You're not an assistant teacher, you're a substitute teacher. I shouldn't be telling you this, but these days you're like hen's teeth.'

That was a pleasant new experience for her; it beat cattle-call auditions, anyway.

She followed the directions down the corridor to the left and into classroom 4B. Once the lights were switched on, it revealed itself as bright and cheerful, a far cry from the overcrowded classrooms she remembered from her own childhood. Still, there was that familiar smell of pencils, markers, rubbers. Collages made with lollipop sticks and glitter lined the walls, alongside a notice about diversity.

That was new – at least nowadays they made a point of including people. In her day, diversity consisted of one poor kid from somewhere else who became a spectacle until finally everyone just got bored and moved on. She took the little chairs down off the tables and looked at her watch. Quarter past eight. In half an hour a crowd of ten-year-olds would be piling in and she hadn't a clue where to start. Help.

She stuck her head out of the classroom door to see a door across the corridor marked 4A and a name plate that said *Miss Traynor* – clearly someone who was important enough to merit their own plaque. She stuck her head around the door to see a head of copper-coloured curls bent over a desk.

'Er, excuse me . . . Hi, I'm Cassie, I'm the sub for 4B.'

The other teacher, about five years younger than herself, looked up from where she was correcting homework in copybooks that hadn't changed remotely in thirty years.

'I was wondering if you wouldn't mind giving me a heads-up about what they're doing. If you don't mind.'

If the other woman felt the slightest flash of irritation, she didn't show it; she stood up with a warm smile and immediately advanced towards Cassie with her hand out.

'Hi, I'm Maggie. It's so daunting the first day in a new school, isn't it?'

'Actually, it's my first day in any school – as a teacher, that is.'

Maggie didn't miss a beat. 'Am I glad to have you! Otherwise, I'd be running between them, trying to cover two classes for the day. Head-wrecker.'

She continued to smile warmly, prompting a glow of gratitude in Cassie, who vowed from that moment onwards to be just as kind and lovely to anyone she ever met for the rest of her life.

'Come on, there's nothing to it, I'll show you.' Maggie showed her the timetable on the wall back in 4B.

'You're starting with English for the first forty-five minutes, then geography, then SPHE.'

'SPHE?'

Maggie looked at her curiously.

'You don't have kids yourself?'

'Er, not yet, I mean . . . no. But I'm a quick learner.'

'I don't doubt it. Here's the books. Just stay one lesson ahead of the kids and you'll be fine. Oh look, Marie has marked exactly where she's got to, so you can pick up from there – simple. I wouldn't bother with "Word Wizard", that's quite technical, I'd start with the reading book and get them to discuss it.'

Cassie smiled gratefully. She chose *Why the Whales Came* by Michael Morpurgo – that was something she could definitely do – and then it was geography, followed by SPHE, or Social, Personal and Health Education. In their regular teacher's book there was a note: *Who am*

I? How do I fit in with friends? OK, she could definitely manage that. In fact, she could do with a bit of it herself. A little role-play or game would be fine and that would get her as far as break time.

Maggie explained that all of the teachers up to Fourth Class had to meet the children at the gate and lead them in a line back to the classroom. Crikey, talk about feeling like an impostor. She gratefully followed Maggie out to the yard, where a bewildering array of children of all sizes were milling about.

'And this is 4B.' Maggie indicated a column of ten-year-old boys and girls. 'Good luck and see you on the other side.'

'Hi, boys and girls, my name is Cassie Kearney and I'll be taking you for class today.'

In fact, it wasn't the children who were intimidating, it was the parents, particularly a small group of women who were eyeing her sceptically. Just keep moving, she reminded herself, never make yourself a stationary target. Modelling herself on the other teachers, she stood at the head of her class and followed the long crocodile into the building.

'Miss, Miss, we're supposed to change tables today, can myself and Liam sit together?' Suddenly, there was chaos, as everyone saw an opportunity to buck the system and sit beside their pals. She realised one good decision she'd made was to wear platform boots. Feck teaching theory, at least be the tallest person in the room.

'Now . . . hold on, boys and girls. Just for today we're all going to stay in our old seats.'

Hanging on to control and being the adult was at least half the job, that much was clear.

'Miss, would you like me to hand out the copybooks?' A tall girl with a smooth ponytail was looking at her expectantly.

'And you're . . .?'

'Sophie.'

'Excellent, thank you, Sophie.'

It was important to spot the allies.

'Now, everyone, as I told you, I'm Miss Kearney and you'll have me for today. Take out your reading books and I'll start reading, then all of you can carry on.'

A small squat boy with a scattering of freckles, who reminded her of a baked bean in a hoodie, piped up, 'Is Miss Upton very sick? Is she ever coming back?'

'I'm sure she will be back, but we won't worry about that just for now, OK? Let's begin—'

'Miss, Miss! Could we make her a card? Like one that said, "Get well soon, but not too soon" – in case she has a relapse like my granda did.'

His voice had the natural croaky tone of a comedian. A titter rippled around the class, but this wasn't Cassie's first time in front of a tough crowd.

'What a lovely idea . . .'

'Rowley.'

'Rowley. So thoughtful, and we must *absolutely* do that.'

Rule one: always keep the comedian occupied, and never take it personally. (Easier said than done.) But public life was full of class show-offs, so don't underestimate them.

Ten thirty and time for SPHE. She felt a surge of hope. Break time was in sight!

'Now, boys and girls, I want you to divide into groups and make up a little scene where one of you is the odd one out. Maybe you're new, maybe you're different in some way, but I would like you to show how you can include the new person. OK?'

She smiled broadly, conscious of projecting a massive amount of energy towards the doubtful children. As expected, the 'good girls' group organised themselves straight away and began assigning roles to each other with great enthusiasm.

The lads' group, with Rowley at the centre, had already started guffawing and kicking each other, which seemed to be part of the preparation. Oh Lord.

'Now, boys, keep the noise down, please, we don't want to disturb the other classes.'

They glanced at her momentarily then carried on exactly as before. She should've got everyone sorted out before dreaming of letting them leave their desks, that was obvious.

To her horror the noise from Rowley's group had reached the approximate decibel level of a cup final. She dodged her way to the top of the classroom and had just raised her arms in a desperate attempt to reclaim some order, when the door was flung open.

A silence fell on the room.

Roger Newcombe stood glaring at them like a high court judge ready to pass sentence. Cassie's heart sank.

'Do you realise that you can be heard at the other end of the school?'

'Yes, yes, sorry. We'll be quieter from now on, won't we, everyone?'

Roger Newcombe fixed her with a chilling stare through his no-nonsense square glasses. The pause was ominous.

'I hope so. We want a nice quiet atmosphere in this school, don't we, boys and girls? None of this chaos now.'

He swept out the door, leaving a waft of rebuke in his wake.

'Right, boys and girls, you heard that. Pipe down or there'll be trouble.'

For her, not them, but she wasn't going to tell them that.

Rowley's role-play was an outrageous multi-generational family caper with a farting granny, a super-intelligent dog and Rowley, of course, as the hero, complete with bionic anorak and power potion, all of which was met with hilarity and rapturous applause from the class. Just then, the bell went and the children piled out of the classroom, buzzing with excitement. Cassie sank onto the hard plastic chair and tried to breathe mindfully, when a head of copper curls popped around the door.

'Don't mind him,' Maggie reassured her as they headed up the corridor. 'Between ourselves, he's a bit of an arse. He's of the opinion that discipline is the foundation of an effective school.'

'Sounds more like prison.'

Maggie laughed. 'You'll get used to it.'

Cassie rather hoped she wouldn't. Just then they arrived at a door marked 'Staffroom'. Cassie felt a jolt of anxiety, especially as Maggie seemed not to be stopping.

'Are you not coming in?'

'Afraid not, I'm on yard duty. Just relax, they're a nice bunch.'

With that, she vanished out the side door, leaving Cassie alone, which felt about the diametric opposite of relaxing.

She was met with a diverse group of mostly women, ranging from the Miss Marple lookalikes to trendy young girls who looked barely out of school themselves and alternative types in eclectic outfits. She'd tell that to Mam. They all seemed deep in conversation. There was nothing random about a school. You had a rigid timetable, worked with the same people every day and paced yourself from holiday to holiday. Quite a contrast to her old life, which was pretty much the complete opposite. She made for the kettle unnoticed and helped herself to a coffee and digestive biscuit, trying to look busy and not too much like Nellie-no-friends in the corner.

She overheard two teachers, each of whom had a lunchbox in front of them.

'Did you hear that racket?'

'Who on earth was in charge of that? I thought there must have been a riot. Disgraceful.' Own up, Cassie thought, better to be talked to than talked about.

'That was me, sorry. I'm subbing for Miss Upton. We did a role-play thing, but that's the last of the ruckus, I promise.'

They exchanged glances and seemed to agree on an attitude of sympathy.

'I'm Denise. Would you like a flapjack?' the younger one broke in. 'We've worked out a science for getting through to lunchtime. Slow-release oatcakes and dried fruit.'

'We teach Fifth Class; you don't get away with anything,' confided the other lady, who had a Joan Rivers hairdo and introduced herself as Babs. 'By the way, have I seen you somewhere before? Your face is very familiar.'

The thought of explaining herself in the staffroom on her first day was more than Cassie could cope with.

'I don't think you recognise me. I just have one of those faces.'

Chapter 18

Pulling out of the car park, she experienced conflicting feelings of elation and exhaustion. Too wired to face an empty apartment, but not up to making adult conversation. There was only one thing for it.

'Mam? Are you home?'

'It's Monday, of course I'm home. I'm taking delivery of the new mattress. How long will you be? Eric is out, so pick up a cake and I'll put the kettle on.'

Cassie sighed with relief at the gift of not having to explain.

Just then her phone rang. 'Well, how did you get on?' For a moment she was confused by the upbeat voice. 'Phil?'

'The very one. I always like to phone my clients after the first day to check how it went.'

'Great, I think. Well, it was, but Roger Newcombe barged in this morning because it was a bit chaotic at first. I mean, *I* knew exactly what we were doing but—'

'Don't worry! That was all part of the learning curve, I'm sure. He was delighted and he wants you back tomorrow.'

It appeared that short of actually setting the school on fire, she was going to be kept on for the moment.

She baulked. A single day was one thing, but the idea of facing 4B as their main teacher every day was an exhausting prospect. Still, the money was good and it certainly felt nice to be in demand. There was something about Phil that made everything feel safe and manageable.

'Fantastic, Phil, thanks for the call. I'll be there tomorrow.'

'Do you know something? I think you have a flair for this . . . It's just a feeling, but I believe in you. I'll say no more.'

And he was gone, leaving a whiff of positivity in the air.

* * *

'Eric is mad about him,' said Mam, 'and don't be fooled by that little office. He does very well, he just doesn't bluster and brag like some people without an arse in their trousers.'

She was busy was filling their mugs with steaming tea.

'Mam, are you trying to set us up?'

'All I'm saying is, sometimes you can end up looking for romance in all the wrong places. I don't want to drag up the past . . .'

'Oh, why change the habit of a lifetime.'

'But that fellow in England, the Scots one . . .'

'Gavin was his name, I was with him for fifteen years.' She paused. 'You might as well know, I just heard from Josie that he's getting married to a young one.'

'Oh no, love. I'm sorry, that's desperate.'

'Yeah, I'd a pants of a weekend but I think I've made my peace with it.'

Mam reached out and squeezed her hand. 'You're better off, love, I mean that. We only met him twice. Don't take this the wrong way, and I'm saying this as your mother and I care about you, but did it never occur to you in all the time you were with him that he'd leave you high and dry? Because it was there in big flashing letters six-foot high to the rest of us.'

'Well, you could have said something at the time rather than hitting me with it now.'

But even as she said it, Cassie knew only too well how she'd have responded.

'I loved him and I just thought it would work out.'

'Things don't just "work out", not for most people anyway, and it's not "uncool" or whatever you call it to want to know what's going on.'

Cassie felt her heart sink but there was something about the starkness of Mam's words that felt like a relief. It was all true. She had to stop hiding from herself.

'I was afraid to push too hard in case I heard something I didn't like.'

'For the love of God, you always lived in cuckoo land. You're not a stupid girl, in fact I always said to your daddy that you'd brains to burn. But there was always . . . something missing with you. Reality maybe. Maybe that's what made you choose that crazy career. Sure, isn't that what created the whole rift with Maxine in the first place?'

Cassie began to cut thick wedges of the Swiss roll she'd picked up on the way. 'I'm whacked, can we not just have our tea?'

'Please yourself, all I'm saying is I'm delighted you've started a nice sensible job. And you've Phil to thank for that.'

'Mam!'

'All right, then, let's talk about your new chap. The one with the three kids. How's that going?'

What sounded like an expression of friendly interest, Cassie could identify as an emotional bear-trap. Any offer of information could be used to chastise her. Still, the desire to talk won out. 'He's . . . I can't describe it. You know when there's just something attractive about someone, but you don't know what it is. Chemistry, I suppose. Plus, I babysat his two younger kids last week and I really enjoyed it.'

Mam's mouth looked as flat as a hyphen.

'You're only thirty-seven, Cass, it's still not too late. Don't forget, chemistry has a danger of blowing up in your face.'

She'd a knack of expressing Cassie's secret fears. Still, awareness was everything, right? Once she had her eyes open, surely to God she could avoid falling into the same hole over and over again.

'I only took care of them once, in an emergency.'

Mam's mouth morphed from a hyphen to a dash.

'And what did their mother think of that, I wonder?'

'Well, she didn't know, obviously.'

'I'd keep it that way.'

Why was Mam being so negative about Finn all of a sudden? 'I could do with a bit more support, Mam. He is unattached, after all. They're separated. It's not like I'm doing anything wrong.'

'That's not the point, love. You've always been the one to make sure everyone else was sorted. It's time to look after yourself. Not that you'll take a blind bit of notice, but I have to say it.'

'I know, Mam.' For a moment she felt tearful. In a world where everybody seemed to have someone, Mam was the one person for whom she would always be special.

'And another thing, you're going to have to contact Maxine sooner or later. Those bridesmaids' dresses won't pick themselves.'

* * *

Finn was busy for most of that week, so she didn't see him but they exchanged texts at night.

> *Missing you. Kids loved you, keep asking when you'll be back.*

Mam's words kept sounding in the back of her mind, but she pushed them away.

> *Loved meeting them too. When you around? Love to see you.*

> *Have kids all week. Their mum's away. Can't wait to see you.*

That was OK. The kids had to come first, that was a given, but she would've loved to curl up with a bottle of wine and tell him all about her new life. Time enough, she told herself. Mam was obsessed with old-fashioned ideas of what to expect from a man but life just wasn't that simple anymore.

In the meantime, she was undergoing a crash course in managing 4B, without a single day of teacher training, and her strategy of 'fake it till you make it' was starting to wear thin. Nevertheless, Rowley, Sophie and the rest of the class seemed to have accepted her, and once she mastered the confidence to give everyone clear instructions before they left their desks to do tasks, she just about managed to retain a decent level of order.

She'd realised after the first day that it wasn't necessary to dress exclusively in costumes from old bank commercials, and had relaxed a bit into jeans and jumpers. Every evening, she went home with her books and planned the lessons for the following day.

She'd become quite pally with Maggie, the form teacher for 4A, so she was pumping her for some background info on Miss Upton over lunch.

'So, what's she like? When the kids talk about her, they almost seem a little scared.'

'Marie . . . Well, she's a nice person, but let's say I probably wouldn't be having this conversation with her, I'd be a little more formal. But you'll find out, she'll be back on Monday.'

Cassie's heart sank. 'That'll probably mean I won't be needed anymore.'

'Are you kidding me? Comb-over won't let you go that easily. He's been frantically trying to get staff, he's only short of jumping out into traffic to offer people jobs. I'd bet my lunch on you going nowhere.'

Cassie felt a glow of relief; it wasn't exactly job security but at least it suggested she mightn't be out on her arse at the end of the week.

* * *

Late April it might be, but the weather was still chilly. Cassie was curled up on Finn's sofa in front of the fire, finally enjoying their long-awaited Saturday night.

'It's weird, all my life I was afraid I couldn't do anything useful, but that's not true. I just say to them, "This is the magic space where nothing can go wrong," and all this stuff comes out that they've never dared share before in case they'd be mocked. Sorry, I'm ranting.'

Finn refilled their glasses and stroked her cheek with the back of his hand.

'Not at all, I'm proud of you. You've gone from dog walker—'

'*Impostor* dog walker to *impostor* teacher.'

'To managing a class full-time on your own for a week. That's really something.'

'Do you really think so? I've been waiting all week to tell you. I just hope when Miss Upton gets back, she won't try to squish all of this. What I'm hearing about her is a bit iffy, even though they're all being super diplomatic, now I come to think of it.'

Did she imagine it or did Finn momentarily flinch?

'Finn, are you OK?'

He seemed to be processing her words, but he was inclined to do this, wasn't he?

'I'm sure whatever hits you, you'll be able to handle it,' he said at last and the moment passed.

'God, I hope so, Finn. How long does it take to feel real? I'm thirty-seven and I still feel like a fake.'

'Don't ask me, I've always had impostor syndrome. But maybe that's because my parents left us to it, they weren't big on encouragement.'

'You mean they weren't around?'

'My dad had businesses – property development, conservatories. He'd his finger in that many pies, and my mother did the books. They were what you'd call a power couple, I suppose. I mean, we were fine, we'd plenty of minders and babysitters.'

'And what was that like?'

'I used to spend time in my room making models. We lacked for nothing . . .'

'Except what you really needed. Like, being noticed.'

It made sense that despite Finn's urbane exterior, sometimes she found herself searching for him as though he were stuck at the bottom of a deep well and she were calling down to him.

'Well, I notice you.'

'You don't know how much that means.'

Cassie was surprised at the intensity in his voice.

'We never felt ignored. The opposite. Mam kept coming up with business ideas, like her party catering company Party Poppers – you can imagine what that got changed to. I remember myself and Maxine shelling prawns for hours till our hands went red and chapped. Still, I remember it being fun. Crazy, but fun.'

Finn did his sudden laugh then became serious. 'Promise me you won't let that school turn you into something you're not.'

'Why would I?'

'Don't give up on your dreams.'

'What dreams? I dreamed of being a TV star and going to red-carpet events in spangly frocks and having my photo in the tabloids and going on those silly ITV quiz shows for celebrities, but it hasn't happened. I never got past the stage of being "pencilled in", which is a nice way of saying "fuck off". I couldn't keep that up, it was just too painful. At some point I had to find something to make myself useful. That's the one thing I've loved about the past week. Maybe being a star wasn't something fate had in store, but this is OK, it really is, so please don't make me second-guess it.'

'I wouldn't do that for the world. I see you as this beautiful, kooky free spirit. There are too many people who've given up on their dreams.'

Cassie couldn't help wondering who he was really talking about.

'You make me sound like Jennifer Lawrence falling up the steps for her Oscar. Can we stop talking about work now? It's just us and Thor, and I want to relax.'

'Let's leave Thor out of it.' He pulled her to him, so she could feel the soft flannel of his shirt and instinctively slid her hand inside to caress the smooth, warm skin underneath. She felt him responding as the outside world melted away, leaving only each other's touch.

Chapter 19

Cassie pulled into the school car park before eight o'clock to get a jump on the morning, which was not normally something she did willingly. She'd uncovered a flair for Irish and her head was buzzing with plans around the little role-plays she'd worked out involving new words they'd learned last week.

As she approached the classroom, she could see from the transom window above the door that the light was already on, and she was taken aback by the racket of chairs being slammed impatiently onto the floor. She peered round the door to see a tall, slim woman in an expensive-looking midi dress and boots, her hair in an elaborate updo, organising fiercely. There was no doubt she'd been up at six to get that outfit in place. The woman swung round to face the door, causing Cassie's heart to lurch.

'Can I help you?'

'Oh, er . . . Hi, I'm Cassandra Kearney, I'm the substitute teacher and I've been taking—'

'Thank you, I appreciate your help, but as you can see, I'm back and there's no further need for you in this class. I suggest you go back and speak to the principal, who's in his office. He can reallocate you for the day.'

With that, she turned on her heel, leaving Cassie speechless, mortified and furious. Technically, Miss Upton was right but there was something about the dismissive tone in her voice that stung Cassie like a late-summer wasp.

Right now, she'd no option but to head back up the echoey corridor to the office where Helen, the school secretary, was hanging up her limp blue anorak.

'Hi, is Roger— Mr Newcombe here?'

'There's been a leak in the back toilets over the weekend, so he's trying to fix it with Mr Daly.'

Just then, the flap, flap, flap of Roger Newcombe's all-leather shoes could be heard approaching along the tiled floor.

'Mr Newcombe, there seems to be a small bit of doubling up here,' announced Helen.

'Yes, yes, Marie's back and, as fate would have it, nobody's phoned in sick. Pure fluke. You couldn't make it up.'

He appeared, as usual, to be mainly addressing himself. 'Still, if I let you go, someone else will get you.' He paused. 'Are you qualified as an SNA? Special needs assistant: reading, writing, dyslexia, autism, ADHD?'

For a split second she contemplated spoofing, but she gave it up as a truly terrible idea.

'I won't lie to you, I'm not trained.'

'We can sort that out later. Come with me.'

Cassie baulked. The last thing she wanted was to go back within a mile of that intimidating woman. It turned out she couldn't have been more wrong.

'Good morning, Roger, how can I help?' Miss Upton's tone was warm and engaging, as though she were working the room at an embassy cocktail party. The headmaster's manner had softened correspondingly.

'Cassie will be your assistant just while we're sorting a few things out. Any problems, you know where to find me,' he said, making himself scarce and leaving Cassie to face Miss Upton, who reverted to her previous tone as soon as the door closed.

'If you wouldn't mind setting out the tables, I have an Irish project planned.'

Without thinking it through, Cassie blurted out, 'That's so interesting, Miss Upton. I've some ideas myself I'd been working on for the class. Perhaps we could compare notes.'

A flash of irritation crossed Miss Upton's face but then, unexpectedly, she broke into a smile like the sun coming out from behind a cloud.

'Oh, call me Marie. Well, it sounds like you have some experience. Tell me all about yourself.'

She had to acknowledge that Marie was charismatic and had a quality that made you really want her to like you, even if a secret part of you felt uneasy. As she laid out the equipment, Cassie found herself chatting away about London and her acting career, and what a rollercoaster it was proving to start all over again at thirty-seven. Marie was a fabulous listener, you had to hand her that; her laser-like gaze softened to close attentiveness, which gave you the impression she'd heard and understood every word like nobody else, and invited you to confide in her further.

'Gosh, that's fascinating, Cassie. To have that sort of talent. That'd be a great help for teaching too, I'm sure.'

'Funny you should mention it . . .' Cassie poured out her ideas, delighted to have such a receptive audience.

'Sounds wonderful. Unfortunately, I find myself constrained by the curriculum.'

'Constrained' was such a Marie word.

'Cassie, I'm going out to collect the class, say hi to the parents, all of that. Would you mind taking two kids down to the small classroom when we get back? They're excused Irish, so you can do some extra reading practice with them.'

Cassie agreed readily. She was a little crestfallen at her loss of autonomy with the class but, hey – reality check – she was the rookie and Marie was turning out to be much nicer than she'd feared. Perhaps this wasn't going to be so bad after all.

For most of the next hour, she worked patiently with each child, then headed back to classroom 4B, only to hear eager voices coming from inside. She pushed open the door and saw a group of children enthusiastically doing a role-play that was exactly the same as she'd described to Marie. Cassie felt sick, not just at the deliberate plagiarism of her idea but also the sense of betrayal from somebody she'd chosen to trust in spite of her misgivings.

'Hi, Cassie, Miss Upton did plays with us too, even better than last week,' volunteered someone.

'Really, they seem so familiar.' She stared at Marie, who met her gaze without a flicker. For a second Cassie wondered if she'd imagined the whole thing. Did she spot the ghost of a smile? But what could she do?

Just then the bell went for break, and they headed out to the yard.

'Er . . . Marie, can I just check something with you? You used my material . . . I mean, the role-plays I told you about, but I thought you said . . .'

Marie turned to her with an almost amused expression. 'It's all about being flexible in this work . . . all about collaboration. That's just how it works.'

She sounded so reasonable that, in the moment, Cassie felt guilty for even mentioning it and found herself agreeing hastily. It was only afterwards that she began to ask herself when something shifted from collaboration to plain old ripping off of someone's ideas.

At lunchtime, in the staffroom, a small group of teachers seemed to crowd around Marie to welcome her back and protest that the place hadn't been the same without her. Well, that was for bloody sure. This was all too familiar from her own school days. It still was with her old gang, if she were being honest. Marie was the popular girl in the class, and popular girls existed in staffrooms just as they did in schoolyards. But was she the person everyone wanted to be friends with or just the person they least wanted to dislike them? A bit of both, possibly. Even Maggie seemed less available, so Cassie ate her lunch quietly at the end of a table and tried to stay inconspicuous.

* * *

Driving home that afternoon, she scanned her contacts at the traffic lights for someone to buzz for a bit of reassurance. Josie – no, she was deep in baby-land; Mam? No. The person she really wanted to text was Finn, but he'd be at work. So, that left Philip. Would phoning him be overstepping professional boundaries? At the same time, he'd sent her for the job, so presumably she could check in with him. She found herself hitting call, her heart pounding a little.

'Cassie, how are you? It's great to hear from you.'

She sighed with relief. There might have been times in her life when she'd have thought of someone like Philip as 'uncool', but right now his warmth and enthusiasm felt like balm to her jangled nerves. She burst out about Marie and how she'd confided in her, only to find she'd shamelessly nicked her idea and then behaved as though nothing had happened.

'She gaslighted me, Phil.'

'Don't talk to me, you wouldn't believe how common that is. Boardrooms, presentations, pulpits even . . . I'm hearing about it every day.'

'But what can I do? I can't stop her, I haven't even any qualifications. I'm a nobody in there. I'm powerless.'

'Ah now, go away out of that. You've just had a bad day,' he said kindly. 'You've learned the hard way to keep your ideas to yourself. But now you come to mention it, an SNA qualification wouldn't be the worst idea in the world. You could do it online in your own time.'

'Really, do you think so?'

'Sure, Google it. You could start any time and do it from home. It'd push your pay up too.'

Philip had an uncanny way of making everything a bit more manageable. As Mam said, he was a lovely guy. What was it about Phil? He felt like the sort of person you could confess your darkest fears to without being judged. He was handsome, in an almost old-fashioned, genteel sort of way. He was kind and interesting, and what was more, he seemed very interested in her. What was not to like if you'd half a brain?

* * *

That evening Cassie was curled up on the sofa in the sitting-room-slash-pole-dance-studio, munching her way through a black bean burrito bowl she'd treated herself to from the local deli, when Ramona trailed into the room. At first Cassie thought she was on the phone to a particularly exuberant friend. After a few moments of earwigging, she determined that her flatmate was recording a post and was preparing her fans for a big treat.

'Instagram?'

'Insta, TikTok, YouTube, everything . . .' Ramona was dressed in what was, for her, a casual outfit: red tracksuit bottoms and a matching crop top with a tatty dressing gown thrown over it.

'Are you working tonight?'

'Sister, you have got to be shitting me. It's Monday night, not even the cats work on a Monday night. No, I've got a date.'

'Savage, where did you meet him?'

'Tinder.' So that's what all the build-up was about. It struck Cassie that Monday was an ideal night for thousands of followers in their PJs to watch Ramona hauling herself into high-octane glam and heading out to meet a complete randomer for the first time.

'You going out dressed like that?'

'Babe, are you kidding? This lot? I have to start from here so my story has a dramatic arc and the guys can travel with me.'

It sounded exhausting. Fun, but exhausting. Ramona was going to bring her fifty thousand followers through the whole getting-ready process.

'Do you seriously feel like going out on a chilly Monday night when it's starting to rain?'

'Babe, I have responsibilities. I do it so they don't have to.'

She waved her phone in Cassie's direction. When did we all pull back on our own lives and end up watching other people live? she wondered. Ramona was doing reality TV for the tiny screen.

'Where are you meeting him? Or . . . Is it a him?'

'It's a them, but all right, them's a him. The Blind Pig at ten. I'll give them two drinks and after that I'll put it to the vote with my crew. That is, unless I really like them or really hate them, in which case I decide and everybody else can fuck off.'

'So, if you're "ish" the viewers can decide.'

'Exactly.'

'Sounds fair.' If a bit baffling, Cassie thought. She couldn't imagine her life witnessed by fifty thousand people, who all felt they owned a piece of you. Trying to live just for herself was stressful enough.

'Anyway, you keep watching tits and abs on *Ex on the Beach*, and I'll go get ready.'

'Don't dare leave without showing me your outfit. Do they get to vote on that too?'

'Are you kidding me, there'd be chaos. I'm an influencer not a dress-up doll.'

Half an hour later Ramona sashayed in, wearing loose flowy trousers and a skimpy crop top that revealed an enviably defined midriff over which she'd thrown an aviator jacket. The effect, along with her white-blonde hair, was stunning. Cassie could imagine an army of women on sofas round the country frantically doing searches for her gear.

'Opinion: shades or no shades?' She stuck on a pair of round John Lennon sunglasses.

'It's dark out.'

'So?'

Cassie shrugged. 'Go for it . . . Wait, you're meeting this person for the first time, late night, in a bar? Are you sure it's safe?'

'That's kind of sweet that you care about my safety, but you actually sound like a public service announcement. Get out of your comfy pumps and live a little, because being good all the time's not going to earn you shit, trust me.'

With that, she swung out the door, which slammed behind her, all the while talking confidentially to her phone. Cassie wondered if she too wasn't a character in Ramona's world by now. Hardly. She wasn't nearly cool enough to feature in Ramona's story.

Chapter 20

The following morning Cassie pulled into her parking space, reminding herself that she was only a lowly assistant and her wings had been clipped.

At 8.40 a.m. there was still no sign of Miss Upton, so Cassie threw on her spring jacket and trudged out to collect class 4B.

The column was ready to snake indoors when, out of the corner of her eye, she caught sight of Marie, looking more hassled than the previous day and holding the hand of a little girl. There was something familiar about the scene and it was only as they came into focus that realisation dawned. The child was Cici.

'Mummy, look, it's our babysitter! Hi, Cassie!'

There was no avoiding it. Weakly, Cassie raised a hand and returned the wave. Oh crap.

The pieces fell into place. What sort of a mess had she got herself into?

She met Marie's gaze and realised she seemed to be having a similar epiphany. Marie, it was obvious, was Marisha, who used her maiden name for work. Of course, she'd already spoken to her on the phone that night in Finn's apartment, without realising it. But more than that, Finn must've realised that she'd be working with Marisha and, for some reason, had chosen not to warn her.

What the hell? That explained why he'd seemed cagey about her excitement at getting the job. She didn't even have the thirty seconds necessary to fire off a text demanding an explanation. Now she was going to be stuck in a room for what felt like all eternity with Marisha and the thorny question of just why her ex-husband had chosen Cassie to babysit for her kids at the last minute.

Cici had joined her Senior Infants' class and trundled off happily in the opposite direction.

Struggling to look calm and professional, Cassie tried to focus her attention on the children. From behind her, Marisha's voice hissed in her ear. 'We need to talk. At break time.'

Cassie felt a cold hand clutch her stomach. A conversation like this promised to be all shades of shite.

Break time arrived, and in an attempt to delay the dreaded confrontation, she checked her phone, only to see four missed calls from Ramona. What the hell? Ramona never called her. Alarmed, she hit call and waited – she was ready to ring off, when a voice answered, 'Well, hey, do you never check your phone?'

Cassie could tell she was attempting her usual sass, but her voice sounded muffled and downbeat.

'Where are you?'

'Mater A&E, thanks for asking.'

'What? Oh my God, I'm so sorry, Ramona, I didn't even know you weren't home. I feel terrible.'

'Then that'd be two of us, so chill. Point is, they won't let me out alone, so either you come to collect me or I sit here like part of the furniture.'

'What happened?'

'Long story – so, can you come?'

It was funny that out of all of Ramona's legion of followers, there didn't seem to be anyone else she could call in an emergency. Cassie could see Marisha eyeing her across the desk, tapping her manicured nail impatiently. Well, feck her.

'Yeah, course I can. See you in half an hour.'

Filled with a burst of righteous courage which trumped any intimidation, Cassie marched up to Marisha and announced she had a family emergency and wouldn't be back until lunchtime. Marisha didn't look one bit pleased – she'd likely been rehearsing the roast she was about to deliver – but Cassie realised she didn't give a shite. Let her stew.

'I'll be back as soon as I can,' she said, without waiting for a reply.

* * *

Ramona had a black eye and some pretty angry-looking bruising down one side of her face.

'Hey, kid, thanks for showing up.'

'I'm sorry, Ramona, I didn't even realise you were missing. Are you OK?'

'I'm fine. Can't you tell?'

She looked exactly the opposite to fine.

Cassie helped her down to the car and, once inside, she took a breath. 'What the hell happened? Was it that Tinder date? Were they a psycho?'

'Naaa, it wasn't them. They were OK but the guys gave it a thumbs down, so they had to go.' Cassie nodded, trying to appear neutral.

'But then I got talking to these two guys in the bar.'

Seriously, Ramona, most people would've called it a night at that point, Cassie reflected.

'They were on holiday . . . They seemed fun . . . I think. So, we were doing shots, having a laugh . . .'

Cassie was starting to feel like her mother, but forced herself to keep her trap shut.

'What went wrong?'

'I was stupid, I know . . . I went back with them to their Airbnb . . .' She seemed to be trying to reconstruct the scene in her brain. 'It all seemed pretty chill . . .'

'*Chill?*' Shut up, she warned herself. The last thing Ramona needed right now was to be reminded that the whole situation hadn't been the world's greatest idea.

'We were goofing around and having fun . . . then I don't know, the atmosphere changed somehow. One of the guys was kind of sitting behind me, and I thought he was OK . . . but the other guy started to creep me out and then I spotted the two of them exchanging glances . . . I'd had a few drinks, but I'm not stupid. I shot to my feet and made for the door. The creepy guy grabbed me by the arm, but I shook him off, pushed him as hard as I could and just ran . . .' It seemed like she was struggling to reconstruct the events. 'And I made it out into the hall, but I must've whacked my head on the way, even though I don't remember feeling any pain. Hurts like hell now, though. Anyhow, I got out onto the street and . . . it was busy, they didn't try to follow me.'

Cassie realised she had both hands covering her cheeks in horror.

'I knew I was concussed because I felt really dizzy so I hailed a taxi . . .'

'Oh my God, Ramona. That could've turned out so much worse.'

It made sense, in a way, Cassie reflected. All her life Ramona had felt unprotected in spite of her family's wealth, like a high-wire act with no safety net.

They drove back to the apartment as the radio played 'Raspberry Beret' by Prince.

'Someone was looking out for me last night,' said Ramona. 'And when I find out who it was, I'm gonna give them a big hug.'

Cassie smiled, and as she sang along with the chorus, she found herself filled with gratitude for the nurses, for the sun, for what really mattered and, especially, for the world of second chances.

* * *

Cassie arrived back at school just in time to answer discreet enquiries from the other staff.

'I saw you flying off in your car, I thought, God help us, is someone dead?' said Babs.

This was a clear invitation for Cassie to fill them in. She managed to give the crowd at the table just enough information to seem trusting and collegial, but not quite enough salacious detail to fan the gossip. All the while, she spotted Marisha circling the staffroom like a silent shark. It was ten past one – five more minutes of break to go.

'Cassie, have you a moment?' she hissed.

Just get it over with, Cassie thought. She really didn't have the energy for Marisha's vendetta. Marisha ushered Cassie into the guidance counsellor's room, flipped the 'Do not disturb' sign round and slammed the door.

'Sooo . . . you were the babysitter I spoke to that evening on the phone. I knew there was something familiar about your voice, but I couldn't quite place it.'

'Look, I'm really sorry about how that worked out, I acted in good faith. I hope the children weren't upset.'

'On the contrary, they appear to have had a fine time, kept asking when they could have you again.'

Cassie cringed inwardly – that was no help to her right now.

'So, it seems . . . you are in some contact with my husband?'

Her 'husband'. That wasn't exactly how Cassie understood the situation but, admittedly, she hadn't had a chance to contact Finn yet. There hadn't been enough space in her head for two emergencies at once. What if he'd already revealed their relationship? What if Marisha already knew all about them and was just testing her?

All of a sudden, after everything she'd been through, this situation just felt so tiresome.

'Look, yes, I did end up babysitting your children on one occasion, but I didn't make the connection either. I was as surprised as you were this morning. If you want me to leave the job, I will. It's been a very upsetting morning and the last thing I need is . . . insinuations about . . . whatever it is you're insinuating about me.'

Cassie knew exactly what Marisha was itching to ask her and had no intention of making it easy. She seemed to be sizing Cassie up. She doesn't want to expose herself either, she thought.

'Well, I'm sure you were glad of the money.'

Just then the bell went right outside the door and the tension snapped. Cassie guessed they were both equally glad to get out of the room. For the rest of the day Cassie found herself trying to stay invisible at the back of the room. In spite of her composure in the moment, the confrontation with Marisha had shaken her. The experienced teacher expertly brought the class through a double period of maths, totally on top of each child's progress. There was no rowdiness, no messing. How had she ever imagined she could fill those shoes?

Chapter 21

Cassie pulled into the underground car park of her apartment block and texted Finn:

> *Need to talk. Crazy shit has happened. Call me ASAP?*

Ten seconds later the phone rang on video call.
'Hey, what's up?'
Finn was at work, she could see what looked like an office behind him; he appeared mildly concerned but nowhere in the same league as she was feeling.
'Why didn't you tell me your ex worked in my school, for God's sake?'
He shifted awkwardly. 'OK, yes. First of all, I wanted to tell you but . . . But it's a big school, so there was every chance you wouldn't have come up against her at all, and I thought, why create something, if there's no need.'
'Finn—'
'Wait. And then when I realised you were actually working with her, I-I didn't want to freak you out. I thought you'd be better getting on with it yourself.

You're so good with people, I wanted you to have your own relationship with her.'

'Well, turns out I do. A shit one.'

In a way he was right, what use would it have been knowing in advance? The situation was as awkward as hell, and nothing could've changed that, but still . . . come on. That was a pretty massive omission.

'Don't bullshit me, Finn, you were trying to avoid an awkward conversation. Why would you not tell me something that important? Were you deliberately trying to keep your life compartmentalised? Because I'll tell you now, I can't live like that. If that's how you're going to play it, we're over. Done.'

'Stop. Cassie, please. Look, I'm sorry, this is all my fault, you're right, I should have told you. How can I fix it?'

Finn was talking about the situation like it was some sort of faulty machine. She was about to shout back, 'You can't,' but thought better of it. OK, he might have been trying to avoid confrontation but, knowing Marisha as she did now, she could hardly blame him.

'Another thing: she referred to you as "my husband". Finn, you call her your ex, is there anything else I need to know?'

He seemed very positive on this one. 'No, honestly, that's just how she talks.'

Finn was on the move at this stage and seemed to have found a dingy store cupboard to wedge himself into.

'Are you sure?' After all, what else might he have glossed over?

'She's . . . very possessive about things. Like her pupils, the children, me.'

'Even though—'

'We're over. Yes.'

This whole situation was turning out to be way more complicated than she'd realised.

He went on, 'It's not that she wants me back, believe me, just that she's not prepared to . . .'

'Let someone else have you?'

'Something like that.'

'Fuck. You really should've let me know about this. This is big, Finn. How many more things are you hiding?'

'Nothing, I swear. You know everything. All the . . . mess.' He looked uneasily towards the door. This wasn't a conversation to have where someone could barge in at any moment, looking for photocopier ink.

'Should I tell her straight out about us, Finn?'

'I don't know. If you think that's the best thing?'

'How do I fucking know what the best thing is? Both options are awful. Like having to choose between being caught in an earthquake or hit by a tornado.'

'We're not obliged to tell her. Strictly speaking, what I do is none of her business.'

'Strictly speaking, I know, but I still can't sit in her class for the rest of the term living a lie. I know that means that I probably won't be sitting in her class at all, so I'll be back to dog walking, but there you have it. How come no matter what choices I try to make, I always find myself out on my arse?'

Cassie was aware she was feeling sorry for herself.

'It's not fair to leave all this to you. I'll deal with it. I'll tell her the whole thing this evening.' This felt like the worst possible option, portraying her as 'the other woman' – at least if she dished the dirt on herself, she might have some hope of control.

'No, please, just trust me to sort this out.'

Finn looked more than a little relieved. 'Can I see you tonight? I really miss you.'

'I'll see. I forgot to tell you, Ramona was beaten up, I'll have to go home and check on her first. I'll come over later.'

'God, I'm sorry. I can cook something. And get wine.'

'Going to your place feels . . . weird now, as though we're being watched.'

It wasn't reasonable but it was true. Marisha's energy was stalking the place even if she wasn't there herself.

'Cassie, please, she's never set foot in this place, she leaves the kids at the door.'

No, but I bet she wonders about it, thought Cassie. I bet she has a picture of it in her fantasy.

* * *

When Cassie got home, Ramona was sitting up on the sofa, wrapped in a fluffy rug and looking considerably better.

'About time, I thought you were never coming back. I had a shower and got dressed, but turns out I'm going to have to adjust my colour scheme to tone in with the bruises. They're turning a lovely greeny-yellow.'

'You're unbelievable, Ramona, you don't have to act tough with me.' She sat on the end of the sofa and gave her friend's feet a hug. And filled her in on the Marisha drama, which she loved.

'Oh God, don't make me laugh, my ribs ache.' Behind her bravado, Cassie sensed that Ramona was feeling a lot more vulnerable than she was letting anyone see.

'It's a fucking mess. What am I going to do, Ramona?'

'Honey, look at the state of me. Do I really seem like a good place to get life advice?'

'You're pretty good about other people.'

'Why thank you, I'll take that as a compliment. Be brave. If you lose the job, so what, get another. If you like this guy, screw her, it's worth it.'

'I suppose. Even though that is pretty much the diametric opposite of what my mother would say.'

'And she's happily engaged to be married for the second time, whereas I'm lying here thanking God I still have all my teeth, so what does that tell you?'

'That she's right. For her.'

'Exactly, and you've got to do what's right for you.'

Cassie looked around. There was no sign anyone else had visited. No cards, no gifts, no sign of family. Ramona, it seemed, picked up on her thoughts.

'So, I called the old bird, filled her in on the drama. Turns out she was less than sympathetic, surprise, surprise, but she sent me some cash so, go Granma.'

'Be honest with me, Ramona, how are you doing? Are you in pain?'

'I'm fine. Don't sit here looking sorry for me. Go get laid by what's-his-name, chief engineer of the Starship Enterprise or whatever.'

'OK, I'll see you tomorrow.'

'Oh and pick me up a pastrami roll from Donny-brook Fair on your way back. God, I love those things. You've got something good going. Don't let anyone trash it.'

And that was the closest Ramona came to being real.

* * *

She'd bought a nice bottle of Pinot Noir. Sod that it was Monday night. In fact, the more she thought about what had happened since that morning, the more it felt like an entire week had passed, and on that basis, it was already at least Thursday. For the first time she let her shoulders droop, and the full stress of the day hit her.

Finn hadn't taken any chances and had a bottle of white chilling when she arrived.

They sat on the plush sofa, gazing out the window with her head on his shoulder, and didn't say much for a moment. But the air was full of unspoken feelings, so better to come straight out with it, thought Cassie. 'Is it all too hard? Is there just too much in the way for us?'

'Don't say that. All of today I've been thinking that you won't want to stay with me, that I'm dragging too much baggage with me and . . . that's part of why I didn't tell you about Marisha before. It was cowardly and I'm not proud of it.'

'It's OK. In a weird way I'm glad I know her. Now it all makes sense. I don't think I'd have believed it otherwise. She's . . . tough.'

'Thank you. That's the first time I've been able to talk to anyone about it.'

It became blindingly clear that the reason she found Finn so hard to fathom was that he was exactly that. For everybody. And that included himself.

'Can you imagine what it'd have been like if we'd met back at the beginning, when we were in our twenties? What would you have thought of me?'

He laughed ruefully. 'I didn't know too many aspiring actresses back then. You wanted a very exciting life, full of spontaneity and excitement, I suppose. I wouldn't have stood a chance.'

Cassie considered this. 'I'd have thought, this guy wants a super-normal life. He'd never consider a flaky proposition like me.'

'So . . . the moral is, be careful what you wish for.'

'Well, I chose someone just as flaky as myself and look how that turned out.'

Enough time had passed for Cassie to accept that much of what happened with Gav had been of her own doing. She'd been afraid to commit in case she was wrong, afraid to settle in case she regretted it, afraid to grow up in case she grew old. Well, turns out time isn't selective, it's quite happy to pass, whether you're acknowledging it or not.

'Hey, let's go on safari. I'd love to sit in a jeep in the heat and watch lions and elephants . . .'

Finn brightened. 'Let's save up all our money and go into space for twenty minutes.'

Cassie laughed.

'That's the most bonkers, tech-bro idea I've ever heard. But you would have that view of Earth forever in your mind's eye.'

'I'll look into it.' Finn reached out and stroked her hair. 'Thank you.'

'What for?'

'For not mocking me.'

'Of course not, why would I?'

'I grew up in a house of very loud, very busy people. There was no time for dreamers. Nobody did anything different. So, once I wasn't causing any trouble, they just let me get on with it.'

'That's sad.'

'They were so busy with the business, they didn't have time to pay me that much attention, so I grew up not really paying myself much attention either. I just felt kind of . . . invisible.'

'According to C.S. Lewis, "Children are not a distraction from the more important work. They are the more important work,"' said Cassie.

'My kids loved you.'

'Really? I was only with them for a few hours.'

'I heard all about it. Especially from Conor, and he rarely says anything.'

Cassie flinched. 'I'd say Marisha loved that. OK, I'm going to stick my neck out and say she seems to be a very committed mother, but hard on them.'

Finn nodded. 'Everyone else seems to think she's perfect. I fell in love with her because I thought she was the first person who really saw me. She has that way about her. It was only later I realised she never did anything else. I felt under surveillance, judged 24/7. I worry now for them.'

'Sssh . . .' She put her finger to his lips. He leaned in and kissed her, as a full moon hung like a pale opal above the Dublin skyline.

Chapter 22

Driving into school that morning, Cassie wondered about levelling with Marisha. There was PE first, so that would give her a bit of time to nurse the white-wine hangover that was starting to settle just above her eyes, despite the glass of Dioralyte she'd downed before dashing out the door.

She arrived in to find Marisha wearing athleisure bottoms and a hoodie by some upmarket brand, with not a knicker line or a bulging zip in sight. She took centre stage at the top of the class and raised her arms like an evangelical preacher.

'Now, boys and girls, as you all know, there's only six weeks until the summer holidays.'

A big cheer rocked the classroom.

'I know, I know, we're all looking forward to it. But wouldn't it be great if we had something *fantastic* to show your mummies and daddies?'

There was another cheer. This was way more user-friendly than Marisha's usual no-nonsense tone.

'So, you know what we're going to do? A *play*. Won't that be great fun?'

Cassie was shocked, then furious. Marisha knew exactly what she was doing, she knew Cassie's background. Was that how Marisha was planning to punish her? By completely sidelining her?

'And Cassie, who we all know used to be an actress, will assist. It's quite a common thing, you know, children, that when people have tried to do something and maybe it hasn't gone as well for them as they might have wished . . .' Here she allowed a little aww. 'They find themselves teaching it.'

Cassie was stunned. This was jaw-dropping, even for Marisha. Little Sophie put her hand up.

'My mummy says she saw Cassie on TV on the ad for a deodorant.'

Suddenly, there was a clamour in the class, as the children all piled in to share, 'So did mine.'

'That's quite enough. Now, children, you have to understand that doing ads is what some actors do when they can't get proper acting parts, like in a real theatre or a television programme.'

A forest of hands shot up.

'Or like in the movies?'

'Exactly.'

'Like *Transformers*?'

'Or *Maleficent*?'

Cassie felt the pressure building up in her chest. She couldn't just sit and listen to this slanderous rubbish. 'Actually,' she projected, 'I think you'll find that lots of very famous people do ads. That's how they can make a lot of money very quickly.'

This was a direct dig at Marisha and her government salary.

'So, Cassie, are you minted, then?'

Cassie laughed kindly. 'Unfortunately not, Rowley, but I would argue that ads can be an art form. Some of them can look as good as – or sometimes even better than – the movies.'

Marisha picked up that she was starting to lose the room.

'All right now, boys and girls, I've chosen a lovely play. We'll know all our words and when to say them and where to stand. Won't that be great?'

The way it was presented sounded to Cassie more like the changing of the guard than a creative endeavour, but what the hell, Marisha was the one in charge.

The rest of the day passed uneventfully. The children didn't seem to notice that there was a stand-off between their two teachers, but Cassie was acutely aware of the chilly atmosphere. Marisha had a way of aiming her charm like a laser beam, so she could sparkle at the children on either side of her, while leaving Cassie out in the cold – a classic bullying technique where nobody else would even notice.

Just before the end of class, at two thirty, she made the announcement. 'Boys and girls, listen up now, tomorrow after lunch we'll be holding auditions for the play.'

Was it her imagination or was Marisha trying, and possibly succeeding, in nicking her identity? She was regretting more and more her unguarded openness on the first day.

* * *

Even on the screen, Josie looked visibly tired. She was now seven and a half months pregnant.

'God, this baby weighs a ton. I think it's going to be a sumo wrestler.'

'Even if it's a girl?'

'It's an equal-opportunities pregnancy.'

'Boom boom,' finished Cassie.

The quip hung limply in the air, neither of them having the energy to snigger.

'How's the chest of drawers?'

'Still yellow.'

'Bit like me.'

'Cassie, why are you staying in that job and putting up with all this shit? It can't be the only one around.'

'If I leave now, it'll be just another thing I haven't stuck with. I know it sounds stupid but if I can stick this out . . . I can stick anything out. It feels like a . . . test.'

'Really? You sure you're not making excuses to avoid confronting Cruella de Vil?'

'Of course I'm making excuses, she's incredibly intimidating, but if I don't stand my ground now, I'll always be trying to dodge the hard stuff. She's important in a way I can't describe.'

Josie shifted uncomfortably and took a sip of Appletiser, her latest go-to obsession.

'I'm not disputing it, but you seem to be giving her a lot of power.'

Cassie shrugged. Josie continued, 'Don't let her bully you. Remember she only has power in that schoolroom – outside of it, she's nothing.'

But that wasn't totally true; like it or not, it felt like her life and Marisha's were tangled up together like two old pairs of tights in a washing machine.

'And what about Finn? When are we going to get to meet him?'

'Yes, well, it's a bit complicated. Josie, what does he sound like to you, really?'

'Nice, sensitive . . . a bit avoidant. But then, some of the nicest people in the world are avoidant. Just make sure it's not about the things that matter most to you.'

'You're right, Jos,' Cassie said, though what she could do about it wasn't clear.

The Zoom call moved on, and Josie turned sideways to show her the bump and wail about the silver stretch marks that no amount of slathering on of Bio-Oil would magic away.

'It's like someone else has taken over my body . . . it's out of control. But it's kind of thrilling at the same time. Pal has started this ritual he calls "bump watch" every evening, when it wakes up and starts to kick off. He says he's going to buy a tiny Arsenal strip so it can get started right away. He's jumped straight to the "footie in the park" stage. I mean, forget all about pushing the baby out and the screaming and the nappies and the puke and poo.'

Cassie burst out laughing at the thought of goofy Pal transforming into a doting dad, but there was something truly miraculous about the change in her friend's body.

'It actually suits you. It looks totally natural, even though I could never have imagined it. Remember back when we shared the flat, we used to imagine what each of us would look like pregnant and stuff pillows under our jumpers, laughing ourselves silly about it . . .' She couldn't help the rueful tone creeping into her voice. A little V of concern appeared between Josie's eyes.

'It's still not too late, Cass. You're only thirty-seven. If you really want to do it, don't wait, for God's sake.'

'Have you and Mam been talking?'

The last thing she wanted was to steal the joy from Josie's special time. She daren't mention the emptiness she was feeling behind the shared delight, like gazing down a lift shaft when the doors open by mistake. An emptiness that feels all wrong because it's where something else ought to be. She wasn't going to mention that. It just wouldn't be fair.

* * *

The next morning at 7 a.m. Cassie opened her eyes and allowed the fragments of her thoughts to fall into place. She thought of the conversation with Josie the previous evening, her pregnancy bump and the words, 'Don't leave it too late.' She'd given up hope of having a baby after the split with Gav, accepted that that boat had sailed and there was nothing more to be done. But maybe that wasn't true, maybe she'd more options than she'd once believed. A thin shaft of hope lit up the back of her mind like the sun on winter solstice . . . Crikey, the big numbers on her digital clock now blinked 7.17 a.m., so she'd better get cracking. In the bathroom, lined with dark-green veined marble tiles, she dropped her oversized T-shirt on the floor, turned sideways, and for one private moment allowed herself to imagine what she'd look like with a bump. A stab of pain in her chest made her gasp and rub the spot with the heel of her hand. No time for that now. She swiped the thought away and stepped into the steaming luxury of the rain shower.

Marisha would be holding her wretched auditions today. That promised to be a pain in the arse. It felt so unfair and bloody frustrating, considering the whole thing had been her idea. She remembered something that Da, who loved nothing better than a good cliché, had said to her: 'Sometimes you're hot, sometimes you're not. It's a long road that has no turning.' Well, Da, right now that's exactly where she felt: on a straight road to nowhere.

She made a pot of strong coffee and treated herself to a bowl of high-fruit muesli with a banana, on Babs and Denise's advice. They'd learned a thing or two about making it through to lunchtime. Just then her phone buzzed – it was a text from Finn.

How you holding up with Cecil B. DeMille? :)

Ha ha. Not.

Missing you

You too

Don't let it get to you. Storm in a teacup.

I know. Xxxxx

Xxxxxx

That was all fine, except if you were stuck in said teacup, it still felt like you were drowning.

* * *

Hurrying down the corridor towards the classroom, she spotted her friend Maggie up ahead, her copper ringlets bouncing with her energetic gait. Cassie ran to catch up with her.

'Maggie, I don't like to be a pest, but can I ask you something?'

'Of course.'

'You have an SNA . . . I mean, is she your assistant, or . . .?' She couldn't help herself. 'Junior or sort of . . . servant?'

Maggie gazed at her in astonishment, then a look of realisation dawned.

'God, no. I couldn't do my work without her. We're a team. I see her as my equal, of course. We're colleagues.'

Why, oh, why hadn't she been assigned to 4A? Where things would've been lovely and friendly and . . . respectful.

'That's what I thought. Thanks. See you at break time.'

Marisha was dressed all in black: leggings and a T-shirt dress, with her hair in a bohemian-looking messy bun. Cassie had no doubt the whole image was carefully assembled.

'Good morning, boys and girls, Cassie will go round and collect your homework and then we'll start on the auditions for our play.'

This promised to be about as much fun as an ice-bucket challenge, thought Cassie grimly.

Marisha had chosen a traditional fairy tale, *Jack and the Beanstalk*, nothing too controversial to piss off any of the fussy parents. The script appeared to have been written some decades ago and there was certainly no mention of diversity; however, it was a solid enough idea and they might as well get on with it. Marisha, of course, was highly conscientious and had photocopied a pile of scripts for the children.

'Now, boys and girls, I want you all to move your chairs around in a circle so we can all see each other.'

Crikey, this was shaping up to be a nightmare for the shyer children. Marisha started out by asking the boys, in turn, to read for the part of Jack, so the whole process turned out to be more of a public reading test than a search for acting ability. To her dismay, it became clear that Rowley wasn't a great reader and was possibly dyslexic, which wasn't uncommon in creative people. He stuttered through his lines, obviously wracked with nerves. Halfway through the scene, Marisha raised her hand in exasperation.

'That's enough, Rowley. Thank you, you can play villager 2.'

His whole body slumped. A wave of indignation surged through Cassie. Moments like this were life-defining. All they did was show a child what they couldn't do – how many talented people's dreams had been dashed by moments like these?

The part of Jack's mother was almost automatically given to Sophie. The part of Jack was given to Trevor – a quick, talented lad – while Ahmed, who sang boy soprano in the school choir, was cast as the harp. It all made sense but, at the same time, the whole affair had a dispiriting feel that the kids who were already doing well were being given more, while everybody else was relegated to the back row.

The part of the giant was assigned to Martin, the tallest boy in the class, who blushed beetroot every time he had to open his mouth. The poor child delivered his iconic *fee-fi-fo-fum* line in a flat, conversational tone more suited to the stock-market report than a boisterous fairy tale. All in all, fairly standard stuff for a school play. Cassie sighed to herself. Shame, there was potential here for something spectacular.

* * *

'Well, did you bring my favourite chocolate Swiss roll?' said Mam the moment she opened the door.

'They only had the lemon one, sorry.'

'Sure, isn't that the way of it. We all have to make compromises.'

Cassie could tell from experience that Mam was in a no-nonsense mood. As soon as she'd made them two cups of coffee and sat down, she started. 'When are you going to phone Maxine? You've been putting it off for months, and it's already last minute for the dresses. Typical you. I don't want to find myself sitting here at 2 a.m. the night before my wedding with the eyes hanging out of my head hemming bridesmaids' dresses.'

In fact, there was nothing Mam would've loved more, not to mention recounting it to anyone who'd listen.

'Look, love, I know there's been all of that between you and Maxine, and it breaks my heart that we can't all meet together, but surely now is the time to fix that.'

Cassie nodded uncomfortably. Mam was wonderful but she did have a tendency to place herself at the centre of everything and genuinely felt that nothing could happen effectively without her. She'd whipped out her phone and was scrolling madly to find the number.

'God, Mam, stop, please. You're taking over again. I'll do it tonight, OK? I promise I won't let you down.'

'Then that's all I need to hear. Have another piece of cake.'

Cassie was starving after spending her lunch break on yard duty.

'We can't, Mam, remember we've got to look like Kate Moss in less than two months.'

'That girl always looks in need of a good plate of sausage and chips. And what about your poor friend that got beaten up? I must drop over and visit her. I'll bring her a bedjacket for receiving visitors. Do you think she'd like that?'

'You know what, Mam? I think she'd love it.'

'Great. So . . . what about this new chap, will he be at the wedding?'

Maybe it was the tension of having to stifle herself around Marisha all day, or light-headedness from hunger, but Cassie found herself blurting the whole story out to Mam. At the end there was silence, which was astonishing in itself.

'So, you're working with this woman, and she doesn't know what's going on?'

'No, but I think she might suspect.'

'Look, I might be very old-fashioned in all of this, but I'd say honesty is the best policy. I mean, *if* they're living separately and *if* she doesn't want him back, then why are you keeping it a secret in the first place?'

Mam tended to see things in black and white, which was fine for her but really didn't work out for Cassie.

'Right, I'll have a word with her,' she said, just to keep Mam happy.

'These blended families . . . all I know from cooking is some ingredients just don't mix.'

Chapter 23

Cassie arrived home to find the apartment in darkness. That's odd, she thought and pushed open the door to the sitting room, where she saw Ramona lying on the sofa, her face barely illuminated by her phone. She switched on the wall lights and was greeted by the sight of the day's dishes. Obviously, she'd barely moved. That wasn't like Ramona.

'Hey, I've brought your pastrami roll, though I was tempted to scoff it myself.'

She'd anticipated a quip but Ramona was silent. Her white-blonde hair lay flat on her head, and her face, normally made-up to meet the world, was pale and scrubbed. She looked almost unrecognisable. It wasn't that she looked bad – just different, younger. Cassie couldn't help wondering how many people ever saw behind the mask. She sat by the sofa and gently asked, 'Hey, how're you doing?'

Ramona shrugged but didn't reply.

'Is something wrong?' She hardly needed to ask. Cassie could see from the set of her jaw that Ramona was fighting to hold back tears. She pulled a tissue from the box and handed it to her.

'I don't want to pry but . . . you can tell me . . . if you want.'

'I can't do it anymore . . .' She broke down and sobbed.

Cassie shifted to the side of the sofa and hugged her, as Ramona's bony frame shuddered. For all her swagger and uber-sophistication, inside she was little more than a kid, out in the world on her own.

'Sssh . . . It's OK,' Cassie said, rubbing the girl's back like you would an inconsolable child, for whom words have no meaning beyond the sounds. 'Let it all out.'

'In that house, when that guy caught me, I thought he was going to kill me. I really thought I was going to die there.'

'I know. But you didn't. You're here now and you're safe.'

'And then it hit me: who was even going to care? My mom never wanted me . . .'

'I'm sure that's not really true.'

'Oh, you'd better believe it. You can't imagine it, because things aren't like that for you. She was seventeen when I was born. So, poor Grandma got stuck with me. She was delighted. *Not*.'

'Your grandma wasn't maternal?'

'Are you kidding? Being stuck with me really cramped her socialite lifestyle. I don't blame her, she never asked for it.'

Cassie didn't know what to say, so she just sat, holding Ramona's hand.

'And I wonder why I'm such an exhibitionist, and so . . . fucking stupid sometimes. I get it. I keep trying to matter.'

'We're all trying to matter.'

'I've been posting about what happened, and people were commenting and sending love, blah-blah, but . . .'

'They mean well, they just don't know the real you, do they?'

Ramona shrugged. 'If I stopped posting tomorrow, they'd just scroll on down to the next face. I'm just a . . . thing . . . I'm content. I'm not real.'

'That's not true. You're really important to those people, a lot more than you're giving yourself credit for. And you're real to me. You're real to Mam. By the way, she's coming to see you and bringing a bedjacket to keep your shoulders warm, she says.'

Ramona gave a throaty laugh. 'You're kidding me, that's so cute. Does it have feathers round the neck and cuffs like Doris Day in *Pillow Talk*, with Rock Hudson? "What a marvellous-looking man." That's one of my grandma's all-time favourites.'

'I think it might be pink crochet.'

'I could make it work.'

They both laughed, feeling a bit better.

'Is this the moment for gin and tonic? I bought two of those little tins.'

Cassie took two glasses out of the cabinet and filled them with ice.

'God, these things are so fucking weak,' commented Ramona, unimpressed. 'What am I going to do, Cass? I've wrenched my stupid shoulder and I can't dance like this. Everything I do depends on my body. Without my act, who am I?'

'You're plenty – you're you.'

Ramona was silent. 'Cassie, I'm afraid that just being myself isn't good enough. And I can't do anything else.'

Cassie felt at a loss – what was she supposed to say?

'You can be anything. OK, maybe not in this precise moment, but don't make my mistake. I'm only realising now that my value isn't just from one thing, or what other people think of me. And you're right: at the end of the day, nobody really does give a damn apart from the people who love you.'

'I've always been kinda short on those.'

'Well, not anymore. And if you can make your living as a pole dancer, I'd say there's not much you can't do.'

'I'm not going to overanalyse that, but thank you.'

'It'll be all right. I promise.'

'Here's to being a nobody.' Ramona drained the last of her gin and tonic.

'Now you're talking.'

* * *

Later that evening, Cassie was curled up on her favourite chair by the window, sipping a mug of tea and contemplating the conversation she'd had with Mam. The prospect of phoning Maxine felt like a grey cloud hanging in front of her, but Mam was right, she really couldn't leave it much longer.

She scrolled down to the number she hadn't used in years, that she'd even thought about deleting more than once.

Don't think about it, she scolded herself. Maxine probably won't even pick up. She'll be ferrying a team of kids in her bungalow-sized SUV to an ice-hockey game or something. Cassie allowed the phone to ring eight or nine times before knocking it off in relief.

Look, she'd been brave, she'd phoned, she'd done her bit, fair and square. Now it was up to her sister. The wedding wasn't till July, there was still time . . . just about. It was a cop-out and secretly she knew it, but that was as much as she could face tonight.

* * *

Rehearsals were in full swing. Marisha had marked out the floor with coloured tape, 'like the professionals do', and was constantly shouting directions which meant bog-all to any of the children.

God, with her grandiosity you'd think she was directing *Hamilton* on Broadway, but Marisha was the diva of 4B and revelling in her position.

Marisha pointed at each character in turn and read the line out for them to repeat with exactly the same intonation. As a result, all the actors parroted their lines with the same, God-awful, stilted delivery. The other children shuffled around, trying to manage their frustration, rotating on one toe or picking their noses.

'Villagers, stop fidgeting!! Now, what is the most important thing in our play?'

Silence.

'That the audience, your mums and dads, can hear every word and that they go home knowing exactly what happened. Clarity. Well, in this show, children, we'll all be clear as a bell.'

As though on cue, there was a knock on the door and Roger Newcombe's head appeared. Cassie remembered the first time he'd barged into her classroom, his face like an angry lightbulb. This time he couldn't have been more different, his tone mild and solicitous, although even from across the room, Cassie could spot the spaghetti sauce from lunch on his lapel.

'Ah, Marie, I'm just checking in to see how you're doing with the drama. Well, I must say this all looks very organised . . . very professional. Are you enjoying it, boys and girls?'

'Yeeeeaaaaah,' they droned.

What the feck else could they say? Marisha glowed as he went on, 'Well, it's marvellous to see all this creativity in the school.'

Jeez, she'd seen more creativity spray-painted on a bus shelter.

'And I see you're ably assisted too.' He nodded in Cassie's direction.

She could've puked. Was anything worth this humiliation? Feck salary or security! The old Cassie had always stuck to her dreams – they mightn't have been great dreams, or lucrative dreams, but they were hers. Feck it. She was going to hand in her notice. Mam would be disappointed, of course, and even lovely Phil would be disappointed, which felt bad, but she couldn't let that stop her.

* * *

By lunchtime, she was still shaking with fury. Maggie sat down opposite her, as they took out their tubs of salad.

'Are you OK? How's the famous play going?'

'Shite. Sorry, that just came out.'

'That bad?'

She nodded, realising in horror that she was close to tears.

'I can imagine, if you've been a professional in that world all your life . . .'

'It's awful. It sounds mad but it's like she's enjoying sticking it to me. Am I imagining it?'

Maggie shook her head. 'I didn't like to say, and it wasn't my business, but that's why the last SNA left. It was because she couldn't stand it.'

'Thanks for telling me that, really, at least it's not just me.'

Maggie glanced around to make sure that nobody was listening. Behind her, at another table, Cassie glimpsed Marisha, who seemed uncharacteristically quiet, nibbling a banana and sipping an Actimel.

'She's really, really charming to anyone her level or higher, but anyone less important . . .' Maggie didn't need to finish that sentence – they both knew how Marisha treated those she perceived as inferior.

Cassie couldn't help wondering where Finn featured on that scale.

* * *

When Cassie pushed open the door into the apartment at the end of a long day, instead of the previous hush, she was met with high hilarity. Mam was sitting on the armchair, holding forth about her wedding plans, while Louise was perched on the end of the sofa, now looking visibly pregnant. God, pregnant women were following her everywhere, Cassie thought, but then quickly dismissed that and hugged Louise warmly, genuinely delighted to see her.

Mam was on top form. 'Go on, Ramona, try it on. I think pink is a great colour on you, it throws light on your face.' She was tactful enough not to mention the heavy bruising across her forehead and one cheek that was morphing from green to brown. Ramona dutifully slipped into the crocheted bedjacket, looking so incongruous that Cassie could barely contain her giggles.

'What do you think?'

'It shows a whole other side of you, Ramona,' observed Louise with her usual tact.

'It's a little old-fashioned but these things come back in, sure, you see it every day,' said Mam optimistically.

'That is one hundred per cent true,' agreed Louise, which made Mam glow.

'So, tell us all about this wedding.' Louise had a marvellous way with mothers, and Cassie dreaded being compared to her pretty friend, who seemed to have achieved everything Mam would wish for in a daughter.

'We're having a wedding arch and a marquee in the garden. When it's not your first time, we-ell, you want to keep things simple.'

This was a complete fantasy. 'Mam' and 'simple' inhabited two totally separate universes.

'So . . . spill the beans, what's your dress like, Iris?' said Ramona.

Mam lit up. 'Secret, it's a secret, and so are the bridesmaids' dresses, *if* somebody would actually get it together and get them organised.'

Cassie cringed. 'I'll talk to you about that later,' she muttered.

Shortly afterwards, Louise excused herself on the pretext of having to make her husband's dinner, even though Cassie knew she was likely going home to an empty house. Mam happily agreed to go down in the lift with her.

Once the door closed behind them, Cassie and Ramona looked at each other.

'You're so lucky. Your mom is great.'

'Maybe. She lives in her own little version of reality, and other people just seem to go along with it. Maybe that's the secret to a happy life.'

'How's the job?'

'Unspeakably shit. I've decided to leave on Friday, so that'll be something to celebrate.'

'Attagirl, no job's worth that. It'll all work out, you'll see.' They smiled bravely at each other.

* * *

That night, in bed, she texted Finn.

> Can't wait to see u. Need to talk. Had enough of that poxy school. Leaving on Friday.

> Brave girl, proud of u wish I was with you now.

> Me too. Miss you.

> Night night

☺

She clicked off her phone and turned over. Still, the feeling of emptiness stayed with her. Was this what was in store for her? Nights alone, longing for their next snatched moment together.

* * *

Next morning Cassie drove into school, switched off the engine of her car and took a deep breath. What more could Marisha do to her? Nothing. She couldn't touch her anymore. Cassie felt liberated. In fact, she felt a lightness she hadn't for weeks. Helen, the secretary, was met with a Colgate smile and a cheery hello.

The classroom was empty. Relax, she told herself, just make the most of the next two days and then drop into Roger Newcombe on Friday afternoon and tell him you're leaving. She felt a bit guilty about that, because she did love the kids and he was pretty desperate but . . . Sorry, not her problem.

Just then, Marisha shuffled in, looking strikingly different from her usual glamorous self.

'Cassie, love, would you mind going out and picking up the kids? That'd be great,' she said in a tone normally reserved for people she liked, which was odd.

The children followed Cassie back in, chirping and chatting, buzzing with the bliss of summer holidays just over the horizon. She couldn't help feeling a pang of regret at the thought of leaving.

Marisha was sitting at the desk, looking washed-out, and suggested that everyone open their books for some quiet reading. 'We'll come back to the show this afternoon,' she promised in a lacklustre voice.

At lunchtime Marisha, who normally snapped her books shut and hurried out the door, remained slumped at her big desk with the excuse that she'd some marking to do and would stay in the empty classroom for lunch. Cassie was tempted to engage her in conversation but thought better of it.

The odd atmosphere continued throughout afternoon rehearsals when Martin, the giant, shifted awkwardly on his too-big feet and tried to parrot the lines Marisha was feeding him. It was obvious to Cassie that the poor child was struggling to remember each line he was being fed, let alone remember them all at once for the performance. He wasn't the only one who was struggling: Marisha seemed to be dragging herself through the rehearsal and at 2.25 p.m. she seemed to stagger slightly. Cassie jumped forward to catch her, and a couple of the girls squeaked with alarm.

'Get a chair for Miss Upton, quick, Rowley.'

'I'm fine, honestly, don't make a fuss, there's no need,' she breathed, though she looked quite grey. Cassie was pouring her a glass of water when, mercifully, the bell for the end of school blasted outside the door and the children scrambled for their bags. Five minutes later the classroom was empty, apart from a couple of floating bits of paper.

'Marisha, would you like me to call somebody to come and collect you?'

Even as she said it, Cassie's heart lurched. What if she named Finn as her person? She could, easily – it was the most obvious thing in the world.

'No, no, thank you, Cassie, I'll be fine.'

'I'm not trying to be rude, but you look bloody awful.'

Surprisingly, Marisha smiled. 'That sounds about how I feel.'

There was something off about her demeanour; it was only then that Cassie realised she was straining to stop herself from crying.

'Marisha, are you OK? Sorry, stupid question. What's going on? Is there any way I can help?'

'You're very kind, even though I've been such a bitch to you.'

Wow, she hadn't expected that. One thing Cassie had learned about Marisha was that nothing she ever said was without purpose. She leaned back and breathed deeply. 'That's a bit better. I thought for a moment back there I was going to be sick.'

'Nightmare. You sip your water and I'll open another window.'

Marisha smiled weakly.

'You've probably picked up a gastric bug from the kids. I don't know how I've escaped so far.'

'That's not it.' There was an edge to her tone.

For a moment Cassie was alarmed. Could she be hinting at a serious illness?

'Cassie, can I trust you?'

Cassie nodded.

'You see, sometimes I think that when a person's made a bit of a mess of their life – and you won't be offended if I say that to you – it makes it easier to confide in them because they mightn't judge you so harshly.'

Cassie nodded mutely. There was simply no answer to that.

'I'm pregnant.'

Oh. My. Jesus. She'd been so wrong. She'd actually thought there was nothing more Marisha could do to her. For a moment there was a ringing in her ears and everything felt very, very far away.

'I'm sure that might come as a bit of a surprise.'

Surprise didn't come within light years of what Cassie was feeling.

'And does your . . . husband . . . know?'

'My husband?' she burst out. 'Oh . . . him, God no. Can you keep a secret? Really?'

Cassie nodded. She was so relieved at the last remark that she'd have agreed to anything.

'I mean, it's all going to come out sooner or later . . . I have to tell someone and it may as well be you.'

Cassie decided to ignore the implied insult. 'Right.'

'It's Roger's.'

'Roger . . .?'

'Roger Newcombe, the principal. We're obviously . . . a thing.'

Cassie nodded – for longer than was normal, she realised. 'Rrrright. So, if you don't mind my asking, how far along are you?'

'Oh, not long . . . nine weeks. I mean, it's a mess because it's all happened so fast, but it's wonderful at the same time. We've both secretly known for ages but we couldn't act on it because of family situations. I know I shouldn't really be telling you all this but . . . Oh, who cares. We're in love and obviously you can see what an amazing guy he is. He's such a . . . fucking adult. It's so attractive.'

Wow. That was one way of describing him. Not everyone's.

'That's amazing, congratulations, I'm delighted.' Which was absolutely true. Also, she wasn't imagining it: pregnant women were actually stalking her.

'Thank you, Cassie, that really means a lot.' Marisha actually squeezed her hand. 'Look, I'm going to be honest: at my age, I'm forty-three – I know . . . it's hard to believe – I'm finding it a little exhausting. I've really enjoyed directing the children, and I know they've loved it, but I'm going to have to hand over most of the play. I know it's not really fair to ask, but d'you think you'd be able to manage? Roger knows that I may be taking a bit of time off here and there.'

'Of course, Marisha, I'd be happy to do it, don't you worry about a thing.'

And there it was, the solution to everything, and all she'd had to do was keep turning up.

* * *

Cassie was heading home, trying to process what had happened. She drove down the N11, turning the situation over and over in her mind as though it were a Rubik's cube, and heaven knows, she was never much good at those.

First of all, this was great. Marisha had moved on in no uncertain terms. The only problem was, from a purely selfish point of view, it could totally upend her relationship with Finn. If he'd felt unavailable before, surely that was only going to get worse? You could be sure Marisha would be unshipping the younger children onto him now that it suited her. She could just imagine Mam rolling her eyes. Had she a point? Was their relationship going to become just another experience of her feeling bottom of the list? The thought was dispiriting. Also, what was she going to do about Marisha's confession? She now knew this huge fact about Finn's ex-wife – should she tell him or not?

Just then the sudden blast of a car horn made her jump, and as she looked up, she realised she'd been sitting in front of a green light for ages. She waved an apology before speeding off down the road with a stream of angry drivers behind her.

* * *

Finn phoned around seven that evening. 'Hi, babe, what're you doing?'

He sounded distracted and it turned out he was mashing potato for the children's meal, which she remembered had to be more-or-less identical every day for Conor. In the background she could hear a female voice yelling, 'You pair are driving me fucking crazy. Dad, I'm *not* sitting in there anymore. They're *fucking mutants*!'

'Samantha, will you calm down, please. Put your headphones on or go into the bedroom.'

'This place is driving me fucking crazy. I'm fourteen, why can't I just stay at *home*?'

The last word was delivered at such volume that even Cassie winced. There was some more muttering to the effect that she was going out for a walk and a warning not to try to stop her.

'Sorry . . . Sorry about that. Listen, I have the kids tonight, obviously, and . . . Look, I'm really sorry but Marisha's asked me to take them tomorrow evening as well. She's not well, I don't know what's wrong with her. I know we'd planned—'

'It's fine, honestly, it's absolutely no problem.' Oh God, this was awkward. She was on the verge of blurting out, 'I know exactly what's wrong with her,' but something stopped her.

'I promise . . . this is not my choice,' he said.

'Look, it's fine, I totally understand,' she said warmly. She actually felt relieved. No way could she be in Finn's company and not tell him about Marisha.

'We could do Saturday instead?' she suggested.

'You're being really understanding about everything. I'll make it up to you, I promise.'

Poor Finn, no matter how well-meaning he was, he always seemed to find himself wrong-footed when it came to Marisha.

Chapter 24

'Excuse me, could I speak with you for a moment?'

Cassie had gone out to the gate to pick up the children, when she was approached by a very tall woman around her own age. There was no need to introduce herself – her height and features meant she could only be Martin's, the giant's, mother.

'The thing is, he's not very good at public speaking. He's hardly slept at all these past few weeks. I really don't want him to miss the opportunity to be involved in the show but . . .' Her voice dropped and she took a step closer. 'He's not able for it. Please don't make him do that big part.'

Yet again it seemed that fate was intervening in the best possible way.

Cassie felt a surge of warmth towards this anxious mother. 'I understand, leave it with me. We don't want any child doing something that causes them upset.'

Relief flooded the woman's face. 'Thank you for understanding. I'm not sure that certain other people – who we won't mention – would have been so kind.' She jerked her head in the direction of the school building.

Cassie wondered if perhaps Marisha wasn't as universally loved as she imagined herself to be.

'Don't give it another thought.'

Poor Martin had obviously been going through hell over the past few weeks and finally here she was in a position to help. She'd just arrived at the door with the class when she was met with Roger Newcombe. He looked agitated but was struggling to hide it.

'Cassie, Miss Upton isn't that well. She's phoned to say she'll be in for eleven.'

She panicked at the thought he might have heard about Marisha's confession the previous day, but he showed no signs of awkwardness towards her.

She did notice he'd been wearing the same rather-worse-for-wear brown jacket all week rather than rotating them as usual, which was a clue something was going on.

On a positive note, she now had carte blanche to organise the 4B play so that everyone would get a chance to shine, though if there was one valuable lesson Cassie had learned from Marisha, it was organisation. All the inspiration in the world would only end up in frustration without it. She did wonder if that hadn't been her own problem all along: all impulse and no proper planning. Well, it was high time she became a grown-up. In fact, the success of 4B's production of *Jack and the Beanstalk* depended on it.

'Now, boys and girls. Miss Upton will be out for the first part of the day and you'll be having me instead. I know, very exciting,' she quipped, to a few grins. 'So, we're going to make a few changes at this point in the show – tweaks, they're called, and that just means we're going to make it even better than it already is. First of all, we're getting a new character . . .'

There was a buzz of interest.

'And it's going to be . . . *the beanstalk*! And it's going to be played by . . . Martin. Martin, you're going to need a new green costume with branches. So that means we'll need a new giant, who'll be played by . . . Rowley.'

The round freckled face lit up like he'd been plugged into the national grid. His friends all cheered, while the other kids reacted with a mixture of hilarity and outrage.

'He's smaller than me, he can't be a giant,' piped up a little girl from under a fringe like a Yorkshire terrier.

'It's called acting, you don't have to be the person . . . You just have to make your audience think you are. If you believe it, they'll believe it. You'll see.'

Rowley barrelled up to the front of the class and launched himself up on a desk, to Cassie's consternation. Still, this was important, health and safety be damned for the moment.

'Fee-fi-fo . . . bleedin' fum!'

'You're not a giant, you're only a little scut,' roared one of the class bullies. Oh no, was this going to backfire horribly? But if there was one place Rowley could handle himself, it was in front of an audience.

'Whaddy'a talkin' about? Enough o' that or I'll stick yez in a kebab for me supper.'

What followed were a few exchanges to the effect of, 'Oh no, you won't,' and, 'Oh yes, I will,' in classic panto style. Cassie's heart soared – this was exactly what she'd hoped to achieve. Rowley's inventiveness and lack of fear pulled the others along with him and instead of the usual spiritless delivery, even the shyer kids edged forward to find their place in the fun. Trevor, who was playing Jack, had been worrying her, as he came across stiff and self-conscious, which wasn't at all what Cassie knew he was capable of.

He confessed that his hero was Spiderman, so she helped him to imagine Jack being Tom Holland playing Peter Parker, Spiderman's real-life identity. Immediately, something seemed to click with the boy and all his awkwardness fell away.

Sophie, Jack's mother, spurred on by the overall excitement, seemed to be drawing dramatic inspiration from *The Playboy of The Western World* to great admiration from the rest of the class, while the Bondarenko twins were delighted to be cast as the cow, though where Cassie was going to find a cow costume, she dreaded to think. That was for another day.

When break time came around, the children erupted out into the yard. Rowley hung back.

'Me granda has a little stepladder at home . . . I can have it under my arm for the show for lookin' tall. And, eh, d'you think the show will be at night, 'cause my ma works nights an' I know she wouldn't want to miss me?'

Cassie reassured him that every effort would be made to make sure all the families could come. It was only afterwards she panicked at the responsibility for making every kid and their families' dreams come true.

That lunchtime Cassie sat quietly at the end of a table, when she overheard Babs and another teacher sniggering to each other. 'I can't believe it either. What on earth does she see in him, with those musty suits? And, apparently, the husband's a dish.'

She could see Marisha at another table, nibbling what looked like white bread and a banana, plus the obligatory Actimel. Poor thing, she was probably feeling hellish and trying to behave as normal. Cassie almost felt sorry for her. Almost.

* * *

As they were leaving on Friday evening, Marisha called her aside. 'Cassie, could I ask you a favour? I hope you won't think I'm being inappropriate, but I know my children have met you before and you seemed to get on with them. It seems my ex has an arrangement on Saturday evening, so I was wondering if you might be free to babysit for me? I know it's short notice . . .' Oh hell. This was her longed-for night with Finn that was going to make up for all the last-minute cancellations. She felt on the verge of blurting out everything. Mightn't that be the best thing to do? Once you let an opportunity to tell the truth pass, it became a lie by default. Don't be a fool, she decided, go home, phone Finn, tell him everything and clear the air.

'I'm really sorry, Marisha, I've already made plans for Saturday night.'

She hated these half-lies but what else could she do?

Marisha shrugged. 'That's a pity, I was really looking forward to a night in. And you seem to be so good with Conor. He really needs someone who can understa—'

She suddenly looked horrified.

'Are you OK?' Cassie asked, alarmed. The dust motes tumbling in a shaft of sunlight seemed to freeze.

'It's you, isn't it?'

All Cassie could do was nod dumbly.

'I'd a hunch he was seeing someone. So, it's you. I'm not surprised, I can see you'd be his type. So much for choosing a safe person to confide in,' she added bitterly. 'Well, it seems like you know pretty much everything about my life now. Congratulations.'

Cassie's shoulders collapsed. 'I'm so sorry, I never wanted this to happen. I hated not being able to be truthful.'

'No, you were able. You just chose not to be.'

Cassie nodded miserably. What could she say?

'On the other hand, you're obviously discreet, because if you'd told Finn already, all hell would've broken loose.'

'I hadn't a clue what to do but in the end I just . . . cleaned my apartment to keep myself busy,' confessed Cassie.

'Could've done worse.'

'Look, I'll leave. I can't see another way. I never meant to be deceitful. Please believe me. I'll just tell Mr Newcombe that I'm finished and that'll be it.'

'Don't.'

'Sorry?'

'You might as well stay. You know everything now, what more can happen? By the way, my ex-husband is an overgrown adolescent. You do realise that?'

Cassie reflected that that was exactly what she liked about him.

'That's if you still want to stay – I fully understand if you don't.'

'No, I do . . . I really do.'

'Well, then, we know each other's secrets. Let's call it quits?'

Cassie nodded. 'Quits.'

'In case you're wondering what to do next, please let me tell Finn. My call. I haven't even shared it with the kids yet, so that's next on the list.' She sounded weary but resolute.

In fairness, it was true what Finn had said about her: Marisha really was a grown-up.

'OK, I'd better go. Have a good weekend.'

'I doubt it, but thank you.'

* * *

On the way home, Cassie's head was buzzing, so she stopped off in Georgian Fare and grabbed an irresistible slice of baked cheesecake. When she got home and opened the door to her apartment, she was met with a blast of music coming from the back. She was happy to see Ramona curled up on the small plush sofa in the kitchen, cradling a mug of coffee.

'You're looking chipper, so what's up?' she asked.

Cassie made herself a cup of coffee and recounted the whole story to Ramona, having first sworn her to secrecy.

'Wait . . . stop . . . stop . . . Let me get this straight, she actually confessed that whole pregnancy thing and the stuff with the headteacher to you just because you've made such a screw-up of your own life?' Ramona looked at her wide-eyed. 'That actually came out of her mouth?'

Cassie nodded. 'She meant it in a nice way.'

'Really? Holy crap, imagine what she'd have confessed to me.'

They both cackled with laughter.

'Seriously, though, underneath she's actually kind of a good person.'

'Honey, underneath I'm Little Miss Muffet but who's going to dig that far?'

'Well, the good news is, she didn't get me fired.'

Ramona's light seemed to dim a little.

'Good for you, sister,' she said.

Attempting to lighten the moment, Cassie whipped the cheesecake out of her bag, cut it in half and placed it onto two plates, before refilling their coffee cups.

'It'll come right, Ramona, just give yourself a chance.'

Her eyes lit up. 'This is such a relatable golden moment for the guys,' she said, referring to her followers, who apparently hadn't abandoned her en masse, as she'd feared. On the contrary, since the accident, her followers had soared and now they numbered almost seventy thousand. You had to admit, she'd a genius for marketing. From Cassie's perspective, she was just sitting on a boring kitchen counter, eating a piece of squishy cake, but in Ramona's Instagram story, especially with the filters on, the same picture became aspirational and inviting. It just showed how daft it was to take people's social media personas literally. Real life happened moment to moment, without the special effects.

Chapter 25

Cassie lay on her bed, with very little going through her mind, for a change. She knew she should get up and go for a walk or do something worthy, like going to the gym, but somehow her limbs just didn't want to move. A tree branch swayed in the breeze outside her window and, perched on it, a small crowd of starlings were gathering for an evening gossip before huddling up together for the night. It all seemed so simple and cosy. Just then her phone buzzed – Finn's number flashed up on a WhatsApp video call and instinctively she braced herself. God, Marisha must have broken the news. He looked stressed. Her heart went out to him.

'Hey, are you OK?' she said.

'Pretty shocked . . . No, stunned, if I'm being honest. Marisha told me her news, both parts, and said she'd told you already.'

'Look, before you say anything, I'm so sorry, it was really awkward. It felt like something I shouldn't have known and I couldn't say anything because it really wasn't my news to tell.'

'No, I get it, I'm sorry you were put in that position. Anyway, Cici and Con are in bed, and Samantha's stormed off to stay with her friend. I didn't tell them about the baby or anything, I just wish you could come over.'

'I know, I wish I could too.'

'Can I ask you something? Be honest, d'you think I'm a bad father? Have I let them down?'

Cassie took a deep breath. 'Of course not. Life's complicated but this is on a whole other level. I was floored by Marisha's news.'

'I can't stop thinking about it . . . I'm so angry . . . with her and myself and that pompous arse. I mean, is he attractive? I always thought he reminded me of Mr Burns from *The Simpsons*. I don't know what to do. I can't imagine how the kids are going to react.'

Cassie could picture him pacing up and down. She cast around in her mind for something that might help. 'It's awful and I can't imagine what you must be feeling . . . But . . .'

'Go on . . .'

'There is one thing you could do for now. You could reach out to Samantha. She's going to slip between the cracks if you don't.'

'Samantha? How?'

It obviously hadn't occurred to him.

'I don't know, buy a bloody sofa bed for yourself and let her have your room. Let her do it up the way she wants. You can't leave her sharing with an eleven-year-old boy, it's not right.'

'Fuck, why didn't I think of that?'

'I don't know, but you're thinking of it now. It's not too late. Text her right now and tell her you've had an idea and you're happy to pay for anything she wants. After that it's up to her.'

'You're right, Cass, you're the best. I really owe you.'

'Never mind that, just text her now and get back to me. Bye.'

She ended the call. The starlings had settled onto the big branch, out of sight behind the young green leaves, and were twittering companionably. Why was it that everybody's life from a distance looked so normal and together, but once you got closer, you found it was just as fucked-up as your own? The starlings had it right – or maybe, if you looked closer, there was a top starling in the best spot on the branch and a loser starling stuck down the wobbly end?

A few minutes later the phone went again. Finn ploughed straight in, 'Samantha replied to me about having her own room. I was afraid she'd gone into town to get pissed or something, but she's just at a friend's house, watching a movie.'

The relief in his voice was palpable.

'So, what did she say?'

'I'll read it out to you . . . *Could be OK. Can you Revolut me €50*. What d'you think?'

'She knows you're feeling guilty about moving out and she's going to shake you down for all she can get. Just be glad it wasn't a hundred. Still, she's accepted your offer.'

'At least it's one thing I can do for the poor kid.'

'Well done. You put her first. That's exactly what she needs right now.'

Finn was shaking his head and re-reading the text. 'Little wagon . . .'

* * *

The next morning Cassie opened her eyes to a sun-drenched glorious Saturday. She lay there for a few minutes, allowing herself to enjoy a peaceful moment when she had actually nothing to worry about. She was going to start the day with a lovely coffee sipped on the balcony, as people in bright summer clothes hurried up towards the big exhibition in the RDS and the place began to buzz for the rugby match later that day.

Feeling the holiday mood, she pulled on leggings, an oversized T-shirt, flip-flops and sunglasses. Nice. She'd just helped herself to a big bowl of berries and yoghurt from the fridge, and settled down in the sun, when her mobile buzzed.

'Cassie, is that you?' Her heart sank.

'Hi, Mam.'

'Are you busy?'

Cassie sighed. 'Not really.'

'Listen to me, I woke up this morning in a panic. If I don't get my dress now, I might as well throw my hat at it.'

Oh God, this was totally fair, she'd really let Mam down around the wedding.

'Eric has gone for a hike with a priest friend of his, so I was wondering if you could drop out this morning and we could go looking for a dress. I thought we could've all done it together with Maxine but it's not turning out like that.'

She sounded crestfallen, and Cassie's heart went out to her.

'Of course, Mam, just give me a chance for a quick shower. I'll meet you in Marian Gale in an hour.'

'Good girl. There's no point in looking online, sure we'd be quicker taking the plane to China ourselves.'

Bloody hell, she thought, the only time she ever felt there was nothing to worry about was when she'd forgotten about something. Thank God for the luxurious rain shower. She pulled on a dark-green flowy midi dress teamed with last year's leather sandals and the sunglasses, which elevated every outfit. A wipe of lip gloss and she was out the door.

Mam was already prowling the bridal racks when she arrived.

'I thought you'd never get here.'

'What, I'm bang on time—'

'Hi, how can I help?' A very beautiful girl, who would have looked stunning in any of the dresses, beamed at them. 'Sooo, we have bride and mother of the bride?' she cooed.

Cassie felt Mam bristle. 'No, actually, we have bride and bridesmaid.'

There was just the faintest hesitation as the girl processed this, then she lit up.

'Fantastic, this is so beautiful, daughter is helping mama. What had you in mind?'

Somewhat mollified, Mam stepped forward. 'Well, I was thinking of something light . . . it's for July.'

'Next July?'

'God no, we could all be dead by then. This July.'

The beautiful girl blinked. Cassie could see her bracing herself for the next demand.

'Perfect. And what colour?'

'White.'

Cassie gave just the faintest hint of a shrug. Mam did Mam and nobody was going to persuade her otherwise. They gazed in trepidation at the racks of backless, frontless, strapless, see-through bridal gowns. Surely in all of that there'd have to be something suitable that'd only need a bit of a hem?

In the end the assistant proved to be worth her weight in gold. She found Mam a long white satin sheath dress teamed with a stunning embroidered organza wrap. Matching shoes and a floral headpiece were chosen next. Mam stood gazing at herself in the mirror, entranced by the image. Cassie could feel tears welling up.

'You look beautiful, Mam.'

'I do, don't I?'

'Eric will be stunned when he sees you.' She felt a small ache in her heart as she said the words.

'Ah thanks, love. I'll have a little word with your daddy later on, let him know what he's missing.' She gave Cassie a gentle elbow in the ribs, before regaining her composure. 'Will you, for the love of God, try phoning Maxine again? I know you tried once. You're dodging it, I know you.' Mam was back on top form.

They hugged outside the shop and Cassie agreed to bring the dress home with her to hide it from Eric.

For feck's sake, she thought, it was like hiding the Santa presents.

* * *

By eight thirty that evening, she couldn't make any more excuses – she was going to have to make that call. Oh well, get it over with . . . She pressed call and waited five rings, six . . . She'd already lowered the phone from her ear when she heard, 'Hello?'

Cassie's heart sank.

Maxine's voice sounded familiar but different, older. Of course it was, what was she thinking? Maxine was a forty-three-year-old woman. For some irrational reason she'd expected her to remain exactly the same as when they'd last spoken.

'Maxie? It's—'

'I know.'

She could envisage Maxine in her Toronto house, with the lakeside view, surrounded by her children and her pets, with Ownie, her husband, a fine man and a good provider. Cassie could imagine she still felt justified in her opinion, still right.

'I thought I should give you a call . . .' she began.

Silence.

'On account of Mam's wedding.' She'd started out with a surge of energy, which was rapidly ebbing away. 'Look, Mam asked me to call you because . . . we need to sort things out.'

There, she'd said it. She could do no more. Another long silence ensued.

'Right. I suppose this is all about the bridesmaids' dresses for this absurd wedding?'

Trust Maxine to deflect everything.

'That's part of it, yes.'

'We're far too old to be bridesmaids. It should be the girls, obviously.'

Cassie was struggling hard to keep her temper. 'Well, Mam suggested it and it's her day, so . . .'

'What do you want, Cassie?'

She felt stung by the abrupt tone and for a second was afraid she was going to cry. 'We do have to decide on these dresses somehow.'

'That's no problem, I can choose something online and send it on to Mam for her approval. Nobody's going to be looking at us anyway.'

Cassie felt utterly dismissed by her tone, but something in her just had to fight back.

'Speak for yourself.'

There was an icy pause.

'Is that everything? I've to pick Eoin up from hockey so I can't hang around. Tell Mam I'll send some options on to her, she can show them to you, OK? Bye.'

And that was it. Annoyance and frustration surged through Cassie.

'Bitch!' How could a well-intentioned, open-hearted attempt to reach out to Maxine be met with such a cold, dismissive response. Bugger Mam for putting her in this position.

She paced distractedly up and down the floor, and then picked up her bag and swept out of the apartment.

On the way downstairs she phoned Finn, who would probably still be relaxing in front of the TV with his feet on Thor, waiting to hear from her.

'It's me. Can you meet me in half an hour on Sandymount Strand?'

'Sure, babe. I'll be there.'

* * *

Cassie was already pacing up and down the path when he pulled into the car park, the shallow sea a smooth sheet of silver.

'Hey, this was a great idea. By the way, you were right, I've arranged to pick Samantha up tomorrow for a trip to Ikea,' he called cheerfully, until he saw her face. 'What's up?'

'Can we just walk? I'm too upset to talk.'

They set out across the beach, where little curled worm shapes dotted the ridged sand as far as the eye could see. Cassie stomped along with her eyes fixed on her feet.

'So, are you going to tell me what happened?'

'I tried, I really tried.'

Finn had the sense not to press her on whatever the hell was going on. Eventually, after they'd walked about a half a mile across the beach, she explained about the conversation with Maxine.

'Mam has insisted I make the arrangements, but that means she gets a chance to express to me what a useless piece of shit she thinks I am. And it really upsets me.

270

And, OK, we were never *really* close, but we used to get on fine.' She could hear her voice tightening.

'That's lousy,' he said, slipping his arm around her shoulders.

She nuzzled into his shoulder. 'Thank you.'

'What happened between you? You don't have to tell me if . . .'

She stopped dead in her tracks. 'I might as well. I haven't told anyone this, not even Gav, I was too freaked out and, honestly, too ashamed.'

'I'm not forcing you.'

'No, It's OK . . . It was the first summer after my graduation from drama school, and everything was going great: I'd got my first professional job, I was feeling like the person I always wanted to be. Bea had got me an audition for a new sitcom scheduled for the following week. It was all amazing. It was the day before I went back to London and Maxine had reluctantly agreed to allow me to take Miri, her two-year-old daughter, to do the supermarket shopping while she was at the hairdresser's. This'll be fine, I thought, just pop her in the trolley and push her around like other women I'd seen . . . Why are you laughing?'

'Nothing is simple with a two-year-old.'

'Oh, shut up. Anyhow, she was grabbing everything, driving me crazy, so I unstrapped her from the seat and popped her inside the trolley to distract her. Then I remember stopping at the bakery counter and my phone rang, and it was Bea changing my audition time . . . She said they must be really keen, and I'd have to be back

271

early for it. I just got totally distracted. I know there's no excuse. And the next moment, I looked round and the trolley was empty. I'll never forget it. I just ran and started calling and calling her name. And it was around the time of some of those awful child abductions. Then Maxine turned up and started shouting at me in front of everyone, calling me selfish and irresponsible and unfit to mind a child. The next thing . . . I'll never forget it, this woman just appeared, carrying Miri. I remember she was holding a handful of crayons she'd picked up. I burst into tears. But Maxine just snatched her up without a word and walked off. She never apologised and I was afraid to say anything to her. I went back to London the next day and we never really made up. Sounds ridiculous but that's it.

'I didn't go for that sitcom audition, or any of the other big jobs Bea had me lined up for. I suppose I didn't I feel I deserved them. I just sort of sank and, looking back, I'm sure it affected my relationship with Gav. How could it not? I was still raging with myself that I lost concentration, lost myself in that stupid, vain world. I still hate myself, it's that simple. And so, I deserve to be hated.'

'Maybe that's what she's picking up,' Finn remarked levelly. They walked in silence for a while, before he went on. 'You do know that what you're describing is something I've feared myself: you turn your back for a second and they disappear. Sure, it's every parent's nightmare.'

'Thank you, Finn. That makes me feel a bit less of a pariah.'

'Come here.' He stopped and hugged her close to him, rubbing her back as though she were a distressed child. 'Let it go. Miri's fine. It's all fine. You just need to forgive yourself.'

The tears were running down her cheeks, and she angrily wiped them away.

'That's what I tried to tell Maxine, but she still despises me.'

'That's probably an exaggeration. Someone's got to start the forgiving, so maybe start with yourself.'

'I'm sorry, I've just got snot on your shoulder.'

'It's OK, I'm pretty used to it.'

'You're a freaking genius, d'you know that? My friend Norah's right. If you want a problem solved, go ask an engineer.'

He smiled shyly. 'Come on, let's go home. I've been thinking about you all week.'

'Me too. It's been a long week.'

'Too long,' he whispered, taking her face between his hands and kissing her slowly.

At some point night had fallen and the sky ranged from pale orange right up to inky darkness. The tide had turned, shifting the vast flat beach into sea once more. They picked their way back across the ridged sand, hand in hand, as Cassie felt her panic melt into the wide-open sky.

* * *

After arriving back at her apartment the following day, she slumped down on the bed and listened to her phone messages. There was only one and it was from Maxine. She pressed redial.

'Hi.' Maxine's tone sounded impatient.

'Look, can we please have a conversation?'

'About these dresses? Why? It's not that complicated, is it?' Her tone was abrupt.

Typical Maxine. Don't let her get to you, she reminded herself.

'OK,' Cassie said, 'the truth is I'm afraid you'll choose mauve and I'll look like I'm diseased or having a fucking heart attack, and you'll look gorgeous because you're dark-haired.'

There was a pause.

'I'm not dark anymore, Cass. I'm grey.'

'Really? I'm sorry, I didn't know.'

'Hey, it's a few greys, not cancer.' Maxine's semi-Canadian accent was trying to sound brisk but just sounded so sad, such a pointless waste of precious time.

'I didn't mean it like that. Maxine, I don't want this shit between us . . .' A sob rose up from deep inside her. There was silence from the other end.

'I don't want it either.'

'I'm sorry for what happened. I really am—'

'Cass . . .'

'Is she OK? Does she remember?'

'Not at all. She's perfect. She's getting ready for prom. I think she'd really love to meet you.'

'That'd be amazing. I've missed you,' she blurted out.

The relief she felt was like dropping a heavy rucksack from her back.

'Missed you too.'

There followed the fastest catch-up in history, as fifteen years of news criss-crossed the Atlantic in ten minutes. Finally, they drew breath.

'So, what colour should we choose?'

'White, of course, that'd really piss off Mam.'

They burst out laughing and in that moment the years melted away.

'I'll leave that to you, Maxie.'

'OK, but I gotta say, I still look hot in mauve.'

Chapter 26

'Babe, I need your help.' Finn sounded stressed.

Cassie was sitting propped up on her bed on Sunday evening – not her favourite time of the week – preparing for next day's classes and feeling a dread that had no particular centre.

'Babe, guess what, I'm here doing your ex-wife's work that she's still getting paid for, despite not turning up half the time, so how're you doing?'

There was a sharp intake of breath from the other end of the phone. She felt a pang of guilt.

'Sorry, that was mean. Don't mind me. I'm like a bitch, I'm pre-menstrual.'

'I'm sorry, Cass, I really am. I've just got a request to cover nights next week and I'm stuck for Tuesday. I hate to ask you but . . .'

'It's fine, honestly, I'd really like to see them again. I sort of promised.'

'Er . . . Just to give you a heads-up, you'll have Samantha this time.'

She baulked. The younger children were a pleasure, but a raging teenager . . . well, it'd be an experience. Surely teenagers couldn't have changed that much in . . . what, twenty years? She realised with a jolt that she still thought of herself as reasonably young and trendy, but to someone who genuinely was young, she'd seem exactly what she was, an almost middle-aged woman. That was something she'd managed to avoid facing up to now.

Aside from that, he'd made no mention of Marisha copping on about their relationship. It was possible that she'd so much else going on in her life that she didn't really care.

'Thank you, you've no idea what that means to me,' he murmured in a voice that caused a glow of heat to rise from deep inside her. 'I'll make it all up to you, Cass, I promise.'

'I can't wait, babe, one of these days there's going to be a bonanza . . .'

She heard him breathe a laugh. 'Trust me . . .'

She really wanted to – she really wanted him – but there was no escaping the fact that most of it was out of her hands.

'Babe, I've got to go.'

'Yeah. Night night.'

Deep in thought after her call with Finn, Cassie padded into the kitchen to find Ramona in her off-duty, flat-hair persona. Her bruises had all but disappeared, but she was definitely hitting a slump. Cassie made a mug of tea and sat down at the table opposite her. There was a half-eaten pepperoni pizza in a box – nothing like Ramona's usual high-protein diet.

'What's up?'

'Nothing.'

Cassie sighed. Ramona could turn into an overgrown teenager sometimes.

'Maybe this is just an opportunity for a rethink.'

'Thanks, Cass, if I wanted a pep talk I'd have looked on TikTok.'

'Your shoulder will heal, then you can go back to dancing.'

Ramona swung around and fixed her with a glare through her long, bleached fringe.

'To take the sort of strain the pole puts on it, we're talking months.'

Privately, Cassie reflected that this mightn't be the worst thing in the world.

'If I don't have my lifestyle, I don't have my followers. If I do nothing but buy groceries and do laundry and shit or just putter out to a normal-ass job – no offence – then nobody gives a rat's ass. I'm just a basic bitch like everyone else.'

Cassie was tempted to say 'Welcome to my world,' with just the smallest hint of schadenfreude, but she recognised underneath Ramona's arrogance just how fragile she really was. She knew better than to make any further helpful suggestions; Ramona would have to feel that way until she didn't have to feel it anymore.

* * *

Cassie arrived at Finn's apartment on Tuesday evening, hoping at least for a chance to pick up from where she'd left off with the younger children. To her disappointment, Cici only smiled vaguely and Con barely acknowledged her at all, which left her crestfallen.

Come on, she chided herself, did she seriously expect them to remember her and make a fuss? Kid-time was different to adult-time. It was weeks since the evening when she'd turned up to the apartment in that disastrous outfit – this time she wore her green suede Doc Martens and a summer dress.

Finn had filled the fridge and explained all about their food choices, as if she didn't remember.

'Are they OK? They seem a little . . . subdued.'

Cassie noticed him flinch at her words.

'Kids pick up on an atmosphere. I think they're worried. Cici's missing spending time with her mum and Con is obsessed that there's something seriously wrong. I tried to reassure him, but you know, he gets fixations. And as for Sam . . .' He made a gesture of resignation as he pulled on his jacket.

She gave a reassuring smile. 'I'll see what I can do.'

He went to kiss her but remembered himself just in time. 'Good luck,' he said pointedly.

Samantha was due home at six, after hockey, and in the meantime, Con spread his homework books out on the table. He was finishing Fifth Class and had a surprising amount of work to do. Cici was in Senior Infants but was very self-important about her little tasks. She plonked herself right next to Con's elbow and he pushed her away roughly.

'I can hear you snorting like a pig,' he growled, making her little face crumple into tears.

'That's enough, now, I'm going to sit between the two of you,' Cassie exclaimed.

She felt herself quite comfortable with the children; it was hard to imagine the anxious rookie she'd been only a few months previously. She recognised Cici's books from school – her little bit of homework involved a few sums, a passage of 'fill in the missing word' and finally drawing a picture. Rather a lot for a six-year-old, Cassie reflected. Nonetheless, Cici was revelling in her tasks and laid everything out in straight lines, which she proudly called 'organdising'. It was striking to see, even in a young child, how the basic qualities that would characterise a life were clearly visible. Don't rush it, thought Cassie, none of it's as much fun for real.

The door buzzer went off like a fire alarm. How could someone's attitude communicate itself through an electronic device? The door swung open and a tall, dark-haired girl glowered at her. She would've been pretty if her expression hadn't been quite so hostile. Could this be a teenage version of Marisha?

'Hi, I'm Cassie.'

'The babysitter, yeah, I know . . . like, I'm fourteen, I don't know what you're even doing here, I don't need a babysitter.'

Yikes. When in doubt, be nice, she reminded herself.

'I know, but your brother and sister do, and I'm sure you don't want the job of looking after them.'

Her lip curled with disdain. 'No fuckin' way,' she muttered, flinging her bag on the ground and flouncing into the kitchen.

Cassie was taken aback at the upfront cursing at an adult, but reminded herself, *She's testing you.*

'Sammie, do you want to see my drawing?' wheedled Cici, to whom her big sister was clearly a goddess.

Samantha barely grunted and flopped down on the sofa, eyes fixed on her phone.

'When's dinner?'

Did all teenagers speak to their parents like servants?

'Ten minutes. You must be starving.'

No reply of any kind.

She finished preparing the children's dinners: mashed potato with butter, chicken and the de rigueur mashed turnip – everything separate, of course, for Con's benefit. Finn had warned her against anything too colourful, especially red, and absolutely nothing spicy.

When, finally, they all sat down to eat, Samantha kept her phone propped up against the fruit bowl, scrolling and texting throughout.

'Sammie, Mummy says you're not allowed,' whined Cici.

'*Shut up!*' roared Con, his hands covering as much of his head as he could manage.

'Well, go and phone Mum, then, squirt,' said Samantha, causing Cici to telegraph an anguished plea for help. Cassie shrugged. It wasn't her job to police a teenager and it was likely that any attempt was liable to cause an eruption.

By the time dinner was cleared away, Cici was watching her half hour of screen time that Cassie suspected only her dad, rather than her mum, allowed. Predictably, Samantha flounced away from the table, slamming the door of Finn's old room behind her and leaving the air behind her fizzing with animosity. Still, at least it left the rest of them in peace.

Cici sat curled on the sofa with St Teresa of Avila on her lap, still watching a cartoon of Cinderella, when the door swung open and Samantha strode into the room, an unnerving expression on her face.

'Cassie, there's something I'm curious about . . . If you're the babysitter, how come you're so *old*?'

Cici looked alarmed and Cassie felt blindsided. She'd been prepared for moodiness, but this full-on confrontation was on another level.

'Well . . . you can be a babysitter at any age.' Cassie was deflecting but the teenager was moving in for a direct attack.

'Are you my dad's girlfriend? And if you are, do you know what that makes her, Cici?'

The marmalade kitten with the big, trusting eyes shook her head.

'It makes her the wicked stepmother.'

The eyes swivelled back round to Cassie in shock.

'Is that true?' she whispered.

'Of course not. Samantha's only joking, aren't you? Now, come on, time to get ready for bed.'

Over Cici's head she shot a stern look to Samantha, who met her gaze defiantly.

Cici seemed to have accepted Cassie's explanation and had moved on to her bedtime routine. Tucking St Teresa into bed, she confided that the doll had a new job: looking after her mummy, who went to bed in the afternoons and didn't like eating chicken curry anymore.

Con was crouched awkwardly on the edge of the sofa bed, clearly uncomfortable at the change of furniture as he played his game, which seemed to involve jaw-dropping co-ordination skills. She'd learned from their previous encounter not to try and engage Con in real-life conversation, though he could be approached through the medium of fantasy. She sat beside him for a few minutes.

'It's called *Starfield*,' he volunteered. 'You have to do up your own spaceship and you have all these options to customise it.' He flicked up a list of properties on the screen.

Cassie was struck by the contrast between the anxious, pale boy he was in normal life and the confident gamer he transformed into with the controller in his hand.

They sat together companionably as he blasted other ships to bits and appeared occasionally as his avatar, a muscled figure in futuristic armour.

'Do you think my mum's going to be OK? I mean, is she going to die or anything?' he blurted out. He didn't even try to look at her.

'No, Con, absolutely not. Put that thought right out of your head.'

He barely reacted but nodded his head and carried on. It was painfully obvious how much turmoil he was in underneath the unreadable surface. At eight thirty, give or take, he went to bed, after a lengthy session of tapping, counting and checking.

Cassie had finally slumped down on the sofa with a relaxing mug of tea when the door swung open. Samantha perched on the arm of the sofa, staring down at her.

'I was being serious earlier. Are you?'

Oh crap, this really wasn't her call, but outright lying just didn't feel right.

'Yes.'

'Knew it. Are they getting divorced?'

Despite the bravado, there was an underlying fear in her voice.

'I honestly don't know, Samantha, you'd have to ask your dad.'

Samantha picked at her shoelace distractedly. 'Where'd you get your boots?'

'London.'

'A girl in my class has a pair of shoes that cost a thousand euros.'

'Bet she's lying,' said Cassie.

'That's what I said. She lies about everything anyway.'

Cassie really wanted to reach out and tell this kid that she understood what a confusing, shitty situation this was, but feared anything she said was going to come across horribly wrong. Following the least empty silence she could remember, Samantha stood up to leave, and as she reached the door, she swung round. 'You're a schemer. The little ones mightn't see it, but I do. Don't think you can take our dad away from us.'

She slammed the door behind her, leaving Cassie winded. The problem wasn't what she did, it was how she was seen. The wicked stepmother.

Chapter 27

Louise's house was filled with pink and blue balloons for the baby shower. A table was decorated with pink and blue camellias, and laden with finger food and flute glasses for Prosecco. The French windows opened on to the terrace and a pile of beautifully wrapped gifts sat on a side table. The girls were dressed in summer frocks or flowy trousers and silk tops, while Louise wore a soft pink dress that flattered her eight-month bump.

'I'm on a child-free day so I've decided to wear the most stainable clothes possible, just to celebrate,' announced Bryony, waving a full glass. The handsome Mike had manhandled the garden furniture into a suitable arrangement on the patio and then made himself scarce, but not before planting a brief kiss on Louise's cheek. They presented the picture of happiness.

'This place is gorgeous, what a lucky little babe it's going to be, with a view of the sea and all . . .'

The fact that the baby wouldn't give a shite about a view of the sea wasn't mentioned by anybody. Cassie was feeling irritable, and fakery in any form was getting right on her nerves. Ramona had been extended an invitation by Louise, who didn't like to leave anybody out, but she announced that she'd rather have a nipple piercing without pain relief than go to Louise's baby shower and feel like a freak.

It was only a few days since the evening babysitting for Finn's children, but an ominous feeling had been haunting Cassie all week. She picked up a miniscule hamburger and nibbled it thoughtfully. Let it go, she urged herself, there's not a solitary thing you can do right now, so she accepted a refill of Prosecco from a young teenager, who'd obviously been paid a few bob to help out for the afternoon and seemed delighted with herself. Why couldn't Samantha have been more like this girl, friendly and obliging? She hadn't mentioned anything to Finn because, well, there was a conflict of interest, wasn't there? She didn't want to be the one turning him against his own daughter, not that he'd want to hear what she had to say. And yet, the teenager inside her wanted to protest the unfairness of it and how mean Samantha had been to her. Side with me, not her. Wasn't that exactly what Samantha was so afraid of? And how would she have felt in the same situation, if her beloved Da had found some other woman? Awful.

'Hi, how're you doing? You're looking great. How's the doggie walking going?'

Babe-a-licious Bryony was looking lightly tanned and untouchable.

'I'm teaching now, actually.'

'Really, what?'

'Children.'

'Cool.'

A glass was rung with a fork by Celine, who appeared to have volunteered herself as MC and had arrived early to offer her 'help', which apparently included downing most of a bottle of Prosecco. She began, 'Hi everyone, excuse me, I just want – on behalf of our lovely Louise – to say a few words to celebrate our years of friendship and the imminent arrival of Louise's baby, the last of us . . .'

Here, there was a small hiatus as someone whispered to her that there was someone else – oh, for fuck's sake, Cassie thought, like she cared.

'Sorry, Cassie, *almost* the last of us . . . to have our babies, and I'm just thinking about all of us, how in the future our little ones will be able to play together, and in the years to come there'll be a whole new generation . . . of us.' With that, she gave an alcohol-fuelled sob.

'Tissue alert,' called someone good-naturedly. 'First tears of the day.'

There was an emotional round of applause as the others, apart from Norah, wiped their eyes. Cassie felt close to tears herself, from boredom. Or at least, that's what she told herself, sipping her way through yet another glass of bubbles. Norah appeared immune to the tidal wave of sentiment. 'I wouldn't inflict my pair of little horrors on anyone,' she muttered.

The presents were opened and admired: a T-shirt with *Mama* on it from Celine, a vegan mother-and-baby pamper kit from Bryony, and from Norah a very large parcel which turned out to be her own postpartum doughnut cushion, in the interests of recycling, along with a box of chocolates – quite how the two combined, it wasn't clear.

'If you're anything like I was, you're going to need it,' she explained grimly.

Cassie's gift was a pair of fluffy cashmere socks and a little wall plaque that said: *Anyone can be a mother, but it takes someone special to be a Mum* – Louise was so touched and Cassie felt humbled.

'Honestly, that is *so beautiful*.'

Just then the charming teenager was given a nod and reappeared with a pink and blue iced cake. Evidently, they were keeping the gender reveal a surprise. Without wishing to be mean-spirited, Cassie thought it all felt so . . . conventional. She just hoped for the poor child's sake that it fitted neatly into either the pink or blue category.

It was strange how observing something completely separate from yourself could bring you face to face with your own truth. Suddenly, it all became blindingly clear. It wasn't fair but, as obnoxious as Samantha might have been, she had a point. The kids had lost their stable home, they were just about to find out that their mother was expecting someone else's baby, and now here she was, swooping in to take their dad. She was the interloper. It couldn't be clearer, and she had to tell Finn, right now. It just didn't seem right for her to take her happiness at other people's expense. Thankfully, the tearful toasting was over, and she was able to slip off to the loo and surreptitiously phone a taxi.

* * *

'You're sozzled.'

She was standing in his apartment, her jacket slightly off-centre, a cross-body bag askew across her chest.

'That's not the point, it's all true, admit it, it's all my fault. Samantha hates me and the other two only don't because they don't know what I am yet. I've betrayed their trust. That's what I am. I'm a traitorous bitch. We're finished.'

'Cassie, that's horseshit. You are not responsible for Sam's appalling behaviour; you should hear what she calls me. The only reason she doesn't abuse her mother is she doesn't dare. This is not *all your fault*, so don't imagine you're specially chosen for her ire.'

'You're just saying that because you feel sorry for me.'

'You're actually very gorgeous when you're rat-arsed.'

'I'm ser-us. Don't patronise me . . .'

'Come here.' He pulled her in towards him and kissed her hungrily. This wasn't what she'd intended at all, but still . . .

* * *

She woke at about 7 p.m., with the beginnings of a hangover, beside Finn, who was scrolling on his phone. He seemed to find the whole thing pretty funny.

'I can't believe a baby shower was that dramatic. You should go to them more often.'

'Oh God, was I crazy? I'm so embarrassed. I will never look at a cocktail hot-dog again as long as I live.'

She got up and trailed into the shower in the hope of feeling a bit fresher. Her headache was beginning to kick off and she was in urgent need of painkillers so she padded back into the kitchen, where Finn was sipping on a glass of red wine and expertly chopping chicken and vegetables to add to what smelled like a Thai green curry. Cassie remembered that she'd had very little to eat since breakfast. She slipped her arms round his waist and breathed in the aroma.

'Yummy, that's exactly what I need.'

He raised an eyebrow. 'Glass of red?'

'I'll need something to wash down the Panadol.'

They sat on the sofa and ate with the plates on their knees. He really was a fantastic cook when he put his mind to it.

'This is exactly what I don't let the kids do.' He smiled.

'It's great being a parent, isn't it?' Cassie leaned against Finn's shoulder, feeling as safe as she'd felt since . . . Well, since she was little. 'You get to make all the rules.'

'Do you ever wonder about how everything came together for us to meet that morning, with Phyllis and randy Napoleon that kept trying to bonk Patricia's Bichons?'

They laughed at the ridiculous memory.

'If either of us had been half an hour either way, we might never have met. Do you ever regret it?' he asked.

'Well, my life is a lot more complicated than it used to be, but no, I don't regret it.'

'And you never regret leaving London?'

'No.' She sighed, aware there was a note of sadness in her voice. 'I mean, I regret how things ended with Gav. But I suppose it was the end of an era. I gave it everything I had. It just didn't repay me.'

'Cass, I owe you an apology. You were put in a rotten position with Samantha, and you shouldn't have been. It was my responsibility, mine and Marisha's.'

'Being called the wicked stepmother was a first, I'll admit.'

Still, she had the niggling feeling that he hadn't put a stop to Samantha's behaviour. He hadn't actually stood up for her. She took a deep breath.

'Finn, I've never asked you this before but . . . what am I to you?' She cringed. It really was one of those questions men hate being asked. But she had to confront it.

'Cassie, you know what you are. You're my girlfriend.'

'I know, but sometimes I feel like the girlfriend of . . . a part of you. The other part I don't feel like I've much connection with at all.'

There, she'd come out with it.

'What do you want me to say?' He sighed.

She wanted him to say that he loved her, that she was the most important thing in the world to him and everything else would work out around that.

'If you have to ask, I can't help you,' she muttered, aware of sounding petulant.

'Come on, Cass, you know how difficult things have been . . .'

'Sure, of course, I'm sorry,' she said, though underneath the doubts still niggled.

Chapter 28

Roger Newcombe was definitely wearing the same jacket again this week, and definitely the same pair of shoes, God love him, as Mam would say. He met Cassie in his office on Monday morning, looking sheepish, and explained that Miss Upton wasn't well but would be in by break time. She replied agreeably that it was no problem but did notice Helen, the secretary, shooting a jaundiced expression towards his back. Not to worry – no Marisha meant a hassle-free morning, although Cassie had to admit that her attitude had softened considerably in recent weeks.

The class began rehearsing. Cassie had composed a rock 'n' roll routine which included Rowley belting out some early Elvis-style lyrics through a crackly microphone. He and Ahmed, who was now playing the part of the giant's electric guitar, rather than the harp, were learning what could potentially be a show-stopping routine, if only Rowley could remember the steps and Ahmed didn't keep tripping over both of their feet.

The show was scheduled for two weeks' time and shaping up to be a far cry from the original sedate affair. It might veer in the direction of outrageous, but look, wasn't that what everyone dreamed of, a bit of excitement in an otherwise mundane world?

At break time Cassie spotted Marisha's car pulling into the car park. She traipsed into the classroom, looking tired and wan, as Cassie tidied up after the set builders.

'Cassie, look at the marvellous work you've all been doing. Listen, I really wanted to catch you on your own. My daughter Samantha told me this weekend what had transpired between you last week. She didn't tell me at the time because I think she felt guilty. I know she can seem a little . . . harsh, but she's a good girl. It's all just been very hard on her, you know, at fourteen you're not one thing or another, it's such a difficult age.'

'Marisha, I get it. I'm not trying to take anything from anyone. That's what I wanted to tell her. I would have been exactly the same if my parents had split up, worse probably.'

'Well, mine did split up when I was fourteen so, unfortunately, I know exactly what she's going through.'

Nonetheless, there was something about the streetwise Samantha that put Cassie on alert. Although she was undoubtedly a vulnerable, remorseful teenager underneath, Samantha was clearly taking advantage of her parents' guilt and calling the shots. It wasn't that long since Cassie had been fourteen herself.

Marisha, in the meantime, seemed to have flipped back into professional mode.

'I think you might need to collect the children, the bell is about to go,' she announced briskly.

Cassie really wanted to like Marisha; the only problem was, how could you like someone who was treating you as a confidante one minute and a minion the next?

* * *

Shortly after three o'clock, Cassie was reversing out from her parking space in the school car park, when a call came through. The number was familiar, though she hadn't seen it for a while, so she quickly pulled up to a safe spot at the side of the road.

The projected voice practically leaped down the line. 'Hi, darling, it's Sunita from London, remember me? Surprise, surprise. How're you getting on in little old Ireland?'

Cassie was genuinely delighted to hear Sunita, who'd taken over the agency after Bea's passing.

'Sweetie, what a pleasure to hear from you. All good here, what's up?'

'Well, if you're not sitting down, find a chair. I just got a call from the BBC ten minutes ago to say they'd seen an old tape of yours and they're interested in you trying out for a part on *Wentworth Way*. How about that?'

'You're kidding me?'

'Not at all, I'm going to ping you over the details. And absolutely no disclosure, complete confidentiality, I know I can trust you. They want the tape for Wednesday, close of business, all right? Get back to me later, sweetheart.'

And she was gone.

Wow. That came from outer space. Cassie should've been delighted, she realised, but right now, with everything else that was going on, the whole idea felt exhausting. On the other hand, it was a fantastic opportunity.

She waited until the email came through and scanned the script. It was a good storyline. Great, in fact. It wasn't just a blink-and-you-miss-it affair, this was actually the really meaty, really nice part of a woman who'd just got out of prison and was trying to restart her life. She began to feel a fizz of excitement and a surge of possibility. Just then the familiar, creeping doubt raised its head. How many times had she been in this situation? Endless audition tapes, endless hopes, only to have them dashed yet again.

All of a sudden, she felt a wave of loneliness and yearned to talk to someone who'd understand. Mam would tell her to have more sense, and anyone else she could think of would have some sort of a vested interest. Then it hit her, the last time she'd been phoned at home by her London agent was that horrible day when she'd lost little Miri in the supermarket and thought she'd ruined everything. But that had been a lifetime ago. She needed someone whose judgement she trusted but who'd give her sound professional advice . . . There was only one person she could think of.

'Phil?'

'Cassandra, I'm hearing nothing but great things about you from Roger Newcombe.'

'About that, Phil, it might all be getting a little complicated.'

She explained to him about the phone call from her agent and her confusion. He listened carefully, without interrupting.

'And the thing is, Phil, it's a really good part.'

'And do you want to do it?'

She sighed audibly.

'Or maybe d'you not want to put yourself in that position again?'

Philip really got it, in fairness.

'Something like that.'

'OK, what if I said to you that it wouldn't be the same as before, because now, whether you get it or not, it can't make or break you.'

'You think I should do it, Phil?'

She braced herself for an evasive answer, but after a long pause he replied, 'What I'm hearing is that you'd love to go for it but you're afraid. And what *I* think is that it's come to you, you've earned it, so don't turn away from it. Sure, make the tape, send it off . . . and let it go. Isn't that what Ecclesiastes says: cast your bread upon the waters?'

'I thought that referred to doing good without expecting a definite reward, sort of thing?'

'Let's just say, your talent is a gift to the world, so if you're asked to share it, don't question too closely, just do it.'

There was something about his words that reached beyond the surface. She felt a wave of peace.

'Thanks, Phil, that really helps.'

* * *

296

She trailed in the door of her apartment that evening, hauling a big bag of art materials to make props. Ramona was scrolling on her laptop with an unusual intensity.

'What're you doing?'

'Booking flights to my new life.'

Cassie's heart jolted. 'What? You're leaving?'

'No, I'm starting a new business. It's going to be a clothing and accessory line based on my online presence, and it's going to be aimed at women twenty-five and upwards who aren't afraid to dress for their fantasies.'

'Wow!' Cassie privately thought that sounded a little risky, given that people's fantasies were inclined to vary; however, what Ramona actually meant was that she'd define the fantasies, and her customers would buy the outfits. Well, it'd worked so far with her influencer career, so she was perfectly poised to launch the clothing line. In fact, it was a bloody great idea.

'Yah, I've been on to Grandma and she's all over the idea. So, I'm going to China to source a pattern cutter who'll prepare my designs and then, of course, I'll need a factory for manufacture and distribution . . .'

'Jeepers, you decided all of this since . . . what, ten o'clock this morning?'

She was clearly out of her funk.

'When I go, I go.' Ramona glanced over the top of the screen. 'You look chipper, what's up?' After swearing her to secrecy, Cassie explained about the BBC soap that she wasn't allowed to name, and how she was going to need help videoing herself and sending it off.

'And you think present company might help you with that?'

'Please?'

'Are you kidding me? Wotcher, me old China plate,' she began, in an excruciating cockney accent.

* * *

That evening, when she was supposed to be crafting an electric guitar out of cardboard and twine, she started learning the three scenes she had to record. The accent required was her own, so she decided there was no point in over-stressing about it. Instead, she focused on learning the lines so thoroughly that she could forget about them, which generally took more time than she had. Miraculously, Ramona came up with the solution.

'All you gotta do is record the scenes on your iPhone, then you tap share, then you select "Loop Playback" and then you can play them on repeat all night at low volume as you catch your Zs,' announced Ramona. 'It's how they teach dudes foreign languages for the military, scientifically proven. You're welcome.'

The following afternoon she and Ramona set up the phone camera. Cassie was dressed in a hoodie and ripped jeans, and had rubbed a bit of Vaseline into her hair to look downbeat. She'd almost forgotten the excitement of creating a character. Ramona assembled the impressive collection of lights she kept for her posts and created a professional-looking corner where she'd be well-lit.

'Boy, you look like shit, it's perfect,' Ramona commented.

'OK, you have to read the in-between lines to give me the cues. And not in that atrocious accent you put on, for feck's sake.'

'Aw, please? Can't I just throw in, *"Cor blimey, she's been banged up in the Rusty Nail!"*'

'*No!* Now stop messing.'

There was something about Ramona's cockiness and irreverence that leeched the stress out of the situation. It turned out her tip about the sleep had been spot on and the lines felt securely in Cassie's head so that she could just play the scenes as spontaneously as possible. After two takes, they had it.

'That was really good, really natural. I'd have believed you'd done time.' Ramona sounded mildly astonished. Between them, they uploaded the clips to the appropriate platform and hit send.

Cassie punched the air with her fist, feeling strangely at peace. She'd made the decision not to hope and stress, as she'd done in the past. She'd cast her bread upon the waters and that would have to do. She wasn't going to tell anyone either; the last thing she wanted was well-meaning people constantly asking if she'd heard any news. Say nothing and let it take care of itself, she decided.

Chapter 29

'They've arrived, are you going to drop round and open them?'

Mam sounded like an overexcited ten-year-old. So, the dress she was going to be decked out in for Mam's wedding, chosen by Maxine, had finally arrived. It could go either way: she was an autumn-colouring type and Maxine was winter, so there was going to have to be a compromise somewhere. Frankly, she'd more pressing things to attend to. The Bondarenko twins' mother hadn't been able to find a cow costume to fit them, so Cassie had volunteered to make it herself, and time had become dangerously short. She veered left off the N11 and headed up towards Mam's.

There was a large cardboard box sitting on the sofa, like an unexploded bomb.

'Don't touch it while I make tea. I picked up a Black Forest gateau, will you have a slice?'

'Mam, we're supposed to be trying to look our best, we can't be scoffing cake every day.'

'Ah, well, we'll all be dead long enough. We can cut down the fortnight before, that'll do it.'

After they enjoyed a slice of cake and a cup of tea, Mam couldn't contain her curiosity any longer and approached the box with a pair of scissors.

'Right, let's have a look.' She cut open the sticky tape and folded back the lid to reveal . . . pine-green fabric . . . with silver piping. Mam's horrified expression mirrored Cassie's. It was a July wedding.

She pulled the first dress, her size, out of the cellophane bag and stared at it. The fabric was cheap and shiny, and she could see Mam beginning to panic.

'I'll try it on, it may be one of those garments that doesn't have . . . what do they call it? Hanger appeal.'

She slipped out of her clothes and into the slithery polyester dress, which clung to her but definitely not in the right way. Eric bustled in gamely with a full-length mirror. He caught sight of her and there was no mistaking his look of dismay. Mam was starting to cry.

He couldn't restrain himself. 'Oh dear, I've seen classier-looking fertiliser bags.'

'They're awful, just dire.' Mam sobbed.

'I'm phoning Maxine, she'll be around at this time. They must've looked completely different online, that's the only explanation,' Cassie muttered, aware of rising fury. She video-called her sister's number and paced up and down, waiting. Surprisingly, Maxine picked up almost immediately.

'Hey, how's it going?'

Cassie tried to control her voice. 'Maxie, you stay right there, don't move, and I'm going to show you the dress.'

She propped the phone up on the mantelpiece and stepped back into view. It took a moment for the shock to register on Maxine's face.

'Oh. I mean, I was a little unsure about the colour, but the dresses looked gorgeous.'

'Well, they're not. Maxine, they're poxy. We're going to look like Santa's elves' mammies.'

'Oh God, Mam, I'm sorry.'

By this point Mam was helping herself to a second wedge of Black Forest gateau, but Cassie whipped it out of her hand.

'That won't help, trust me. OK, what's going to happen is, I'm going to pack this dress into the box and send it straight back. Then Mam and I are going straight back down to Marian Gale, this very minute, and we're going to buy two new bridesmaids' dresses.'

'Cass, I'm sorry, I was genuinely thinking of your colouring.'

'I know, stick around, I'll need you later. It's all going to be fine,' she said confidently, feeling the exact opposite. If things didn't fall into place fast, they were in big trouble.

* * *

'And do you have an appointment?' enquired the formally dressed assistant, flicking through a large diary. They both shook their heads guiltily.

'It's an emergency.'

Cassie relayed the slithery-dress debacle in as few words as possible, more for her own benefit than the assistant's, who smiled politely but clearly couldn't give a toss.

'Well, never mind, let's see what we can do.'

They were shown a range of bridesmaids' dresses suited to women closer to half her age.

'Would you like a little peep at our mother-of-the-bride selection, just for options?'

'We would not, thank you very much, we'll make this work,' growled Mam. She could say what she liked to her daughters, but let anyone else dare to cast shade and they'd feel her wrath. In the end, Cassie tried on a silvery lavender-blue strapless gown which, thankfully, looked great on her slim frame.

'And what about Maxine?' said Mam doubtfully. 'I'm not sure I can see her in strapless.'

'I have an idea,' said the assistant, who – having realised she stood to earn some commission – had thawed considerably. 'We call it the rescue section.' She pulled out a length of the same shade in tulle and created a halterneck effect which rendered the dress slightly less girlish while maintaining the lightness of the design.

'I *love* it,' breathed Mam. 'Come on, let's get Maxine on the phone.'

Maxine appeared to be in a grocery store but managed to wedge herself into the quietest corner she could find, so Cassie could model the dresses to the incongruous vision of Maxine framed by beer cans. She looked crestfallen but agreed that the dress would be lovely. Cassie felt sorry for her.

'On the bright side, Maxine, it's close as dammit to mauve.'

* * *

303

Following a successful shopping expedition and having deposited the bridesmaids' dresses safely at Mam's house, Cassie landed through the door of her apartment and collapsed in the hall.

'Cass, is that you?' came a voice from the kitchen.

'I can't remember. I'm emotionally drained.'

She pulled herself to her feet and trailed in to find that Ramona had taken over the entire table with a sketch pad and a desktop computer on which she'd created a variety of designs in an astonishingly short length of time.

'You can't buy this stuff. Not now. But I'm betting it's how a truckload of people would dream of dressing if they could. Like, not all the time, obviously.'

Cassie picked up a sketch from the table; it was a top made of what looked like armour, with leather straps, and worn with some sort of skirt and chunky lace-up boots. It looked like something out of one of Gav's computer games.

'Wow, these are kind of . . . sensational. They'd have a cult following, they really would.'

'Sure, they're not cosplay costumes, they're club clothes. It's not like I'm planning on opening a shop. These are niche, pricey and highly desirable to a certain clientele.'

'OK, you really seem to know your market.'

'Honey, I've been secretly dreaming of this for years. What else am I going to think of while spinning upside-down on a pole.'

'So, how're you going to get it all made?'

'I've found a manufacturer in China who can source the materials, seeing as they're not mainstream fabrics.'

'Sounds like it's going to need a ton of money.'

'Grandma's a feisty old bird. Most of the time she'd freeze your blood on the spot, but when she likes something . . . stand back.'

'And she likes . . .?'

'You betcha, she's already planning her outfit for the launch. It's going to include a limited makeup range – very futuristic, male and female – incredible footwear . . . I swear to God, you will never have seen anything like it. It's going to be like Biba was in the 1960s in London. The original.'

'Ramona, this is so exciting. Are you covering it on TikTok or Instagram?'

'Are you fucking kidding? And let some other douche get the jump on me? No way.'

'So, what happens now?'

'Tomorrow at 6 a.m. I've a flight to London and from there to Beijing. I've an interpreter meeting me at the airport, so sayonara, baby. But enough about me, what've you been doing?'

Cassie's heart sank a little. How to follow that? She explained about the disastrous bridesmaids' dresses and their dash to replace them with something decent. In fairness to Ramona, she wasn't the least bit snobby and laughed heartily at the online slithery horrors.

'Oh, man. Some people have a neck like an armadillo with the stuff they'll try to pass off. Just make sure she gets her refund.'

Spoken like a pro, Cassie thought.

* * *

The apartment felt empty over the next couple of days, although that meant Cassie had plenty of time in the evening to cut out the black-and-white cow costume from a pattern off the internet and then start the tricky job of piecing it together without accidentally sewing the legs to each other. She was settling in for the evening, when her phone buzzed. It was Finn.

'Hey, what's going on?'

There was a rueful laugh from the other end. 'Guess?'

'Er . . . OK. The guy at work who should be on call tomorrow night was abducted by aliens, so you need me to babysit?'

'You don't have to, I can find somebody else. But if you do, I'm going to bring you out for dinner on Saturday to make up for it.'

'Shut up. You can't afford to keep bringing me out for dinner every time you get an emergency. That guy seems like a lazy shite, with his endless excuses, and deserves to be fired but apart from that, it's fine, I'd like to. I've been sewing together a cow's arse all week and I could do with a change of scenery. See you tomorrow at six thirty.'

It was only when she put the phone down that she reflected on how she'd got used to what was actually a pretty weird situation, when you took a step back. Far from being furious that somebody else was stepping in to look after her children, at this moment Marisha didn't seem to have the energy to care. She was obviously coasting until the end of term. Nonetheless, a wave of unease passed through Cassie, what Da used to call a goose walking on your grave. Come on. Was she just looking for something to worry about when everything in reality was fine?

* * *

Only Cici and Con were there when she arrived. Finn stopped her in the hallway.

'Just to let you know, Samantha is expecting her period so she might be a little salty when she gets back. Don't be surprised.'

'Got it, it's a tricky time,' she said, while what was going through her mind was, *Feck that!* Teenagers could have particularly dramatic period symptoms, true. Nonetheless, this smacked of a Samantha Special. She was being granted a pass to hold the family to ransom. How was she getting away with it? Imagine if she'd tried a lark like that with Mam or even Da at fourteen? Cassie had vivid memories of being given two Feminax and a hot-water bottle, and told to lie down and stop moaning.

She slipped into the routine. Cici's homework seemed to consist mostly of drawing pictures of what her summer holidays would be like. Yikes, she thought, here's hoping all the kids had something exciting planned. Con glanced at her neutrally and then continued with his maths, which wasn't unusual for him, and not to be taken personally, she'd recognised.

Cici vanished for a moment and returned with St Teresa, who was kitted out in a dress made entirely of tinfoil, including a tinfoil hat. Cassie knew better than to even crack a smile but there was no doubt the doll had a new and important role.

'It's armour,' she explained gravely. 'She has to protect my daddy.'

'I see . . .'

'Samantha says we have to protect him from you because you're the wicked stepmother.' Cassie was not totally surprised, but something about Cici's innocence made the situation even more upsetting.

'Cici, I'm not trying to take anything away from anyone. St Teresa is very special at protecting the family, and I've no doubt she does, but she doesn't need to protect it from me.'

Cici's round hazel eyes were unsure. 'Is that true?' she whispered.

Cassie felt a surge of fury. What did the teenager think she was doing, manipulating the younger children? And yet, she'd to remind herself, Samantha was technically still a child too.

As though on cue, the buzzer sounded and a minute later Samantha flounced into the hall and flung down her bag, coat, hockey stick and a bottle of Lucozade in a jumbled pile.

'Hi, what's for dinner?' she called breezily.

Feck that, she wasn't going to get away with causing devastation and then pretending it'd nothing to do with her.

'Samantha, have you a moment?'

Cassie followed her into the bedroom that used to be Finn's but was now Samantha's, although there was little evidence she'd actually moved in, apart from an oversized yellow check duvet cover.

'What?'

'I think you know what, Sam. You've been saying rotten things about me to the younger ones and upsetting them.'

Cassie could see her bristling.

'You're not my mother and I can say anything I want to my own little brother and sister.' This was veering way off target; she needed to change tack or she was only going to make things worse.

'Look, Samantha . . .' The girl had exactly the sort of defiant look she could imagine her giving a teacher. 'I know it's tough when your parents split up, and even more so when they meet somebody else. I'm sorry this is how you feel, and in your shoes, I'd have probably felt something similar.'

'Well, you're not me and I don't care what you'd have done at fourteen, so fuck off and leave my family alone. And don't think you can get to my dad behind my back, because he'll always pick me over you.'

Cassie picked up that, underneath, the girl was very unsure of herself, but another part of her recognised that what she said was true. No wonder Marisha could afford to be so magnanimous – she'd somebody far more effective to fight her battles for her. On the other hand, if Samantha thought that Cassie coming into her dad's life was bad, just wait for what was coming down the tracks from her sainted mother.

For the rest of the evening, Cassie kept very quiet, serving the food and helping Cici with her night-time routine. Con still wouldn't meet her eye. She busied herself tidying away the dinner things – because apparently teenagers didn't do chores anymore – but the truth was, she felt like shutting herself in the bathroom and breaking down in tears. Teenager or not, Samantha was old enough to know exactly how to wound an adult but had learned nothing of the complexities of life that might have softened her attack.

Finn arrived back at eleven and Cassie met him in the hallway, already in her jacket.

'Hey, why the big rush, what's wrong?'

Cassie briefly explained to him the conversation with Samantha, who no doubt was straining her ears to the max behind her door.

'And you know what, Finn, maybe she has a point.'

Right now, Cassie felt too exhausted to talk any more about it. Finn looked disturbed, though he certainly didn't jump to her defence with a burst of indignation, but then, had she really expected him to? *Stop me leaving*, a little voice inside her was crying out, *tell me she's wrong*. But nothing happened. Cassie stepped out into the corridor and the door closed behind her like the end of an era.

Chapter 30

Cassie climbed the steps up from her apartment block car park with a leaden feeling in her gut. When crossing the foyer, a flash of movement from outside caught her eye. She did a double take but the view through the code-protected glass door was empty. No, she hadn't imagined it – she glanced back quickly and this time there was no mistaking it. Someone was loitering at the edge of the outer door. Her heart quickened; had the security man seen them? She whipped out her phone to dial the number, when the figure lurched into full view: battered leather jacket, narrow scarf, pork-pie hat . . .

'Gav?'

The shape raised his arm in a gesture reminiscent of Antarctic explorers glimpsing long-awaited rescue.

'Cassie. Let me in.'

His Glasgow accent sounded so familiar. Oh, for fuck's sake. A couple of possibilities occurred to her, but only one stuck: I can't leave him out there. She keyed in the code, and he staggered in the door and theatrically sank to his knees.

'First things first, I don't know what to say,' he proclaimed, which was clearly untrue. 'I owe you an apology. I am . . . beyond sorry.'

She gazed at him in disbelief.

'Get up off the fucking floor, Gav. Sorry for which bit? For dumping me by text after fifteen years? For wasting my life?'

'All of it. I know . . . you're absolutely right.'

There was a pause as he rolled a cigarette with supreme attention.

'You can't smoke that here,' she said. How were they even talking about smoking? This was ludicrous.

'Nice place, by the way. Classy.'

He looked mildly wretched. She sighed. It all felt so familiar. Teflon Gav.

'You'd better come on up.' Oh no, was she going to regret this?

'I can't bear the idea of putting you out . . .' He looked sheepish but definitely not crushed.

'Bit late for that I would've thought.'

They traipsed upstairs, and after closing the door behind them, she took in the incongruous sight of Gavin mooching in Ramona's apartment.

'Gav, you stink. I'm not even going to talk to you till you've had a shower.'

'Honeybee, you read my mind. I came overland, you see.'

'Second on the left, and don't call me that.'

Gav was cocky but he knew when not to push his luck. While he was in there, she contemplated what looked like a hurriedly cobbled-together tangle of his belongings in a holdall on the floor. God only knew where the rest of them were. At the same time, she was having the surreal experience that he'd never actually been gone. They'd never had an actual row; she'd never even received an explanation, apart from that last weird cryptic text about him staying with his mate. And now here he was, back, as though the intervening months had only been a bizarre hallucination. But this was reality. She didn't even know where he'd got her address from.

Don't, she warned herself. *Don't get sucked back into this*. It'd be all too easy. Dear God, after her broadside from Samantha, which was already feeling like light years ago, was there any more that life could hurl at her this evening? She wandered into the kitchen, opened a bottle of Sauvignon from the fridge and poured herself a glass. Gav looked like he'd a few on board already. Of course, it wasn't good to self-medicate in times of stress but, on the other hand, screw that. In the hierarchy of needs, this was the very moment for a glass of wine. She longed to phone Josie but it was after midnight, so whatever happened, she'd have to deal with it herself.

She heard some scuffling from the hallway and a few minutes later Gav appeared, clean-shaven and wearing a T-shirt she didn't recognise and a pair of combat trousers which she did. She poured him a glass and pushed it across the table.

'Mmmm, lovely, cheers. What're you sewing?'

'Cow.'

'Nice. You're looking well, Cass, I'm really proud of you.'

There was always this wonderful ease with Gav, but bloody hell, he really had some neck.

'Honeybee, I hate to ask but I'm starving. You couldn't rustle me up a little pasta carbonara?'

She looked at him in disbelief.

'If that's too much, plain tomato sauce would be lovely.'

This was exactly how he'd evaded every attempt at big conversations. Marriage, kids. And in fairness, maybe she'd let him.

'Gav, what the hell are you doing here? And don't do me the indignity of trying to justify yourself.'

'I should have come ages ago. I realised that as I was crossing the Irish Sea.'

'Really? That soon?'

'Now, now ... I had to come. I realised that when ... OK, I'll explain. Right, Kirsty's parents arrived down from Scotland. Very nice people and all that, but then the three of them started having this ... conversation about combining the wedding and the christening. Can you imagine?'

'*What?* Wait. Stop. Did you say *christening*? She's fucking pregnant as well? I do not believe this.'

She felt herself involuntarily standing up and pacing around the room.

'Oh, right. Did you not know?'

'No, Gavin, I did not. I only knew about the wedding. And that was a big enough shock. How could you do this to me? Turn up here and tell me she's pregnant?'

She felt a huge lump in her chest, making its way upwards.

'But it wasn't planned, honeybee, it just happened. The whole thing.'

'But Gav, things don't just happen. They didn't happen for us. Why was that? Was it me?'

'No, honey, never. Maybe it just wasn't the right time.'

'That's bullshit. It could've been.'

'I know and I never meant to hurt you.'

Which was true; he probably never gave it the slightest thought.

'Cassie, how can I make it up to you?'

'Is that supposed to be a joke? Have you got a time machine so I can go back fifteen years, get out and dump you?'

'Now, now, we had lovely times. I can't let you trash what we had together. They're precious memories. I just don't think I valued you enough.'

'You reckon?' There was such a note of nostalgia in his voice that, in spite of herself, she felt her anger ebbing away.

'Absolutely, we had some special times. Here, give me a hug.'

And that's exactly how Gav tried to work his magic. 'No.'

'Just . . . hear me out . . . This whole wedding palaver is a total mind-fuck, Cassie. All the table plans, and the bride and groom fucking fruit cake . . . It all feels so bloody bourgeois.'

Cassie thought of Mam and Eric. 'That's weddings for you.'

'You understand, Cass. I felt . . . trapped. It wasn't . . . like us. That's why I'm here. I knew you'd get that.'

She could feel herself being reeled in: suddenly, she was the only person who understood him.

'Gav, she's due her baby . . . when?'

'On 20th July, I believe.'

He made that sound like the baby of a distant acquaintance.

'Why did you do it?'

'I mean . . . she was young, gorgeous, I was flattered – what man wouldn't be?'

'Gav, you're an idiot.'

'I realise that. She's twenty years younger, for God's sake. She doesn't know my music, she doesn't get my references, my jokes, and her friends are kids. I mean, they're a pain in the arse. But then . . . obviously, there's the baby.'

When Josie had broken the news about the wedding to her, she'd imagined it as a massive occasion of joy and triumph. Evidently, real life didn't quite match up.

'What'll I do, Cass? You were always my rock, you were always the one with the sense.'

That wasn't saying much, she thought.

'Last Tuesday I made the decision to call off that . . . travesty of a wedding. I emailed everyone, it was awful, I won't lie to you. People were pissed off with me. I just knew I had to get away, go somewhere . . . and I said to myself, where's the safest place? Where's the one place in the world I want to be? And it hit me: *I need to get to Dublin, to Cassie.* And I took a taxi to Euston station.'

I can't explain it, I didn't want to fly, I needed to be on the ground.'

'Oh, Gav.'

'Cass, d'you think there's any hope for us to get back what we had? It was good. I was too stupid to recognise how good.'

She should be feeling vindicated and all sorts of yummy feelings, she reflected, but all she could feel was tired.

'I think once you've cracked an egg, Gav, there's really no way to stick it back together.'

'Leaving you was the biggest mistake of my life.'

'The time to say all of this was last October. Oh, sorry, by my calculation that's right about the time your young lady was getting knocked up. How could you dump me by text, Gav? You didn't even face me.'

'I know. I'm a shit. Hands up, I admit it. I felt claustrophobic. I needed a change. How d'you put that into words?'

'Well, you know what I think? I think you should go straight back to Kirsty and try a bit harder.'

He looked crushed. 'That's it? That's all you've got for me?'

'So fucking what if your music is different? So what if you don't like her friends? You're not living with them, or her family. Man up, for God's sake.'

'Cass, we really had something. You'll always be the one that got away.'

'Funny, that's not quite how I remember it. You can sleep on the sofa tonight, but you'll have to go tomorrow. I can't have you staying here.'

He seemed to accept this. 'You've really come on, Cassie, I'm really proud of you.'

'I'll get you a duvet. And a pillow.'

Lying in bed later, she half-expected the door to creak open – would she have secretly welcomed that? Everything she'd dreamed of in the months after he left. It was all coming to pass. Gav begging for forgiveness, her being *the one* after all. But the baby. He was going to be a father with some young one, and all he wanted to do was run. If it had been herself in that position, he'd have done exactly the same thing. Gav was an emotional magpie. He simply couldn't resist the next shiny thing. Even if she took him back, she would inevitably become part of his past again.

It occurred to her that she'd tried to be the solution to enough people's problems and, always, it seemed at her own expense. She was just drifting off to sleep when a text flashed up on her phone. Finn.

Feel awful 'bout this evening. Need to talk tomorrow

Oh God, she thought, why couldn't everyone just leave her alone to sew her cow costume in peace?

* * *

The next morning was a Saturday. Cassie woke early to a halo of sun pouring in around the curtains. She came to and lay there for a couple of minutes, reconstructing the events of the previous night. Oh no. Gav. Here.

It was 8.50 a.m. She knew Josie and Pal were early risers, so she shot off a text:

> *You round for quick vid call? Won't believe it . . .*

The reply came back instantly.

> *Hell, yes.*

Josie looked puffy and tired, and Cassie felt guilty for hassling her.

'Well, guess who turned up last night? Gav.'

'Shit, no way. Can you believe his pure cheek? We got a garbled email from him. To be honest it looked like a circular to say the wedding was off.'

'And you won't believe what else. She's pregnant.'

'Pregnant? No. You're shitting me. Are you OK?'

Josie took a moment to relay the information to Pal, who she could hear whisking eggs off-camera.

'Pal says he half-expected him to turn up at ours. Look, Cassie, she was going to get pregnant at one stage or another. She's twenty-six. That's what twenty-six-year-olds do. Pal says you dodged a bullet.'

'Tell him thanks.'

Cassie felt a surge of love towards her friends, who were always there when she needed them most.

'I've told him to get his arse back to that poor girl. I know I should be raging but, honestly, with every hour that passes I'm counting my blessings that things worked out the way they did between us.'

Josie laughed. Just then Cassie heard the buzzer. There was only one person it could be. Oh, God, this couldn't be happening . . .

'Jos, I'm so sorry, I've got to go . . . I'll explain later.'

Even as she was ending the call, she could hear Gav's voice answering the intercom. She scrambled into a pair of zebra-print leggings under her T-shirt and made for the bedroom door just in time to see Gav cordially welcoming Finn as a guest at the door, as though he owned the place. She could see the confusion on Finn's face and could only imagine the horror on her own. Gav, however, seemed perfectly relaxed, as though he'd lived there all his life and was entirely expecting Finn. He volunteered to make a pot of coffee that would be very pleasant to drink out on the balcony, given the rare blast of Mediterranean weather. And the weird thing was, unless she kept reminding herself that Gav was wildly spinning his own version of things, she found herself almost being sucked in. Time to take charge.

'Finn, this is Gavin. He turned up unexpectedly late last night.'

'And I was very kindly taken care of, I might add. Nice leggings, by the way.'

Bastard. He was deliberately trying to muddy the waters.

'No, he wasn't,' she broke in.

'Er . . . maybe I should come back later?' Finn was looking as uneasy as she'd ever seen him.

'No, no no, not at all, sit down . . . take a load off,' insisted Gav, exuding largesse.

'Gav, shut up. Finn and I have been seeing each other since January.'

'Well, you little dark horse, you . . .'

'Actually, I've heard a lot about you,' said Finn.

'Well, word does get around.' Gav was in his most ebullient form, but Finn was having none of it.

'It actually seems that you're a bit of an arsehole and I'd say the last thing Cassie needs is you landing in on top of her. So, the best thing you could do right now is not prevail on her good nature any longer and get the fuck out of here.'

Cassie felt a mixture of gratitude and unease.

'Well, excuse me, the last thing I'd want to do is step on any toes . . .'

Finn's face was implacable. 'There's a sailing from Dublin port at two o'clock, you'll be in plenty of time for it.'

Cassie couldn't help feeling a pang of regret. 'Let's have breakfast first, at least.'

Finn glared at her. Oh well, she'd put up with enough from his side.

After they made coffee and warmed the croissants brought by Finn, they sat around a small wrought-iron table on the balcony as Gav lit a roll-up to celebrate the mini-heatwave and leaned back, exhaling smoke as though he owned the place. Viewing Gav through someone else's eyes was actually very enlightening. He was highly persuasive, and that was to someone who'd been on the receiving end of his misdemeanours. No wonder as a naive young woman she'd been bewitched. She felt a wave of sympathy for the kid she'd been, the little piglet in the house of straw – no match for the charming wolf who'd blagged his way in.

Gav was engaging Finn in a conversation about the well-known bands he'd worked with. She had to admit he was very impressive, very good at his job of organising difficult people, often with massive egos, inveigling them to do what was needed. Once you saw past that, it was just him doing his job. For the first time since she'd met him, she didn't feel the lesser one.

Thankfully, by eleven Finn stood up and offered to drive Gav to the boat.

'You're a gentleman, sir. I won't forget it.'

He would, of course – instantly – but that still didn't stop you feeling good when he said it. Standing in the hallway with his miscellaneous baggage assembled about his person and a faint whiff of tragedy in his manner, he hugged Cassie warmly as though they were long-lost friends.

'Maybe the two of you can come over and visit us, when the baby arrives?' he said in all sincerity. Evidently, he'd reimagined his future once again.

An hour later Finn reappeared, looking exasperated.

'Well?'

'Oh, we're best friends. He actually suggested that I buy a return ticket so I could come with him and have a "bit of a hooley" on the boat.'

Cassie burst out laughing. 'That's about the least "you" thing I could ever imagine.'

'I don't know, for a moment I was tempted. A part of me thinks I should do a bit more of it.'

'Now you're scaring me.'

She filled another cafetière, heated some milk, filled two oversized cups and sat down.

'I'm sure you feel like a relaxing coffee after your mercy dash.' She was picking up that he didn't look relaxed at all. 'Actually, there was something I wanted to ask you. Would you like to come to Mam and Eric's wedding as my plus one?'

Finn winced.

'Look, Cassie, I need to talk to you . . .'

There'd been a tension in his manner ever since he'd arrived this morning, she'd just been too distracted to notice.

'I was speaking to Samantha . . . She came in to talk after you left last night.'

This did not sound like good news.

'She's very upset about us. And that's without—'

'Even hearing about Marisha and the baby, I can imagine.'

'The thing is . . . I don't think I can do it to her. She's been through enough. It's not that I want to, believe me.'

A wave of exasperation engulfed Cassie.

'She's manipulating you, forcing you to choose her or me, and you're giving her that power.'

'As a parent, I have to put my kids first. I'm sorry if that's hard for you to understand.'

Ouch.

'Well, fuck you for saying that. You do know it's only Samantha who feels like this? She's competing with me. The younger two were perfectly fine.'

But even as she said the words, she knew she'd already lost the battle. It was obvious some things went way beyond a convincing argument.

'It's not what I want.'

'No, but it's what you're getting, Finn. Maybe I'm delusional, that is entirely possible. But from where I'm standing, this is not good. It's not good for a fourteen-year-old to be given that much power. Whatever she looks like, she's still a kid. I know, I've been a four-teen-year-old girl. I didn't merit being given everything I demanded. Looking back, I know I needed to be pro-tected from some of my own convictions. Not that I'd have taken a blind bit of notice at the time. But, OK, forget about me. Think . . . What about the next per-son who comes along in your life, and the next? Is she going to block everyone? You're going to end up resent-ing her.'

Finn looked uneasy; she could see a twitch in his jaw under the pale, freckled skin.

'I'm not going to be looking for anyone else. Look, I'm so sorry, I saw a future for us. I really did. But that's just how it is, I can't see any other way round it.'

With that, he put down his half-drunk coffee, stood up and left without another word.

Cassie was shell-shocked. It all felt so final. This couldn't be happening.

It seemed that no matter which path she chose, her happiness was doomed.

* * *

'That's bull and you know it.' Josie was eyeballing her as best she could through puffy eyelids. Apparently, the high pollen count was causing a devastating allergy, and because she couldn't take antihistamine, it was running riot and she was blowing her nose constantly.

'Well, that's all I can see in it.'

'He was bullied by his wife, now he's being bullied by his daughter . . . it couldn't be plainer.'

'Samantha called me the wicked stepmother, Josie, and all I ever did was try and help. You know something, that whole stepmother thing is a pile of shite. Most of the time it's just a woman in a bloody difficult situation doing the best she can.'

'Hear, hear. I'm sorry, Cassie. I know you really liked him, but it was just so complicated.'

There was something about Josie talking in the past tense that stung her more than anything.

'If I'd known what was coming, I mightn't have given Gavin the bum's rush so fast. He actually asked me if there was any hope for us, said that he hadn't ever realised how good we'd been—'

'*Stop!* Cass, I can't believe I'm hearing this. No, just *no*.'

'I can't hate him.'

'No one can hate him, he's Gav. That's how he can cajole crews and manage tours all over the world. It still doesn't mean you should get back with him. You're in shock, that's what's wrong. Just don't make any sudden moves.'

'I don't think I'm capable of making any moves right now.'

Josie had to go then to help Pal put up a blind in the baby's room but agreed to chat later in the week. Cassie gazed around the apartment that up to a couple of hours ago had felt full of life and possibilities. Now it was as empty as though the tide had gone out, leaving her like a beached jellyfish drying in the sun.

She sat watching the happy figures bustling up and down Ballsbridge – everyone busy, everyone with somewhere important to be and friends to meet. It was only herself that was so alone, so directionless. She picked up the cow costume, examined it from every angle and then started sewing again from where she'd left off.

Chapter 31

Jack and the Beanstalk was counting down the last few rehearsals to opening night on Thursday. It seemed to have gone backwards from the previous week, though she reminded herself of how that always happened when you tried to put everything together. On the negative side, Rowley and Ahmed still hadn't gotten through their routine without crashing into each other, but on the positive side, the Bondarenko twins fitted perfectly into the cow costume, to their shared satisfaction.

One of the dads had turned out to be a whizz at carpentry and, using his jigsaw, had cut plywood into exactly the shapes needed for all the scenery and was now apparently busy painting them in his garage. She'd assembled all of the costumes from potato sacks, aided by Martin's mum, who was a most obliging woman and an excellent seamstress. Cassie felt a surge of gratitude towards heroic parents.

Trevor had provided his own Spiderman costume for Jack, and Rowley's granda had provided a small stepladder for him to stand on to look tall. The goose would be dressed in an ingenious costume made out of chopped-up old net curtains dyed brown.

In theory, the whole thing should work – the children knew their lines, they'd learned the songs – it was just that when it was all put together, everything fell apart. She really had forgotten that these weren't professionals, they were children, most of whom had never stood on a stage before, apart from Sophie, who had her speech and drama certificates framed on the wall at home and never let anyone forget it.

Cassie's heart sank to see Roger Newcombe sidling in the door to watch a Monday morning rehearsal which was predictably woeful. She could've told him that in advance.

'It's in four days, you do know that?' he muttered darkly.

'It'll be fine,' she chirruped, although right now she would have done anything for someone to reassure her.

Marisha arrived in at eleven, looking a lot more rested than Cassie felt. She couldn't help wondering if part of her improved mood had been the news that Finn had dumped her. Well, Da was very fond of quoting the Chinese philosopher Lao Tzu: 'Care about what other people think and you'll always be their prisoner.'

It wasn't about Marisha or Samantha in the end – it was about Finn, and if he wouldn't stand up for her, did it even matter what anyone else thought? Every time she let in what'd happened, she felt lost, devastated. She hadn't heard a word from him, nothing. It was as though a door had slammed and he was inside with his family, while she was left standing outside in the cold.

* * *

Cassie opened her eyes on Tuesday morning with a jolt of fear. Only three days to go until the mammies and daddies, staff and pupils – not to mention Roger Newcombe – would be in their seats, watching the show. She had to hold her nerve and pull it all together somehow, but everything felt like swirling chaos.

She reminded herself of Olympic athletes who completed the full race in their imagination before they ever set foot on the track. So, she'd to clarify the whole show in her head until it ran like clockwork. She sat on the side of her bed and focused her mind on every move, from the first moment to the last, then went through it, again and again.

After forty-five minutes, she was feeling a lot more confident but was running extremely late so had to scramble into the shower and would have to eat her breakfast at the traffic lights – so far so good.

On the way to work, her phone rang. It was a UK number and her heart leaped.

'Darling, I didn't wake you up, did I? Sorry to phone so early but it's an emergency.'

'Sunita, hi. What . . . what is?'

'Turns out they adored your tape, no surprise there, and they want you to come in for a camera audition.'

'What, where?'

'Well, here of course, London.'

'That's amazing . . .'

'I know, darling, on Thursday at 3 p.m.'

The very day of the show. Oh. My. God.

'Right . . .'

'I'm thrilled for you. Only thing is, there's rather a lot of script here and you'll have to be off-book.'

'How much?'

'Around thirty pages.'

Holy crap. How on earth was she going to learn that much, even without everything else going on?

'Thanks, Sunita, I'll call you back.'

Oh shit, shit, shit. What was she going to do? There was *no way* she could let everybody down. She needed help. Help! There was only one person she could ask.

'Phil? I'm so, so sorry to call you this early.'

'Ah, Cassandra, it's yourself, isn't it a glorious morning?'

Was Philip beyond being fazed by anything? She had the phone on speaker and was in the process of weaving through rush-hour traffic, while trying not to spill her bowl of cereal. She explained the situation, and how if she wasn't there to direct the show, it'd be a disaster, but at the same time, this was the break she'd been waiting for all her life. Even before she'd finished telling him, the solution was clear. She couldn't let down the little faces, the kids who'd already surpassed their own expectations, the people who'd put aside days of their time to help. The parents to whom it meant the world to see their kids step out for their big moment. She was holding a whole community of people's hopes and expectations, however cheesy it sounded.

'I can't go.'

'Now, now, don't panic. You're doing an all-or-nothing on it. I do it myself if I get in a pickle. Don't limit yourself, though – first of all, check whether they can see you the following day. Now, of course, there's always the risk they'll have made up their minds already, but what can you do? If that doesn't work, get back to me.'

She redialled Sunita, who sounded horrified.

'Oh, darling, I don't know. All I can do is ask, but I can't make any promises. They don't usually work around people, you know. You work around them.'

In the past Cassie would have been stressed out of her mind and obsessively waiting for Sunita to call back, but this time, she thought she'd done all she could. *You can't control everything. If it's for you, it'll work out. If not . . .*

The morning crawled by. Rather than focus on the vagaries of the BBC, she decided to stick with what she could control and rehearsed the group songs again, so the kids all sounded reasonably in tune. In the absence of perfection, they'd have to rely on enthusiasm. All of a sudden, a flash of crisis swept over her. Was she out of her mind not to cast this aside and put her career first? How inconsequential was this little show beside a behemoth like the big series? Just then, for no particular reason, words came to her from Da's favourite poem by Patrick Kavanagh: 'Gods make their own importance.'

There was her answer. Thanks, Da.

As soon as break time arrived, she checked her phone messages. Nothing. As the day wore on, her confidence ebbed. She had jumped to an impulsive decision, where she put other people's needs before her own. Again. She tried to block it from her mind and concentrate on the kids. She didn't even care that Marisha was looking smug. Too bloody busy for that.

It was only that evening at six, long after she'd given up checking, that the phone rang. 'Darling, we're very lucky and they can see you on Friday, but you'll have to be there by nine thirty in the morning. Can you do that?'

Could she do that? Oh hell.

She managed to book a 6 a.m. flight into Heathrow Airport, which cost a small fortune but was her only hope of getting there on time.

Next problem was the daunting task of learning what amounted to half an hour of dialogue virtually overnight. She'd use Ramona's trick, she decided, but they'd obviously called people at such short notice to see whether or not they could cope with the pressure.

The next day passed in a blur of trying to watch and encourage the kids, while sewing extra leaves on the beanstalk. They were using the stage for the first time and, as she knew perfectly well would happen, everybody forgot the lines and all the songs, not to mention which side of the stage they were meant to come on from. That would hopefully change once they did a couple of run-throughs and got used to the new space. Dress rehearsals were famously shambolic. Better chaos today than tomorrow.

At the same time as all of this frenetic activity, she was running the audition lines in her head, scene by scene. Astonishingly, she was capable of more than she would've thought possible. Phil's words came back to her: 'Don't limit yourself.'

Finally, two thirty came around.

'Right, everybody, great work and a big well done! Leave your props and costumes in place, with your names on them, and I'll see you all tomorrow.'

* * *

That evening she packed her case for London. She'd be staying with Josie and Pal while there, which promised to be a delicious break after all the madness. Thank God the character she was auditioning for was the opposite of a glamour puss; at least that took the pressure off her to look perfect, considering she was starting out from home at four in the morning. What she needed now was a long soak in the bath to relax. Standing in the spacious, dark-green marble bathroom, watching hot water from the big tap fill the bath, she relaxed. In that moment, it all fell apart. All of it: the little show, the big audition – it was all so pointless. She found herself sitting on the edge of the bath, sobbing into a towel.

There was no point in kidding herself. Her life with Finn was over – his awkwardness, his solidity, the way strands of hair flopped forward onto his face. His long, lean body. He was gone from her. Maybe she could've done more, or said less? Been less eager to please? What else could she have done to create a different outcome? Nothing. It was beyond her control. From the emptiness inside, a sob rose up, muffled by the gushing tap. It was all lost . . . lost. After a long cry, she blew her nose on a strip of loo paper and climbed gingerly into the bath.

There was something very comforting about the deep warm water that seeped into every crevice, enveloping her like a fleecy blanket. The many bubbles popped gradually, leaving bald patches on the surface. The water was gradually growing cold. There was only one way to go: forward.

Chapter 32

'Sorry, you're . . . what?'

The round freckled face gazed up at her.

'I'm not going to be able to be in the show tonight.'

'Rowley, what are you talking about? Without you there is no show. Do your parents not realise that?'

'No, see, the thing is, me granda has got sick and me ma is doing a wedding at her job, and somebody has to be there to look after him, in case his oxygen levels get too low. 'Cause then he could die.'

Oh, for God's sake. She could feel the whole edifice wobbling like when you slide the last Jenga block out from the bottom . . .

'Don't worry, Rowley, that's quite understandable, these things happen. Martin knows the lines and can easily step into your part,' Marisha purred.

Cassie was horrified. Poor Martin had forgotten the few lines he ever knew. He was prepared to dress in the green costume his mother had made, and his only job was to give people a leg up onto a raised platform, which was supposed to be in the clouds. More than that, he couldn't do it: he couldn't sing, he wasn't funny, he'd be a disaster. But Marisha really didn't seem to care about the impact this would have on him.

Cassie knew some people would say she was being fanatical, and illnesses happened – or maybe it was the soothing tone of Marisha's voice, exuding satisfaction, that she couldn't stomach, but something had to be done.

Break time came and, without a word, she slipped out and made her way to the office. To her relief, there was no sign of Roger Newcombe. Helen, the secretary, was sitting listlessly on the swivel chair, which was patched with masking tape, dunking a custard cream in her coffee. She jumped guiltily when she saw Cassie.

'Helen, I need your help, it's an emergency,' she hissed. She explained the situation and how she needed Rowley's mam's phone number; at the prospect of a bit of intrigue, the secretary looked more energised than Cassie had ever seen her. Strictly speaking, Cassie explained, this was an educational call for a student's benefit. She copied down the number and address, and slipped out to her car. It was a long shot, but she was past caring.

'Mrs Adams? I'm so sorry to bother you. This is Cassie, Rowley's substitute teacher, I don't believe we've met. The thing is, I don't know if you're aware of this or not, but your son is an extremely talented performer,' Cassie began.

In that moment, Rowley's mam's voice rose an octave. 'That's what I always said. I've *seen* that in him as a little tot.'

'Mrs Adams, if he doesn't take his place on this show, it could alter the whole course of his life.'

She was giving it welly but if there was ever a time to speak up, it was now.

'I know, love . . . but what am I to do? I have to work. My father can't be left alone.'

'We'll collect him.'

'What?'

'I'm sure your father would love to see his grandson on stage. We'll pick him up with his wheelchair before the show and pop him in the front row. He'll have the best seat in the house. I give you my word I'll keep an eye on him myself to make sure he's all right and, afterwards, I'll drop them both home.'

The voice sounded quite emotional. 'You'd do that for us?'

'It'd be my pleasure.'

'You really think he's that good?'

'Mrs Adams, I know it. He's a natural. I only wish you were there to see him.'

'His daddy passed away three years ago and since then it's been hard.'

She could hear the tough facade cracking.

'I'm so sorry to hear that and I understand.'

'But if you'd do that for my son . . . that'd mean the world to me.'

And so, it was settled. Rowley would go home as usual, and Cassie would pick him and his granda up at six.

* * *

Marisha wasn't impressed. She'd been busy rustling together a costume made out of several sacks tied with a curtain cord for Martin, who looked wretched.

'You've just violated GDPR with that call. This is a disciplinary offence. I hope you realise that.'

She'd never come closer to telling Marisha to fuck off. Don't give her the ammunition, she reminded herself.

That lunchtime the staffroom was buzzing. A second microwave had been purchased following a whip-round and there was intense controversy around who'd contributed and who hadn't, and therefore wasn't entitled to use it.

Further down the pecking order was gossip about tonight's show. This included opinions ranging from 'Well, at least that racket will be over' to 'Isn't it great that such a young class are doing something so ambitious? Let's hope they don't fall flat on their faces.'

Nonetheless, they were all going to turn up to support. Babs and Denise had organised their Fifth and Sixth Classes to help out and serve refreshments.

An intermittent drilling sound was coming from the assembly hall as the carpenter dad had taken a day off work from his job as a kitchen fitter to assemble the set, which wasn't improving the headaches in the staffroom.

* * *

Back at her flat after school, Cassie had just about managed to jump in the shower and wash her hair, and was wrapping herself in towels, when her phone buzzed a notification. Her heart leaped when she saw it was Finn.

> *Missing you. Hoping tonight is as good as you deserve. xxx*

What she deserved? What did anyone deserve?

> *Thank you. I hope so too* ☺ *xxx*

She hesitated about adding 'missing you' but then thought, *What's the point?*

It said so much less than she felt, but maybe that was just as well. She really didn't have the energy for any extra drama today.

She chose a dark floral-patterned maxi dress to go with her green suede Doc Martens and styled her hair half-up, half-down. Not bad, she thought, finishing off her makeup with a mulberry shade of lipstick, even if tonight's not all about me.

* * *

At a quarter to six she pulled up to Rowley Adams's home, a battered-looking terraced house in front of a scraggy green space where children were playing. His mother emerged through the door, a broad-shouldered grey-haired woman wearing what looked like a professional waitress outfit under her anorak. She looked like someone who, under other circumstances, could be formidable, but underneath you could sense the weariness. She waved at Cassie.

'Ah, there you are, I'm off to work. I'm after giving the two of them their tea. My father has his oxygen canister and the mask if, God forbid, he needs it. Rowley will show you everything. God love him, he's up to ninety about tonight.'

She stopped by Cassie's car. 'And thanks, for what you've done for Rowley, for all of us. Not everyone thinks like you. I won't forget it.'

'Thank *you* for trusting me. I'm only sorry you won't be there.'

'Me too, but sure, the money won't earn itself.'

With that, she bustled off towards a desolate-looking bus stop in the distance as Cassie went through the open front door to have Granda's care explained to her by his ten-year-old grandson.

Not a bother to Rowley. The wheelchair was set up with Granda Anthony installed in it, a blanket round his knees, the oxygen canister stored underneath.

'I love a show,' he wheezily explained. 'I used to manage the cabarets on the cruises.'

Cassie glanced around the house. It was spotlessly clean but everything looked old: the sofas, the TV, the wallpaper – it looked like no money had been spent on anything in years. They were just living day-to-day, she reflected guiltily. Some of us don't know we're alive.

*　*　*

The school hall was buzzing when they arrived. Mr Daly, the groundsman, had volunteered as technician and was up on his tallest ladder focusing the lights, based on where everyone would hopefully stand, if nothing went disastrously wrong.

Class 4B were getting into their costumes, aided by Fifth- and Sixth-Class girls. Cassie swung into action. She set up the mirrors and her makeup box, and distributed sponges and makeup for the oldest, most confident girls and one absolute whizz of a boy to do their bases. The next hour felt like ten minutes as they got the children ready for their characters – and, she was delighted to observe, they all looked very distinctive. The children were wild with excitement and nerves. A few of the younger ones were overwhelmed and burst into tears, while a bucket had to be grabbed for someone who was sick. Cassie had a supply of tissues and allocated the older children, who were delighted with their responsibility, to look after them. Granda was already in place with a mug of tea, shouting genially up to Mr Daly as best he could, despite the oxygen cannula. Roger Newcombe was hovering around nervously as Mr Daly proceeded to run through the sound cues with each child. Whether any of these would materialise at the right volume or in the right order on the night was anybody's guess.

There was no sign of Marisha. Surely she wasn't going to boycott the event?

From seven thirty onwards they could hear mammies, daddies, siblings, other pupils and a very decent showing of teachers, some of whom had taken the opportunity to make a night of it and head to the pub before the show.

'I can hear my daddy's laugh,' squeaked one little villager. Inevitably, at ten to eight, everyone needed the loo all at once.

At five to eight there was a ripple in the atmosphere: through a crack in the curtains, Cassie could see Marisha approaching up the centre aisle. She was dressed in a long purple dress, sailing through the audience, smiling graciously to left and right as parents reached out to shake her hand. Cassie practically laughed. There really were two ways of looking at the world: you did the work or you looked for the credit. Sometimes they coincided; mostly they didn't, but right now she couldn't give a hoot.

At 8 p.m. she gave the 'go' signal to Mr Daly on the walkie-talkie and the opening music started. A huge cheer rose up from the audience. Oh help, Cassie thought, that's really going to throw them. Not a bit of it. This was not Sophie's first show, not by a long shot – the girl waited for the applause to die away then surfed the wave, full of Celtic tragedy: 'The Lord save us, Jack, but there's not a red penny left between us and the poorhouse . . . There's nothing for us in this world but *hunger* and *desolation* and *death*.'

The Bondarenko twins stumbled on in the cow costume, which didn't look too bad, but they lost their coordination and tottered around a bit, causing hilarity from the children in the audience, not to mention the back row of slightly blotto teachers.

The play continued more-or-less as rehearsed, which was a miracle in itself. Trevor as Jack delighted the kids with his homage to Spiderman; Sophie was excellent as the mother and Cassie could hear lots of appreciative whispers of 'She's very good, isn't she?' to her parents' pride.

Jack came on in one scene, lamenting what a terrible day it'd been and how he'd been scammed out of his cow by a conman. In despair, he threw a handful of jelly beans out the window. At this point Mr Daly managed to dim most of the lights apart from one bulb, which blazed away merrily, in spite of his efforts.

Martin, as the beanstalk, had been lying behind a plywood bush since before the show, and was starting to get bored and fidget, but thankfully he remembered his cue and scrabbled to his feet to the wonderment of the smallest children.

'Miracle-Gro!' roared Babs from the back to the whole row's amusement. Oh hell, once hecklers got going, they'd only encourage each other. She spotted Roger Newcombe sniggering behind his hand. Trevor as Jack appeared in his Spiderman pyjamas to climb the beanstalk, which everyone loved.

'This is lit!' he announced at the sight of the beanstalk. 'We've got to make a TikTok video.'

Again, Mr Daly had to hit a music cue, which was correct, except deafeningly loud. After everyone yelled, he pulled it back down to a level where the reedy voices of the few kids who actually knew all the words could be heard. The rest were clearly miming nervously. They shuffled through a few hip-hop moves, at which point Jack announced that he'd got half a million likes already. Which seemed unlikely, even to the Junior Infants.

Jack got a leg up from Martin to the upper level, which was supposed to be the castle in the sky, and hid himself in a cupboard before Rowley, the giant, made his entrance, dressed in a silver Elvis suit complete with cloak.

'You're not a giant!!'

'Oh, yes I am!' he replied, setting up his stepladder. 'D'ye like me new ladder? I'm after nickin' it from Woodie's,' he began. 'I'd a terrible job hidin' it under me jumper. I had to nick a sunlounger to hide it. But, listen, do yez ever get bored? I do get very bored up here in the clouds, and the Wi-Fi's no good, even with me hotspot on, so I have to play me guitar. Do yez want to hear it?'

There was a chorus of 'Yeaaaah,' and a few rogue 'No's from the wits in the audience.

'Right then, Ahmed, you're on!' he yelled.

Ahmed and his electric guitar struggled to make their entrance through an unfeasibly narrow door, and were accompanied by a wince-inducing splintering sound. Cassie gritted her teeth but, mercifully, the scenery wall held.

'Hit it, Mr Daly . . .'

Mr Daly was clearly starting to enjoy the celebrity status his job was affording him and responded with a thumbs up.

For the first time ever the two boys tore through their routine without a single mistake, Ahmed daring to play his four chords with panache and Rowley rocking the vocals like someone four times his age. The audience were on their feet, dancing. Granda, on the verge of leaping out of his wheelchair, had his fist in the air. Cassie was horrified. If he collapsed, she'd be totally responsible.

The goose waddled on and announced she laid Gold American Express cards.

'Would she lay one for me?' yelled Babs from the back to hoots of laughter.

At the end, just as Jack was straining to cut down the tree, a group of younger boys and girls came out with placards, chanting 'Save the beanstalk!' and 'We don't want a has-bean-stalk!' and tied a red ribbon around Martin. Then the people and the giant agreed to share the world together, so long as he could piggyback on their Wi-Fi, and they all started singing the old Three Dog Night rock anthem 'Joy to the World', with new words to include the beanstalk. The whole audience were on their feet with their arms in the air, swaying in unison.

Finally, the show came to a close with Sophie tearfully declaring how, now she had a Gold American Express card, they'd no longer be poor and destitute and she could shop online for the rest of her life.

Rowley's granda was accepting compliments from all around and basking in reflected glory. Ahmed's parents were glowing with pride at their son's guitar playing after a year of lessons. Sophie's parents quietly thanked Cassie, before loudly praising Marisha. But Cassie knew that, if you hadn't done the work, then compliments felt meaningless. Something had changed for her, she realised: the kids' success was her success. They'd way surpassed their own expectations, and that meant everything.

* * *

By 11 p.m., Rowley and Granda were delivered back home, and between herself and Rowley they lifted the frail body out of his wheelchair and onto the sofa. He'd be able to boast that he was at Rowley's first gig, he announced. Though, looking at Granda, with his ancient veined hands clutching his blanket, Cassie was painfully aware that he mightn't see too many more.

By midnight she finally hauled herself through the door of the apartment, which felt deafeningly quiet after the mayhem of the show. For an instant she felt the compulsion to text Finn and tell him how the show had been a blast, that the kids had been a revelation, but she realised, even before the thought had fully formed, that it was pointless. As she was staring at her phone, a notification buzzed and Philip's name flashed up. It was a text from him:

> *I heard it was a triumph, big congrats!*

Phil had obviously heard all the gossip from his pal Roger. She smiled.

TKS. *What a rollercoaster! Airport 4.45 a.m. tomorrow . . . Today!*

You'll do it. Keep it simple. ☺

As she collapsed into bed, it registered briefly in her overstuffed brain that Philip had never once let her down.

Chapter 33

She was completely disorientated when the alarm went off. It was still pitch-dark and all she could remember was that she had to get moving. After a thirty-second shower, she gradually came to and was halfway through pulling on her clothes when her phone buzzed to say the taxi was at the door. It was 4.10 a.m. A flash of panic ran through her. Check everything: passport, money, phone, earphones, scripts. Anything else was replaceable.

Five minutes later she found herself and her little case pinned against the back seat of the taxi, speeding towards the airport in the pre-dawn light. She was conscious of the exhaustion dragging at her limbs, but adrenalin would have to substitute for her meagre hours of sleep. She glanced down at her outfit – scraggy jeans, runners, T-shirt – over which she'd thrown a lightweight trench coat which served in the early-morning chill but was liable to become roasting hot in the heatwave of central London.

Once at the airport and through to the departure gate, she'd settled herself into a corner of the café beside a plate-glass wall through which she gazed at the sun rising over a runway which shone with a pinky silver light.

She'd ordered scrambled eggs and fresh orange juice, with the idea that high-protein, slow-release energy food was her wisest choice. Glancing around her, all she could see were dazed-looking people in business clothes sipping Starbucks and flicking on laptops. Along the walls lounged long-haul travellers in sandals and runners, with rucksacks or massive cases, making connecting flights, chugging energy drinks or the occasional pint of beer – good luck with that, she thought.

The big digital clock on the wall showed 5.37 a.m. Oh God, what if her flight was delayed or, even worse, cancelled? There were just so many stages where all of this could go horribly wrong. She needed everything to run like clockwork to arrive at the studios on time but, realistically, what were the chances of that? Panicked, she swung around, looking for someone official to ask, though nobody else seemed the least bit bothered. Just then she heard her flight being called and felt her body sag with relief.

Once settled into her seat on the flight, she felt like one of those children on a mechanical ride, frantically rocking, trying to make it work without putting any money in the slot. Again, nobody around her seemed overly fussed that they were running a few minutes late. Cassie, she told herself, you're stressing, you'll only burn yourself out. She put in her earphones, switched on her lines loop, and lay back in the seat and waited for the familiar feeling of taxiing down the runway, the pause, turn, the moment of held breath, and then the roar from the engines.

'We're up,' cheered the lady in a pink flowery dress in the seat beside her to her husband, who looked slightly ill.

Hallelujah, they were on their way.

* * *

Heathrow was packed and sweltering.

Cassie elbowed her way to the front of the queue to get off the plane as politely she possibly could, without actually trampling over old ladies, and then made for the terminal, scuttling along, passing everyone on the travelator, excusing herself and trying not to run over their feet with the wheels of her case. Her watch was already showing ten past eight . . . Oh God, this was getting tight. How could time just vanish like this, when it looked on paper as though she should have oceans of it?

She sweated through passport control then burst through the sliding glass doors into the arrivals hall, oblivious to the bored-looking people standing around, holding name signs. She glanced around wildly and spotted the sign for taxis. Oh no, imagine if there was a massive queue or even a Tube strike? Could easily happen. Nightmare. What if she'd made it this far, only to be hit by one of an infinite number of obstacles? She rushed out the exit in a panic and almost wept with relief to see the row of trusty taxis lined up like well-trained black bears. She waved at the first one, who nodded to her. She climbed in, basking in that familiar sense of safety as the door slammed behind her.

'Elstree Studios, please, how long should that take?'
she gabbled.

The cabbie brightened up at that. ''Bout forty-five
minutes, give or take. You in a hurry, then?'

She burst out about her audition and how she absolutely had to make it in time for nine thirty. He pulled
away steadily.

'Should make that, no problem, barring accidents,' he
remarked sanguinely.

'Don't mention that word, please.'

She was aware of her hands leaving sweaty prints on
the screen as she scrolled through the contacts on her
phone.

'Sunita?'

'Darling, where are you?'

'I'm in a taxi heading for Elstree.'

'Fabulous, well done you.'

'The only thing is, Sunita, the place is massive – how
on earth am I going to find *Wentworth Way*?'

'Don't worry, I'll phone through and let them know
you're on your way—'

'Not a bother,' volunteered the cabbie cheerfully.
'I know where it is. I'm in and out of there all the time.'

'Really?' said Cassie. 'And there was me, thinking I
was the only person ever to have to find my way there.'

He laughed at this and suddenly it all made sense. There
was a whole world going on around her and, no, she wasn't
the only person in it to have done this. Just calm down.

A few moments later, her phone buzzed. 'Hi, this is
Judy, I'm PA on *Wentworth Way*. Just head for the low

office buildings beside the lot and I'll be looking out for you.'

She felt a surge of gratitude towards this Judy, even though she didn't know her from a hole in the wall.

Finally, they pulled up to the big gate, and in front of her was the original building with the words 'Elstree Studios' printed across it in massive letters. Her cabbie seemed to know exactly where he was going and to be enjoying pointing out the various sights to her.

'That's where the *Big Brother* house was, that's the studio where they shot *Star Wars* . . .' Cassie wasn't capable of focusing on any of this, but nodded politely. He swung round a corner and pulled up to an unprepossessing office building outside of which a blonde girl in jeans, with a lanyard round her neck and a clipboard, was waiting. Judy. Oh. My. God. She'd one hundred per cent made it with exactly twenty-five minutes to spare. Judy welcomed her but seemed quite businesslike. As far as she was concerned, this was just an actor turning up for a reading, not a pioneer who'd toiled from the far reaches of the Earth, against all the odds, to reach the impossible dream.

She was shown into a smallish green room with a sofa and a TV, and for the first moment since her alarm had gone off that morning, she allowed herself a minute to exhale. A young runner stuck his head around the door. 'Can I get you a coffee? Did you have far to come?' he enquired breezily.

'A coffee would be fabulous.' She smiled with the sort of gratitude people normally reserve for emergency medical personnel.

She nipped to the loo, where she caught sight of herself in the mirror and realised with a shock that every screed of makeup she'd put on at home had worn off long ago and, in fact, her face looked as bald as a newborn gerbil. She reapplied eyeliner but kept her lip gloss minimal and mussed up her hair. All in all, she looked just about the right level of dishevelled.

Perched on the edge of the sofa, sipping her coffee and leafing through her scenes, she realised the lines felt familiar . . . really familiar, she actually knew them. She resolved to buy Ramona a fabulous gift on the way home for that golden tip. She replayed in her head what Philip had said, *keep it simple*, when Judy appeared at the door.

'Would you like to come in now, Cassie?'

Her heart jolted but she deliberately took a breath and released it slowly as she followed behind the PA.

The audition room turned out to be an office with a grey space set up for filming. She picked up from their energy that they were in a hurry but allowed herself to let it go. That wasn't her concern; meanwhile, the director, Alan, explained to her that they couldn't use any of the sets because they were constantly being used for filming. It was a machine that never stopped needing to be fed, he said with a rueful laugh.

Polly, the casting director, explained that they were going to film four scenes with her.

They really didn't seem overly concerned about what acting jobs she'd been doing lately; thankfully, they seemed overwhelmingly focused on what she could do right now. Alan smiled a businesslike smile and asked if she was ready to begin her audition. This was exactly the moment where, in the past, she'd always come unstuck. She'd be fine up to that point, but then, unbidden, nerves would attack from nowhere, she'd freeze and find herself overcome with self-consciousness. She'd have begun judging herself, running a self-critical inner monologue while trying to mind-read what the casting people were thinking about her. None of which resulted in a positive outcome. Ever.

This time she felt none of that. Something had changed. Between then and now, that fear seemed to have washed away. She felt free, calm and focused. All the stress of the journey melted away and she simply stepped into the character. She sensed her feelings intuitively, responding naturally and truthfully to her cues. After she finished, there was a long pause.

'That was great. Thank you,' said Alan with a look of relief.

She realised they needed her to be good, just as much as she did.

'Thanks, Cassie, we'll be in touch,' said Polly warmly.

They all looked pleased, and even though the glances between them were unreadable, she didn't focus on that. Again, that was their business, not hers. She shook hands with them and walked out the door into the blinding sunshine.

* * *

Cassie felt lighter than air as she towed her little case along the path, out past the historic studios, feeling free to fully notice them for the first time. She walked the fifteen minutes to Elstree and Borehamwood station in the glorious morning. It was only ten thirty and already she'd accomplished the impossible. She bought her ticket and found a bench beside a few older people waiting for the train to St Pancras, taking their time. She'd done her best, her absolute best. She hadn't dried on her lines at any stage, which was a miracle in itself. She wasn't kicking herself for going over the top or for holding back. Her phone buzzed.

'Darling, how did it go?'

'Great. It went great, actually, Sunita.'

'Oh, well done . . . that was the one to get right, wasn't it? Well, let's wait and see.'

She could hear the genuine excitement in Sunita's voice. 'Let's hope our Bea's up there keeping an eye out for you. Bye, darling.'

What about Finn? she wondered, she felt the urge to text him . . . but he hadn't texted to see how her audition went or to wish her luck. Of course, she remembered, he didn't even know about it. So much had happened in the last few days. She'd been so busy, it hadn't fully registered. That such a huge thing had happened in her life without him knowing seemed to open up a yawning gap between them. There was Time Before the break-up and Time After.

Settled on an inside seat, she leaned against the window and sank into a daze. The surge of adrenalin that'd carried her this far was starting to drain away, and for the first time since she'd arrived in London, she began to feel her own exhaustion. It was early, but already the day felt endless. She was moving into that speedy, jet-lagged state where she couldn't trust her own judgement. The best thing she could possibly do was nothing.

Wait until she got to Josie's, where she could reality-check everything, and in the meantime avoid any sudden moves that would screw up her life.

Chapter 34

At last, feeling she could barely walk another step, she trailed up to Pal and Josie's door and rang the bell. She heard the clumping of somebody coming down the wooden stairs quite slowly.

Josie opened the door, looking the same, but different. It was one thing seeing her friend in two dimensions, but Cassie found the physicality of Josie heavily pregnant quite overwhelming.

'You're here!'

'I'm here.'

'Oh my God, look at me, I'm the size of a house.'

'You look amazing.'

The two hugged as best they could. Josie's face was fuller than usual but her eyes sparkled and her smile was as warm as ever.

Seated at the kitchen table, tucking into a slice of carrot cake and a mug of java, Cassie gazed around her friend's so-familiar apartment which, not unlike Josie herself, looked the same, but different. The little painted yellow chest of drawers was wedged in the hallway, waiting to be filled with tiny vests and socks and Babygros, while through a doorway, she could see the second bedroom painted a dove grey and with stencilled little white clouds. This was now a family home. Six months ago, she reflected, that would've made her sad, but no longer was she feeling like life was passing her by; instead, she was feeling, well, that she was up to her neck in it, whatever happened. There was only so much you could control, and that was a fact.

'We got an email last week. Gav's wedding's back on. You won't believe this, but he blamed the whole thing on an "administrative error"!'

The two women rocked with laughter at the sheer neck of it.

'You know, when he turned up in the middle of the night, he asked me to make him a carbonara.'

That set them off again.

'I don't know why I'm laughing, Josie. If I didn't, I'd be bawling.'

'Wow, Cass, you've come a long way.'

'Thanks.'

'So . . . what about Finn?'

'You know, I asked him to Mam's wedding but . . . It felt like Gav all over again.'

Josie's face was concerned. 'And his kids?'

Cassie shrugged and tried to explain in a garbled way what'd happened: about Samantha's rage, about Marisha, about how he felt he'd no choice but to finish with her and how she still felt constantly on the verge of texting him every time something good happened, or something bad. And how she was still in love with him. It was only as she described the events to Josie that she had time to really hear them herself. Despite the morning's euphoria, a bleakness crept over her.

'Oh, sweetie, I'm so sorry. He sounds . . . how can I put it? In a difficult position, but a bit . . .'

'What? Please tell me.'

'Mmm. He's lovely . . . He's just a bit . . . slippery, like mercury,' said Josie.

'Slippery?'

'But I mean it in a nice way. Look, none of us are perfect, we're all something, for God's sake.' Josie was trying to backtrack on the shot that had accidentally hit home.

Cassie nodded. 'He could've stood up for me a bit more, but then, what do I know? I'm not a mum.'

The words hung in the air.

'I'm so glad to be here, Jos.'

'Me too, sweetie, I've really missed you.' She rubbed her round stomach protectively. Babies or no babies, they would always be friends. Of that, Cassie was sure.

That evening the three of them cooked a meal together. As Cassie chopped a salad and crushed garlic, while sipping a glass of wine, she was reminded of the old days. Josie was long past morning sickness but still gagged at the smell of anything too strong.

'I can't wait for this sprog to land,' said Pal. 'I haven't cooked a decent curry in months.' He winked at Josie, who would've playfully kicked him in the bum if she hadn't been liable to tip over. This was how it should be, thought Cassie sadly: two equal partners in it together, not snatched meetings here and there, and compromised loyalties. But Jos was right earlier, and no situation was perfect, second families most of all.

'Hundred per cent, Pal, get the priorities right.' Cassie laughed.

God, she'd missed these sessions. They sat at the old pine table and made their way through a mountain of fish pie and salad – or at least Pal did, who no amount of food seemed to fill. Cassie felt like she'd run a marathon and tucked in enthusiastically.

'So, how did it go?'

'Oh, Pal, don't ask her. You know that's like asking someone to read the future from, like, a leftover hamburger.'

'What?'

'People claim they can do that. I've seen it on TV.'

'From a hamburger? What people? That's the most irrational thing I've ever heard—'

'Just people.'

'The art of divination. It used to be cow entrails in ancient Rome,' said Cassie helpfully.

'Please, I'm eating.'

'You started it.'

'You never know with castings, it all depends on who else went for it,' said Josie.

'Come on, give me your glass, Cass. I've been on fizzy water in sympathy with preggers here. Let's have a toast just in case you get the part.'

The three of them toasted everything that had happened, hadn't happened and might yet happen, if they were lucky. Cassie felt a pang of melancholy that here was one of those rare snapshot moments when everything comes together on a silly, random night.

Pal was all in for a quick game of Scrabble, when Cassie felt tiredness wash over her, as though her battery had just died.

'It's only a quarter past nine but I'm done.'

'Thank God I'm finally not the only one saying that,' said Josie.

Between them they made up the sofa bed in the spare room and she flopped down, every fibre of her body collapsing with relief and exhaustion. *What a day*, her mind began, but something bigger, darker, warmer enveloped her and that was the last thing she remembered.

* * *

'Smashed avocado on toast with crispy bacon and possibly a sausage?'

Pal's narrow face appeared around the door above an apron with a Tarzan body printed on it. It took her a moment of bewilderment before she remembered where she was.

'Oooh, yeah, great, just give me a minute.'

She did love that about Pal, his Labrador-like enthusiasm and excellent cooking skills. His head disappeared and as she sat up in bed, her head swam. Oh God no, she wasn't going to be sick, was she? Dangling her feet on the side of the bed for a few minutes, the wobble steadied. She shuffled into the kitchen to be met by Josie in her oversized T-shirt and leggings and could see from the back that Pal was naked under the apron, apart from boxer shorts, a concession to having a guest.

'Wow, Pal, you covered your bum, I'm honoured. Somebody really important must be visiting.'

He grinned at her and, without asking, filled a mug of coffee and pushed it towards her. Her stomach heaved.

'I'm sorry, I don't think I'm going to be able to manage this. By the way, did we get royally rat-arsed last night?'

'No, sweetie, it must be yesterday catching up with you, that's all,' said Josie.

'Oh well, all the more for me,' declared Pal, piling up a plate.

Cassie wasn't sure exactly what she felt like eating and wandered over to the fridge for a mooch. It was only after she sat down that she noticed the look on Josie's face.

'Cassie . . .'

Only then did she register what she was holding: a strawberry Actimel. Their eyes met.

'Are you late?'

'No. I'm only due this . . . No, wait, it must've been . . . last weekend. Oh shit.'

'Pal, babe, as soon as you've got through that lot, we're going to need you to do a run . . . to the pharmacy.'

* * *

'Is it showing yet?' shouted Josie through the bathroom door. Cassie was sitting on the loo, leaning forward on her elbows and staring at the white plastic stick in her hand.

'Yes.'

'Great, well open the door, then.'

'No, I mean it's a *yes*.'

From outside the door, she could hear Josie scream, Pal saying something and then him screaming too. She unlocked the door and they both burst in and jumped on her.

'Oh my God, oh my God. I know when it was. It must have been after that sozzled baby shower.'

'OK, OK, everybody calm down,' said Josie, looking anything but calm. 'Cass, you were meant to be here today, this was meant to happen.'

Cassie nodded dumbly. Apart from feeling as seedy as she could ever remember, her life was now in free-fall, totally unrecognisable. She looked at Josie, who was struggling to look confident.

'What am I going to do?'

'You're going to do . . . nothing right now. Have a nice shower and we'll let the dust settle, then we'll see.'

Which sounded like something she could manage. Just about.

They all sat in the sitting room, Cassie in a pair of jeans that already felt constricting.

'I don't understand, Jos, how can you not feel pregnant one day and then, the next . . .'

'I don't know, that's just how it is. I was the same.'

On the one hand, this was amazing, beyond belief; on the other, she wasn't naive enough to think that there wasn't a fair chance something could go wrong, especially at her age. In that case, she thought, all the more reason to savour every moment of being pregnant, as this might be the only chance she'd get.

'Should I tell Finn?' She already knew the answer.

'Do you want to?'

'Yes. But d'you think it'll seem manipulative?'

'Pal, if it was you, would you feel manipulated?' said Josie.

'What? You're asking me to imagine something I haven't done, as though I was somebody else. I don't freaking know.'

'That's such a guy thing to say. Cass, I mean, d'you feel what happened was a mistake?'

'God no, it was a really fun time. I just thought we were being careful . . . Who am I kidding? We totally weren't being careful.'

'Well, at least it's nice to think this baby had a happy conception.'

They both laughed ruefully.

'That'll sort everything.'

'You know what I think? Do nothing for the next couple of weeks, then decide. It's all going to be OK. I have a feeling.'

'Thanks, Jos,' said Cassie, without a hint of certainty.

* * *

The following day, before Cassie set off for Heathrow, she felt a wave of unease. As long as she'd been with Pal and Josie, she'd felt safe and understood, but now, heading out into a world that mightn't be so kind, she was overcome with panic.

'You guys, you've been so amazing. I'd be nothing without you. And your baby's going to be amazing too.'

'We love you, Cass, we're always here for you, no matter what,' said Josie, hugging her as best she could.

Outside, the street was full of people in fashionable clothes; the weather was cloudy but still sweltering, and the sky dark with a yellowish tinge. Just then an eerie violet flash lit up the sky, followed by an earth-shaking crash, and the first giant drops of rain began to fall. Was this a portent of things to come? Stuff and nonsense, she thought, rushing for the shelter of a shop awning as huge drops of rain plopped down on top of her.

Chapter 35

Sitting on the Aircoach, she scanned her messages.
Mam:

> Hi, hope you'd a super time.

Crikey, if only she knew.
Ramona:

> Hey, ya, be back at the end of this week, or maybe the next. Still China time. Awesome trip.

Nothing from Finn.

She tried to stifle her disappointment by shoving the phone in her bag and looking out the window at the all-too-familiar scenery, but there was nothing familiar about it anymore. This time she was looking at it as a pregnant woman. The world was transformed. She was carrying this huge secret but had no one to share it with.

What was it about late Sunday afternoon that was so bloody depressing?

There was nobody she felt like contacting, nothing else to do when she got in, so Cassie climbed into bed while the starling colony still chattered away while holding what sounded like a birdie barbecue in the tree outside. Tears rolled down her face. She should feel euphoric, lucky, but right now all she could feel was scared and very, very lonely.

* * *

She had discovered that anything with a high-fat content seemed to help her morning sickness so the next morning she grabbed a strawberry milkshake and a croissant in the deli. All of a sudden, Marisha's attacks of the vapours made sense. If the poor woman was feeling anything like herself, she could offer nothing but sympathy.

Marisha was already at her desk when Cassie trailed in, and she was looking a little perkier than previously. Could that be an indication that this ghastly nausea would ease up after a few weeks? She eyed Cassie finishing her milkshake but made no comment.

The week passed slowly. Thankfully, the children had finished their coursework so all there was to do was fun activities like painting and sports day, where she could stand holding one end of a rope for the morning, an activity which didn't require too much initiative.

Finally, the last Friday crawled by and at twelve thirty they waved the wildly excited children off for the summer holidays, and heaved a sigh of relief as the last pair of feet scampered off down the corridor, leaving a few stray bits of paper floating in their wake.

All that was left to do was tidy around and meet the rest of the staff for lunch in the local pub. As if that was going to happen. She became aware of Marisha watching her closely. Cassie was conscious of moving very slowly.

'You are, aren't you?'

'Sorry?'

Marisha gave her a weary look. Should she deny it? She actually felt relieved.

'Yes, I am.'

'And I'm guessing I know whose it is?'

Cassie nodded. She simply hadn't the energy to think up anything more creative than the truth.

'Sit down.' Marisha pulled over chairs for both of them, and Cassie sank onto one gratefully, regardless of what was going to be said.

'He doesn't know yet, does he?'

Cassie shook her head.

'To be honest, he ended it with me,' said Cassie miserably.

Marisha nodded. 'Yes, and I think I know why.'

There was a lot that Cassie was sorely tempted to say but she only had enough energy to keep her trap shut.

'Well, he's a bloody fool, he should know a good thing when he sees one.'

Really? She hadn't seen that one coming.

'Let me explain something. My ex-husband's mother was a selfish cow. Mine, on the other hand . . . was just hard to please. But anyway, he always says his parents were lovely, but that's rubbish, they vanished off to live in Spain the week he did his Leaving Certificate and never came back. And believe me, they couldn't wait to go.'

OK . . . this was news.

'I'll be honest with you, Cassie, because it's something I recognised very early in my marriage. We made a huge mistake. I should've been with a guy like Roger, who's decisive and together, and Finn would've been happy with someone like you, who wouldn't have tried to boss him around. Honestly, I was only trying to organise him, but that's for another day. The point I'm trying to make is that, in spite of himself, he's vulnerable to women who dominate him, and that includes my older daughter.'

'But he needs to face her himself.'

'Of course he does. But he won't, he's got this mortal fear of abandonment. Sure, even the dog's picked it up from him.'

'Marisha, I really appreciate you telling me all this, but I'm not sure what good it'll do.'

'Leave it with me.'

With that, she picked up her beige Ugg cardigan. 'Best of luck, Cassie, you deserve it,' she said and swept out the door towards where Roger Newcombe was loitering around his maroon Volvo. How was it that Marisha could be so awful in some ways and inexplicably generous in others? People really were the weirdest set of contradictions.

* * *

'You have got to look at this catalogue. It's sick,' Ramona bellowed, barely in the door on Saturday morning, before tearing open her case and pulling out brochures and fabric samples until the floor looked like a landfill site. 'I bought you perfume from the duty free!' she projected.

'Got you perfume too. Only, don't bring it near me.'

Ramona eyeballed her for a second, but then got distracted and produced a stunning top constructed from leather and metal from the bottom of her case.

Cassie felt guilty for holding back her secret, but she just wasn't ready to share the news with anyone else. Equally, Ramona was so tied up with her own excitement that they spent the rest of the morning going through her new collection, which seemed to have been assembled at breakneck speed and to exactly reflect her vision. Ramona, she had to admit, could really get shit done.

'Go to China if you want something done fast and right. This isn't a sweatshop deal, by the way. This is high-end. The launch is gonna be June next year. Hey, I totally forgot, how'd the audition go?'

'Great, thanks, it actually went great.'

'Any news yet?'

That was the least of her worries at the moment, but as the days had turned into a week, euphoria was starting to give way to disappointment. She shook her head.

'Fuck it, come and work for me.'

'You know what, I just might.'

Chapter 36

Mam and Eric's wedding was a week away. The weather was shocking and Maxine was due home in four days.

'I can't believe it,' said Mam. 'God hates me.'

The plan was for a marquee on the garden lawn, which was currently accommodating a flock of seagulls who were sailing around contentedly.

'The weather forecast says it's due to dry up on Tuesday,' said Eric, as the three of them gazed out through the French doors at the sheets of rain.

The caterers were confirmed, as well as the makeup and hairdressing lady. On paper, it should've all been fine but Mam was beside herself.

Cassie was sipping weak tea, which was averting suspicion, but anyway Mam had her wedding filters on and seemed incapable of noticing anything else.

'Don't worry, Iris, we've both done this before, it'll all work out in the end,' soothed Eric unwisely.

'For feck's sake, what use is that when it's now, today, and we should be going out and buying sixty pairs of wellington boots for the guests, by the looks of things. Don't be annoying me about years ago.'

Cassie met Eric's eyes behind her back as he made an 'oh, blimey' face. Well, if the relationship survived the week of the wedding, they were set for life.

* * *

'You're so skinny, I hate you' were Maxine's first words as she picked them up from the airport. Just you wait, thought Cassie. Behind her was Miri, who she hadn't seen since she was a toddler, but here she was, seventeen years old. Five-foot-eight, long dark hair, baggy jeans and looking remarkably like Cassie remembered Maxine at that age. To her mortification, she found her chin wobbling. 'Hormones!' she heard Josie's voice in her head.

'Auntie Cassie, hi.' Miri stepped forward and they hugged. Feeling the warmth of the young woman's body, it finally hit home that she was forgiven.

'I look like shite,' declared Mam.

'You do not. Give over,' said Maxine, who'd always had a less guarded relationship with their mother. 'At least you don't have to worry about acne, be thankful for that.'

'No, but I have to worry about eye bags from stress, and that's worse,' Mam countered, refusing to be comforted. 'I've been living in my eye mask, day and night.'

'Will I make you a cup of tea, Granny?' said Charlotte, Maxine's younger daughter.

'That'd be lovely, darling, thank you, you're so good.'

'They really should be the bridesmaids, not us pair of crocks,' said Maxine.

It was funny, Cassie thought, just how quickly they'd reverted back to old patterns. In one way it was lovely and nostalgic; on the other hand, it reminded her just how feisty Maxine could be. She wasn't the angry young woman who'd left Ireland all those years ago; she'd become a confident mama bear, as she referred to herself, and Cassie was conscious there was a whole new person to get to know.

Eric appeared from the garden, looking businesslike and carrying a sweeping brush.

'Had a gander at the ground, I'd say the going's soft to fair. But, given there's another day to go . . .'

Mam was not to be mollified.

'Yes, but they'll be putting up the marquee tomorrow, tramping round and hammering pegs in . . . Sure, by the end of it this place will be like the Okavango Delta. Cassie, love, will you pop out and get me forty sets of those plastic things you stick on stiletto heels to stop them sinking.'

Cassie's heart sank. First of all, popping anywhere felt quite beyond her, and secondly, where in the name of God was she going to find that lot? Maxine must have read her face. She winked and said, 'Come on, Cassie, we'll go on a mission. Girls, you can look after Granny.'

They trailed around the Dundrum shopping centre for an hour, finally managing to locate enough wretched heel protectors, which they had to admit would be badly needed. Finally, they slumped down in an airy café and ordered tea.

'Hell, the jet lag's getting to me, I feel like I got up at four in the morning. It's like I'm actually being pinned to this chair,' said Maxine.

Cassie was going to reply, when her phone buzzed with a text from a number she didn't recognise. She read out the text:

> Sorry I was mean. You are a nice person. S

She looked at it in puzzlement for a few minutes and then the penny dropped.

'Samantha. Bloody hell, talk about too little, too late.'

'Am I allowed to ask?'

Cassie explained the situation to her, about Finn and his children. Maxine listened intently.

'Trust me, thirteen- and fourteen-year-olds don't know shit but they think they're Oprah.'

Cassie was conscious she hadn't mentioned the biggest thing of all. Somehow, with Pal and Josie it'd been totally different but there was absolutely no way she was going to steal Mam's thunder, nor was she ready for the avalanche of opinions that were bound to land on her head.

'I'm sorry it's worked out like that and if there's anything I can do . . . I know things haven't been so great between us . . . and I'm sorry for that, but I'd like you to feel you could come to me.'

Cassie nodded. Actually, Maxine's awkward offer meant the world. She didn't have to tell her sister everything, but just knowing that she could felt like an old, empty space had been filled. She smiled.

'Come on, sis, let's go home and try on these wretched bridesmaids' dresses. And if they're too long . . .'

'Gotcha. Too late for hems. From here on in, it's platform shoes.'

* * *

The day before the wedding dawned cloudy but dry. The seagulls had migrated out of the garden, so that at least was a good omen. At 10 a.m. the truck with the marquee arrived, accompanied by a few of the neighbours, who came out to have a gawk. They'd been invited to the afters, so thankfully there was no embarrassment. Cassie, Maxine and the two girls were busy hoovering and dusting.

'Never mind about the plates and silverware, the caterers are bringing all of that,' said Mam. 'Now, we're all going for a manicure at three, so look nice.'

They were all sitting in a row in the nail bar, when Cassie's phone rang. Oh, bloody hell, she thought, could the timing be any worse? Her lavender-coloured nails were still gloopy under the drying light. She could hear Mam tutting beside her and contemplated ignoring the call. Maxine, on her other side, gave her an encouraging look. She gingerly flipped open her phone case and saw the agency number displayed. Her heart leaped. There was absolutely no way she could discreetly slip away; all she could manage was to stab the screen with the pad of her finger. Sunita's jubilant voice rang out over the speaker.

'Darling, I've just heard. You got it.'

'What . . . What? Are you serious? Oh my God, what did they say?'

She was conscious of virtually shrieking down the phone.

'They loved you. They said you were so authentic and natural. That's exactly what they said. That you were a natural.'

'I can't believe it. I can't believe it.'

'What? What?' everyone was shouting.

'I just got the part in *Wentworth Way*.'

Mam was not to be outdone.

'She said you were a natural! D'you know what the part is, girls? A convict.'

One–nil to Mam.

Cassie was inwardly thrilled but conscious of not making too much of a fuss. It wasn't as though she was feeling like knocking back a load of champagne, anyway. This was Mam's big moment; hers could wait.

It wasn't until that night, as she lay in bed, that she allowed herself a moment to bask in her success. She was only too aware that they'd have to be ready for the makeup lady at nine thirty tomorrow morning, including Ramona, who was coming to get dressed with the rest of the girls. All her adult life Cassie had waited for this moment, but now the person she most wanted to share it with was gone. How ironic that she'd got exactly what she wanted just after she'd stopped wanting it.

Five years ago, this would've felt like the answer to a prayer. Now, it was just one more complication. She put her hands on her belly and addressed the person whose existence almost nobody else in the world was aware of. 'Whatever happens, little one, it's you and me now.'

Chapter 37

The wedding morning dawned, and in keeping with Eric's meteorological predictions, the garden was reasonably dry. The guests were to begin arriving at two thirty for the ceremony at three.

Mam's bedroom had been transformed into a boudoir, complete with illuminated mirrors and rails of dresses. They each had a sateen robe and their hair was done first, while they waited for makeup. Maxine had brought the traditional bottle of champagne and all the girls, apart from Cassie, were sipping excitedly.

Ramona had changed from her tracksuit into a black snakeskin-pattern minidress, embossed with gold, teamed with gold cowboy boots which showed off her mile-long legs. She eyed the lavender-blue frocks with her head cocked to one side.

'Don't say anything,' muttered Maxine.

'Naaa, they're not so bad. I mean they're cute, they're just a little hokey—'

'And now is not the time to say "but they suit you",' hissed Cassie.

Maxine sniggered and topped up her glass.

'Iris, you look like a goddess,' Ramona announced to Mam's delight, as everyone else crowded round and toasted her.

Just then, Eric popped his head round the door with his hand theatrically covering his eyes.

'I didn't see anything, ladies, I swear. Cassie, there's someone here to see you.'

Careful not to catch anyone's eye, she followed Eric downstairs to find, standing on the doorstep, Finn, looking sheepish but just as she remembered him . . . except his hair looked slightly longer.

Her heart practically leaped out of her chest.

'Hey,' he said.

'Hey,' she said.

Which was, admittedly, pretty minimal but all she could come up with in the moment. He seemed a little unnerved at the family drama he'd blundered into, what with the caterers tramping in and out with crates of food, while flower arrangements pirouetted past as the two of them dodged out of the way.

'I'm so sorry to interrupt your mother's wedding. God, is this the worst possible timing or what?'

'No, it's fine, I mean you were invited but . . .'

She gazed at him in silence. There was so much to say, she simply couldn't fathom where to start.

'You look great, by the way. Your hair's . . . fancy.'

'Yeah. Thanks. Finn, why are you here?'

'I-I . . . I needed to see you.'

'OK . . . Well, now you have.'

The pain in her heart was so bad that she had to rub between her breasts with the heel of her hand.

'Sorry, wedding nerves. And it's not even my stupid wedding.'

She was conscious he was eyeing her body.

'Shouldn't you be . . . sipping champagne or something?'

She looked pointedly at him from under her fringe.

'Sorry, that was a dick thing to say.' He seemed to be in one of his acutely awkward states.

But before she could reply, Miri appeared behind her. 'Sorry, Auntie Cassie, Grandma says if you don't come back up and finish getting ready, she's going to develop a migraine and we'll have to cancel the wedding.'

'You have to go, Finn. You can't be here today. I'm going to have to finish getting ready.'

'Look, before you go, I know I'm a total arse turning up, but I've been thinking . . . a lot, in fact. I've been doing nothing else.'

Finn reached out his hand to touch her face, his expression unreadable.

'*Cassie!*' Mam's voice reverberated from upstairs, jolting them out of their trance. They both stepped back.

'I have to go.'

'Yeah, me too.' He nodded.

She was aware of him backing away, his gaze full of unspoken feelings, before she turned away and closed the door.

'So . . . is that the chap?' muttered Eric, who had been hovering just out of sight.

'He was . . . Oh, Eric, I don't know, what am I going to do?'

He reached out and squeezed her arm then vanished into the other room. Upstairs, Ramona met her on the landing.

'Hello, girlfriend, was that who I think it was? Yummy. Will he be joining us later?'

Cassie suddenly found herself overtaken by that awful feeling when you realise you're going to cry, and there's absolutely nothing you can do to stop the tears. A sob came out, unbidden. 'No. He won't.'

Ramona, a good head taller than her in her gold platform boots, flung her arms around Cassie.

'Honey, it'll work out. Look up, quick, look up! Whatever you do, don't smudge the mascara,' she soothed, whipping a tissue out from her cleavage and expertly soaking up the tears. 'Let him go for now, it'll all work out.'

At that precise moment, that felt painfully unlikely. Still, this was Mam's big day and there was nothing for it but to push down her feelings and slap on a smile.

* * *

The wedding went off better than anyone could have hoped. Nobody sank in the mud, Maxine and Cassie didn't look too comical, and Mam looked radiant in her classic satin sheath dress and floral headdress. She'd decided to walk herself up the aisle, on the grounds that at this stage in her life she was her own woman.

Philip was the best man; standing beside Eric, he looked perfectly at home in a silver morning coat, and Cassie realised there was something unmistakably old-fashioned about Phil.

For a moment, standing to one side with her sister, as Mam and Eric made their vows, Cassie felt Da's absence like a hole in her heart. He was the one person whose down-to-earth sense could make any crisis manageable.

A brisk westerly wind picked up during the ceremony, causing the wedding arch to list perilously to one side, while Auntie Patricia was overheard commenting, 'Isn't it wonderful how much you can fit into these gardens in their original size?'

During the drinks reception, Ramona sidled past Philip, who was getting drinks for everyone at the bar. Observing this, Maxine hissed to Cassie, 'Who's the best man who keeps staring at you like you're his winning lottery ticket?'

'Shut up, he's called Philip and he's a lovely guy.'

'I don't know,' Ramona drawled, as she joined them. 'I think he's a hottie. Like if Fred Astaire had a love child with Harry Potter. I would do him, definitely.'

Cassie wasn't sure whether this was terrific news for Philip or if it meant he was in mortal danger.

Just then a gong rang somewhere, calling them to dinner. She'd been put sitting beside Philip at the top table, which was customary for a wedding party, and Mam kept looking over and winking at her.

Thankfully, the meal included poached salmon and asparagus on creamed potato, which Cassie found exactly the kind of plain, wholesome food that soothed her all-day morning sickness. She was starving but forced herself to at least preserve a bit of decorum and not make a show of herself by shovelling the food in too hungrily. This was the first time she'd been with Phil in a social situation and she was feeling unexpectedly self-conscious at such close quarters.

'I love your dress, by the way,' he said in a tone that made it clear he meant it.

'So, Phil, how come you know Eric?'

He laughed. 'If I told you, you wouldn't believe it.'

She smiled warmly, feeling slightly less ill after some food.

'Try me.'

'We were aid workers in Rwanda in 1994, during the genocide. I mean, we were just young fellas, or at least I was.'

'My God, sounds terrifying. For a moment I thought you were going to say you were priests.'

'No, but I thought about it. Still do . . . sometimes.'

She was getting the distinct impression that now was not one of those times.

He paused for a moment and seemed to be searching for words. Oh dear, was he planning to declare himself? Just then there was a wave from Eric.

'Oh, I've just got the nod,' Phil muttered and stood up, tapping a glass with his fork and causing a wave of shushing.

'Ladies and gentlemen, I'm here today to talk about my good friend Eric, and Iris, who I now count as a good friend also. I'm afraid I don't know enough embarrassing stories about Eric's youth to entertain you, and we didn't have a stag do, so I don't even have that to draw on. But I will say one thing about Eric: he taught me to be the man I am and for that I owe him everything. Eric has the quality of common decency in a world where it is anything but common. At a very difficult time in my life,

Eric was there for me, although he'd never remind me of it. He doesn't push himself forward, but anyone who knows him recognises that he can't be pushed back either. He's a man who knows his mind and stands his ground.'

Mam was glowing with pride at Eric, who was fiddling with the tablecloth sheepishly.

'In a world where we've so many superheroes in the movies, but so few in real life, I'm proud to say that I have one true hero, and it's my friend Eric Morton.'

Everyone was delighted with the speech, particularly as it was so short, and clapped warmly, beaming at each other.

'Well done.' Cassie smiled at Philip. 'That was just perfect.'

As he sat back down, she was surprised to see tears in his eyes. 'Thank you,' he said, grasping her hand and raising it to his lips. 'You've no idea what that means to me.'

Out of the corner of her eye, she could see Mam elbowing Eric frantically. The whole event was taking on a surreal air. Cassie felt for him, but there was a knot in her stomach. Phil was polishing his glasses and seemed to be trying to compose himself. He placed them back on and turned the full gaze of his large, pale blue eyes on her.

'Cassie . . . I don't want to miss this opportunity to say just how much I've enjoyed our . . . connection over these past few months.'

'Thank you, Phil, I've really enjoyed it too. There's no way I'd have made it this far without you.'

'You're an exceptional woman, you know . . . It's a long time since I've met anyone like you.'

Cassie found herself secretly glancing around, hoping somebody would cut in, but everyone seemed to be keeping their distance.

'Without wishing to bring the mood down, you may have heard that my wife—'

'I did, Phil, Mam told me. I hope you don't mind, and I am so, so sorry. I can't imagine what that must have been like.'

He nodded gravely. 'Who knows through what rocky terrain our paths may take us . . .'

'Well, that's certainly true. Is that a quote or did you just . . . make that up?'

'Essentially . . . yes.' They laughed. 'See, that's what I love about you, Cassie, your . . . lightness.'

'Thank you.' Oh gosh, he'd just said the L-word.

Thankfully, by now the tables were cleared away and the disco was beginning. The neighbours crowded in – even some, Cassie suspected, who hadn't exactly been invited – and the party took off. Her ambition had been to somehow make it through the wedding without looking too much like a washed-out pair of weekday knickers, but things were starting to veer off-track. She'd completely forgotten about the dancing. Oh Lord, she couldn't be seen to be a complete killjoy, but jigging around was pretty much guaranteed to bring on a wave of nausea. She would've given anything to creep home and close the door on her nice, cool, quiet bedroom. There was a glow from Eric and Mam – not euphoria, exactly, but gentle happiness, and some of it definitely pointed in their direction.

'Excuse me, Cassie, would you like to dance?' Philip broke in on her reverie.

It was a slow song: 'Can't Help Falling in Love' by Elvis. They couldn't have picked a smoochier song if they'd tried. Mam was winking madly across the floor and Eric was unsubtly giving his speciality thumbs up.

'Of course.' She smiled. She could feel Phil's arms tentatively reaching around her, and the scent of some sort of pleasant woody aftershave rising from under his collar.

'This is a great favourite of mine. By the way, you're looking very beautiful this evening,' he murmured.

'Thank you.'

'I've been waiting for a chance to . . . talk to you.'

Her heart sank. Oh God, she just didn't have the energy for this.

'I wonder if maybe we could go out some time . . . doesn't have to be formal . . . just spend some time together, away from work.'

She could feel him struggling to sound casual. 'Aaaah . . .'

There was no faking it. What was wrong with her? Stupid, stupid girl who was only ever able to choose the path that would lead to unhappiness. Phil was a wonderful man, in every way. And attractive. Ramona could see that, so why couldn't she?

But all she could feel was absence, the desperate yearning for Finn's arms, his voice, the fact that it was his child she was carrying inside her body. She couldn't lie to herself. Her head might try but her body insisted on telling the truth.

And if that meant going it alone, then so be it. Glancing around at the joyful, heaving dance floor, she realised she'd never felt so utterly alone. Philip could feel her reticence, but no amount of guilt or wishing things otherwise could change that. She tried to concentrate on swaying to the music but somehow it felt tense and clunky. As the song ended, she stepped back, trying to avoid the look of disappointment on his face.

'Phil, I would love to spend time with you, but, er . . . as a friend. And I'm not sure that's what you want . . .' she petered out.

'No, Cassie, it isn't. I have to be honest.'

Her heart broke for him.

'I'm sorry if I embarrassed you.'

'No, you didn't, it's me. I'm sorry, Phil, but I'm going to have to go, I'm just not feeling too well.'

At least that was true. Suddenly terrified the dinner was going to make a second appearance, she put her head down and made for the loo, ignoring Mam's devastated looks.

Ramona, despite not quite having her arm back to full strength, was ripping up the dance floor with her moves. She caught Cassie's eye on the way past.

'Hey, what's up? You look kinda peaky. I thought you were getting cosy with the best man.'

'Ramona, please, don't slow me down.' She groaned. 'He's all yours.'

'Are you crazy?' Ramona's parting shot echoed in her head as she wound her way through the crowd.

Mercifully, there was no queue for the loo, and she sank down onto the floor and leaned her cheek against the cool tiled wall, allowing her heaving stomach and spinning head to settle. All she could think of was her quiet bed, and leaving all the noise and expectations behind. She felt sorry for Phil, sorry for herself, sorry for Mam's hopes.

On her way back to the table, she realised just how sober she was and everyone else decidedly wasn't. Auntie Patricia, who'd a few gin and tonics on board, trapped her against a large speaker which was blasting out 'Dancing Queen' by Abba.

'God, but aren't you all very brave, in your little frocks. I'm only saying . . . And Iris in white, isn't she gas? But look, she's happy and he's still got his health, for the moment, God love him, and that's the main thing.'

There was no sign of Phil.

It was midnight by this stage, which was just about a respectable time to slip away. Trekking up the stairs to her old bedroom, she could hear the disco sounds fading into the background. She closed the door and leaned against it in relief. Alone was OK. If this was to be her fate, she could go it alone.

Just then her phone buzzed. There was only one person it could be.

Have to talk.

Where are you?

Outside.

Her heart was pounding out of her chest.

There was a knock on the door. It was Ramona.

'Chick, you OK? You looked kinda green. You're not gonna barf?'

'If I haven't by now, I'm probably over the worst.'

If there was one person Cassie could actually face right now, who would be non-judgemental as hell, it was her. She poured out the whole story, about the baby who, despite its microscopic size, was dominating every moment of her life.

'Plus, this dress is about to explode at the seams. Help me, please, Ramona, what am I going to do? I keep telling myself I can go it alone, but the truth is I want him but I don't know if he's up for any of this.'

'So, where is he now?'

'Outside, in his car.'

'Are you shitting me? Honey, the only person you need to have this conversation with is him.'

Not for the first time Ramona had deftly sliced through her confusion.

'Would you sneak down and let him in? Please. And try not to let anyone see you.'

'I'll be tact personified,' she hissed, although that would definitely be a first, Cassie thought.

A couple of minutes later there was a tentative knock.

She opened the door slowly to see Finn standing there in the half-light, wearing the same clothes as earlier. His eyes met hers with such intensity that her heart jolted as though an electric current had shot through her.

They gazed at each other in silence for a moment. He seemed unsure.

'Cassie, I—'

'Finn, I'm pregnant.'

He took a breath. 'I know.'

'Before you say anything, I get it. I get the whole thing with Samantha, I get how crazy your life is, and I don't expect anything from you. I can do this on my own. I just needed you to know about it, that's all.'

Finn gazed at her incredulously.

'Is that what you think? You think I'm going to just walk away and leave you?'

'I don't want you feeling sorry for me. I can handle this.'

She could feel the tears rising.

He reached out and caught her face between his hands.

'Cassie, I'm crazy about you. I've never felt this way about anyone, ever. I'm scared of how much I feel for you.'

'Me too.'

'Being with you is like finding my way home. I'm not letting you go again.'

Tears were pouring down her cheeks. 'Really?'

She felt his mouth searching for hers, felt the taste of him, his familiar smell that felt so right.

There was one thing, though. 'Finn, how did you know I was pregnant?'

He smiled. 'I've been here before.'

Course he had.

'You're not drinking and your breasts are . . . notice-ably bigger, which is gorgeous, by the way.'

He slid his hand into the bodice of her dress and cupped her breast, making her gasp.

'Careful, they're really tender.'

'Sorry, but your being pregnant with my baby just feels . . . really hot.'

'Really?'

'Oh yeah.'

'I know it's complicated . . .' she began, but his lips silenced her words.

Chapter 38

The next morning, around eleven, as the only un-hungover adult, she set out a buffet of croissants, fruit, freshly squeezed orange juice and a big cafetière of coffee on the patio table. She contemplated bacon but felt her stomach heave at the very idea. She made herself a mug of weak tea, closing her eyes in the sun which had mischievously decided to split the stones the day after the wedding.

After a few minutes Maxine trailed outside. A short time later, Mam surfaced in a flowy silk kaftan over jeans and oversized sunglasses, looking chic if a little fragile. Eric, it turned out, was having a lie-in.

They helped themselves to breakfast and sat back down. Mam eyed her suspiciously.

'Aren't you marvellous, darling, doing all of this, though for heaven's sake, where did you go last night so early? Philip ended up with your friend Ramona. Now, there's a girl with her head screwed on. And you see now why he was answering your calls morning, noon and night for the past couple of months? I tried to tell you. That poor man had *hopes*.'

'Well, Mam, if it makes you feel better, he looked pretty hopeful to me when I was going to bed,' said Maxine, smiling reassuringly at Cassie.

The sun beat down as though they were on the French Riviera. Now was as good a time as any, thought Cassie. She sighed; the prospect of hiding her secret was becoming even more untenable than sharing it, there was nothing else for it.

'Look, I was waiting for the right time . . . I have some news. I didn't want to tell you before the wedding, obviously . . .' Something in her tone made them perk up despite their hangovers.

'I'm pregnant.'

A stunned silence fell around the table, and Mam sat wide-eyed, a croissant suspended halfway to her mouth. Maxine spat back her mouthful of coffee and, despite her hangover, launched herself at Cassie, enveloping her in a powerful hug and hollering, 'My little sis is pregnant! My little sis is pregnant, and not a minute too soon.'

'Don't squeeze me!' She gasped. 'I'm not feeling—'

'Sorry! That's a great sign, though,' declared Maxine joyfully. 'The sicker you feel, the more hormones are flying around.'

'*Well* . . . that explains *a lot*,' exhaled Mam at last. 'That's why you shot down poor lovely Philip and let him get away.'

'Mam, will you *shut up*,' shouted Maxine good-naturedly.

It only took a moment for Mam to recover her decorum.

'Actually, there's somebody I'd like you to meet. Sorry for the short notice.' Cassie vanished into the house and then reappeared with Finn, who was sheepishly holding a bunch of flowers.

'Mam, Maxine, this is Finnian, Finn . . .'

She met Mam's and Maxine's gazes.

'Heavens above, Cassie, did you ever do anything the simple way? Finnian, you're most welcome to our house. Please take a seat. Now tell me, how are all the kids?'

Maxine rolled her eyes while Mam surveyed Finn thoughtfully, before commenting, 'Well, you're very good-looking, I must say.'

'Jesus, Mam,' said Maxine.

'Maxine, for the love of God, will you get me a Bloody Mary. This is far too big news for anything else. A big family is a blessing, of course. Three, is it? But I'm sure they're all very good, are they?'

Finn laughed. Surprisingly, he didn't seem too fazed by Mam's grilling. He exchanged a glance with Cassie.

'Some of them.'

'But, sure, isn't that always the way. Children go in phases. These two were always like that.'

'Mam, will you stop talking about us as though we're still children,' said Cassie.

'Ah well, he knows what I mean, don't you, Finn?'

'I do, Mrs Kearney.' He smiled.

'Morton now, since yesterday. But call me Iris,' she purred.

It was becoming ever clearer to Cassie just how Mam had managed to bag herself two husbands.

Finn reached down and took Cassie's hand.

By this time, Maxine had returned with a tray of Bloody Marys.

'Still feeling like crap?' Maxie nodded sympathetically at her.

Cassie's main focus had switched to why, in her distraction, she'd knocked back a glass of fresh orange juice, which was now curdling in her stomach.

'How long are you gone, Cass?' she asked.

'Seven or eight weeks.'

'Well, a new baby is always a joy,' announced Mam, as though she'd just read it off the side of a passing bus. 'I'm thrilled for you, I truly am. But tell me, Finnian, how are you going to manage, with all your responsibilities?'

He was now having the experience of being nailed by Mam.

'The way I see it, Iris, when you love someone, you just make it work.'

All of a sudden, Mam's face lit up. She gazed at him fondly. 'Well now, Finnian, isn't that the pure truth?'

For all her bluster, she was a hopeless romantic at heart.

'But, wait now, what are you going to do about your part in *Wentworth Way*? I mean, Finn, she's only after spending her entire life waiting for something like this. Even if Eric says the BBC pay is rotten . . . But that never stopped you before, did it? It's the honour, I suppose . . .'

'Oh, Mam, I can't think about that right now,' said Cassie.

'But sure, wasn't it Michelle Pfeiffer who played Catwoman when she was eight months pregnant?'

Maxine rolled her eyes.

'No she didn't, Mam. Don't be ridiculous.'

'Well, somebody did,' said Mam. 'Look, love, Finnian is right, you put the most important things in life first and let everything else work around them.' She got it in one. And that's what made her Mam.

Chapter 39

Two weeks later, Cassie climbed into Finn's car outside her apartment.

'All set?'

'This is going to be fun when I'm eight months pregnant,' she groaned.

He leaned over and kissed her lightly.

'Come on, the scan is at half past. We don't want to be late to meet this sprog of ours.'

'Finn, I'm nervous, is that stupid?'

'No, it's not stupid, it's natural. Wait, I've got something for you.'

He reached back and produced a gift bag, placing it on her knee.

'What's this for?'

She opened it to find the tiniest soft teddy and a pair of beige bootees.

'Unisex colour, so whoever we get, we'll be prepared.'

He really was all in, after the months of indecision.

'Oh Finn, they're so beautiful. Thank you.'

He gave her a pointed glance. She'd realised that sometimes he could become very serious.

'No . . . thank you,' he said, as he pulled out into the traffic.

'For what?'

He shrugged awkwardly. 'Just for being you . . . and because I never thought it could be like this.'

She stayed silent so he went on, 'I mean, when things are really good between us, it's different . . . that's all.'

'I know what you mean,' she said. Having seen both sides, she reflected, made their second-chance love all the sweeter.

Epilogue

13th February

> *Perfect timing for Valentine's*

read the WhatsApp from Norah.

> *Massive congrats on baby Benny. Welcome to the Sleepless in Stillorgan club. Ha ha ☺!!*

from Bryony.

> *So thrilled for U both. Enjoy glass of bubbles at last!! ☺*

from Louise.

'You better believe it.' Cassie gazed down at her two-day-old boy asleep in the Moses basket.

'Look at him, Finn, he's so good.' She reached out and caressed the impossibly tiny cheek, causing the infant to stir.

'How are the others doing?' she murmured.

'Conor is surprisingly good, says he's glad to have a brother at last. Samantha has warned everyone not to think she's some sort of unpaid nanny.'

They exchanged a rueful smile.

'Tough negotiator. Sounds like we'd better start saving up,' she said.

'Thor is the most traumatised. After me, that is.'

She punched him playfully in the side.

'But St Teresa's been getting the worst of it, I believe.'

'Oh no, tell me.'

'Apparently, she's been working double shifts.'

'Dreadful.'

'She's been kitted out in a blue plastic apron made from a sandwich bag. And what with two baby siblings to look after, Cici says, St Teresa never has a minute to herself.'

'Poor St Teresa.' She laughed, nuzzling into his shoulder. 'Finn, how am I going to manage? Sometimes it all hits me. I've to bring him with me to New York for Ramona's launch in June, I have to be there . . . I swore to her I wouldn't miss it, and of course Mam'll turn up in her fancy suit as the European Marketing Manager, so I'll be baby-wrangling on my own.'

'I'm coming.'

'What?'

'Well, I have to, seeing as dishy Phil will be floating around. I don't want him to run off with you.'

'No! Finn, you just are the best. You know that?' She flung her arms around him as he tried to contain his grin.

'Well, I am pretty special, that is true.'

'Plonker.'

She curled up against him. 'And Finn . . . you know I got a call from Sunita to say my *Wentworth Way* character will be coming back for three episodes before Christmas. Well, how am I going to manage that? The last time was hectic enough, trying to play all my scenes behind tables and oversized handbags to hide the bump!'

He looked down at her and raised an eyebrow.

She smiled. 'I know, I know . . . stop angsting, we'll sort it out.'

And it was true. If anyone had told her a year ago what the future held, well, she'd have been on her knees with joy . . . and she was, honestly. But that's not quite how life works, she mused. When a dream comes true, it also becomes a reality.

And every happy ending is, after all, just another beginning.

Acknowledgements

First of all, I would like to thank Mark, my chap, and Jessica, my daughter, who have put up with catching me acting out bits of the book to myself. Where would I be without you? Muffin the dog for non-verbal encouragement, sometimes that's enough. Thelma, my mum, for always believing in me; James, my big brother, and Anne, my sister-in law, for everything.

My agent, Ger Nichol of The Book Bureau, for her support and unflinching belief in my work. From Embla, Stephanie Carey, my editor, for hilarious suggestions and fabulous insights, this book would not be what it is without you. Daniela Nava for her stellar sub-editing job (not to mention her LOL memes in the margins) which sharpened and clarified this book. Emma Wilson who over saw everything, Beth Free at the studio Nic & Lou for the beautiful cover design, Emma Dunne for proofreading, Vishani Perera for the great marketing job. Big thanks to Chelsea Graham for audio editing and to Amy McAllister for the fabulous narration that brought all the characters to life.

Vanessa Fox O'Loughlin and Mary Stanley from Inkwell.

Huge thanks, too, to the Irish Department of Tourism, Culture, Arts, Gaeltacht, Sport and Media for the Basic Income for the Arts scheme, your bursary has been invaluable.

I also need to thank my friends who encouraged me in my many moments of doubt and that mattered more than you could ever know: Mary McEvoy, Chris Delaney, Shanta Choudhree, Emer O'Neill and Jac Broder and Claire Roberts.

Also, Helen Gilmartin and Sheila O'Callaghan for their moral support. The SGI Buddhists in Wicklow Wexford who were there for all the stages, thank you.

About the Author

Isobel started acting in Trinity College Players and from there moved into professional theatre, where she was awarded 'Best newcomer to the Irish Theatre' and went on to work in theatre and TV, including playing a fantasy-prone barmaid in the series *Glenroe* for sixteen years. Isobel has written for TV soap, radio and theatre, including *Party Face* which ran off-Broadway with a star cast. She is also a qualified psychotherapist and worked for several years as a TV agony aunt #AskIsobel on *The Afternoon Show* for RTÉ. She has written another novel, Learning to Fly (2022).

Underneath it all, her loves are: dancing to eighties club classics or old Eurovision hits with Muffin the dog or drinking coffee while staring blankly out the window. Isobel lives in Dublin with her partner, Mark, and daughter, Jessica.

About Embla Books

Embla Books is a digital-first publisher of standout commercial adult fiction. Passionate about storytelling, the team at Embla believe our lives are built on stories – and publish books that will make you 'laugh, love, look over your shoulder and lose sleep'. Launched by Bonnier Books UK in 2021, the imprint is named after the first woman from the creation myth in Norse mythology. Embla was carved by the gods from a tree trunk found on the seashore; an image of the kind of creative work and crafting that writers do, and a symbol of how stories shape our lives.

Find out about some of our other books and stay in touch:

X, Facebook, Instagram: @emblabooks
Newsletter: https://bit.ly/emblanewsletter